STONE TOWN

Also by Margaret Hickey

CUTTERS END

STONE TOWN

MARGARET HICKEY

BANTAM

SYDNEY AUCKLAND TORONTO NEW YORK LONDON

BANTAM

UK | USA | Canada | Ireland | Australia
India | New Zealand | South Africa | China

Bantam is part of the Penguin Random House group of companies whose addresses
can be found at global.penguinrandomhouse.com

Penguin
Random House
Australia

First published by Bantam in 2022

Cover photography courtesy of Adrian Campfield/Trevillion Images
Cover design by Christabella Designs
Author photograph by Benjamin Dowsley
Internal design by Midland Typesetters, Australia
Typeset in 12.5/17.5 Adobe Garamond by Midland Typesetters

Printed and bound in Australia by Griffin Press, part of Ovato, an accredited
ISO AS/NZS 14001 Environmental Management Systems printer

A catalogue record for this
book is available from the
National Library of Australia

ISBN 978 0 14377 727 4

penguin.com.au

We at Penguin Random House Australia acknowledge that Aboriginal and
Torres Strait Islander peoples are the Traditional Custodians and the first storytellers of
the lands on which we live and work. We honour Aboriginal and Torres Strait Islander
peoples' continuous connection to Country, waters, skies and communities.
We celebrate Aboriginal and Torres Strait Islander stories, traditions and
living cultures; and we pay our respects to Elders past and present.

For my boys, Alexander, Eddie and Ben

PROLOGUE

He shouldn't have brought them here.

It was hard to navigate the bush at night. He ran through the landmarks in his head; the edge of the road, the path by the stream into the bush, and then crossing over the tape the council had put up warning people to go no further. He'd been here less than a week ago and the hat he'd left behind must be here somewhere . . .

Slowly he turned 180 degrees, the phone torch shedding a jagged beam of light, making the trees jump out, appear too close. He took a deep breath, rubbed his free hand down his jeans. Despite the cold, he could feel a thin sheen of sweat rise on his forehead. He breathed out slowly, spun the torchlight again, this time behind him in a wide arc.

The girls' faces appeared ghost-white in the spear of light and they covered their eyes with their forearms.

'Are you lost?' the younger girl, Sarah, asked. 'Evan, are you lost?'

'Quiet,' he said. 'I need to listen.'

1

'What even is this?' Sarah's older sister Emma, the one who mattered, asked. 'You bring us all the way out here with barely any light and you tell us we'll hear something cool, and now you don't know where we are?'

'Quiet.'

'Jesus, Evan, I'm going. C'mon, Sez.'

Emma turned, but not before Evan heard the disgust in her voice. She probably thought he was making it up just to impress her, or worse, so that he could . . . well . . .

'Wait!'

'Enough, Evan.' Emma's voice was sharp and it made him shrink. She'd probably tell everyone at school he was even more of a loser than she'd first thought.

The girls began walking back in the direction they'd come.

'Wait!' he said again. 'I—'

And then they heard it. At first, a low moan. The girls turned back to him open-mouthed and in the light he could see their horror plainly written. He felt it too, a dark turning in the pit of his stomach. The moan grew louder and the girls rushed to him so the three were almost hugging. Louder still as Emma tried to pull them all back along the track.

'What is it?' she whispered. 'Who's out there?'

Abruptly – silence.

'I want to go home,' Sarah said, and the two girls started walking quickly along the darkened path.

'Is this some trick?' Emma turned, vicious, towards him. 'You think this is funny?'

Her face was not as he thought it would be. Instead of huddling up to him, she was as against him as always. He'd got it wrong again.

'I'm sorry,' he said, faltering.

'What was that sound?'

Evan hesitated. 'I don't know.'

And then the screaming began. A high-pitched scream, from somewhere out in the bush, and all three started running blindly, away from the noise, the uneven torchlight making strange, panicked patterns on the spindly gums and shrubs. The screaming, it seemed, came from all around, and above it were their own breaths, ragged and panting.

They ran through the screaming bush for what may have been seconds but felt like years, the trees distorted, limbs reaching out and scratching at their faces.

And then, just as suddenly, it stopped.

The teenagers kept moving. Evan thought they must have passed the council lines and were back into familiar territory, when Sarah called out in pain. He turned to see the younger girl lying on her stomach and sobbing.

'Get up!' Evan cried, harsh against the wails, but the girl did not move. He gave the phone to Emma and reached down to grab Sarah. He pulled her up in one movement and she stood there, swallowing sobs and wiping snot across her face.

'Let's go,' Evan said, still rattled. The screams had been different tonight. More intense. Higher pitched.

But Emma had not moved. Instead, she was staring down the length of the torchlight's beam and the other two followed her gaze.

There, curled up in the brush, was the body of a man.

The rain, when it came, was torrential. Fat surges of it, racing into gutters, rivers and streams. No rain for three years, then this.

Young kids marvelled at it, tree-changers had long baths outside in it, and the old farmers muttered about the strangeness of it; the timing, the intensity. Not a drop in winter; now it was almost the end of spring and the clouds were exploding with the stuff every few days.

Jacqueline Matteson lay awake, listening to it pelt on her tin roof. Even if it had come when they needed it, it still wouldn't have been the right sort. Too sudden, too damaging for pre-harvest. Gushing rain and now the berries ruined, the crops probably flattened.

A sound from outside – not the rain: sludging, running? The porch creaked. Jacqueline sat up in her bed and reached automatically at the empty space beside her. A sound at the front door now, a muffled shout and, was it . . .? Yes – low whispering. Frantic. Her first thought was the girls. She swung her legs over the side of the bed and reached for the chair.

'Who is it?' she called, and with effort raised herself off the bed and lowered herself into the chair, manoeuvring the wheels around the bed. The sound was definitely her girls and now she felt a fear rise in her throat, because it's every farmer's nightmare: an accident on the farm. Before she could reach it, the door was flung open and her two youngest daughters, Emma and Sarah, stood there drenched. And who was that behind them? Evan?

Sarah was choking back sobs, the other two pale and shivering.

'What is it?' Jacqueline asked sharply.

'There's a man . . .' Emma said. 'Along Stoney Creek . . . he's . . .'

'He's what?' Jacqueline felt a deep dread – she'd been through this before. 'Has there been an accident? Where? Tell me!'

'It's Aidan Sleeth,' Evan said. 'I think he's been shot.'

CHAPTER 1

Detective Senior Sergeant Mark Ariti stamped his feet hard on the front porch of Jacqueline Matteson's house. Outside was raven black, rain pelted hard. Inside, though it was barely 2 am, the living room was lit up like a showground and filled with people young and old. Mark recognised no one. Stone Town, barely twenty-five kilometres from where he lived in Booralama, may as well have been another universe. Consisting mainly of old farming families and an influx of tree-changers, the area was known for its mines, remnants of settler stone houses scattered about the bush, and significant wheat yield.

Riveting, Mark remembered thinking, in Year 10 local history. *Take that, Machu Picchu.*

But the gold from Stone Town was long gone and it had been years since farmers' sons returned from boarding schools to make a life on the land.

Stone Town now had a different footy team from Booralama, different netball team, different CFA, CWA. But not a different police station.

In the lounge, three girls sat huddled on a couch and a wiry older lady nursed a drink beside the fireplace.

Mark introduced himself to the tired-looking woman who opened the door to him.

'Morning. Detective Senior Sergeant Ariti, Booralama. I'm here to speak to the three kids who found the body.'

The woman's face was metal-grey in the bright light of the room. 'Can't it wait till the morning? We're exhausted.'

Mark made an apologetic noise and indicated the notepaper and pen in his hand. 'Procedures.'

The door from the kitchen swung open, and with a burst of energy an attractive woman in a wheelchair entered the room.

'Jacqueline Matteson,' she announced, holding out her hand.

He shook it. 'Detective Senior Sergeant Mark Ariti.'

'Well, Sergeant, do they need a lawyer?' She tipped her head towards the girls, who were now staring up at him with tired and tear-stained eyes.

'That's up to you,' Mark said. 'But I'm just here to ask a few questions.'

The old lady with the drink piped up. 'You're Helen's son, aren't you?' She didn't wait for a reply. 'I'm sorry for your loss, dear. Helen was a lovely lady.'

'She was.' Mark cleared his throat. 'Thank you.'

Jacqueline's face shifted, softened. 'You can talk to them

in the kitchen. Evan's just gone in there. Girls?' She nodded to her daughters, gave them an encouraging glance. 'The policeman here needs to speak to you about what you saw. I'll be just in here.'

Two of the girls untangled themselves from the couch and walked past Mark into the other room. He said his thanks to the women, and followed.

In the kitchen, a young boy sat at the table, head in hands. 'Evan?' Mark asked.

The boy looked up, red-faced and anguished. 'It *was* Aidan Sleeth, wasn't it?' he said.

'Yes, I'm afraid it was.'

'I thought it was, but – his head. It was . . .'

'Yes.'

The face remained Aidan Sleeth from the nose down, but the back of his head was an explosion of gore. Bits of brain, skin and bone matter on nearby shrubs and trees, blood soaking into the wet earth. The rest of the body appeared unharmed and strangely comfortable, huddled into the side of an acacia tree, knees up to the chest. Cream chinos, brown brogues, a light blue shirt and a navy Country Road jumper. Wallet in the jeans pocket. Aidan Sleeth, forty-one. Successful farmer and property investor. Ex-wife, on good terms. Beyond that, Mark knew little else. He'd safe-guarded the crime scene, set up barriers, taken photos, arranged for the body to be taken away. Tomorrow, Foren-sics and Homicide would arrive from Adelaide.

The teenagers were frightened. Each had the look of a face not quite put together, features pained and uncertain.

'Names and ages?' he asked, pen held high. 'Just for the official stuff.'

The older of the girls answered. 'I'm Emma Matteson, fourteen. This is my sister, Sarah Matteson – she's twelve – and our neighbour, Evan Williams. He's fourteen too.'

'That's great. Now, can you tell me – and take your time – how you came to see the body?'

There was a slight pause, a shift in the air.

'We just saw it there, in the torchlight – all crumpled up on the side of the path near the creek,' Emma said.

'Did you touch the body at all?'

'No way! Why would we do that? No, we just came back here and woke Mum up. Then she called Sue – that's Evan's mum. My grandmother, Beth Matteson, lives in the house out the back, so she came in too.'

'Was it only you three out there tonight?'

'Yes, only us.' Emma was firm.

Mark thought for a moment. 'There was another girl in the lounge room. Was she not with you?'

Sarah gave a snort. 'That's Isabelle, our other sister. She only got out of bed when we came in.'

There was a silence and Mark wondered if their mothers had broached the subject yet.

'What were you doing out there in the bush after midnight?'

Emma looked hard at the table. Sarah, the youngest one, mimicked her sister's action, but not before she threw Evan a quick sideways glance.

'You were sneaking out, weren't you? I get that. But why?'

'Are we in trouble?' Sarah asked in a small voice, eyes still cast downward.

'Not by me you're not. I'm only interested in the body – but still, I'd like to know why you were out there and if you saw or heard anything.'

At 'heard' the boy flinched.

'Did you hear something, Evan?'

'We heard screaming.' Sarah spoke for him.

Mark straightened, tried to keep his voice casual. 'Screaming?'

'Yeah. I was so scared and we were running and running, and that's when I fell over and we saw the dead man.' Sarah's face crumpled.

'This screaming, was it like someone in pain, or someone frightened, or someone screaming, you know, for fun?'

'For *fun*?' Emma was scornful. 'Yeah, the screaming was like fun, fun, fun. That's why we were running in the opposite direction.'

The girl had a point. 'Was it a woman's scream?'

The three went quiet, then Evan muttered something.

'What was that, Evan?' Mark had to bend down towards him.

'I said, it was a bird.' Evan raised his head and looked blank-faced at Mark. 'A Barking Owl. Their cry, it sounds like a woman screaming.'

'It didn't sound much like a bird,' Emma said, doubtful.

'It was.'

Barking Owls. Mark had heard the tales; the screaming bird that wakes you in the night thinking a woman is being raped and murdered just outside your door. 'Those birds common round here?'

'Not really.' Evan's head was drooping. 'But it's breeding time and there are a few out there in the bush along the creek.'

'You know a bit about birds, do you, Evan?' Mark kept up his light, friendly tone. The one he used for kids and belligerent drunks. God, he was tired. And cold. He realised he hadn't yet taken off his coat after standing outside in the dark, in the rain, staring at Aidan Sleeth's shattered head.

The boy muttered in response.

'What's that?' Harsher than what he was aiming for, but couldn't the boy speak up? *Shoulders back, son!* he wanted to say. Mark repeated, 'Could you say that again, mate?'

'There's this person who sometimes stays near here, he knows a bit.'

'He's a twitcher,' Sarah said, and she mimicked a bird, her arms flapping, then cupping her hands to make binoculars. 'Not Evan, I don't mean him. I'm talking about the man from the co-op.'

Out of the three of them, she now appeared the brightest, eager to help, her little face aglow. She was probably over-tired, bordering on hysterical. His two sons got like that after a party or a movie about superheros. He should go. His doona called like a beautiful siren.

'Twitcher, okay.'

'They're people who watch birds, like *a lot*.'

'Shut up, Sarah,' Emma said, irritated. 'He's a twitcher, so what? There's weirdos everywhere.'

'Nothing wrong with birdwatching,' Mark said, and looked at Evan.

The boy shrugged, turning his face away.

'That why you were out there? Listening for birds?'

Emma laughed, a short bark. 'Evan said there was something cool in the bush and that we should go there with him to check it out. He made it sound really good and Sarah kept nagging me, so we met him at the bottom of the driveway and walked there, into the bush. It's not like there's anything else to do around here.'

'Okay.'

'Really cool, wasn't it, Evan?' Emma turned to the boy. 'Thanks for that, arsehole.'

Evan's face, anxious before, now sagged and his eyes welled up.

Mark reached out and patted the boy's hand. 'No need to blame anyone.'

Just then the door opened and Jacqueline Matteson entered, her eyes bright despite the hour.

'Time for bed, kids,' she said before turning her chair back into the lounge room. 'Sue, want Isabelle to drive you home?'

Mark pretended not to hear. He'd only seen her briefly, but Isabelle did not look old enough to own a licence. That said, she was a farming girl, probably been driving since she was ten, and it *was* just next door. He said nothing. Went to say something. Said nothing.

Jacqueline caught the look. 'She's fifteen. And it's just up the drive and across the paddocks. A track, not the road. I'd

11

never let her drive on that. It's okay. Issy knows to drive slow, I'm very strict about it.'

Mark raised his eyebrows in a helpless gesture, then gave a sigh. It was an act: Frustrated Rural Cop.

'Yes, please,' Sue called back, listless. The woman had all the features of cardboard.

Evan stood up and Mark shook his hand, then watched his drooping shape leave the room. The two girls followed: Emma defiant and without glancing back, Sarah giving a small wave.

With the teenagers gone, the kitchen expanded and became lighter.

'Here.' Jacqueline was offering him a towel and a coat. 'You're still soaking.'

'Yup. Bit wet out there.' Mark took the towel and gave his hair a rough dry, rubbing it over the back of his neck and behind his ears. He wrestled off his wet coat and mimed where to put it – back of the chair? Or the table? Jacqueline nodded towards the chair. He put it there.

The new coat, much too big, was a great relief. Its dryness seeped into his bones. Comfort. He felt like curling up right then and there on the Mattesons' kitchen floor.

'What do you think happened?' Jacqueline picked up two empty cups from the table with one hand and wheeled them to the sink.

'Difficult to tell. City detectives will be arriving soon enough, they'll be able to give us a clearer picture.'

'Surely there's no clearer picture than the back of a man's head blown off.'

He couldn't argue with that. 'What about you? What do you think happened?'

'It sounds pretty obvious that the man has been shot. Maybe by accident, I don't know. Probably a hunter, there's deer out there.'

'We can't rule out suicide.'

'No, you can't.'

Mark caught the tone, recognised it in his own thoughts. Rural men suicided all the time, twice as often as their city counterparts. Depression, the fishbowl existence, divorce, loneliness and drought. Factors that didn't seem to fit with what he knew of Aidan Sleeth, but even so. Rural men weren't generally talkers. Counselling? Maybe in a blue moon. *Maybe.* Still, why go into the bush, far from your home, in the dead of night, in the pouring rain, and shoot yourself? Most rural men suicided on their properties, had planned for it, practised even.

There was nothing so far, in the little he'd learned about Sleeth, that suggested this scenario was likely. Sleeth's farm wasn't failing. His divorce, according to Brian, the paramedic from Booralama whom he'd met at the scene, was reputed to be amicable. This rain wouldn't dent Sleeth's bank balance – his farm could withstand the rough seasons – but still, suicide could not be ruled out. The stats were clear on that. Police in rural stations across the country told grim tales of cutting people down from ropes, unhooking gas pipes from cars, and prising the family gun from fingers grey with death.

'The kids mentioned screaming, a Barking Owl. You ever heard it round here?'

Jacqueline gave an exaggerated shudder. 'Yes. Horrible! First time I heard it, I made Rod get up with me and go out looking for some woman I was convinced was being strangled in the bush.'

'Can't have been fun.'

Jacqueline shook her head. 'Took me a while to get used to the call, but I did – sort of.'

'They rare, Barking Owls?'

'Endangered I think, but I'm no bird expert. I haven't heard it for at least a couple of years. Doesn't mean they're not out there, of course.'

'You think that's why the kids were in the bush tonight, to hear it?'

'They said that's why. With Emma, though, I'm never entirely sure. She can be a bit wild.'

Wild. What did that mean? Reckless, fast? Different connotations for males and females.

'They've had a rough night,' he said.

Jacqueline yawned, ran a hand through her hair. 'Word got out pretty quick, as you can imagine. Emma and social media . . . People are already messaging to let me know what type of casserole they'll be dropping around. I'll take a few days off, see how the girls go. It's actually Evan I'm more worried about.'

Mark thought of the boy, slouched over the table, a portrait of misery. And something else – fear?

'Better be off.' He felt in his jeans pocket for his keys. 'Thanks for the coat. And for letting me talk to the kids so late.'

'I hope Emma wasn't rude to you. She can be a nightmare.' A dark curl bobbed at the side of her cheek.

Fetching, Mark thought. He coughed. 'Fetching': a funny word to think of right now. 'Three teenage girls, don't know how you do it.'

'Three! I've got four. Georgia's at university.'

Mark gave a low whistle. 'Hats off. That's impressive.' He walked out the swing door into the lounge, Jacqueline following. He lingered a moment in the warm room. A photo on the living room wall showed a family of six: four girls, a younger Jacqueline, and a big man in a blue polo shirt and jeans. A happy shot. Mark pointed to the man. 'That your husband?'

Jacqueline looked up at the photo, head tilted in a fond expression. 'Yep, that's Rod. He died four years ago.'

'I'm sorry.'

'You weren't to know.' She fiddled at her hair, pushing the errant curl back into line behind her ear. No use, it sprang out again.

Mark stood awkwardly, studying the photo. He coughed into the crook of his elbow and thanked Jacqueline as she opened the door for him and said goodbye.

He gave a quick wave and stepped onto the dimly lit porch, clicking the button on his keys. The mention of the dead husband had made things awkward, though it needn't have. He knew, after all the stilted conversations about his mother, how difficult it was for people to talk naturally about what was the most natural of progressions.

Most natural, that is, unless you were shot in the back of the head.

The police HiLux lit up like an old friend as he hurried towards it, sludging through the puddles. Headlights on, he pulled out onto the dirt driveway, now a moving thing of potholes and running streams. It was another freak storm with flash flooding, crops lost, old gums falling. Dangerous for anyone caught out in it. Why choose such a night to impress the girls? Wouldn't Evan's bird be there tomorrow?

On his way home, in the darkness along Stone Town Road, then the lonely stretch to Booralama, Mark listened to radio updates about the missing woman, last seen eight days ago. No real news as yet, neighbours were shocked, leads were thin. He switched it off.

In the quiet of early morning, Mark thought about the Matteson family photo. Rod standing proud in the centre with a small girl on his shoulders, Jacqueline beside him holding another. No wheelchair. Two older girls were laughing into the camera. Four children. Oldest away at university, the youngest two in the kitchen, the ones to find the body.

So why, Mark asked himself, was it the second-born daughter, Isabelle, who was sobbing?

In the brief seconds his headlights had lit up her face as their vehicles passed each other on the Mattesons' driveway, Mark had seen the girl's distraught face; her expression anguished and full of woe.

CHAPTER 2

Kookaburras woke him. Mark lay for a moment in bed, looking up at the fading stickers of Transformers in formation around the window. Barely there, but he could make out their features still: Bumblebee, Optimus Prime and Megatron. The stickers had been placed there by his mother, who'd thought it would cheer him up after a bout of the flu. He'd been fourteen at the time, embarrassed by his mother treating him like an infant, but even so . . . the stickers remained. Alien beings that could transform into machines? Their creator was a genius, and anyway, he remembered thinking, some older kids still liked *Ewok Adventures*.

Mark's eyes wandered further around his childhood bedroom. It needed a paint. The faded cream colour was brown at the edges and peeling on the wardrobe side where the western light was most fierce. He ran his fingers along the wall, bubbled now, and was that mould near the carpet? A spider web glistened above the door. It wasn't just this room, it was every room. The house itself needed repainting, restumping, rewiring and a good rethinking. If only it could transform itself into a city apartment over-looking the river, close by to Charlie and Sam.

His boys would still be asleep at this moment. Aged six and eight, and each in a separate bedroom with white walls and walk-in robes and colourful doonas. Kelly's wage had skyrocketed further after they separated, as she moved from family law to corporate contracts. Her new house, bought with the new boyfriend, sparkled with presence and style. Mark was happy for Kelly and Steven; the boys were happy, everyone was happy.

A brief chorus of rain tinkled down the gutters, the tempo upbeat and light.

Outside the kookaburras stopped and the magpies started up, their fluty song a daily pleasure. It gave him pause. His house might be falling down, he might be single, living in his childhood home with stickers on the sills, his kids might be hours away – but in terms of birds and trees, Booralama was about as good as it got.

Mark got out of bed, stretched and rummaged about, trying to find his running things. Footy shorts, still too tight but getting looser, singlet top and old runners.

On his way out, down the front path, the dense garden pressed in, wet and languid. *Add pruning to the list*, he thought. The callistemons were drowning in their own weight. That smell though, that low thickly sweet smell of healthy earth and things growing, he loved it. Above, the eucalyptus trees shook with birds and insects. Already, the low hum of cicadas had begun. His mother's iron fence held firm, and the gate creaked as he opened and closed it. 'An old lady's house' was how his city friend Angelo had described it when he came for his one and only visit. 'All garden and photos and tea-stained china cups.'

Mark couldn't deny it. There were only so many family pics a house could hold and at last count there were seven teapots. There were too many books on historical homes in the region and a lonely piano, like him, losing tune. Mark couldn't work out whether it was grief or laziness that prevented him from cleaning the place up. No doubt a combination of both.

He began a steady jog and headed down to the river path, some twenty metres from his mother's house – correction, *his* house. 'You have it,' his sister Prue had insisted when they'd been going over the will. 'What do I need it for? I live in bloody Canada now, married to a loaded Yank. You're newly divorced and semi-depressed. Have it, Mark, it's yours!'

This close to the river and with such a big yard, the house would sell easily. Tree-changers would be attracted to its size, established garden and high ceilings. There would be a charming way to describe the family of pygmy bats who lived in the roof – and as for the *pressed tin!* He always referred to it as such, ever since his aunt and her posh friends from Melbourne came to visit. While the single bathroom failed to impress, the *pressed tin!* did. Yes, he could ready the house for sale. Move back to the big smoke, buy something small in the burbs and see his sons every day instead of every second weekend and holidays.

The path was empty, no one out walking this early. It was not yet six. The wide river glistened smooth in the morning light, and the reflection of dappled gums on its surface made the whole scene appear tranquil and slow. Not so; he knew only too well the uneven depths, the strength of the current and the danger of submerged logs. At school, a kid in the year above him had jumped off the bridge into the river – they all did it. He had himself countless times, despite the warning sign. But who cares about a sign with a stick figure and a red cross on it when you're fifteen? The kid had got stuck in a dead tree drifting below the surface. Trapped under it and almost drowned, if not for his friends who had dived in again and again to find him. Now, David was a severely brain-damaged quadriplegic living with his parents behind the primary school.

The image of David lying on the side of the river, unconscious, with teenagers scuttling about in shock, brought Mark back to last night's events. Aidan Sleeth, dead in the bush. Teenagers, there on a dare, coming across his body and raising the alarm. What would it do to a twelve-year-old to see such a thing? Mark thought of the young girl, Sarah, and how she'd raised her hands into binoculars to describe the art of twitching. Maybe she would be okay. The other girl, Emma, seemed angry rather than scared. What, after all, did he know about teenage girls and resilience? As for Evan – ashamed, nervous, worried. Mark decided he'd like to talk to him again. And then there was Isabelle, her sobbing face in the headlights. Why so devastated?

Mark looked at his watch, then picked up speed as he crossed the walking bridge and circled back again. The sun was beginning to have some heat in it and the ground steamed with the remnants of last night's rain. Homicide would be arriving from Adelaide at ten o'clock. There'd need to be a crime scene visit, a plan for the investigation, witnesses to formally interview. Last night he went to bed thinking he might head down to the city for the weekend to see the boys. No chance of that now.

Mark slowed to a walk, panting hard. He was getting quicker, but the years were taking their toll. At fifty-one, six k's feels like sixty.

The first of the walkers came into sight. Lee O'Brien and his dog Roxie. Lee liked a chat. Mark waved a hello and focused hard on his watch as the man passed.

'You heard the news?' Lee asked, taking his headphones out of his ears and pointing to them. 'Just on now.'

Already! Mark thought. This town was leakier than Canberra. 'Yes,' he said. 'But we can't say anything in regards to it yet, Lee. There's the family to consider and it's a matter for the police.'

Lee looked at him curiously. 'It certainly is, but you must admit, this new development is interesting.'

Mark shook his head. 'New development?'

The old man leaned in, making his voice louder and slower for the (slightly) younger man. 'The missing woman – they've released information about what she was investigating.'

Mark stepped back and nodded. Now it made sense. Detective Sergeant Natalie Whitsed, the missing woman. Every police officer in the country was invested in her case. It was all the talk in station tea rooms across Australia, at morning briefings, during routine checks and mundane arrests: Natalie Whitsed, a fellow cop. Where was she?

'And?' Mark felt foolish learning this news from Lee, but what was it, six-thirty? He'd had less than four hours' sleep.

'Media says she was in the middle of investigating Charlene Scopelliti. How's that for you?' Lee sounded pleased to be the giver of such news.

Charlene Scopelliti! The twenty-four-year-old Melbourne socialite, former hairdresser, ex-girlfriend of a Brownlow medallist, reality TV star and now the wife of Tony 'The Hook' Scopelliti, fifty-something owner of a chain of strip clubs and fast food restaurants. Recently jailed for drug trafficking, extortion and smuggling stolen goods, Scopelliti was the current kingpin in organised crime.

'What's the betting Natalie Whitsed is still alive?' Lee grinned unpleasantly, pulling on his dog's lead.

Mark didn't answer. But he thought, *I don't like her chances.*

The older man put his earphones back in place, giving Mark a flat-hand wave before moving off at a brisk step.

The sun speared between the trees, piercing bare skin. Mark winced. Next run, he'd wear sunglasses. Taking off his shoes and top, he walked down the riverbank in the bend, where it was sandy rather than muddy. He took two steps before stretching into a shallow dive, the river washing over him dense and cold. He surfaced, already metres down-stream, and had to swim hard to make it back to the bank and his clothes. He'd done this swim hundreds of times but the cold and the strength of the river never failed to impress.

Daily routine complete, Mark walked home refreshed, not bothering with top and shoes. He thought over the day ahead: Aidan Sleeth, homicide investigation. There'd be the usual chatter about Natalie Whitsed, but for him today was all about the local man shot in the Stone Town bush. Already Mark longed for his room, with Optimus Prime gazing over him like a benefactor.

Inside the house, the phone was already buzzing. He picked it up. Homicide, on their way up the highway. 'Inspector Clare Rendell here.' A gruff voice; smoker. 'Heard the news?' It was too early to sound so harried.

'Yes,' Mark answered. 'The Charlene Scopelliti con-nection.'

'Not that.' Rendell's voice was scornful. 'I mean *your* case, Aidan Sleeth. Someone's rung in to say they know who did it.'

'That was quick.'

'Yeah, Waldara Station received the call an hour ago. Got directed to Homicide. Woman from Stone Town, wants to talk with you pronto. Texting you her details now.'

'Thanks.'

'Have the case sewn up by the time we arrive, can you?' The inspector's voice was tired. 'We're all about Whitsed down here.'

'Here too.'

'She was one of our own. Same station, Adelaide.'

Mark heard the stress. 'We'll find her,' he said, meaning 'the police will'.

'Yeah, yeah.' The unspoken words were clear. *Unless Scopelliti's mates already have.*

CHAPTER 3

This was big. Scopelliti's wife, Charlene. Journos would be salivating at the emerging plot line; the glamorous wife of a con being investigated by a female cop, now missing.

What did Natalie Whitsed discover about the young wife and minor celebrity whose husband was in jail for drug trafficking, extortion and theft? Morburn Prison may be holding Scopelliti in solitary, but that didn't mean he couldn't reach out to his mates on the outside who owed him a thing or two. And it worked both ways – the outside could reach in to Scopelliti too, extend its fingers beyond the walls and barbed wire and security measures. What news of the outside was brought to Scopelliti each day? What nasty rumours filtered into his cell?

The text with the details for the person claiming to know who killed Sleeth came through; Mrs Patricia Delaney, Lot 4, Stone Town Road, Stone Town. Mark put the kettle on, standing for a moment and listening to its whistle – Aidan

Sleeth had been shot dead in the bush, *this* was his priority. Leave Natalie Whitsed and the mysteries of Charlene Scopelliti to the rest of the force.

Mark googled the address sent to him by Rendell. It was north of the Mattesons', two paddocks shy of the old Stone Town primary school. He'd have to drive past Jacqueline's house to get there. Something half-forgotten quivered in his gut. Quivered, just for a moment, then rested, biding its time.

A shower, quick breakfast – mug of tea and crumpets – and Mark was headed out again. He'd have around an hour to talk with Mrs Delaney in order to be back in time for Inspector Rendell. The press liked to call Homicide the glamour squad of the force, but Mark knew them only as hard-arsed and able.

In Booralama, traffic was rarely a problem, but at this hour he'd caught the back of a sports bus, the one headed to the private school one hour away. There was a high school in the town, he'd gone to it, but kids were increasingly abandoning it for the more expensive one in Waldara, down south.

The town's sole traffic lights became red and he waited, the students in the back seat of the bus turning to him and waving. He waved back, liking their energy, wishing he had some of it. The lights went green and the bus turned left. Mark steered ahead past a new cafe and a phone repair shop. Booralama, his hometown, had changed – of course it had. Perhaps it was age, nostalgia for his youth, but Mark couldn't help remembering when kids in town and the surrounding farms all went to the same school, played for the same teams and went to the same parties. It was progress, perhaps – all the new people moving in, the new houses, the roundabouts. Choice, that's what was good about it. Where to send your kids to school, where to eat and who to mix with. Choice is a kind of power and who doesn't want that?

The temporary move back to his childhood home in Booralama was a choice. His mum had had a fall and the time spent in hospital did her no good. Something about Helen dimmed when she was away from her garden. His mother had been seventy-eight, but only in hospital did she seem old. It frightened him, the way she'd clung to him and whimpered like one of his own sons. The nursing staff at Booralama base agreed Helen Ariti would be better off at home. And so he'd come up from the city, taken two weeks' carer's leave, then three, then four. Then compassionate leave after the funeral and, after all that, what with the vacancy for a police position in the local station after the old cop got cancer, it seemed just as easy to give up his city rental and stay.

Prue flew out from Canada for the fortnight before Helen died. It had been a privilege, the siblings agreed, to look after their mother in her final days. They were never closer to her than at the end. Now, each part of the house was infused with Helen and their shared life. A cracked teapot reminded him of the quick way she placed things, her gestures haphazard and busy. Empty jam jars in preparation for the plums, the creak in the floorboard where she exclaimed for half a century 'I must get that fixed!', and half-packets of mint-leaf lollies in the pantry. 'I'll use them on a cake!' she'd say, though they'd been solidified for years.

Helen Ariti had had a good life. Even after his father had died when he was young, Mark could remember his mother as active as a wren. Now she was gone, and he was alone in the house, *his* house.

The road north to Stone Town was long and flat, bordered on both sides by wheat fields and, further on, drooping eucalyptus, native grasses and weeds. If not for the recent storms, Mark would be seriously worried about fires. Twenty years earlier the whole region had been up in flames. He could remember the customary photo in the city paper of a useless bloke in stubbies and thongs holding a limp hose in the face of a roaring inferno. He remembered it because he was that bloke. He'd been in Booralama for a rare visit at the time, catching up with friends, got roped into a social tennis comp, became embroiled in the fires.

Mark hit the crossroads and turned left, past an old stone ruin and down a thinner road, darkened by the dense tree line; this was the edge of the Stone Town bush, sixty-odd acres of it, full of mine shafts and birds and, less frequently, blokes with half their head shot off. After the madness of the gold rush in the 1850s, it had somehow escaped the razing into farmland. It was unknown to him, this bush. Booralama people generally headed to the river, or down south to the Waldara hills for weekend walks and swims, not to this countryside with its snarled trees and dry creeks and strange birds. No guidebook ever mentioned walking in the Stone Town bush; there were no designated tracks or huts to stay in, no camping facilities, not even a welcome sign. It was just there.

As Mark drove past the Mattesons' property on Stone Town Road, he could just make out their house down the driveway. Tall birch trees on either side, a ute out the front. His coat was still in that house, he could pick it up. Say he was there to collect it and also have a chat to the second-eldest daughter, the one too young to drive. Find out why she'd been crying. Just the shock of it all?

Mark swerved around a dead roo on the edge of the road, its hindquarters bloated and stiff. Probably been there for a couple of days. He should move it. He didn't.

Mark checked the address for Mrs Delaney again; here it was – Lot 4. A run-down weatherboard at the end of a dirt driveway, the yard littered with rabbit holes and straggly shrubs. Thistles grew around a rusted tractor. A sign read 'EMOH ROU', our home.

Country life, Mark thought. *Now here's one for the magazines.*

He knocked on the door. 'Mrs Delaney? Detective Senior Sergeant Mark Ariti.'

'Eh?' a voice called from somewhere in the darkness of the house.

'Hello? Mrs Delaney?'

A figure thumped down the hall. 'Hold your horses, I'm coming.'

The door opened.

'Mrs Delaney?'

'Pat,' the woman said, huge in her Demis Roussos gown. 'No need for Mrs Delaney unless you're Princess Anne or the bank.'

Mark shook her hand and explained his presence.

The woman stepped outside, her calves a pair of sturdy posts beneath the floral dress. Mark stood up straight; something about the woman garnered respect. She gestured for him to sit on one of the chairs on the porch and he did so, obediently.

Pat flapped at a wasp about her head. 'You're Helen Ariti's son.'

Mark nodded. It always amazed him, the social reach of his mother. He looked at the woman more closely, felt a flicker of recognition. 'You were at Mum's funeral.'

'I wouldn't have missed it.'

A group of older women had made sandwiches and cakes for the reception after the service. Pat had been one of them. Loads of scones and egg and lettuce and jelly slice. He hadn't thanked them properly. Prue did all that.

'Thanks for coming. And for all the food, it was great . . .' He trailed off.

'Her jam never won at the show,' Pat ignored his attempt at gratitude. 'Too many bits of peel in it.'

That was true; his mother would never have bothered with the precise peeling and washing of the fruit.

Pat reached for a tea towel on her shoulder and gave a whack at the wasp. 'But it was always the tastiest. Couldn't convince the other judges though – it was always about the peel, the peel, the peel.'

'I don't think she minded losing every year.'

'And her tea! Never one for a strainer. Tea leaves half the way up the cup and all over the country once Helen poured.'

Mark shifted in his seat. 'You knew Mum well then?'

'Same CWA there for awhile, we all know each other. After Bob died, Helen came here every week, making her terrible cuppas, providing meals. She did it till I had to say stop. That woman! She would have come every week till the apocalypse if I had let her.'

Mark looked out to the Stone Town bush, dark green and grey. Still, in the morning light. There was so much about his mother he didn't know.

'Was Bob your husband?'

'Son.'

'Sorry.' The word was always inadequate.

'Cuppa?' Pat gave the wasp one final swipe, caught it in the tea towel and threw it on the wooden boards, stamping on it. Her weight resounded; the house shook on its stumps.

'No, thank you. I'm here about the phone call you made this morning to the Waldara police, about Aidan Sleeth.'

'Called the Booralama station, you weren't in.'

'I don't generally start work before eight-thirty.'

Pat raised her eyebrows, gave a little shake of her head.

'The call, you said you knew who was responsible for Aidan Sleeth's death.'

'Oh, I know all right.' Pat picked up a pair of boots from the porch and banged them together, shaking off clods of dirt. An axe leaned against the railings, its handle worn with use.

'Well, who was it?' Mark asked, a little desperate.

Pat lowered herself into a chair beside his. It looked a difficult process. Mark stood to help and she refused, face red and determined.

31

Finally, she sank into the chair and an expression of peace crossed her face. 'Getting old's a bugger,' she said. 'My advice is, eat your greens and have a small glass of whiskey in the evening with your smoke. Just the one, mind you, no more.'

Mark waited.

'Lovely day,' the woman said with a sigh.

Mark saw the hint of a smile cross her face and tried a different tack. 'Did you know Aidan Sleeth at all?'

'Not much. One of the in-and-out types. Grew up here, left for university, came back home, travelled – you know the type. Unit in Melbourne I think, there half the time. He was young – I knew his parents a little, nice people. They separated: one moved to Surfers, the other Noosa.'

Pat paused.

'They were very different,' Pat added, and he gave a nod. Noosa and Surfers! Too right they were different, like pearls and jet skis. 'Both dead.' Pat scratched at her face. A flake of dry skin fell off, caught the breeze and flew away. 'Their place here has a tennis court and a garden with tiny hedges. Was the original homestead in these parts. After their divorce they kept it for the son, Aidan. Went around there for a meeting once.'

'What about?'

'I don't know. The community hall? The state of the fire station? What are any meetings about? Usually nothing, but you go.'

It's true, Mark thought. *You go.*

'When was the last time you spoke with Aidan Sleeth?'

'Spoke with him!' The woman gave a laugh, the top of

her body jiggling up and down on itself. 'Probably when he was sixteen and I was telling him off for something. More recently though, when he's been driving in his flash car past here – doesn't stop for a chat, just gives a wave, as you do. That's Aidan, no time for us hillbilly neighbours.'

'Who do you think killed him, Patricia?'

Pat looked at him, then tapped the sides of her chair. 'Put it this way. You live in the city – crowded suburb, more cafes than people. You want a change in lifestyle, you want the bush, you want the peace, you want to make homemade jam and put it in the show. You want your kids to play with sticks and to climb up trees. You want to go vegan and grow your own shoes. You get together with a group of like-minded friends and you buy a block of bush. Stone Town bush. A co-op. You get some alpacas, your kids go to the local primary school, and you love it till you discover it's not creative enough and there's too many kids with names like Zaidan and Jayden who like to ride dirt bikes in said bush. You take your kids out of school, start advocating for a Montessori, and while you're waiting for the funds, you home-school, start teaching your kids about art and the environment and making good choices.'

'So far, so good.'

'Yeah, till the kids start asking when Zaidan can come for a play.'

'Where's this going, Pat?' *I have to get to a meeting.*

'Point is, everyone's relatively happy. It's a good life. Neighbours don't intrude, people are nice enough and the bush is quiet. No one notices the dope plants on the front porch, and if they do, it's only because they need a bit of help with the old arthritis.'

'Okay, Pat, who do you think killed Aidan Sleeth?'

'There's one couple left that originally bought the Stone Town bush blocks and turned it into a co-op. It's all going along very nicely and they don't regret selling their city home for under $400,000 when it's now worth *well over a million*. They don't mind that *at all*. They say that a lot. *A lot.*'

'You like these people?'

'Don't see them much, but they're okay. Murderers often present that way. Bradley Edwards the Claremont killer volunteered, you know – Little Athletics.'

Mark stood. 'Look, Pat, I'm going. Let's wrap this up.'

'Aidan Sleeth just bought twenty acres of Stone Town bush from one of the co-op members and he was planning on getting a subdivision built. Courts and drives and houses that all look the same. Probably call it Sleethville.'

'So, you think . . .'

'I think that it's worth paying Evie and John Renner a visit. The rural dream they invested everything in is about to go boom and it's all down to one man.'

'Sleeth.'

'There you go, you *are* a bright one. Helen always said that.'

Mark caught that knowing smile in her voice again. 'Thanks for the information, Pat. I'm not sure it's conclusive though.'

'Just talk to them. You'll see.'

Mark looked at his watch. 'How'd you find out about

the shooting so early, Pat? You called Waldara at, what – six? Six-thirty?'

'Oh, come on now, Mark.' Pat shook her head in mock frustration. 'You know what this area's like. News spreads like a rash, no matter what the hour.'

It was true. Mark's sister Prue still claimed to have found out about her surprise twenty-first birthday party before it was organised.

The two of them gazed out at the land. Despite the front fence and the road, the bush appeared very close. A wattle, half alive, was leaning over the side gate as if it was trying to find the latch.

'Does it bother you a body was found out there last night – a local, shot?'

Pat thought for a moment, then shrugged. 'This land's been thick with bodies for two hundred years. One more won't change anything. And a local? I'm not sure about that. What's a local?'

'You're a local. Mum was a local.'

'Yeah? Maybe. Maybe you're right. This place does feel like home.'

Bit of a strange thing to say, Mark thought. He looked at the woman beside him, eyes closed, huge, rocking back and forth on her chair, the axe beside her like a pet. Who was she? There was a Band-Aid on her calf, curling at the edges, its centre darkened with blood. He hadn't noticed it before.

'Where were you last night, Pat? I have to ask.'

The old woman laughed, her whole body jiggling about like panna cotta. 'I was at a CWA meeting, the show fundraiser. Over at Sue's house. She never likes holding it at her place, but it was her turn, so we all went there.'

Sue, Evan's mother.

'Who else was there?' Mark got out his notebook and held his pen poised.

'A good number, considering the weather. All the locals: Jacqueline Matteson, Sue Williams of course, Jacqueline's mother-in-law Beth, and Evie Renner, which was nice. She's the co-op owner I told you about. Wants to put in some of her vegan slice so we'll see how that one goes.'

'When's the show?' Mark asked, standing. 'Might go along.'

'Next Saturday, Booralama showgrounds. Good day for the kids – you've got young boys, haven't you?'

It always stumped him, how much locals knew of his life. Booralama and its surrounds were like a web, everyone connected and linked through family, work and experience. No wonder tree-changers often found it tough. The romantic idea that gripped them – of a simple life with friendly folk – soon faded when the old ties were revealed.

'Yeah, two.' Mark stood, walked down the old porch steps, each one creaking with his weight. Another house that needed restumping, re-everything.

'Kids love the show. You used to.'

Mark felt a flicker of recognition. He *did* remember the show – from when he was a child and even into his late teens, when his mother used to drag him along to help out with the produce stall. A vague memory of Pat Delaney and another woman and children rose to the surface like a bubble, floated there, then burst once he climbed into his vehicle and started the engine.

Backing out of the driveway, Mark raised his hand to wave. Pat Delaney was standing, queenly in her bright gown, palm up in either farewell or benediction; it was, frankly, difficult to tell.

CHAPTER 4

On the way back to Booralama, Mark kept the window down and let the cool air blow over him. Outside, after all the rain, it was thick with humidity, and now, with the fresh air filling the car, he felt as if he could think properly again.

He hadn't asked Pat all the questions he should have. When was the last time she'd seen John Renner? How did she have all the information about Sleeth's business dealings? Had she ever heard the Barking Owl? He looked at his watch. Thirty minutes and Homicide would be in town, asking what he'd learned about Sleeth. They were pushy, Homicide, and they'd be keen to wrap this one up so they could get back to their priority: Natalie Whitsed.

An image of the police officer, her face plastered over posters and newspaper and television reports, popped into Mark's head. Young-looking despite her thirty-five years, round-faced, freckles, blonde. Short and sturdy. *Cute*, the newsagent had commented, nodding towards the latest profile picture of

Natalie when Mark bought the morning paper. What good does cute get you when you're a missing person? More press, more public interest, he guessed. Even more when you're dead.

Mark drove past the dead roo again and noted its bloated carcass, the brown stain growing. Crows again. Always the crows. He should do something about it. Some P-plater might swerve around it and hit a tree. He slowed, sighed and reversed. Parked on the side of the road, he opened the back of the HiLux, got out a shovel. Country police always had such tools in their vehicles: rope, crow bars, shovels. *If we weren't cops,* Mark thought, *we'd be the prime suspects every time a body turned up.*

The roo carcass was partially stuck to the road. Scraping was required. Mark levered the shovel under the bulk of the remains and lifted. The tail fell off and he swore. It was heavier than he thought. Averting his eyes from the purple guts and swarming maggots, Mark lifted the remains and heaved them to the edge of the road. The roo couldn't stay where it was, it needed to be moved further from the road, into the bush, beyond the ditch. He'd have to come back. He was in the process of kicking the tail bone off the bitumen when a ute drove up.

'Need some help?' A young man at the wheel of the ute, early thirties maybe, woollen beanie, long hair, flanny.

'Got it covered now, thanks.' There was a bit of grey fur on Mark's boot. He used the shovel to get it off.

'Was going to do that myself,' the young man was saying. 'But didn't have a shovel.'

'Wouldn't want to do it with your hands.'

'Are you the local policeman?'

Mark looked up. 'Yes, Booralama Station. Why?'

'The death of Aidan Sleeth. Everyone's rattled.'

The bush telegraph again. Faster than the internet. 'Did you know him?'

'Not really, he bought my girlfriend's block. Met him just the once, seemed to be a nice enough guy.'

Mark remembered Patricia's story. 'Your girlfriend used to be in a co-op, right? She left it recently and sold to Aidan?'

The young man didn't seem surprised that Mark knew the story. 'Yeah, what a saga that was. I've been up collecting a few of Sasha's things before they turf it all out.'

Mark looked in the back of the man's ute. A spinning wheel, a box of jars, some paintings. A Buddha statue? The little fat man seemed happy enough to be sitting in the tray of a ute heading back to the city.

'She didn't come with you?'

The man shook his head. 'Not a chance. The co-op didn't end on good terms and, man, there's some serious resentment there.'

'Angry at Aidan Sleeth?'

'Angry at Sleeth, angry at Sasha, angry at climate change and politics and the sourdough that won't rise.'

'You're a brave man to go around there then.'

The young man squared his shoulders. 'Well, Sasha didn't want to and so . . .'

The things you do for love, Mark thought. Once he sat through an opera.

The men studied the roo, its twisted and bloody body now stretched out on the side of the road.

'Sure you don't need any help?' the man said. 'Can't stay there, can it? Good it's off the actual road, but it looks like a person if you half close your eyes. It'd freak some driver out big time.'

The carcass *did* resemble a person. Cold and grey and dead. The shock of seeing it there, some tired driver . . . Mark deliberated; he was running late. Homicide were on their way. 'You got a tarp?'

'Yeah, just a small one.'

'Might get a bit dirty.'

'Sure thing.' The young man looked excited. This would be a story for him to tell his mates at some hipster bar, the time he helped out a country copper.

Tarp laid out, the men attempted to roll the dead roo onto it. Maggots squirmed, purple and brown stuff leaked. It stank. Together with the shovel and some serious boot action, they shifted the body onto the tarp and lifted it up, one at each end, carrying it off the road and down into the bush beyond.

'Someone drives past,' Mark said, 'this wouldn't look too good.'

'It's like we're in the skit of a movie.' The young man grimaced with the weight. 'Thing is,' he continued, 'I can't decide if it's a comedy or a tragedy.'

They stopped and dropped the tarp, lifting it so that the body rolled out, mangled now from all the moving. It ended up beside a blackened stump, its small head arched forward as if about to call out.

'Not a romance, that's for sure,' Mark said, and they headed back to their vehicles.

The men put the tarp in the tray of the ute and shook hands. 'Name's Will,' the young man said. 'Didn't think I'd be tossing a body this morning.'

'Mark. Be a story to tell back in the city. Thanks for your help.'

Will got in his vehicle and the two men waved at each other. Brotherly. Mark thought about dead bodies and watched as the ute drove off, the little Buddha in the back jiggling and smiling as if he knew all the secrets of the world.

CHAPTER 5

Back in Booralama, the streets were quieter, old people having a cuppa and a bickie, parents at kids' sports, looking at their watches, wondering if it was too early to order a pie.

A shiny vehicle was out the front of the police station – Homicide's. Mark parked and headed in, wiping his boots on the mat. Behind the counter and in his office, a woman he supposed was Clare Rendell and a male associate were busy setting up home.

'Sorry I'm late,' Mark said.

'Hello, late,' the male replied. 'Country cops not overly fans of watches?'

The young man's humour bored Mark; in his experience the put-down types were usually socially inept or angry men. The cheap dig irritated him further because the man had set up home in *his* office.

'City cops overly fans of dad jokes?' he replied, looking around for his laptop.

'Give it a rest,' the woman said, looking up from a power point under the desk. 'Mark, I'm Inspector Clare Rendell and this is Sergeant Finn Turner. Finn likes dad jokes. I don't.'

'Any sort of jokes you *do* prefer?' Mark asked. 'Just in case we all, you know, reach the joke stage.'

'Humour's not her thing,' Finn said.

Clare's head snapped up. 'You hear the one about the mediocre man who was rumoured to be in line for promotion to Assistant Director of Homicide?'

'No.'

'Neither did I. Cos it didn't happen.'

Finn shook his head slowly. 'That's funny, Clare. Really funny.'

Kill me, thought Mark.

Clare and Finn had set up a computer each, cleared the table and wiped the whiteboard clean. There was a photo of Natalie Whitsed pinned to the corkboard. Finn was busy pinning up others: vehicles, places of work, Tony Scopelliti. Charlene Scopelliti took her place next to the young policewoman. Face made up, long dark hair in luxurious curls.

'Which one you prefer?' Finn asked, indicating the two posters. 'Blonde or brunette?'

Mark sat down at the table, took out his notebook and read through his notes on Patricia Delaney.

'Don't mind him.' Clare looked up from her computer. 'He's okay once you get to ignore him.'

Mark stared at his notes. A little over a year ago up north, he'd been in an office with two bickering cops. But theirs had been the affectionate sort. He'd liked them. *Darryl and Jagdeep*, he thought. *Save me.*

'Can fill you in now on all the Sleeth details, if you like. Got a busy day.'

'Judging a pumpkin show, are we?' Finn asked. 'Local farmers want you to intervene?'

Mark stretched his hands wide, studied them.

'Finn,' Clare said. 'Go to the car, can you? Get me those surveillance files – back seat, in a small box. We'll need them later.'

'Sure, boss, anything you need.' Finn put down the posters and walked out, brushing past Mark as he went. Thin swirls of dark green edged out from beneath the man's shirt sleeves. Tattoos. Cops were allowed to have them nowadays.

'He seems nice,' Mark said as the door slammed shut.

Clare opened a file on her computer and turned it towards him. It was a photo of Aidan Sleeth, lying in the cold night, with half his head blown off.

The image gave Mark a sick feeling, shivery, as if he was coming down with the flu. He wiped his forehead and closed his eyes for a second.

'You need a cup of tea?' Clare stood, eyes on him, busying herself with papers. 'There's a kitchen out the back, right? How d'you have it?'

'White, thanks.' Mark stared at the photo. It was the one he'd taken and sent to Homicide late last night. Already his actions seemed alien: the call to head out to Stone Town in the night, the rain and mud, seeing the body, taking photos, talking to the ambo, Jacqueline Matteson's house. Tiredness tore at his limbs, hacked into his weary brain.

'Never get used to it, do you?' Clare said, leaving the room. 'No matter how many times you see stuff like this.'

Mark averted his eyes from the screen and tried to think about good things; his sons, the river, gum trees. Every scene in his head, however, was overlaid in red. A bit of Aidan Sleeth's skull had dangled from a shrub, a flexible jigsaw piece, the man's hair on it, thin and light grey like a mouse.

Clare returned, put the cuppa before him and sat down again. 'What did the woman who called have to say?'

'Nothing much. I think she wanted to chat. Seemed to think we should visit the new people in the area, ones whose land will be affected by Sleeth buying up the bush.'

'Interesting.'

'Yeah, Sleeth planned a new development. Tree-changers not too happy.'

They studied the photo. Sleeth's head was a mess – was that bone? Dirt and leaves clung to red clumps.

'Doesn't look like he shot himself,' Clare said. 'Although we can't rule it out.'

Mark nodded. It was true. However implausible, it *could* have happened. Sleeth went into the bush to blow his brains out and slipped. Or held the gun behind his lowered head and shot it that way. Mark tried to mimic the action, reaching his arms behind him, an invisible gun, one hand on the trigger. Clare watched. She'd probably tried the same thing herself.

'It's unlikely,' Mark said. 'Looks like he's been shot from behind, at close range to me.'

Clare peered at the screen. 'We'll need Forensics to confirm, but the entry point does seem to be smack bang in the middle of the back of the head . . . But close? I'm not sure . . .'

Clare didn't finish. *Not sure about what?* Mark didn't ask. Homicide, they'd seen it all.

'Initial thoughts?' Clare asked.

'Accident: fox, pig or even deer shooter most likely. Killer panics, does a runner.'

'Secondary thoughts?'

'Business deal gone bad. Although that's less likely. Aidan Sleeth wasn't exactly the James Packer of subdivisions. There's richer people around here selling up their land for bigger money.'

'Who's buying it?'

'Overseas buyers, big farming operations, solar farm organisations. You name it. Land's the new gold.'

The two sat with their own thoughts for a moment. It was true. Bugger the house, the inground pool, the designer kitchen and floor heating: what was desired now was land. Acreage to develop, to plant white subdivision sticks in and announce new suburbs, massive corporate farms. The land must be bought and then yield.

'Was there a wallet on him?'

'Yeah. Fifty bucks inside, a receipt for dry cleaning and a few business cards. Real estate mostly. One for the local bank. No phone.'

There being no phone was a problem and the two cops pondered its absence. Everyone had a phone on them all the time nowadays. Where was Sleeth's?

'That all?'

'And a membership card, for Birds for Bush.'

'Environmental group?'

'Yeah.' It was an unnatural alliance, the developer and the Landcare advocate, but plenty of people were card carriers for worthy groups. Mark was a member of the Booralama Food Co-op and had never been there, not once. It was only through his mother, who'd paid up for five years, that the membership carried on to him. He thought about the card in his wallet right now. The little wheat symbol and the stick figures holding hands. It made him feel noble to have that card in his pocket. Never mind that he didn't know what a food co-op was — if he died and someone searched through his wallet, they would think he was a worthy citizen. Probably serve co-op things at his funeral: organic and that.

'We'll check that out too.' Clare's eyes were moving away from his and to the corkboard where the faces of Natalie and Charlene stared back. She tore her gaze away from them and back to Mark. 'We're talking with Aidan's ex-wife and his employee later this afternoon. Just a chat. You're welcome to sit in.'

'Thank you.'

'I want you to know, you're the local cop here. We're technically in charge, but it's you with the knowledge of the people, the background and the town. Finn's an idiot, but he's not stupid. I'll tell him to pull his head in and help. We'll all need to work together if we want to get this wrapped up.'

'Agreed on that.'

'You take on the interviews with the local people, bring them in to us if need be. We'll check out the finances, search Sleeth's office, follow up with Forensics and the autopsy. I'm very keen to see the spot where he was shot, check out the area.'

Again, Clare's eyes turned to the faces of the women.

'You working the Whitsed case?' Mark asked.

'Yeah, along with the rest of the force.'

'You know her? Natalie?'

Clare's face drooped. 'Yeah, worked alongside her for a while there, when I was in surveillance and she was just starting out. Nice kid. Desk in the next office to ours. Finn and her are close. The search for her, it's full on, no time to scratch ourselves – and now we get this, a shooting death in the middle of no—'

'The town's name is Booralama,' Mark said, weary. 'So how come, if you're so busy with Whitsed, you got this gig?'

'Finn's young in the job – he got told to come up here, I put my hand up to supervise as long as I could continue working on the Whitsed file.'

The implication was clear. The death of Aidan Sleeth was small fry compared to the biggest case in years.

'Besides,' Clare shrugged, 'with everyone going nuts in the city looking for Natalie, it's good to have some space to look at it on my own, at least for a while.'

Finn Turner walked back in, carrying some folders. Clare nodded at them. 'Been sent these from surveillance.

Nat was working on the Scopelliti case, trailing Charlene.'

'You trying to work out what she uncovered?'

'Steady on. More like trying to work on where she was up to. See if this surveillance and her going missing are linked.'

Finn snorted. Mark knew what he was thinking: *As if they aren't.*

Clare frowned at her associate. 'We can't leap to any conclusions. Slow and steady, Finn. Slow and steady's what wins the race.'

'How do you reckon that's working out for Nat?' Finn asked, no longer jokey. 'Reckon she'd appreciate your glacial approach?'

'Slow and steady,' Clare repeated, firm, and Finn scowled.

Slow and steady was an understatement. Police everywhere were dedicated to the case and not only for the connections to Scopelliti. Cops didn't tend to be treated nicely at the hands of criminals. Female cops, well – it didn't bear thinking about. Searches of Natalie's city apartment, door knocks, interviews with colleagues, phone tapping, camera checking, bin checking, fingerprint analysis, call-ins – slow and steady it may be, but a colossal effort nonetheless.

Mark stood; his left knee creaked. Were the morning runs worth it?

'Leave you to it,' he said. 'I'll get onto those door knocks, call a few people. I'll be in the side office, just off the hall.' He gathered his papers, unplugged his laptop and walked to the door.

'Your cuppa.' Clare half stood and passed him the barely drunk mug of tea. He accepted it in the crook of his finger.

'Sorry to kick you out.' Finn was straight-faced. 'City business.'

'What's that on your pants?' Clare was staring below his knee as Mark backed out the door.

He looked down. There was a dark smudge of blood and mud on his navy trousers.

'Roadkill,' he said. 'Country business.'

CHAPTER 6

Door shut, out of his old office space and into the new, Mark surveyed the state of his clothes. Mud, blood residue and what else? Was that more fur? Yes, that curled brown congealed stuff was a small lump of animal hair. He sniffed his hands – not good. Rather than calling back in to his new colleagues, he texted Clare as he made his way out of the station and to his car. 'Getting changed,' he wrote. 'Back in fifteen.'

A thumbs-up in reply and he was in the HiLux, headed home. He put the local radio station on and caught the end of 'Eagle Rock' before the news. They loved that song on River FM. The tune reminded him of his twenties, blurry nights in pubs with bad carpet and a hangover looming. There was some sort of dance to it, wasn't there? He couldn't recall.

God, he was tired. The 11 am news came on: Aidan Sleeth's death first up. The newsreader was claiming 'suspicious death', and she wasn't wrong. Mark recalled Sleeth's head.

'Found by a group of children!' The newsreader would

get told off for her tone, Mark thought. Too jaunty for a body in the bush, and a local at that. Now she was talking about the weather: 'Severe rainstorms on the way! Flood alerts for Stoney Creek, Wyamma Creek and Eleven Mile Creek!' *Jesus*, Mark thought. The state of the world.

He pulled up in front of his house and was surprised to see serial walker Lee O'Brien stride around the block. Mark hot-footed it to his front gate, half ran up the path and onto the steps of the porch when: 'Mark! You were a sly one this morning!'

Mark sighed deeply, and turned. 'Hello there, Lee.'

'Aidan Sleeth, eh? Shocking.'

'Yep.'

'Any clues on how it happened? Accident maybe?' The man's thin face was fox-like, alert and interested.

'Can't give out any information yet, Lee. Press release will be coming soon.'

'Adelaide police up, I see. Homicide squad, is it?'

Mark nodded and walked up the steps to his front door.

'Any suspects as yet?' The man was relentless. Worse than one of those reporters on *A Current Affair*.

'Should check out that Stone Town lot,' Lee was almost shouting. 'I bet Patricia Delaney knows a thing or two.'

Mark spun slowly on his feet. 'Why would you say that?'

'That woman's got her fingers in every pie.'

'Pies? What pies?'

'CWA, Landcare, foster care, home care, Meals on Wheels, CFA, you name it. Walking advertisement for an OAM.' Lee didn't look happy at the idea.

'Sounds like a good citizen.'

Lee checked his watch, probably his pedometer. 'Don't want to get on her bad side, Mark. Makes Idi Amin look like Mother Teresa.'

'Bit harsh.'

'You don't know half of it.' Lee gave his usual flat-hand wave and moved on at his steady pace, beating age or death or redundancy: whichever came first.

Mark took his boots off, put them by the door and went inside. The house was cool with the blinds in the living room down, the hallway cold on his feet. He went to his cupboard, looking for clean clothes, and decided on a shower, a quick one to wake him up. Under the running water, he thought over what Lee had said about Patricia. *Don't get on her bad side.* He remembered the way the old woman spoke about her neighbours, the nonchalant response to Sleeth's body in the bush, not far from her home. What was it she'd said? *This land's been thick with bodies for two hundred years.* His next visit to her would be different, less deferential.

The water was steady, warm on his tired body. He put his face up to it and felt a relaxation in his limbs. He closed his eyes, let it wash over him.

Mark was shaken from his reverie by the sound of the phone. An old-fashioned ring; the landline. He turned the tap off, put a towel around him and padded down the hall again, the sound jolting. The landline almost never rang. Another remnant of his mother that he'd failed to change. The ring was sharp, insistent. It had rung that way when his father died, the call from Dalgety's, *Heart attack at work*. The phone kept ringing. He picked it up.

'Mark, good, you're home.'

Assistant Commissioner Angelo Conti, his friend, his former colleague, high up in the force and climbing.

'Angelo, why this number?'

'You're not answering your mobile.'

'I was in the shower.'

'Shower? At this time?'

'Bits of dead animal on me.'

Angelo didn't respond.

'How'd you get this number anyway?'

'Kelly gave it to me.'

His ex-wife. Of course.

'What's the emergency?'

'No emergency. A heads-up.'

Mark felt the dread. A heads-up from head office meant strings attached. Heads-up, the signal for collusion. 'What?' His voice was flat.

'Your new colleague, Finn Turner. Little shit.'

'Gathered that.'

'His father's a crim. Assault, theft, attempted murder.'

Mark waited.

'In Morburn Prison. Fifteen years.'

Morburn. That prison up the Barrier. High risk, maximum security.

'You can see where I'm going with this, can't you, Mark?'

He could. He could see it and it hurt him in the marrow of his bones. He knew what was coming and wished himself away, far away, Perth or Broome or Portugal. Norway. Mars.

'There's someone leaking information to Tony Scopelliti. Nothing major, but it's not good. They knew beforehand about a raid we conducted on a Scopelliti business, an associate knew we were bringing him in for questioning – had all his answers down pat. There's a leak. We think it's Turner.'

Mark didn't speak.

'Keep an eye on him, will you, mate? We want to keep him working, see what leaks and what doesn't. Could be helpful down the track. The other colleague up there, the woman, she's aware too.'

'What am I keeping an eye on exactly?' Mark suddenly hated his job.

'Phone calls, emails. Things he brings up about Scopelliti.'

'I don't like being your snitch, Angelo.'

'You're not a snitch. Turner could be the key to finding Natalie Whitsed. You want that, don't you?'

'Course.'

'It's just for a few days. We've given them the green light to keep working on the Whitsed file while they're in Booralama. Mind you, your homicide's their priority for now.'

'Okay.'

'How're you doing, Mark?' Angelo's voice took on a cheerful tone. 'What's the word on the street regarding your shooting? Any chance it was an accident?'

'Your attempt at small talk's not working, Angelo.'

'I'm just—'

'And never say *word on the street* again.'

His old friend sighed. 'I don't like asking you to do this, Mark. Believe me, I don't. But it's not a big thing, just keep your eyes and ears open. They'll be gone soon.'

'Okay,' Mark said, looking at his watch. 'Got to get back to the station. Get snitching.'

'Come on, mate. I'll call you soon, okay?'

'Yeah.' Mark hung up, headed back to his bedroom and got changed. He checked his phone. No missed call from Angelo. The senior cop knew the landline couldn't easily be traced. A clever cop, tidy habits. Well liked. A walking advertisement for an OAM, a finger in every pie.

Back at the station, Mark walked into the small kitchen and took out some leftover lasagne from the fridge. He heated it up and ate it overlooking the concrete yard and back fence, which bordered old-age residential units. A bird landed on the roof of the units then flew off. Crow? No, maggie. The lasagne needed salt. A second maggie joined the first and Mark watched them while he chewed.

Clare poked her head in the door and asked where the coffee percolator was. He pointed to the jar of International Roast and she poked back out. Once his meal was finished, he washed his plate and fork and put them in the dish rack to dry. The office door to where Clare and Finn were working was shut firm so he walked into his own little space and fired up his laptop. There was the paperwork in regard to the finding of Aidan Sleeth; confirmation of a school visit – talking to the Year 10s about traffic safety. There was the break-in at the church, some new graffiti on the side of the IGA, and two bikes stolen from a house in Beaumont Drive. Added to that there was last week's incident with the three teenagers who'd been caught selling and buying weed, and two infringements for speeding. Reports. Police work.

At 1 pm Finn Turner stepped into the office without knocking. 'Sleeth's employee is here. Clare says to join us if you want.'

Mark nodded and stood up, stretching. His lower body ached; his knee cracked. It was a long time since worms on the dance floor.

In the interview room, a young man – twenty-one, perhaps twenty-two years old – sat on a chair, doleful. Clare introduced him as Luke Howsley, resident of Booralama, employee of the deceased. Luke was dressed as if he was attending a job interview: white shirt, tie, ironed pants, polished shoes.

'Now,' Clare said, 'we're going to be taping this conversation, just so that you're aware.'

'Do I need a lawyer?'

'I don't know, Luke, do you? This is just a chat about your dealings with Aidan Sleeth and your relationship with him.' Clare sat back in her chair and yawned. Her air of boredom, manufactured or imagined, was vaguely distasteful to Mark.

'Okay.'

'Do you want a lawyer?' Mark asked. 'Be easy enough to call someone up.'

'Nah,' the young man said. He pushed a finger into the neck of his shirt and pulled hard at it. 'Go on.'

'You don't have to say anything if you don't want to,' Mark added. 'No pressure.'

A nod from the young man.

Clare indicated that she was about to begin taping. 'This okay?'

'Yeah.'

'Interview commenced at 1.05 pm. Luke Howsley, present without a lawyer, understands that anything he says may or may not be held against him in a court of law. Is that clear, Mr Howsley?'

Luke cleared his throat. 'That's clear.'

'Please tell us how you came to know Aidan Sleeth.'

Luke told them the story in a sad drawl: how he'd known Aidan from when he moved to Booralama from Warrnambool in Victoria two years ago. Followed a girl, she broke up with him, went off with some fitter and turner from Nhill. He got a job at Aidan's real estate office in town, started playing footy for the seconds, liked the town, liked the job, liked Aidan well enough. Stayed.

'Well enough?' Finn broke in. 'What's that mean?'

The young bloke jerked his head up, startled. 'What, I didn't mean . . .' There was a beat. Luke Howsley glanced around him, as if only now realising where he was. An uncomfortable pause followed.

'You play footy for Booralama?' Mark broke in. 'Mack still coaching?'

Luke gave him a half-smile. 'Yeah – and playing.'

'Numbers low?'

'Yep. You play?'

'A bit, not for a while.'

'Pull the boots on.' Luke spoke with new enthusiasm. 'Thursday, training. Few of the old blokes turn up.'

Thanks. Mark could sense the smirks.

Finn cracked his knuckles. 'We going to get anything done here besides fill the bench next game?'

'What was Aidan Sleeth like, Luke?' Clare gave a brief nod to Mark and spoke in a new, friendly voice. 'He play footy with you?'

'No, he was more of a gym guy, I think. Not really interested in local footy. Fit though.'

'You knew him well?'

'Not really, not as a mate. As a boss, yeah. He'd come and go. In the city mostly. Checked in on the office when he was up here, looked over the books. Made sure I was keeping monthly targets.'

'Targets?' Finn asked.

'With selling houses and that. In Booralama and surrounds.'

'And were you, keeping targets?'

'Not really.' Luke was glum again. 'Not much in the way of residential home selling. People want to buy houses here, not sell them.'

'Aidan was unhappy with you about that?'

'Yeah. Not that he'd go off or anything, but you could tell. Like, he wouldn't talk much, just look through the books and go . . .' Luke pursed his lips and made flipping motions with his hands as if he was reading notes.

'So, the business wasn't doing well?'

'Are you kidding me? It was doing great! All those land sales, farmers selling up excess paddocks, council approving land from rural to residential, subdivisions, surveying – you name it. People ringing up all the time, dying to sell their lots, make their one-acre block into four. And then there's the rush of people from the city who want to buy up here and build. It's like a tsunami or something, they all want to get the hell out.'

There was a pause from the city police. A reflective one? Maybe.

Clare cleared her throat. 'What about Sleeth's big buy-up of Stone Town bushland? You know much about that, Luke?'

'Other than he seemed really happy about it, I don't know. Twenty acres, it's a good buy. I was in the housing side, so I couldn't tell you much. Aidan said the greenies out there went psycho when he got it approved with the council to go from rural to residential.'

'How'd he do that?'

'I dunno. Take the council members out for lunch? Talk about growth and development over a beer and a steak? Those words'll get you anything. Growth and Development. It's real estate's equivalent of Inclusion and Diversity. People can't get enough of it.'

Luke looked at his phone. He was a millennial and it had been at least ten minutes; he'd done well. 'Aidan made some concessions around the powder magazine – that's like, this old building out there where the miners used to store their explosives. The gold rush and that.'

Mark gave Luke an encouraging nod. Clare and Finn looked bored.

'But still,' Luke continued, 'those greenies out in Stone Town were going sick.'

'Sick as in . . .' Mark thought he knew what kind of sick Luke was referring to, but for clarity's sake, it needed to be distinguished. Wild with excitement sick, angry and frustrated sick, or sick, as in ill?

'Sick, as in not happy. Phone calls to Sleeth all the time, letters to the office, letters in the local paper – that sort of stuff. Didn't do any good.'

Clare cleared her throat.

'Any real problems you know of, with the Stone Town deal – any threats made?' Mark asked.

'Not that I'm aware of. I mean, those greenies, they weren't happy. But threats? Nah.'

Finn piped up. 'What was Sleeth doing all the time in Adelaide?'

'Dunno. Networking? He had an office there. I never went.'

Clare asked Luke if he knew what would happen to the business now that Aidan was gone. The younger man shrugged. 'Maybe his family will sell it? His parents are dead, I know that. He's got an ex-wife . . . Look, got no idea to be honest. Doesn't really bother me, I'm almost qualified to be a PE teacher.'

'How're you studying and working full-time?' Mark asked, aware of Clare eyeing him. 'Asking for a friend.'

'It's all online.'

'For teaching?' Mark was incredulous. 'Wouldn't you need to go and talk to kids at a school? Be in classes?'

'Nope. Everything's via Zoom.'

What a world. Cyber space felt close rather than vast.

'Been doing a bit of tutoring and that,' Luke explained. 'Gives me some experience.'

A moment's reflection. Mark pictured his Year 8 woodwork class, his friend Stitcher carving BALLS into a table, a girl with an asthma attack, kids fighting in the halls. Would tutoring suffice?

'What do you think Aidan was doing in the Stone Town bush around midnight on a rainy Friday night?' Clare's new friendly voice was strained and she looked at her watch.

Luke lifted his shoulders, raising his palms up in a gesture of helplessness. 'I really couldn't tell you. He have traps there or something?'

'Traps?'

'Like, rabbit or something? I dunno. Doesn't seem like something Aidan *would* have – but like I said, I didn't know him real well.'

Traps. Mark considered. Maybe Aidan did have traps. Unlikely – but why not? Who knew what sorts of hobbies or preoccupations people had. Still, he couldn't imagine Aidan skinning an animal, cutting it up and eating it.

'Maybe he had dogs?' Finn sniffed. 'Rabbits make good dog meat.'

Luke turned his head sideways. 'His ex has a dog. Small one. Looks like a rabbit itself.'

The question of why Aidan had been in the bush in the early hours of that morning bothered them all. Was he there to meet someone? Who? And why in the rainy Stone Town night and not somewhere more comfortable?

'Did you see Aidan on the day he died, Luke?' Clare's voice was flat now. Her friendly tone ran to three minutes.

'Yeah, but only for a minute or two. He stopped by the office yesterday, came to get the mail.'

'How did he seem to you then?'

'Normal.' Luke did that *I don't know* expression. 'Didn't talk much. Looked at himself in the mirror a lot, read his mail, sniffed his armpits and left without saying goodbye. He never gave much away, didn't let on if anything was bothering him.'

His body did though: *sweaty*.

'Sleeth a sweaty man?' Finn asked, and Mark looked at him, startled. Did Homicide train in mind-reading now?

'What?' Luke was puzzled. 'I don't know.'

Mark wrote down some notes. What did a perspiring Aidan Sleeth see in that mirror on that day? A man on the rise, or something entirely different?

'Any other clients come to the offices yesterday or the weeks prior? I mean anyone you didn't know, or someone who struck you as being out of place, angry, or demanding or something?'

'No, I pretty much know everyone who comes in and there was no one out of the ordinary. Yesterday there weren't even any appointments. It was quiet as.'

'It must have been difficult hearing your boss has died suddenly.' Mark used a tone of regret. 'How're you taking it?'

Luke looked at the three of them. He had a boy's face. Mark felt a pang of despair for the kid.

'More like I'm shocked. He was shot, right? Back of the head? That's serious shit. Who *does* that? I dunno what he was into, but I want to get out. I'm not gonna lie, it's scary. Sooner I'm in the classroom the better. This has all been, like, so disruptive and I can't wait to just move on. It's not that I hate real estate, but I know I can do better.' Luke looked at his hands. He held one over the other as if he was posing for a group photo.

Clare pushed the stop button on the tape. 'Sounds like a school report,' she said. 'I give you an A.'

Mark escorted Luke Howsley out of the police station and onto the front porch. The air was heavy with dewy heat and the young man scratched at his shirt collar. 'Don't even know why I wore this. Thought it would be a bit formal or something.'

'It can be intimidating.'

'Feel like I'm at a Deb Ball.'

'Got your corsage sorted?' Mark asked. 'Remember to buy the girl a gift?'

Luke gave a short laugh. 'Spoke to Mum, she said to wear a shirt.'

Again, Mark was struck by how young Luke seemed. And soon to be a teacher? He felt ancient. Luke put his hands in his pockets, then immediately took them out again and shook with Mark. 'You should come down to training,' he said. 'The seconds are struggling.'

'Might do that,' Mark said, thinking, *No, I won't.*

'Could help us out, we need numbers.'

'I'll see.' Even thinking about it, Mark felt the familiar twang in his heel bone. *Troy fell because of Achilles and I won't do the same to the Booralama seconds.* 'Good luck with the teaching.'

'Better than real estate.' Luke was undoing his top shirt buttons. 'Investors from the city' – he flicked his thumb back at the station – 'having to deal with that type.'

'Not all like that, surely.'

Luke gave a shrug, *whatever*, a short wave and then he turned, walking up the footpath.

Mark had a thought. The card in Sleeth's wallet. He called out to the retreating figure, 'Luke!'

Luke turned.

'Did Aidan ever talk about the environment? Like, even though he was in conflict with the greenies, was he maybe interested in those sorts of causes; bird or trees or . . .?'

Luke gave a short laugh. 'You must be joking! A real estate investor interested in the environment! If Aidan saw a patch of trees he'd be calculating how many quarter-acre blocks he could fit in it, not marvelling at the general beauty.'

Mark nodded. 'Thanks.'

'But as I was saying in there,' Luke added, 'Sleeth did relent on the land around the powder magazine, six metres each side of it. Birds for Bush, local group, got that at least. Some endangered species there, so yeah – Aidan agreed never to build around there. It's probably what got him over the line with his planned subdivision.'

Mark wrote the point down in his notebook. 'Thanks for that.'

'Tell you what,' Luke continued. 'Aidan didn't mind talking about his time spent in the Stone Town bush as a boy. Anyone'd think he was Huck Finn the way he went on.'

Mark was impressed, must have looked it.

'Studied it in teaching.' Luke shrugged. 'Boring as batshit.'

Back in the station, Clare was putting notes together; Finn was at the end of the hall, on the phone.

'Sleeth's ex-wife sent an email.' Clare slid photos from the crime scene into an A4 paper folder. 'She's not coming in till Monday and when she does it will be with a lawyer.'

'Interesting.'

'Yeah.' Clare looked weary. 'Nowadays the moment you ask someone in for a chat they think it's *CSI*.'

It was true. Mark had pulled people over for speeding and they'd got out of their car, arms up in the air. If he threw them against the bonnet and cuffed them, they wouldn't be surprised. Once a man marched into the station brandishing a Coke can with a story about it being thrown at him from a car, demanding Mark send it to the lab for testing. *The lab? Sure. I'll send it stat. And was it Coke Zero or Diet? Because all my colleagues at the lab here will definitely need to know.*

Mark yawned and closed his eyes a moment.

'Why don't you go home, Mark. Get some sleep. Been a big day for you.'

It had been. The call-out to the bush, Sleeth's dead body, the Mattesons, Patricia Delaney, Homicide arriving. 'Might do that.'

67

'See you Monday. We'll let you know if anything else comes in. Forensics will be here soon. We'll be out at the Sleeth place this arvo and tomorrow.'

Finn's voice rose in the background. 'Just do it, will you? Please!'

Mark leaned against the door frame. 'He on the phone to Telstra?'

'Who knows? He's on that phone all the time.'

Mark felt a flicker of interest. A snitch's type of flicker? Said flicker died down. 'Maybe he's on the phone to a real estate agent, looking to buy up here. Escape the city.'

'Doubt it,' Clare said, turning with a smile. 'See you Monday.'

CHAPTER 7

Cold was her first thought. Pure cold.

But it was pain that woke her. A sharp searing, intense.

There was something wrong with her arm. She tried to move and heard herself scream, a high sound, like an animal.

Wet, it was wet and dark. Black. She smelled mud and the dank thickness of cold earth. Where was she?

Pain. With her right hand, she felt along her left arm. The angle of the limb was all wrong, a bone pointing outward when it should be . . . It gave her a sick feeling in her stomach. Her head throbbed. She ran muddy fingers over her forehead where a thick bump protruded. A sob. Hers? Yes.

She closed her eyes; it was lighter behind her eyelids than the inky surrounds. The deep red was better than the black.

Think. She'd been driving. Where to? A long drive. To see someone . . . Then, a stop, a stop and . . .

Her head pounded now, a rhythmic roar, and she tried to think. Nothing. Where was she?

Her clothes were soaked, jeans sodden and clinging. Water ran down her back in a steady stream. With her good hand, she felt the wall she was leaning on. Dirt, mud. A growing horror – was she underground?

And then, a sound nearby. Close. A movement in the darkness, slight. A deep unfurling rose within her and she pricked up her ears. Nothing but the sound of water dripping and her own unsteady breathing.

Nothing.

Nothing.

And then, something.

She opened her eyes to the darkness, peering, a deep panic rising. And then, she saw it.

There in the thick black, not an arm's length away, someone was sitting, watching.

She opened her mouth to scream and a strange sound came from within her, a high wail born of terror.

The figure shifted, moved closer.

'No,' she mouthed.

'Tweet.' A sound came from the dark shape. 'Tweet, tweet.'

CHAPTER 8

Mark's alarm shrieked. 6 am. He slapped it quiet and lay in bed, lifting the curtain by his window to one side and watching the morning sky.

He didn't run on Sundays. That was the weekly treat he granted himself, but still, he wished he could sleep in a little longer. The day would be stormy. Already, he could see the dark clouds gathering across the grey sky, wind whipping the tops of the gums in his yard. More rain was predicted. Flood warnings in place. Although the day was technically his, he already imagined the calls from the elderly; crossings into town impossible, long driveways rendered useless. The shriek again – he'd pushed snooze instead of the off button. Another slap and, this time, the clock shut up for good.

After he'd left the station yesterday afternoon, he'd come home, lain on the couch, closed his eyes and opened them again to find it was eight o'clock. Then, a quick dinner of scrambled eggs and he'd fallen asleep on the couch for a second time, watching TV. Just after 4 am he'd woken. There was a scratching at the window of his mother's old bedroom down the hall. He heard it from the lounge room, the insistent tapping, maddening if he listened long enough. The old beams of the window rattled and the persistent sound began again, loud in the early morning.

Getting up, and cold, he'd padded down the hallway to where the scraping was coming from. At the doorway to her bedroom, he'd hesitated. Why? A general sadness, but something else too. An unease; the darkened room, the ghostly white of the curtains against the blackened windows. Pulling back the curtains he could see the spindly fingers of a gum branch running down the glass. Mark opened the latch of the window and pulled at it, breaking the thin wood and tossing it to the ground.

Now, back in his bedroom and resting in the gloomy morning light, Mark thought that five years ago, three even, he wouldn't have been so unsettled by such a thing. Something was shaken in him; his divorce from Kelly, separation from his boys, the death of his mother and memories of a reinvestigation up north, one which involved his old school friends and a judgement call he couldn't quite reconcile.

A flock of cockies zipped past in the sky, their white bodies a peace flag and a wake-up call. He yawned, stretched and got out of bed, knee and back creaking in harmony like a sad country and western. In the kitchen, he turned on the kettle and stood, waiting for it to boil. It was too early to ring the boys. He half wished he'd caved at Sam's last birthday and got him a phone. Easier if he could talk to them anytime rather than go through Kelly. Then he remembered the problems at the local primary school with cyber bullying, and the bikes stolen from homes known to be vacant because of snap maps, snap chats, snap whatevers, and savvy teens.

Mark drank his mug of tea, looking out at the garden his mother had spent years of her life in. A large stone bird bath covered in ancient bird shit sat under an oak. Mark watched as a honeyeater flew down and rested on it for a second before flying off. He should clean it out, he really should. The garden was his mother's source of joy. Every living thing in it, flora or fauna, she'd loved.

The calendar on the wall behind him showed January, blank of all appointments. He tore it off and looked at February, equally bare. On March, his birthday month, he stopped. It was bare too – but what was he expecting? A party? There was a photo of a bird – the Crested Shrike-tit. Holding his cuppa with one hand, Mark took the calendar off the wall and moved it to the small dining table. He sat down and read more closely:

The Crested Shrike-tit is a medium-small bird with a striking black and white striped head and neck, a small crest that is often held flattened over crown, a black throat, and a short heavy bill with hooked tips.

Amazing, he thought. *I'm fifty-one and I've never heard of a Crested Shrike-tit. Life is full of excitements undiscovered.*

The calendar was one produced by the local Birds for Bush group. This year's product featured birds of the area;

April was the Spotted Quail-thrush and May the Restless Flycatcher. *Jesus*, Mark thought, looking at the small bird attempting to land on a branch, *I feel like a bit of a Restless Flycatcher myself.* He flicked through the calendar. White-winged Trillers and Rufous Whistlers. *Good names for a band.* August was the *Ninox connivens*: the Barking Owl. Mark read:

> They are a medium-sized brown owl and have a
> characteristic voice with calls ranging from a barking
> dog noise to a shrill human-like howl of great intensity.
> At the beginning of breeding season, they have been
> known to emit a blood-curdling, sobbing scream . . .
> which can be disconcerting to the untrained ear.

Mark pondered: a blood-curdling, sobbing scream. *Disconcerting?* The sound would be enough to send you running, half maddened with fear if you heard it in the still of night, in the middle of the lonely Stone Town bush. The bird itself looked innocent enough. That something so fluffy and round-eyed could make such a terrifying noise . . .

The phone rang; it was Kelly. His ex-wife sounded sleepy but happy. She was always happy these days, it was a good thing. The boys wanted to talk to him – and could he have them from Friday night? They loved coming up to Nanna's house.

'My house now,' Mark said. But he didn't mind.

'Steven's got this work thing in Perth and I'd like to go with him, it'll mean you picking them up on Friday afternoon and having them for three nights. I know it's short notice, but can you? This really is a one-off. They've got the Monday off for reports or something, so it's not like they're missing much school, but I know you'll have to arrange stuff with work so . . .'

Mark hesitated. It would be a busy week and he'd need to take part of Friday off. It would be difficult, but Charlie and Sam – up here for three nights!

'Yeah, sure. Meet halfway to get them Friday arvo?'

'Yep.'

Meeting halfway was what they did. Whether it was up the highway or in marriage counselling, they'd always been good at that. Mutual friends said it was a pity they didn't work out. Close mutual friends knew it wasn't. Mark yawned, wondering vaguely what Steven's work thing was. Good old Stevo, Stevey mate. Some sort of conference perhaps? In a flash joint, with the partners all dressed up and drinking cocktails? A big room overlooking the ocean, king-sized bed and—

'You okay, Mark? I heard on the news there's been a body found in the bush up your way.'

'Yeah, I'm okay. Overslept. Work's been busy.' He knew he sounded grumpy. It was the king-sized bed that did it.

'You should take up a hobby. Play sport again; do something other than work.'

'I'm still running.'

'That's good, Mark, but what about tennis? Something to get you out with other people.'

Mark was only half listening. Something had caught his eye on the back of the Birds for Bush calendar:

Regent Honeyeaters (Anthochaera phrygia), Swift Parrots
(Lathamus discolor) and the Barking Owl are three of
our area's most well-loved and endangered birds. Birds
for Bush is a five-year project funded by the Australian
Government's National Landcare Program that aims to
help landowners create and improve habitat to allow
these birds to thrive.

Birds for Bush is working together with local Landcare
and other key partners to deliver this project, which will
address the key threats for the species. The success of this
project will rely greatly on improved quality and quantity
of woodland habitat. Act now to save Stone Town and
surrounds for three of our most precious birds!

'Did you hear me, Mark? I said, you should find an interest, do something other than work.'

Mark blinked, cleared his throat. 'I think I just have.'

CHAPTER 9

After his cup of tea and a chat to Charlie and Sam, Mark walked into town. On Sunday mornings, he liked to go out for breakfast. The habit reminded him of his city days, breakfast at some cafe with Kelly and, later, with Kelly and the boys. Baristas – young men and women with tattoos and attitudes of cool. Middle-aged women in tight lycra and puffy jackets; Kelly one of them in her own tight lycra and puffy jacket, her hair in a little bun thing, her figure still a wonder. The old days, the past. Coffee, eggs, bacon and sourdough toast. Bit of green on the side? No, thank you. Not ever on a Sunday. Not in the past, not now.

The cafe he chose was named the Fat Bean. It was run by his old school friend Dennis, pencil-thin with hair like an eighties host of *Countdown*. In a former life, Dennis owned a whiskey bar on Hamilton Island before he was made bankrupt in the GFC. Dennis wasn't in on Sundays. He had two young people working for him, siblings who were always bickering over messed-up orders. But even so, the coffee was great, the servings were generous, and it was good to get out of his mother's house. Correction, *his* house.

'Can I get you something?'

Mark looked up and it took him a moment to realise that the young person asking him the question was Isabelle, Jacqueline Matteson's daughter, the one who'd been crying in the car.

'Isabelle, isn't it? I'm Mark. I was at your house in the early hours yesterday.'

Her face was pale, eyes dark with shadow. 'I remember,' she said.

'You doing okay? I didn't realise you worked here.'

Isabelle shifted on her feet. 'I'm filling in for a friend, it's just for an hour. Thought I may as well come in. Not much going on at home. Mum said it'd be good to get out.'

'How are your sisters coping?'

Isabelle gave a harsh laugh. 'They're okay. Back to fighting over who needs to clean up their room. Sarah's enjoying all the cakes people keep bringing around.'

'Kids are pretty resilient.'

'I suppose.' Isabelle looked out the window, the morning light giving her melancholy features a holy glow.

'Did you know him at all? Aidan Sleeth?'

A black car drove at a slow pace past the cafe. Tinted windows, impossible to see who was driving. Isabelle and Mark followed its progress, watched it make an unhurried right turn up the road.

Isabelle sniffed. 'I used to do some cleaning at his office. So, yeah. I knew him a bit.'

Mark thought for a moment. 'I'm sorry,' he said. 'This is hard for you.'

Isabelle gave a sharp intake of breath. 'It's not like I saw the body or anything.'

'But still.'

'I didn't see *anything.*'

A pause.

'So, do you want to order?' Isabelle spoke in a rush.

'Yes, please.' Mark put down the menu that he knew off by heart. 'Big breakfast, mushrooms on the side, no greens.'

'Coffee?'

'Cappuccino, please. In a cup.'

'You don't want like, spinach or rocket or anything?'

'Not on a Sunday.'

'It's against your religion?' There was a hint of a smile.

Mark made a sign of the cross. 'Forgive me.'

Isabelle turned on her heel and Mark watched as she made her way to the counter. So, she worked for Aidan Sleeth a little. Cleaning.

As he waited for his breakfast to arrive, Mark tapped his chest. The binoculars were there, hidden under his jumper. He'd forgotten to take them off back at the house. It was a coup remembering them. After hanging up from Kelly and the boys, he'd wandered out to the garden shed, half aware of what he was looking for: binoculars, the ones his mother carried with her most days, hoping to spot this bird or that. Oh, how he'd been bored by her bird exploits as a young boy. *Look, Mark*, she'd say. *There's a Honeyeater on the grevillea! Look, Mark! It's about to take off!* He'd been embarrassed at the

79

way she'd shout sometimes, grabbing his arm in public and pointing up some tree. *Look! Look!* It was as if, he reflected, she'd spent most of his adolescence trying to get him to see something he couldn't, or didn't want to recognise.

The binoculars had been surprisingly easy to find, hanging on a nail near the door. When he first raised them to his eyes, he had to adjust them; the lenses were too close to each other, the focus too fuzzy for his younger eyes. He'd pointed his gaze at a gum tree and waited. Nothing. The leaves shimmered in the morning sun, glinting on the glass – but as for a bird? Nada. Perhaps they were all hanging out with the Rufous Whistlers.

Now, at the Fat Bean, he lifted the binoculars out of the neck of his jacket and raised them to his eyes once more. The vision was fuzzy again, he had to adjust it. Once clear, he turned his gaze slowly through the windows of the cafe and to the street beyond. Booralama, Sunday morning, was quiet. Three women walked past the cafe along the footpath, and their sudden intrusion into his vision made him blink and pull the lenses away from his eyes. He resettled, looked again. Two people were jogging up and down on the spot, waiting for the lights to change at the road to the left. Was one of them Luke Howsley? He homed in. Yes, yes it was. The young man was wearing footy shorts and a Booralama T-shirt. The person beside him was female, long leggings and a purple top with some logo on it. The lights turned red and they crossed the road, running out of sight.

He turned his gaze around and saw an elderly woman carrying a heavy shopping bag walk with some difficulty along the footpath to the right. Mark didn't recognise her. The old woman put the bag down, rearranged something within it, picked it up again and continued walking, her gait a little easier. A kid on a bike rode past, no helmet, hands off the handles and careering along with all the confidence of youth. Mark turned the focus dial without lowering the lenses, noting the make of bike. He followed the kid right up the street until he was lost from sight. The street was empty once more. With some satisfaction, Mark put the binoculars down.

'What are you perving at?' It was Isabelle, back with his food and drink. *Perving.* The word jarred.

'Nothing.' He nodded down at the binoculars on the table beside him. 'They were my mum's. I got them out this morning.'

'Going to join the rest of them at Stone Town? Search for that bloody Barking Owl?' Isabelle sounded bitter.

'There's a group there?' Mark asked, faintly surprised. 'Birdwatchers?'

'"Twitchers", they call them,' Isabelle said. 'They come to Stone Town, stay at the co-op. The bush around home is meant to be some kind of birdwatcher's heaven.'

'You interested in it too?' Mark asked.

'God no.' Isabelle snorted. 'How boring. I clean for Evie and John sometimes, they own the co-op. That's how I know.' She started to walk back to the kitchen and then stopped. 'Hey, there's that car again.'

Together they looked out the window and, sure enough, the long black car from earlier was moving slowly up the street.

Mark raised the binoculars to his eyes, waited a moment, and then focused. The car was a Chrysler 300c, fitted out with tinted windows. Not your typical Booralama vehicle, not by a long shot. Police senses hackled, he zoomed in on the number plate, noted it down, filed it in the back of his head. No way of knowing if the occupants, as they glided by, saw him staring at them through a lens, and he didn't lower his gaze.

'Interesting.' Isabelle spoke and he started, resting the binoculars down. 'Think they're the press?'

'Maybe.' Mark doubted it.

'Anyway, I'm going. My sister's picking me up.'

'What? Emma!'

'No.' Isabelle gave a half-laugh and Mark breathed a sigh of relief. *There's only so much ignoring a country cop can do.* 'Georgia. She's come back from uni to help us out with all this.' Isabelle gave a sweep of her arm as if it was the cafe, the whole town, the universe, that Georgia had to contend with.

Outside, a motorbike drove past, loud and too fast.

Isabelle nodded at Mark, grave. 'Goodbye.'

'Bye, Isabelle, thanks.'

Jacqueline Matteson's second-born walked out quickly, turning right outside the cafe, and he watched her pass the window, hair streaming behind, young face set hard against the elements.

CHAPTER 10

The pain, if anything, is worse now. It fills her eardrums and screams through her arm. Her shoulder feels hot and she touches it, running her fingers down to the elbow where the bone juts out, still beneath the skin.

She's woken in a haze of red confusion, but when her mind clears, she remembers. She's trapped in a hole. The realisation comes with a deep horror and somewhere in her blurry mind she thinks she remembers someone talking to her, sitting next to her in the hole.

She shakes the memory off. It had been a hallucination and while she is lucid, she needs to think. She opens her eyes, dreading it, and finds once again that her surroundings are in total darkness. So inky, in fact, that only shapes are perceptible – her leg lying there, a hand in front of her face, the walls on either side bearing down.

Her phone is gone. The only possession she has is her Chapstick, and she feels it in her pocket now, wishing it was a torch.

With her good hand, she makes a cup shape, fills it with muddy water from the ground and takes thirsty sips. She does it again and again. If she's to live, she needs to drink.

Can she stand? She tries, groaning, the blood rushing to her arm as she bends over.

With her back against the wall and using her knees as leverage, she attempts to straighten. It hurts, every part of her aches, but she rises up, her jumper stretching down against the wall and catching tight at her throat.

And then, with a colossal effort, she attempts to stand upright before her head hits something solid and dank. There is a wall of dirt on top of her. She lifts her good arm up above her hunched body and feels along it. She bangs at it, bangs again, and the earth thuds, doesn't move.

There is no sky, no sun, no moon. There is no air, no wind, no breeze.

With new panic, she feels along till her arm rounds down in an arc three feet from where she's been sitting. Confusion and then terror overtake her. This isn't a hole, it's a den. Someone has put her here.

Someonehasputherheresomeonehasputherheresomeone-hasputherhere.

For the first time she lets hysteria overwhelm and she screams, one long cry after the other.

It doesn't matter. No one can hear. No one comes.

It doesn't make her stop.

CHAPTER 11

Breakfast finished, Fat Bean paid, Mark walked back home on wide pavements beside a generous road lined with faded elms. After World War I, the grieving Booralama community planted them in recognition of the sacrifice of their young. Now, the big leaves shuddered, wet and heavy, surviving the heat and uncertain climate. Seventy-four elms, one for every local man killed in the Somme or Gallipoli or Ypres. There was a statue too, a bronze soldier gazing into the sun. Every country town had one. Did statues and elms lessen the grief? Mark heard a branch above him creak and he gazed up into the canopy of green. Perhaps the Booralama people saw England or Scotland or Ireland when they looked up into the elms, perhaps they saw some notion of an ancestral home and that gave them comfort.

Repatriated soldiers from World War I reported smelling eucalypt from their boats as they neared the Western Australia coast on their way home. Mark could imagine them crowding the deck, noses raised to the air, a motley choir of sniffers. Nurses in Vietnam took gum leaves with them to chew on when nervous; the perfumed, bitter taste recalling home. Perhaps elms weren't the answer. It was gums, with their fire-loving ways, liquid amber sap and tiny gumnut caps that the war-weary hungered for.

Mark passed a blue gum now and saw a flash of colour in it. A King Parrot? He half thought about taking out his binoculars but decided against. There were things to do.

A white Honda drove past, the family inside waving at him. He waved back, no idea of who they were. It was happening more frequently nowadays. When he first moved back to Booralama, he seemed to recognise only a few faces – the ones he'd been to school with, families of ex-girlfriends and members of the football club. Now, his reach had widened. As the local cop, he was a Person of Interest.

Back at home, he took his boots off and walked along the passageway to his bedroom. It was a habit, taking off the boots. Kelly liked him to do it too, but the practice came from his mother always shouting about mud in the house, the carpet, the dirt on the floorboards. He snorted at the memory. While she had ordered them all to take off footwear before entering the house, Helen herself never removed her gardening gloves or her filthy gardening hat, trailing bits of greenery and cuttings she'd either nabbed or been given by the neighbours.

There were two messages on his phone, which he'd turned to silent during breakfast. Both from friends he knew in the city, their concerned tones – *how are you, mate?* – and vague messages of catching up almost certainly encouraged by their wives, friends of Kelly's. These were men and women he liked. He'd spent drunken nights with them at christenings and fortieth and fiftieth birthday parties. He'd been on a holiday with them in a group of three couples, to Kangaroo Island where they'd rented a house for a week, drinking and eating in easy company. His boys played with their kids. So why the reluctance to pick up the phone and call them back? Part of the attraction of Booralama, he realised, was that no one really knew the life he led in the city and what parts of himself he revealed. The reasons for his marital failures were depressingly mundane: cheating and different interests. Mark had no desire to bring them up again, or be scrutinised for his poor decisions. The calls could be returned at a later date, some vague time in the future.

Mark rummaged around his wardrobe and found an old backpack, got some water, sunscreen and a hat. He took a rain jacket too. It could start pelting again and he didn't want to be in the arse end of nowhere when it did. He removed the binoculars from his neck and put them in the pack, throwing in two apples at the last minute. The pack gave him some satisfaction: he was a man with purpose.

The phone rang again and he looked at the number: his sister Prue. He switched it off; no malice, he just didn't feel like talking. You can do that with sisters, they won't hate you for it.

On the drive out to Stone Town, the third since the early hours of Saturday morning, he listened to the local radio station. Rivers were rising, there was a livestock alert, rain was forecast for the evening. Beside the stretch of road, gullies of water rushed along. Was it La Niña or El Niño or something, which, in conjunction with climate change, caused the weather patterns to be particularly haphazard this year? He'd never known spring rains like it.

There was no mention of Natalie Whitsed on the 11 am news. Was she dead? Mark thought so. That, or worse. He changed gears, slowed as he drove past Jacqueline Matteson's house. Another car was there, a little red thing. Probably Georgia's. He thought once more of the coat that he'd borrowed from Jacqueline and when he should give it back. At some point in the next few days he'd need to talk with the girls again, and Evan most definitely.

There wasn't a sign delineating where the start of the Stone Town bush began, but he could see it to the right, where the paddocks gave way to the trees and scrub thick with blackberry bushes began. He pulled over onto a dirt side-track and turned off the engine. Dark clouds loomed, but the wind was holding off. It was around here somewhere, the path into the bush – but now he couldn't recall exactly where it was. After a while, the bush all looked the same.

Backpack on, car locked, Mark walked into the thickness of the trees. It was difficult to manage. Weeds, sticks, ferns, stones, uncertain footing, fallen trees, some old barbed wire. After ten minutes he wondered what he was doing there, after fifteen he wished he hadn't come. This wasn't the Sunday nature stroll he'd hoped for. And then, just as he was about to turn around and head back to the car, he saw what he was looking for – the orange plastic of the council webbing in front of him. Mark struggled over the foliage to reach it and found, just before the tape, the path. A thin, dirt path, but a path nonetheless, and the one that Evan and the Matteson girls must have taken when they found the body, the same one he had walked down in the early hours of Saturday morning, led there by the local SES volunteer. He'd have to ask again how to find the beginning of the trail. There was no sign now of the crime scene – Aidan's body had been found along the track to the left, closer to the main road – but Mark was interested to know where he'd been. In death, Sleeth was lying down, head pointed to the road. Mark thought it likely that the man had previously been along the other side of the webbing, deeper into the bush.

Earlier rain meant the muddy puddles had settled into mini ponds, forcing Mark to walk around the path rather than sludge his way along it. He could see the curve of the trail, how it led beyond the orange webbing and into a darker section of the bush. A small sign hung from the wilting barrier:

Warning: Dangerous mine shafts in the area and uncertain terrain. No entry until further notice.

Mark knew from experience that warning signs rarely changed people's behaviour, especially ones such as this – where the people viewing it were likely to be local and well aware of the mines and other pitfalls. No entry? Who was going to stop the seasoned walker, the real estate agent who grew up here, or kids on a dare? It was the same kind of arrogance that made country drivers speed on windy dirt roads, kids hurtle off bridges into rushing rivers, and people stay in their houses long after fire alerts called for evacuations.

Mark pushed down the webbing and hoisted one leg over, then the other. Something tightened in his upper thigh and he gave it a rub, digging his thumb into muscle, giving it a quick massage under his jeans. He'd been to a physio a few times, but there were only so many $125 sessions he was prepared to pay for the advice of 'gentle exercise'. The chiro had charged even more and told him to come back at the same time every week for six weeks, or was it six years? He dug at his leg with vigour; didn't pain mean it was getting better?

A low wind started up, catching the tops of the ferns and making the bracken shiver. Wallaby grass rippled, wattle swayed. Mark stretched out his leg before walking up the sodden path, which curved into Stoney Creek, running shallow and at speed. Balancing on a log, he jumped over the water and scrambled up a rise and then down again into a thickened clump of knotted trees, their spindly branches hanging like fingers pointing down. Bleak clouds covered the sun and, for a moment, it was almost dark. Mark paused. From somewhere up the path in front, he thought he heard the faint whistle of a bird.

The sun appeared and he moved on. Blackberry bushes and salt bush lined the sides of the path and, above, the trees: blue gum, mallee and yorrells. The names came back to him, his mother's books and her ramblings on walks about this and that foliage. A river red gum! These trees, with their heavy twisted branches and thin leaves offering dappled light, stood tall and silent in the Stone Town bush. Come fire season, they were bombs: designed to explode in heat. Mark tried to recall if the fires twenty years ago had torn through this part of the bush, decided they hadn't. There were no tell-tale signs of blackened stumps, or regrowth. Everything in the bush looked aged and still.

That sound again – the low trill. It was up ahead. The path became rocky where granite mixed with mud and Mark chose his footsteps carefully. Stopping to tighten a shoelace before continuing, he noted there were other paths leading through the bush. Thin paths, not as established as the rough one he was on, but ones flattened by footsteps or paws or hooves. Where did they lead? The bush seemed to him suddenly to be like a maze, secretive and sly.

He stepped over another deep puddle and was surprised to hear metal underneath his boots. Shoeing aside the leaves and debris, Mark saw that he was standing on a metal grate. He bent down, vaguely disturbed to see that he was, in fact, looking into a covered mine shaft. These, he knew from boring school lessons, were used to separate the shafts – lock them off for the miner who owned the rights. Grates were also used rather than wooden doors in case of flooding.

Mark quickly moved off the grate and to the side of the path. He kneeled in the dirt, taking a closer look at the cavern beneath. It was deep. He couldn't see the bottom. Reaching behind him for a stick, he poked it through the grate and dropped it down – no sound, the depth uncertain. 'Hello!' he shouted into the dank space, feeling foolish. Nothing but the dull echo of his own words came back.

The warning sign from earlier took on new meaning. Here he was, a hypocrite, ignoring the words of danger. Mark found a small stone, pushed it through the metal, and this time he thought he heard it land – a long way down, perhaps ten metres. He stood, straightening his back and looking around. The bush felt closer here; it pressed in. Shaking off a feeling he didn't quite recognise, he continued more slowly. What was he even doing here? Vague thoughts of birdwatching? Trying to see what others saw in this bush? A need to find out what Aidan Sleeth had been doing here late on Friday night?

The sound again! It *was* a bird, and somewhere close now. Mark slipped the backpack off and unzipped it, taking the binoculars out. Hurriedly, he raised them to his eyes and saw immediately how the bush zoomed in. He looked above him, into the canopy of the trees. A flurry of movement across the lens – and he adjusted his line of sight to the left, where, at first in a blur and then more clearly, he caught a bird swooping in to rest on the top of an old Murray pine.

Mark felt a moment of joy, let out a yelp. The bird was brown and white, with a curved beak. It sat dignified on the old branch high above, and then flew off out of sight.

Mark shifted his gaze slowly around, taking his time. No more birds. It was all so quiet. He lowered the binoculars. But then, a slight movement in the trees. He lifted the lens and saw – there, in the trees to the right, some twenty metres into the bush – someone was watching him.

A pair of binoculars was pointed directly at him.

Mark froze, put his own down for a second. 'Hey!' he shouted. 'Hello!' But without the benefits of magnified sight, the bush became a blur of green and grey. Was that a rustling to his left? He swung around. No. He lifted the binoculars again, tried to focus on the same area, but he couldn't be exactly sure where he had been looking. Slowly, he scanned his surroundings.

Another sound to his left now, the swooshing of branches, and he jumped as a man appeared from between the trees, wiping his arms of dew and leaves.

'See anything?' the man said in hushed tones. 'I've spotted Apostles, but the Parrots are hiding out. Might be too wet.'

Mark blinked, confused. 'Where did you come from?'

The man jerked a thumb behind him. 'Where do you think?'

'I saw someone out there.' Mark's voice was shaky. He flung an arm to the right. 'Someone looking at me with binoculars.'

'You think you're the only birder here?' The man raised his eyebrows. 'This time of year, this bush is full of them.'

'Full?'

'Well, three or four maybe. People sometimes camp here too, you know, leave their rubbish around.' He shook his head sadly. 'Probably drunks.'

'It was just that . . .' Mark faltered. 'This one was looking straight at me.'

There was a pause. 'Yeah?' The man rallied. 'And what were you doing to him?'

Mark couldn't fault the man's logic, but his unease remained. He took a drink bottle out of his pack and had a swig. 'You from around here?'

'No.' The man had short spiky hair and was thin, like a sparrow. 'From Gawler – but every weekend I try to get out birding.' He held up his binoculars. 'It's what I live for.'

'Big effort.'

'I usually stay overnight. There's accommodation here – log cabins, nice. At a co-op not far from here.'

Mark focused. 'Owned by Evie and John Renner?'

'That's the one. Cheap, do all right meals too.'

'You ever see a Barking Owl?' Mark asked the question while scanning the surrounds. He turned, so that his back was facing the path rather than the bush to the left.

'Ah, you're after the *Ninox connivens*, are you? Join the club. Well, you'd know they're nocturnal and my obsession only goes so far, especially when the weather's been so poor.' Mark had to lean in to hear the man, his tone low and discreet. 'Seen plenty of Boobooks and Powerfuls, but not the Barking, it's hardly common. I have heard rumours of it up here though. You new to it, are you?'

Mark looked confused and the man held two tunnelled fists up to his eyes, in the universal sign for binoculars.

Oh, birdwatching. 'Yeah, just checking it out.'

'Lots to check out, bird life's full of surprises – last week I saw a Brown Treecreeper.'

'Yeah?' Mark couldn't muster up any enthusiasm. The man looked at him in pity.

'If you're just starting out, maybe check the powder

magazine. There's a nest of Weebills in the tree near the west side.'

'Where *is* that?' Mark recalled Luke Howsley's mention of the building during his police interview.

'Keep going up the track, only three hundred metres or so. You can catch a glimpse of it right here if you look through over there.' The man pointed north-east, to the right of the track. 'Track curves just up ahead – follows the creek line. See it?'

Mark peered through the forest and, sure enough, when his eyes adjusted, he saw the grey outline of a stone wall. The colours of things were all muted in this place. It was difficult to distinguish unless you knew what you were looking at.

'Anyway,' the sparrow man said, 'I'm off. Got to head back home this afternoon and I'm determined to tick off the *Neophema elegans*.'

Mark held up his hands in a helpless gesture.

'The Elegant Parrot!' The man shook his head, smiling. 'You'll get the hang of it. And listen,' he said, leaning in. 'Go quietly. That's the main rule of birding. Go quietly.' And with that, he raised a hand and stepped off the path into the bush again.

A moment later, Mark heard a noise behind him and turned in fright to see a man panting, hands on knees. *What is this, Hindley Street?*

'Was that Gerald just now?' the man asked.

This second man looked of a similar species to the first. Tall, skinny, with hair poking up. Green pants and an old woollen jumper, brown.

95

'I didn't catch his name.'

'Just that I swear I saw a *Pachycephala inornata*.'

'What?'

'Gilbert's Whistler. Need Gerald's Monarch, performs better than my bins in low light.'

Again, Mark had to lean in to hear – like the other sparrow man before, this one spoke in a low voice, breathy and deliberate.

'Were you in the bush just now, about twenty metres in, looking at me through your binoculars?'

The man stared at Mark as if he were strange. 'Why would I do that?' And without a word, he headed off to the right of the path to catch up with Gerald.

Mark took a moment to collect his thoughts. He cricked his neck, took another swig of water. *Go quietly.* Mark began walking up the path once more, where now it curved sharply and continued up a gentle rise. He tried to slow his breathing, to calm his mind. It was a few minutes before he accepted the creeping sense of unease that now enveloped him. He had seen someone in the bush watching him with unnerving intensity through the binocular lens. He told himself it was a twitcher; there were more out there, someone who happened to spot him as he searched for some elusive bird. But the feeling remained, prickling the back of his neck, making him hyper alert.

Through the trees, the powder magazine appeared before him, its solid stone appearance strangely comforting. A sign introduced the old building:

Restored by the National Trust in 1961, this building is a unique addition to the historic precinct of Stone Town. Built in 1859 at a cost of £1300, the Powder Magazine stored black powder used for blasting on the goldfields, and miners were required by law to leave bulk gunpowder in the building overnight. The unique design of the building ensured that any explosion would be minimised by the building's structure.

Today, visitors can see the engineering that created this sturdy and quite rare building, designed so that any explosion would travel upwards rather than outwards.

Made with heavy stone bricks, the powder magazine was a square building constructed inside a buttressed rectangular wall. A door, long broken from neglect or ill-use, hung from one hinge on the entrance. Earlier fears forgotten for the moment, Mark stepped inside, the dark cold of the place making him rub his hands together and put his hood up.

It was a small space, barely six by four metres, and dim with the limited window light. What he presumed to be a vault took up one corner of the room, its iron doors rusted firm. He turned around slowly: there was nothing here, save the quiet cool of stone and a musty smell of old. As his eyes adjusted, he could see that the inner walls were filled with chalked graffiti, initials and words written with abandon across the old stone.

JK sucks cock, I Woz Ere, ST 4 EVA, Faz has AIDS!!

He ran his hands along the wall, wondering at the history of it all. The goldfields, the wealth and the poverty. A dream for some, misfortune for most. And Faz. What had happened to Faz? There was *RD* a few times and, most interesting of all, in the centre of the wall, under the thin windows, *AS*. Now that he could see it, the initials jumped out at him. *AS* was all over, at least ten times – carved into the stone as well as chalked over it. Aidan Sleeth loved this forest like a 'Huck Finn', Luke Howsley had said. It was the stomping ground of his childhood and he was interested in it as a businessman. Was he the *AS* of these walls?

Mark took out his phone, snapping photos of the graffiti.

He stepped outside the powder magazine and again felt it, that sliver of fear. The creeping sensation that, close by and hidden, someone was watching.

The charred remains of a small campfire lay scattered about on the sodden dirt to the left of the building, stones circled around it like an ancient sign.

A loud squawking made him jump and he looked up to see a bird hovering in a branch above him. This was perhaps the mother bird protecting the nest that the twitcher named Gerald had told him about. But Mark felt no interest in birds. The path back to his car lay before him and he took it. Fast.

CHAPTER 12

The predicted storm was coming. Clouds gathered and a light rain began to fall as Mark drove slowly past the house he presumed to be Evan's, that sad boy with the defeated attitude he'd talked to not two nights ago. Then further along, past Pat Delaney's dilapidated house, the bush close, covering it in a mass of green and grey. The route after Pat's turned sharply, up a well-maintained driveway to Aidan Sleeth's large family home. Mark continued straight, on dirt now, the road leading further into the bush and the co-op owned by John and Evie Renner.

The place itself was a hodgepodge of log cabins, large solar panel frames, and impressive garden beds of vegetables and herbs. The first sighting of John and Evie was of them working in the garden, hats moving up and down like a game of bobs and statues. As Mark pulled up into the driveway before the cabins, the couple came to meet him. Evie's wispy grey hair, thin frame and smiley visage was far more welcoming than her scowling husband's.

Mark introduced himself as the local policeman, passing by after a walk in the bush.

'Here about the Sleeth fellow, are you?' John said.

'Such a tragedy,' Evie cut in, resting a hand on her husband's arm.

'Tragedy! I'd have done it myself if I had half the chance,' John said. 'Thought about it often enough.'

This was a surprise. Usually, after a crime was committed there'd be some level of respect for the victim, however disliked they may have been. No, *Look, I'm sorry they're gone . . . but* in this instance.

'You didn't like Mr Sleeth?'

'Like him!' John almost exploded. 'Couldn't stand the man! Him and his shady business deals, offering land prices to our partners that their greedy eyes couldn't say no to, pretending to care about the area – I mean, cry me a river! He had it coming.'

'He was shot in the back of the head at close range,' Mark said, stern. 'People are grieving.' *Are they?*

John snorted. 'I'd have done it face to face.'

Mark looked directly at the man. 'If you've got anything to add to the investigation, I'd like you to come to the station and discuss this further.'

'Fine, fine.' John looked around the place. 'Not as if I've got anything worthwhile to do here.'

'Anything you'd like to tell me now?' Firm.

Evie took off her hat and smoothed down her wiry hair. 'John had been furious at Aidan for weeks – Aidan managed to convince our ex-co-op partner Sasha to sell her share of the land. Twenty acres! Now, we learn he's going to develop it.'

Or was, Mark thought.

'We couldn't afford to buy it off her. Not that she asked!' John exclaimed.

'She would have known we couldn't . . .' Evie smiled hopelessly at Mark.

'Wasn't there some sort of legal binding in the original co-op set-up? Like, you'd have to have all parties agree to any sales?'

John gave a loud snort and again Evie patted his arm. 'No,' she said. 'We were all a bit free and easy in the early days of the set-up. We bought it years ago with Sasha's parents – it was all *let love reign* and so forth. We saw contracts as some sort of evil pact with capitalism. Our primary aim,' she added, 'was for all members to live affordably in an environmentally sustainable community – just small. If we were living or staying here, we had to work voluntarily on the garden and maintain the cabins. It was such a simple premise, but it's never quite worked out as we hoped.'

'You don't live here full time?'

'No, we're back and forth. We've got a small unit in the Adelaide Hills and we still do some work down there. None of us have ever lived here permanently. The most we have ever done so is for six months when we were first setting up and then for a few months straight here and there. But we just love it here, love it!'

John interrupted. 'We sold our four-bedroom house in the city for $400,000 for this. Now that house is worth well over $1.28 million! And any moment now in this place we're going to have bloody kit homes and cavoodles and massive antennas everywhere we look. This co-op is stuffed.'

'That might not be the case,' Evie soothed.

'And agapanthus! They'll grow that too – or worse, standard roses. God! I wish someone had shot *me* instead!'

John raged over to the garden bed and began yanking out weeds. Mark turned to Evie. 'Did you hear anything at all on Friday night when Aidan was killed? Or see anything strange?'

Evie gave a gentle shake of her head and Mark could see, with her emerald eyes and clear skin, how she would have been a real beauty in her youth. 'It was a stormy night, rain and thunder, lovely under the tin roof. We had the two birders here of course – they come up regularly at this time of year. They arrived quite late, about 7 pm, maybe a bit after, but otherwise, there was just us. We had tea early and went to bed and read. John was with me the whole time. I'm a light sleeper, I would have woken if I'd heard anything amiss.'

Mark nodded. Thinking.

'John comes across as all aggressive, but he's not really.' Evie's voice was soothing. 'It's just that we've worked so hard to get this co-op working, and now twenty acres of it have been sold from under us! Just think of all the land clearing they'll do. All the poor creatures who'll die from it.' Her face held real sorrow and Mark could see that, in the garden bed, John's shoulders drooped.

Not ten metres from where they stood the forest began, thick with undergrowth, dark now under a greying sky.

'Beautiful, isn't it?' Evie said, gazing at the trees.

Beautiful? Mark wasn't sure. It was dry, dense, unruly. There were brown snakes, black snakes, tiger snakes and spiders. There were trees that caused rashes, mine shafts to fall down, hard rock to crash against and always, always that sense . . . that you were never quite alone.

'Early settlers called it Stone Town for all the buildings that went up quickly in the gold rush. Later, when the gold was gone, the houses either fell into ruin or were pillaged for their bricks. There's remnants of them everywhere.'

'It's gloomy out there.' Mark wasn't sure why he said it – a general unease about the place – but it was true. The bush on the other side of the road was dense and dark. It was difficult to imagine stone houses, let alone a thriving mining community.

'Yes,' Evie said, 'it's because of the blackwood wattle, an acacia. It's everywhere through the bush. The bark is deep grey, almost black, and the wood stains a dark colour. En masse, the effect is one of tenebrosity.'

Evie's voice had a BBC ring to it, her words knowledgeable, and what did an 'effect of tenebrosity' mean? Time to crack open the Funk and Wagnalls.

'It used to frighten the early settlers,' Evie continued, '"No landmarks" they said, it was all the same, dark and grey and green. Little children went missing in the bush here, never to be found, and their mothers went mad.' A bird wheeled high in the sky and Evie followed its progress as she spoke. 'Settlers dreamed of Wordsworth's dancing daffodils, but what they got was this.'

Ripped off, Mark thought.

'But then, for half the year, the whole bush here blooms and the blackwood flowers in yellow and white. It's amazing!'

'Yes.' Mark didn't find it amazing.

'Watch it though, blackwood can be poisonous. Causes irritation to the eyes and skin. Can make breathing difficult in some. It's disastrous for dogs, hence we don't have any.'

'Are you both originally from the city?' Mark was making assumptions here, he knew. The stereotype: city kids with rich parents, private schools and then university they didn't pay for. Now, fed up with working, they'd settled on the simple life in the country, with country folks, home-grown food and a massive super balance.

'No, we're both farming kids. John's from the Mallee, North-West Victoria, and I'm from the Wheatbelt in WA. We were in Melbourne for university – veterinary studies – and after a stint in New Guinea we bought up this place with another couple. Sasha was born here! I delivered her right in that building over there.'

Mark looked towards a log cabin no different from the rest. He sensed nothing maternal about it.

'We couldn't have children, Sasha was like a daughter – and now she's done this.'

Mark paused. It was a betrayal, but by whom? Was the daughter bound to carry on the wishes of the parents? No wonder the young woman sent her boyfriend up here to collect her final things. The loyalty and the letting go. And what did Buddha have to say about all of this? Mark thought of the little statue, jiggling up and down in the back of the ute. He tried to recall a quote that he'd read years before . . .

Evie was looking at the bush that surrounded their home. 'Fifty million acres of land was cleared in less than seventy years where I grew up,' she was saying, a sad, dreamy look in her eyes. 'It made a few people very rich, but at what cost?' She stared at Mark, intense. 'What cost?'

Was this an actual question he was supposed to answer? He tried to articulate something about his mother and birds and the trees – but he didn't know how to frame it, or what sort of answer was required. It was too big; he was too small.

In the background, Mark could see that John had risen from his weed killing and was poking at something in the corner of the garden bed with his shoe. A tiny round thing was squirming in the dirt.

'A bird!' Evie rushed over to pick it up. 'A baby bird – where did it come from?'

John shrugged. 'Tried to fly and failed.'

'But its wing is broken!' Evie picked it up and carried it to Mark, gazing with concern at her handful.

Mark saw a beak and heard weak and distressed sounds from the fluffy creature.

'Can you save it?' he asked.

John looked over Evie's shoulder, ran a finger over the heaving bird's body. 'Both bones broken in the line across the wing. Let it go.'

'Does that mean no?'

'It's a goner,' John said. 'I'll wring its neck if it makes you feel better.'

It didn't.

'Well, I'll be off.' Mark began walking back to his car. 'I will need to call on you both soon.'

But the two heads of Evie and John were close together like conferring judges, bending over the bird: injured and soon to be dead.

CHAPTER 13

She doesn't know how long she's been in the hole. One night? Days. Days. She might have slipped into unconsciousness. Her head and throat hurt from all the screaming and her broken arm sends shockwaves of pain every time she moves.

She's weak and cold from sitting on the damp ground and the puddles smell bad. But. She's discovered something on the side of the wall, near her feet. A bag, a little backpack. She spends no time wondering how it got in here, whether it was here all along. With her good arm she tears it open, hoping for food and water. She roots about inside the pack, feels the plastic shape of a water bottle and takes it out, unscrews the lid and drinks in fast gulps, hands shaking. She stops herself from drinking the whole thing, although she'd love to, she wants to. Instead, with great restraint, she screws the lid back on and puts the bottle aside, feeling for what else is in there.

An apple. She eats it in big gnashing gulps. She takes no time, it's gone – every bit, the core and all. What else? Small, squishy things in plastic. Rectangular in shape. In the dark, she ponders them briefly before tearing the top of one with her teeth. An ooze spills into her mouth, fruity. A burst of flavour. Artificial. She knows what it is, energy gel. She'd used these when she'd run her two marathons, one a year for the past two years. These sachets, she recalls in her tired mind, are a source of energy and electrolytes. They're mostly sugar, made to replenish depleted glycogen stores. There are six of the packets in the backpack. She eats two more and puts the remaining three beside the bottle of water. The sensation of the gel is like a slug slipping down her throat. It doesn't satiate her hunger, but she does feel a little better.

She searches about in the bag. There's one more packet – a thin rectangle, covered in plastic. She rattles it; it's light and she hears the sound of something loose inside. This one too, she tears open with her teeth, and out fall two inner plastic sheets with the tell-tale lumps of pills. This packet, she's sure, is medicinal. But what sort? Think. Whoever has put her in here plans to keep her for a while. This backpack with the apple, water, energy sachets and this latest find is evidence of that. If he wanted her to die, he could just leave her.

She fingers the pill packet. It could be sleeping tablets. Or pain relief – an Endone would be heaven right now. Without further thought, she pops two of the pills and puts them in her mouth and, taking another sip of the bottled water, swallows. The pills don't taste like anything. They could be Panadol. They could be Rohypnol. She lets that thought settle before carefully placing all the items back in the pack and zipping it up.

The effort has exhausted her. But a thought, which didn't enter her head in the initial excitement of the find, comes to her. The bag was not always here. She is sure she's felt every bit of the floor, the caved roof, the width and depth. It was not there before. Now, with steady resolve and moving about on her knees, she scours again the cavern she is in. When she'd first looked, she was panicked, rushed, confused. Now, she is deliberate in her motions. The dirt walls are damp, everything is, and this scares her. Was it as wet yesterday? Dark, so dark, and the air dank and cold.

Pain and fear come roaring back. She struggles to contain it. Holds it back for now.

She continues to pat the ground, low all around, and then – she feels something. There is a metal grille, maybe sixty centimetres high and the same in width, behind the pack. The three iron bars running down it are maybe fifteen centimetres apart. She traces the edges of the grate, trying to find purchase, but to no avail. She reaches her hand in between the bars, feels a damp wood panel beyond. Another barrier, one she could probably break through. She puts her head against the bars, pushing her face into the space between them, trying to work out if she could squeeze through. She presses hard, her cheekbones aching with the effort. There's no way. She pushes at it with her good hand, rests her shoulder against the bars, shoves with everything she's got. The bars don't budge. She lies on her back and kicks the grille with her heels, hard. It doesn't move. Still, she kicks. Her back is now wet and she feels a deep despondency. Maybe this is it. A wave of inky black clouds ripples through her body. The drugs setting in.

A question, horrible, waits in the deep recess of her mind, and before she drifts into some state of sleep it rears in her frontal lobe: if he doesn't want her to leave, but doesn't want her dead – what exactly is he keeping her for?

CHAPTER 14

In the HiLux on the Stone Town Road back to Booralama, Mark turned the volume up, played drums on the steering wheel. Hoodoo Gurus. The Golden Oldie station, that's what he listened to now, no shame in it. It didn't mean he liked Tony Bennett.

Mark slowed past the entrance to the path leading to the powder magazine and the site where Aidan Sleeth's body was found. A tall, thin man walked out of it now, through the pine poles and onto the road. It was the twitcher he had first talked to in the bush. Mark stopped, kept the engine running and wound the passenger window down. 'Finished for the day?'

The man looked up, startled. Deep in his own thoughts, he seemed totally unaware that he was now on a road. 'What? Oh, yes. Long drive back home now.'

'See anything interesting?'

The man held a writing pad aloft. 'Got my obs all written.

Have to confirm a few sightings, but pretty sure I saw a Black-winged Currawong.'

Mark nodded, unimpressed. 'Did another man find you? He was looking for you – something about a Monarch?'

The twitcher shook his head. 'How could he not find me! Crashing about in the bush like that. I heard him from a mile away. That's Bins for you.'

Bins?

'First rule, you know . . .'

'Go quietly,' Mark added.

The rain started up again, faint at first and then suddenly a white sheet pelting hard. 'Get in,' Mark offered. 'I'll give you a lift back to the Renners'.'

The man opened the door and bent his long body to climb into the passenger seat. He didn't comment on the rain or say thank you or make any gesture at all.

'I still think I saw someone watching me in the bush.' Mark peered into the windscreen as he did a U-turn. 'Staring straight at me.'

His passenger considered, then answered slowly. 'There were at least three of us out there today. I can imagine to the untrained eye it might be unnerving to suddenly see a man in the bush – but that's what we do. We stay off paths, we're still. You have to practise the art of standing without making one movement. We can do that for hours, little to no movement. I've known twitchers who carry CamelBaks so they don't have to lift a water bottle, people who eat sparingly – high-energy snacks that will sustain them through the twitch. I'd say you saw someone, or one of us, in the middle of a deep watch.'

Mark shrugged. 'Maybe.' Doubt lingered. 'Name's Mark.'

'Gerald.'

The HiLux windscreen wipers worked at speed, but it was still difficult to see the road.

'How many of you staying at the co-op?'

'Just Bins and me.'

'Friends, are you?'

'Friends?' Gerald seemed startled at the thought. 'We share interests, if that's what you mean.'

'Is "Bins" his nickname?'

'Yes.' Gerald offered no explanation for the moniker.

'What, does he have a fetish for rubbish or something? He into tips?'

Gerald didn't appreciate the jokey tone. Mark didn't blame him.

'Bins is short for binoculars,' Gerald said after a pause. 'All birders call them bins.'

'Oh.'

The HiLux slid easily over the puddles and around a large fallen branch. Mark stopped, jumped out and dragged it off the road. Gerald didn't offer to help. In the vehicle again, and soaking wet, he drove on, slower now and full beams on.

Mark thought about the other twitcher. 'Will Bins be right out there in this?'

'Back already.'

Mark wondered whether Gerald was aware of the air of otherness he exuded. Conversation was difficult with a man who responded in monosyllables, and only when he felt like it. It had been different in the bush; there, Gerald was in his element, confident.

He pulled once again into the driveway of the co-op – Evie and John nowhere to be seen – and parked outside the main cabin.

'Mind if I ask you a few questions? You don't have to answer right now if you don't want to.'

'I don't mind.' Gerald looked at his watch and blinked, staring out the window.

Mark got out his notebook and clicked his pen on. 'Were you and Bins here all Friday night?'

'Yes.'

'What time did you get up to the co-op?'

'About seven, seven-fifteen in the evening.'

'You travel together?'

'Yes. Bins picked me up, he's from Adelaide.'

'That night, from when you turned up at the co-op, did you see or hear anything strange? A man was killed out there, you know.'

Gerald seemed totally uninterested in the fact and gave no indication that he had heard the news. 'No.'

'What were you doing on the Friday night up here?' Mark could not imagine Gerald clubbing.

'We had the international birdwatching conference. Professor Aberdeen, ornithologist from the University of Birmingham, gave the keynote address, and then there was a workshop on birding and the results of the photo competition. None of us had entered, but there was a fabulous shot of a Willow Tit in the act of catching a fly.'

Mark waited.

'That's incredibly rare, you know.'

'So, does this have something to do with what you were doing Friday night?'

Gerald sighed as if his point was self-evident. 'The conference was held at Oxford University, England. It went from 7.30 pm our time till midnight. The two of us, Bins and I, were there, watching on our laptops.'

'In the same room?'

'Yes, there's a common room – that little cabin just there.' He pointed to a log cottage that was identical to the ones beside it.

'You or Bins leave at any time?'

'What, in order to go and shoot a man in the bush?' Gerald turned, looking at him straight on.

Mark shrugged.

'No. We'd have noticed if the other came back in sopping wet. It was raining most of Friday, remember. Besides, you can check it out. We all had to sign in on the Zoom link and it was live-streamed. I'm under @Gerald44. Just google *International Birders Conference, Oxford.* Bins will be there too. You'll see some great information on new technology in lenses and sightings in South-West France. New Guinea's where it's all happening – the BOPS, of course.'

'The what?' Mark felt weary.

'Birds of Paradise. Extremely rare species.' Again, the man became energised when his favourite topic was mentioned.

'I'll check it out.' *But not for the BOPS.*

Mark's stomach rumbled, and Gerald gave him a sidewards glance before getting out of the car and raising a hand in vague thanks or goodbye. Mark reciprocated, watching as the man sprinted, head down, towards the nearest cabin.

While passing Pat Delaney's house, Mark saw a flash of her bright bulk on the porch and reminded himself to call her the following day. He'd have to do the same for Evan and his mother as well as the Mattesons again. If he was less tired, he'd have liked to head up the Mattesons' driveway and pay a visit now. See those black curls dance up and down around Jacqueline's face, listen to her dry voice as she talked about her girls. But he was worn out and hunger had set in. He reached behind him for his backpack and lifted it to the front seat, pulled out the apple and crunched on it with big mouthfuls.

It was after 2 pm by the time he pulled into his house and hurried up the footpath to his front door. Great drops of rain sloshed down his neck and the first thing he did when he got inside was kick off his boots, then his clothes, and walk naked to the shower. He stood, feeling the full force of hot water, glad of the rain filling up all the tanks. Like most country people, he was ever mindful of wasting the precious stuff and didn't muck around, no matter how luxurious it felt. Towel around his waist and heading into the kitchen to make lunch, the phone rang.

Mark sighed before answering. It was the deep sigh of a hungry man.

'Mark speaking.'

'Heard there's been some action up your way, what's it all about?'

Jagdeep. His former colleague and partner on a case just over a year ago in the outback town of Cutters End.

'Jag! Good to hear from you.'

'Yeah, same. And what's this about Homicide setting up in your station – don't you think that's strange?'

Mark grinned. Senior Constable Jagdeep Kaur . . . how he missed her cool intelligence and easy company. Younger than him by over twenty years, her insightful and well-considered observations proved invaluable in police work, and her straight-shooting demeanour was a relief after the bluster and false camaraderie in squads he knew.

He'd caught up with Jagdeep only a handful of times after her wedding – a huge affair of music and dancing and ceremony that left him exhausted and hyped up for days. Since the move to Booralama, he'd seen her only twice. And as usual, she *was* right: now that he thought about it, there was something odd about the way detectives Clare Rendell and Finn Turner had set up home in his station. A site analysis along with forensics had been carried out, autopsy arranged, key contacts identified. Any other work – financial enquiries, background checks, official interviews – could easily be done from their Adelaide office or by driving up for the day. Why was the force footing the bill for the two of them to stay at the Comfort Inn on King George Street when they could be sleeping in their own beds?

'Yeah,' he answered, phone resting on his shoulder while he turned the kettle on and made a cup of tea. 'They seem more interested in the Whitsed case than the local bloke.' The wan looks on the faces of Rendell and Turner spoke of real grief and concern. They had no skin in the game with the Sleeth case – it was all Natalie Whitsed to them.

'Every cop in the country is interested in the Whitsed case.'

'Where do you think she is?'

'With her being on the investigation of Charlene Scopelliti? Nowhere good.'

They were both silent for a moment, the young policewoman's image foremost in their minds.

'Angelo did tell me that they had the green light to work on the Whitsed case while they were up here,' Mark admitted.

'But still, why the need to *stay* in Booralama? Cops everywhere work on two cases at once, and they're Homicide, right? Their focus should be on your case.'

She was right. As usual.

'How's pregnancy suiting you?'

Jagdeep grunted. 'I go to work for a break. My aunts are here all the time. Poor Adi, nearly drives him mad.'

'You feeling okay?' With each of her pregnancies, Kelly had thrown up for the first three months.

'Not too bad. An aversion to coriander, but that's about it.'

'How many weeks are you?'

'Almost twenty. Why does it take so long? There's a possum that's only pregnant for twelve days. I wish I was a possum.'

'Possums are pests. Their piss makes my veranda reek.'

'Who cares? Twelve days!'

They chatted about Jagdeep's husband Adi, their old colleague Darryl, who still lived in Cutters End, Mark's boys and life in Booralama. Before they hung up, Jagdeep said she'd do a little asking around, check out the two cops now stationed in his town. Her voice hinted at an energy that was not there at the beginning of the call. Work was never far from Jagdeep's mind.

So hungry now that he felt dizzy, Mark crammed a slice of bread into his mouth while he fixed himself two cheese, tomato and salami toasted sandwiches. Only after them, another cup of tea and three Tim Tams did he feel satiated.

He lay on the couch and flicked through his phone, reading the news. Not as much now on Whitsed; the mainstream media was growing tired of the story. There were murders, stabbings, rapes and videos of minor celebrities snorting coke to focus on. Only in police stations was Whitsed's case still being relentlessly analysed. *One of ours.* It was, after all, the core tenet of the force: fierce loyalty to protect the thin blue line. If officers were expected to work in unsafe environments, then they'd have to rely on one another for protection. Any officer must be secure in the belief that, if in peril, others will come to their aid and be willing to ignore danger in order to do so. It's what you sign up for, whether you truly understand it or not.

He remembered Mr Eades, the drama teacher from his school, reciting Shakespeare from some play in a faux English accent to sniggers all round. '*We few, we happy few, we band of brothers; For he to-day that sheds his blood with me, Shall be my brother.*' But despite the nudging and smirks, Mark had been secretly impressed. It's a rare person who doesn't want to be included in a band of something. Now that he thought about it, Mark wondered whether that quote – and one of his friends saying the police force was easy to get into – was the motivation for him to complete the application form and eligibility checks.

We band of brothers.

Whatever had happened, Mark hoped that Natalie's family and friends were reassured that her colleagues were scouring the country, busting budgets and worrying sick. Maybe they weren't. The band of brothers wasn't always fair or just. Old coppers talked about phonebooks under windcheaters, handy for masking bruises after a beating in the cells. There were the deaths in custody, the leaking of personal details in family violence cases, the bullying, the corruption, the association with organised crime.

Mark flicked on the telly. There were no westerns, but there was one of the *Fast & Furious* films. Either four or five or six. He watched the cars speeding along, the beautiful women and the spectacular crashes. At one point, the main bloke crashed his car into a bridge, propelled himself across a gap on a highway and saved his girlfriend mid-air. It was impressive. Mark ate a pie.

He fell asleep, then woke an hour later with a dead arm and the sound of wind lashing against the windows. Another stormy night. *Fast & Furious* was still on. Was it the same one? It didn't matter, he knew the gist. This time the old girlfriend was working with the cops. No one was happy about it.

Later that night, two images came to him before he drifted into sleep. One, the quote he'd been searching for since he'd spoken with Evie Renner, the one attributed to

Buddha. He'd read the words on a poster above some girl's bed at uni. *You only lose what you cling to.* He drifted into sleep, thinking of Evie's intelligent stare and the way she'd lied about being home all Friday night when Pat Delaney had told him she was present at the CWA meeting.

The other image was less philosophical, more sinister: that figure in the bush, half hidden and watching him with a steady, relentless stare.

CHAPTER 15

Early Monday morning, Mark was running by the river again. He never ran fast on Mondays. Big Sunday breakfasts, chips and pies mostly to blame on the one hand, his attitude the other. He'd known men who'd given up, learned to embrace the beer gut, the elastic waistbands, the hoisting of comfortable shorts up under man boobs. Mark put his hands across his chest and felt no puffs of fat. *Not today, Ariti, not today.* He chose a blue gum two hundred metres in front, picked up his pace and ran for it. His father died as thin as a grey lead pencil. His last words in Greek, the language of the country he'd never set foot in: *Óchi tóra*: not now.

A kilometre on and fighting the urge to walk, Mark slowed down once he reached the bend before the footbridge, saw sunlight on the current, shadows of river reds sprinkling light onto water, bringing it from rich chocolate to copper and gold. A few maggies and cockies, quiet now, and others he couldn't identify.

The river was swollen again, reaching the tops of the banks in some places, edging a foot below the path. Old locals told stories of the floods of 1918, how their parents saw the rushing sheet of water spilling over the hillsides and spreading miles over the flats. How bridges, culverts and roads were swept away by water they'd been dreaming of in the decade of drought before. How eight people drowned, two of them veterans of Gallipoli and one a nurse who'd served in Egypt.

Across the footbridge and close to the halfway mark, Mark saw a man sitting on a bench beside the water. A tall man; beanie, black jacket and pants. Mark ran closer and saw that the stranger was on a phone, talking in words he could not understand. Italian? Maybe. Not Greek; he remembered that rapid-fire sound from his childhood, his father talking with relatives on the phone. Never for long. Overseas phone calls too expensive, connections lost and fading.

Mark ran slower now, past the man on the bench. He didn't recognise him. That wasn't strange in itself, but something about his demeanour, his black clothing, the shiny shoes, was distinctly out of place. He turned at the playground of Apex Park and circled back. The man was still there, talking loudly. A fake phone call? People usually spoke louder when they were fake-talking to somebody – he regularly did it himself when he was down the street and couldn't be bothered with someone he knew. Easy to do the hands-up gesture for, 'Sorry, I'm on a call' and then walk into the Fat Bean, talking loudly all the time.

As he passed over the footbridge, Mark looked back again, but the man was gone. Probably nothing and, God, his left knee hurt. His usual sandy patch of beach was now mostly dark with mud and receding with the growing water. Still, he ripped his T-shirt off and shallow-dived into the cold. It hit him as it always did, like hard concrete, pain, and then an awakening and he was himself. Mark opened his eyes for a second and saw only the silver-brown of underwater and his own ghostly arms reaching out.

Surfacing, he saw with a start how far the current had taken him – further today than Saturday with the additional rain. He swam hard, diagonally, using all of his strength to finally reach a point where his toes felt sand and then mud. With a shock, he realised that he was almost twenty metres from his top and runners and had to walk back over the pebbles and sand to reach them, panting hard. It gave him time to vow: no more swimming till the river levels dropped. He was too old for this type of foolhardiness. Even the fact he used that term, *foolhardiness*, meant he was. Not long before he'd be like Lee O'Brien walking his dog Roxie and counting his steps, measuring careful teaspoons of Metamucil into warm water each morning. He was already listening to the Golden Oldie station – it was only a matter of time.

For now, Mark towelled his hair with his T-shirt, shoved his socks into his runners and carried them with him as he walked topless back to his house. Inside, after changing into work clothes, he turned on the television while he drank a mug of tea and ate slightly burnt toast. He liked slightly burnt toast.

In the ad breaks, there was a preview of an extended interview for a true crime show on that night – an interview with Roz Whitsed, Natalie's mother. Using the remote, Mark turned the television up loud. The saccharine voice of the interviewer: 'Roz Whitsed, a Broken Hill mother grieving in limbo. Roz Whitsed, a mother with regrets.' The camera shot to a woman, thin, face lined like a city road map – deep etchings that showed a life lived hard. Her long yellow hair clung limp to a sallow face, mouth a grey slit, with brown stumps for teeth. Only her eyes, cerulean blue, showed a resemblance to the photos of Natalie plastered across the screen now, smiling in her police uniform.

'Natty's a good girl.' The mother was hiccupping into the camera, speaking more to herself than the camera. 'Never done nuthin wrong in her life. Smart too, you know? Smart as a f—' (the interview was beeped) '—whip.'

The interviewer nodded her head, her voice soft and coaxing. 'And she became a policewoman. You must have been so proud.' The false sympathy, it reeked of a Hallmark funeral card.

'Orlways wanted to be a coppa,' the poor woman was saying, nose red and leaky. 'Orlways said she'd join the force no matter what.'

'And that's in spite of your own . . . your own issues?' The interviewer was prodding, gently moving the segment to a direction more favourable with ratings. Really, who cared about Natalie's career ambitions? *Get to the good stuff!* Mark could almost hear it: a producer yelling in the young journo's earpiece during the initial filming.

'I haven't lived a blameless life. Had me fair share'a probs. Drugs and that, family violence . . . Kicked out of home when I was fourteen, stepdad broke me jaw.'

'And,' the journo's voice cut in, with an edge, 'Natalie was removed from you when she was a child?'

'Yeah, can't deny it.' Roz Whitsed coughed into a hanky. 'Department took her off me when she was three. Got 'er back when she was five, then gone again for bits after that. Bits and pieces. With me, not with me. Broke me fu—' (beep) '—heart.'

'You've spent some time in jail yourself, haven't you, Roz?' The journo was needling, persistent. Mark hated her.

'Yeah. Assault. He deserved it though.'

A beat while the journo looked into the camera. Solemn, knowing.

'Is there anything you'd like to say to Natalie, if she's out there somewhere, being held?' Now the hint of triumph on the journo's face. No doubt a long lunch was coming up, maybe an invitation to the Press Club or at the very least a Logies gong.

'Just that, be kind to Natty, she's a good girl.' Roz was crying hard now, two hands clenched on the hanky, nose muzzling it, breath coming in waves. The camera zoomed in, Mark had to look away. Why did they do this? Zero in on pain.

'Bring her back to me! I don't care who you are or what you done, just bring her back to me. Gimme a sign she's safe.' Roz raised her face to look directly into the camera and her features hardened. 'Gimme a sign you piece of sh—' (beep) '—who's got her or knows where she is, let me know what's happened or I'll tear your fu—' (beep) '—heart out.'

The camera swerved back to the journo, now barely

hiding a smile. Her lips had been re-glossed when the focus was on Roz. 'Tune in tonight to hear more about Natalie Whitsed's troubled upbringing and her—'

Mark flicked the screen off, washed his plates in the sink and got ready to leave. The interview wouldn't be good for the campaign to find Natalie. He doubted the police had approved it. Roz was too rough, too uncouth. Her presence would change the way people thought about Natalie, make her less appealing at a time when interest in the case was waning anyway. They wouldn't say so, but in the deep recesses of viewers' minds they'd think that *maybe Natalie did something to deserve it*. Drugs, or hanging out with dodgy people or strange boyfriends. In *The Silence of the Lambs*, the only reason the last girl got any attention was because her mother was a senator. You had to *be* someone, know someone or – best of all – be related to someone worthy if you wanted your cause kept up in the media. Roz failed on all accounts. Viewers would transfer their distaste of the mother to the daughter. And yet . . . Mark felt a flicker of admiration for the woman. In spite of her distress, her obvious grieving, Roz had shown a burning anger born of love, and that would provide energy at least for a while.

CHAPTER 16

Now, when she opens her eyes, she can see. Not well, not like on the surface – but instead of outlines, she can make out the contours of the walls of the den in which she is trapped, the wet earth and, most of all, the entrance – those metal bars. She's becoming accustomed to the dark.

She sucks on the end of the last of the energy sachets and thinks about what she's learned. Because that's important – think methodically, list what needs to be done and be firm about it. It's what makes her good at her job and also why people dislike her. A young woman showing up the old guard hadn't made her popular. There'd hardly be people crying right now. It is up to her.

She drinks a small sip of water from the bottle and jiggles her legs about. Important to keep the muscles moving.

Something happened a few hours before, something that repels her, yet offers a glimmer of hope. He had returned. This time she was aware of his arrival: a scraping, and then a shift in the surrounds, from ink-black to grey and a waft of air, still dank, but new.

She'd sat back at the far side of the den and waited. At first, the sound – a clinking of metal, a scraping, and then he was in, taking up space, too much of it. Tall, bending over like the tip of an arrow to come close. 'Birdy?' he breathed. 'Little bird?' It was a new kind of horror to hear the rasp, low and tentative. 'Birdy?'

And then the movement as he felt all around, unsure and a low crooning, and she saw, in the dimness, a glinting and a point, the dull sheen of a blade.

She drew herself up against the wall, digging her back in, legs ready to kick. His arm was patting her now, her leg and up her thigh. Still, she didn't move. The hand felt her waist, along her chest, not lingering there – and up to her face.

'Are you awake?' He slapped her lightly on the cheek. She smelled foul breath, almost gagged.

He wasn't going to kill her. She'd already reasoned that – after the gift of medicine, energy sachets and water. But what, her mind raced, did he want?

'Why am I here?' she burst out, and felt a stiffening of his features, a drawing back. She held her fear in check and began again, making her voice meek. 'Can you please let me out?'

He relaxed again, she felt it; this was how he liked her. She was learning.

'You're safe in here. I'll look after you.'

Safe? 'I'm hungry.'

Nothing. She shifted, made her voice docile. 'Can I please have something to eat?'

Nothing, and she felt the sharp rise of anger. Who was this weirdo? She wanted to scratch his eyes out, kick him in the head. Instead: 'Thank you for the medicine.'

A pause, and then with her new focus she saw him reach for something out of a bag. Two items. A drink bottle and some-thing else, something fluffy.

Jesus Christ! It was a teddy bear, one of those stupid things with a big love heart on its stomach. Where was the food? 'Here,' he said, placing the items beside her leg, 'for you.'

Finally, a few packets of something – more of the sachets, an orange or an apple? Muesli bars? She longed to grab them and shove them down her throat.

'Thank you.' The thing is, she does feel thankful. Even if as, in the back of her mind, she remembers all those women she's counselled over time who'd been bashed, raped, run over, abused, who said, 'He's nice most of the time,' or 'He can be so sweet,' or 'He was so sorry about it.'

They were grateful for small mercies, and so is she.

CHAPTER 17

The Booralama police station was quiet. State and national flags drooped like weeping widows and a blue heeler sniffed round the lawn till Mark told it to rack off. Inside, Clare's office door was shut. Mark looked at the closed door and for the first time felt truly annoyed by the presence of the other police. *City cops*, he thought, and knew that he was becoming like many of his fellow rural citizens, harbouring resentment for those who lived inside hallowed city walls, who had better access to healthcare and education, who drove on roads not filled with potholes, who had full internet coverage, higher wages and more bargaining power with politicians. Metro types who romanticised the country, bought Airbnb houses for weekenders and visited twice a year, while new school teachers in the same small towns couldn't find a house to rent. *City cops*.

He tapped once on the door and opened it, to see Clare jabbing at her phone. She looked up, guilty. 'Son,' she said, indicating the device. 'Wants to know where the keys to the car are.'

Mark shrugged. 'Where's Finn?'

'Checking out Aidan's office. It's been locked since Friday afternoon, the young guy opened it for us.'

'Luke Howsley.' At least they were working on the case.

'Yeah, him.'

'What did you do yesterday?' Mark looked around the office, where evidence of paperwork and files lay askew.

'Went over the photographs we took of the Sleeth residence on Saturday afternoon. Finn got the spare keys from Sleeth's ex-wife, the one coming in today. We fingerprinted the place, it's enormous. Analysis should be back soon.'

Clare was distracted and Mark bent forward to look at her laptop screen. There, a map of the Adelaide CBD was enlarged.

'What are you looking into – Sleeth's city office?'

Again, the guilty face. 'No, not yet.' Clare continued in a rush, 'I'm checking out the places where Nat was doing surveillance on Charlene Scopelliti. We've got the surveillance recordings to look at and I thought . . .' She caught Mark's look of anger. 'What?'

'Which case are you actually prioritising here?' His voice was hard. 'I know you've been told you can check out the Whitsed file, but I don't need two extra police officers working on a separate case. I get that you knew Natalie, but I've got a station to run and a local man dead.'

Clare was silent for a moment.

'And' – Mark walked to an overhead cupboard and began

pulling out printing paper – 'you've taken over my office in some sort of Lord of the Manor move and I don't have enough space.'

Clare looked at her phone again, and then the laptop screen, where city streets merged and blurred in a confusing thread of colour. 'There's something . . .'

'What?'

Clare stammered, stopped.

'Why are you and your sidekick staying at the Comfort Inn, Clare? Why's the force paying for that?' Jagdeep's questions rang loud in his ear. Mark wished she was here.

Clare sighed and rubbed her forehead. Mark waited, feeling little sympathy for the woman sitting at his desk. A beat. Each of them knew the value in it, the wait. It was human nature to want to speak, to fill in the gaps. In this case, Clare broke first.

'Natalie's phone pinged up this way the evening she left the Adelaide CBD office. We know it was her in the car – toll cameras recorded her on the bridges coming out of the city. We discovered the ping on the day after she was reported missing.'

Natalie was last seen on toll cameras on a Friday night ten days ago. She'd taken the Monday off, so wasn't reported missing till the Tuesday when she didn't turn up for work. The ping was discovered on Wednesday – five days ago.

Mark felt a drumming somewhere deep in his brain. He waited some more.

'Then a couple of days after that her car was found in a back street of Waldara.'

'What?' Mark reeled.

'Yep, parked in a dodgy street on the outskirts.'

'So, it was found on the same day Sleeth was shot. The Friday.'

'Yes.'

'I didn't know this.' Usually there'd be a report, information like this shared over the police network, between stations. Waldara was fifty minutes south of Booralama. A hot spur of anger rose in Mark's throat. He should have been privy to this.

'Drug squad wanted it kept quiet,' Clare said. 'The car is back in Adelaide. It's been dusted for prints, nothing as yet. Investigative cops have been sent to Waldara too – everything on the quiet.'

Of course they wanted it kept secret. When Natalie Whitsed was investigating someone as important as Charlene Scopelliti, all leads, all information needed to be managed, distributed in pieces so as not to disturb any chance of nailing the Scopellitis for what they were suspected of: widespread drug distribution, connections with motorbike gangs, extortion and links with unions. Mark looked at Clare and knew she was thinking the same thing as him: the man in Morburn Prison, Tony Scopelliti, former boxer, head like a Rottweiler, mind as sharp as a blade. What the force would or wouldn't do to find out all he knew . . .

'That's why you wanted to come up here – to check out Sleeth's death *and* see if you could find out more about Natalie's car.'

'Yes.' There was no use in her denying it.

'Where exactly was the ping?'

'Phone tower, south of Booralama.'

'Stone Town way.' Mark was thoughtful.

Clare nodded. 'Yeah.'

Mobile phone pings helped to solve all sorts of crimes. The devices, even when turned off, constantly sent pings to phone towers in search of a strong signal. Only identified with a warrant, the technology of pings couldn't be used as hard evidence but was a definite aid in investigations. The year before, a phone ping signal helped Victorian police to place the husband of a missing woman near the scene where her body was found.

'Any damage to the car found in Waldara?' Mark asked. Crims often torched their vehicles.

'Yeah. Not much. Driver's window had been jimmied. Looks like it was taken for a joy ride at some stage.' Clare rubbed her eyes. 'Not much to go on – kids probably. We're looking into it.'

'See,' Mark said, words weighted, 'here is where the local cop comes in handy. He or she tends to know your petty thieves, your snatch-and-grabs, your free-wheeling pissants.'

'I know! I know.' Clare slumped back. 'But it's not entirely my fault – we had orders.'

We had orders. That old chestnut. Orders, and from whom? Mark thought of his friend Angelo, a mover and shaker, a lunchmate of politicians, the wearer of suits you don't buy in GAZMAN. In his relatively new role as Assistant Commissioner he had the power to issue such orders.

'I saw someone this morning, not from around here. Also – a Chrysler 300c, twice.'

Clare didn't dismiss his observations. 'You get the number plate?' He gave it to her, and she tapped it into her computer, bringing up the rego information. Mark watched while she worked, eyes close to the screen. A certain haggardness was creeping into Clare's features, a woman overworked and burdened with family troubles. He'd seen women like her, not cops, normal women from Booralama, whose kids were in trouble with the law, whose husbands drank the rent money, whose contract jobs were coming to an end. Sometimes, they ended up homeless. There was a woman living in her caravan in Booralama, son attending school periodically, nicking bikes and throwing rocks at passing trucks. Another in a car with her daughter, apparently the best potential for a draft pick the town had had in years.

'You okay, Clare?'

'Yeah.' Her face reddened with self-conscious emotion.

'I'll get us a cuppa, eh?'

He hurried out of the room, afraid she'd begin sobbing and ask for a hug. He wasn't a hugger, not with people he didn't know. His mother had been a hugger. She'd be opening her arms when you were fifty metres away, fingers beckoning, urging you to hurry up into her embrace. He and his sister Prue were more restrained. But perhaps, and he'd observed this, people became less rigid with age. Tears welled when he thought of his boys coming fourth in the cross-country. The Qantas ad on TV undid him every time. Impossible to watch Cathy Freeman's gold medal race without a fulsome sob.

On his mother's death, however, not a tear. His grief had been dry-eyed and bleak.

Mugs of tea steaming, he returned to the room where Clare had now blown her nose and smoothed down her hair. Any trace of vulnerability was gone.

'Put one sugar in it for you.' It's what his mother used to do if he or Prue were feeling sad. Just the one. Two made your teeth ache.

Clare took a sip. 'Plate's come up on the system as being registered under a business: the Crazy Cactus. It's a pole-dancing venue in East Adelaide, part-owned by Tony Scopelliti.'

Mark had a vision of women pole-dancing up and down a cactus, gyrating their way around the spikes. 'What a name,' he said.

'It's because the other owner is Shane Spike. Get it?'

'Yeah.' Mark felt weary. 'I get it.'

So, it seemed that Scopelliti's stooges were here in Booralama, trying to find out what the cops were up to in their leads on Whitsed.

Clare brought up photos on the screen of Spike and other workers at the Crazy Cactus. Mark didn't recognise any as the black-suited man by the river talking on the phone. He thought briefly of the person in the Stone Town bush watching him through binoculars. Felt a chill. He shifted in his seat.

'Hey, listen,' Clare said. 'Maybe don't tell Finn about the car. It's okay that he knows you're aware that we're also looking for traces of Whitsed up here, he knew her probably the best out of all of us – but don't tell him about the vehicle just yet. There's reason to suspect . . .'

Mark turned away, remembering Angelo telling him about Finn and his connections to Morburn Prison. He opened his mouth to ask about it and then thought better of it. No need to get deeper into the mess.

Taking his tea, Mark backed out of his old office and into his new one – the small space he now used in deference to the *city cops*. He found his notebook, clicked his pen and wrote:

Whitsed – Mother is last known contact: phone ping south of Booralama, Stone Town? Car found in Waldara: stolen?

Whitsed investigating Charlene Scopelliti, Tony Scopelliti's wife.

Scopelliti's man in Booralama, sniffing around. How do the Scops know about Nat W and pings/Booralama connection? Finn Turner??

Mark looked at his list. He liked lists. They were neat, they told him what to do. He added ASK SQUIRREL beside the note about Natalie's car having possibly been stolen and dumped in Waldara, and turned to an earlier list he'd prepared on Friday, before Aidan Sleeth was found with half his face blown off. *Two bikes stolen.*

He found a number in his contact list, texted, received a thumbs-up in response.

There were other tasks to complete: the mundanity of police work. A school talk to postpone, a follow-up on the weed bought and sold, a call with Ian Beard, the manager of the IGA, about the graffiti, and one with Father Murcovich about the church break-in.

A loud 'Cheerio' broke his train of thought. Mark poked his head out of his small office door. In the hallway, Clare was staring at a man with the look and smell of a ferret.

'Howzit going in copper land?' the man asked, chipper.

'Excuse me.' Clare straightened and made moves to block the hall. 'I'm going to have to ask you to—'

'Squirrel!' Mark greeted the man and beckoned him into his new space. 'In here.'

Squirrel gave Clare a nod and entered the spartan room with a whistle. 'Hashtag Defunded the Police already, have we? Looking a little dire here, Reets.'

Only people who'd known him since primary school called him Reets, a shortened version of Ariti.

'Got the city colleagues up. Visiting.'

'Checking you out, eh?' He coughed into his hand, looked into whatever had landed there and stuck it in his pocket. 'What you been up to on the sly, Reets?'

'Listen, Squirrel.' Mark leaned with his back to the door. 'I need you to check something out for me.'

Squirrel picked up a stapler from the desk and looked at it. 'Yeah?'

'What do you know about a stolen car that turned up in Waldara a few days ago – a grey Mazda.'

'Sweet FA.' Squirrel opened and shut the stapler, clicked it. Bits of metal spewed on the carpet.

'Can you ask someone, see if anyone knows . . .?'

'What do I have to say, Reets?' Squirrel made the sign with his four fingers overlapped. 'Hashtag, I know nothing 'bout a car.' He flicked the stapler again, bored. A small metal piece flicked onto Mark's shoe. Squirrel could be like this. Wily, out for what he could get.

'Listen, Squirrel – your sister still living in that van with her boy?'

'Dontay?' Squirrel stretched his top lip over teeth like dried kindling.

'Two bikes, Trek Marlins, were stolen last week. Yesterday, I saw your nephew Dontay riding one of them through town.'

'Could have been any kid, Reets. Kids like to ride, remember your shitty BMX?'

'I saw it was him, saw the make, the colour. Red Trek Marlin. No question.'

'Got X-ray vision, have ya?'

'Binoculars.'

Squirrel was silent.

'If you do some searching for me, about this car, I'll forget the bikes – all he needs to do is return them here.' Mark took a risk. 'And I won't press charges for the graffiti on the IGA.'

'Little shit!' Squirrel shook his narrow head. 'His mum said he come home with paint all over him. Looked like a fucken Rubik's Cube.'

'Can you ask around, Squirrel? It's big.' He made the sign with his fingers. 'Like, hashtag big.'

'This to do with Sleeth?'

'Yeah,' Mark lied. 'Think of it as community service.'

'Done my fair share of that.'

None of it voluntary. 'You know what I mean. I don't need names, just where the car was picked up from.'

There was a beat while Squirrel shot out a few more staples. 'Okay. Giss five.'

'Thanks.'

Squirrel pointed to his phone and backed out the door, giving Mark a thumbs-up.

In Year 4, Gavin Mitchell was in a hurry at the toilets and got his balls stuck in his jeans zipper. The whole of Booralama primary school heard the agonised shriek, 'My nuts, my nuts, my nuts!' And so, the name of Squirrel was born.

That loud cheerio again, and Mark looked into the hall-way to see that Squirrel was greeting a tall, attractive woman on the police station porch on his way out. Clare emerged from her room. 'Sleeth's ex-wife,' she mouthed. 'Plus, the lawyer.'

Mark backed into his office to collect his notepad. He waited till the others passed his doorway before following them up the skinny hall to the interview room. Introductions complete, they sat down, a worn table between them.

'Lee-Anne,' Clare said, 'thank you for coming in, we just want to have a chat about—'

'It's Lola.' The tall woman sniffed and looked out the window.

Clare glanced down at her notes. 'It says here that you are named Lee-Anne Sleeth, nee Hetherington, of 16 Spring Street, Boorala—'

'I changed my name.'

'Legally?'

'No. I just go by Lola now.' Lee-Anne/Lola looked at her lawyer and lowered her lids. 'I'm more of a Lola.'

Clare raised her eyebrows and Mark hid a grin. He knew people like this, people who lived in small towns and went to unglamorous schools who wanted to become different people when they left or grew up. There was nothing wrong with it. But still, Lee-Anne to Lola. *Like calling spag bol 'creamy steak fettuccini'.*

Mark wondered how well Lola's lawyer knew his client. For now, the man was assiduously professional in his navy blue jacket, white shirt and light blue tie. Lola sat close by him, her dark orange sleeveless dress tight around her chest and her hair curling down her shoulders in ringlets, as if she was off to a wedding.

'You know we'll be making some notes,' Clare said to the lawyer, who nodded in assent. 'And you know your rights, Lola, yes?'

'I do.' Lola gazed at her lawyer and this time he shifted slightly in his chair.

'Can you tell us how you know the deceased, Aidan Sleeth?'

'Aidan was my ex-husband. We were married for two years and have been divorced for almost five.'

'How would you describe your relationship with Aidan?'

'Fine. We've been a better divorced couple than we were married.' Lola stretched out her hand and looked down, as if expecting to see a ring there. 'We don't actually see each other all that much. I mean, *didn't*. But we were always civil.'

'We're sorry for your loss,' Mark cut in. 'It must have been a real shock.'

'It was!' He saw puzzlement in her eyes. 'Aidan was never, ever depressed or anything.' There was a pause. 'Of course,' she continued, 'you don't think it was suicide, do you?'

'We're investigating all avenues,' Mark said.

'Do you mind telling us where you were on Friday night?' Clare checked her notes.

'I had a few drinks at the Royal and then went home about eleven. Fell asleep watching the fourth series of *The Crown*. And if you're going to ask' – she held her hand up in a stop signal – 'I voted No to a republic. Mother England all the way.'

Mark smiled; Clare and the lawyer did not.

'Who were you at the pub with?'

Lola frowned, her eyebrows pointing down and inward, though her forehead remained taut. 'Well, everyone who was there, I suppose.'

'You didn't meet anyone at the bar?'

'You mean, arrange to . . . no – I just went. I saw loads of people! Just ask, they'll tell you.'

Mark made a mental note to check. It would be easy enough. After a beat, in which Lola picked up a stray hair off the lawyer's shoulder, he asked who had keys to Aidan's Booralama office.

'Aidan, me, the employee – young guy, Luke? – and the cleaners, I guess.'

'Who were the cleaners?'

'I don't know. Local girls. Aidan hired them, not me.' As if cleaning was something she never had to bother with. Or, not since the Lee-Anne days anyway.

'Did you know,' Clare asked, 'that Aidan left his business, plus the family home in Stone Town *and* his city apartment to you?'

'He did mention that a number of times.' Lola looked at her hands again. Stroked her curls, gave them a twirl.

'Why do you think that was?' Clare asked, and the lawyer jumped in: 'You don't have to answer that.'

Clare sniffed and pursed her lips.

'I don't mind,' Lola said. 'Aidan and I had a good relationship, even after the divorce. I saw him quite regularly. His parents are dead. No siblings. Who else would he leave it to?'

The question hung in the small room.

Clare glanced at her notes again. 'According to us, you've been receiving money from Aidan since your divorce – $1000 a month.'

Mark felt a stab of surprise.

A flicker of doubt crossed Lola's face. She fondled a small gold cross at her neck. 'And?'

'What was that payment for?'

The lawyer butted in and this time Lola didn't try to stop him. 'My client doesn't have to answer that.'

'Why was Aidan paying you each month, Lola? What were you doing for him?'

The lawyer stood, nodding for Lola to follow. She looked uncertain before rising to her feet, smoothing down her dress. Her face was shiny – a thin sheen of sweat glistened on her upper lip. Red crevasses ran down her neck like ancient creek beds in drought.

Clare and Mark rose from their seats, said their thanks, which went unanswered, and their goodbyes, which Lola acknowledged with a brief wave.

Once they were out of the station, Clare and Mark looked at each other.

'I'll check out the pub,' Mark said. 'Sounds like a good alibi.'

'She'd still have time to have drinks, leave at 11 pm, drive out to Stone Town and shoot her ex in the head.'

'So, we're definitely ruling out suicide?'

It was the first time she'd admitted that they were looking for a murderer.

'Initial forensic evidence isn't the most accurate – rain made splatter formations near impossible to read,' Clare answered. 'It's early yet, but yes, a cop there I know called earlier. She says the shooting range looks to be around five metres.'

Murder then. In the heat of the moment or premeditated?

'Would have been bloody loud,' Clare added.

'That weather though.' Mark thought of the early hours of the morning when he saw Aidan Sleeth's body lying in the bush. Pelting rain, streams gushing, thunder. The heavy sound of rain on gum trees, weighing them down . . .

'We should get the final report on forensics tomorrow. My contact is going to call me. Jane Southern – know her?' There was a sly undertone to Clare's question. He looked at her, saw the coy glance, and felt a sudden dislike for his new colleague.

'Let me know when Finn's back,' he said, walking into his room and shutting the door. Inside, he tried to open a window, pulling hard on the old wood till it prised upwards. A burst of air hit him, and he breathed in deep. He didn't know about Sleeth's will and his long-standing payments to his ex-wife. So, Clare and Finn had been doing some investigative work. Good. They did say they'd take care of the finances, and the fingerprinting they'd carried out over the weekend was not a small job. Mark's mind wandered to Lola Sleeth, with her long curls and her girlish smile at the lawyer. There was something pathetic about her, a neediness that would either repel or attract depending on intention. And the Royal, he'd go there after work in the next few days.

Mark inhaled another gust of air, took up his notebook and added:

Lee-Anne/Lola Sleeth – sole beneficiary of Sleeth's will.
Paid $1000 each month. Why?
Cleaners
Forensics: 5-metre shooting range

Mark looked out the window again, held his hand up in a gun shape and imagined shooting someone from five metres away. It wasn't exactly execution range, but not far off. Why shoot someone that close and in the back of the head? Shooting someone in the face was personal, it showed a deep level of hatred. In the back of the head at close range – that was more clinical. Now he'd had time to think about it, and the way Aidan's head was blown apart in the bush, Mark believed it

144

most likely the job of a shotgun, good for shooting foxes, the senile family dog, a deer even.

And then that word, *forensics*. He hovered over it, lingered there and was brought back to hot nights in the city, cheap bars and hotels, laughing over drinks and waking up in bed with Senior Sergeant Jane Southern, who two years ago was temporarily placed in his Fraud division. Jane Southern, as tall as him, short dark hair, long and lean. Three years his senior; they called her a cougar. One night a few months ago his finger floated over her number on his mobile, daring himself to ring. She might pick up, might talk to him without rancour, and who knew where that could lead? A car sped past, muffler screaming. Mark let out a heavy sigh and slammed the window down hard, closing off the idea.

His own phone vibrated, and he realised with a start he'd forgotten to check if Squirrel had replied. Two messages: the most recent from Jagdeep asking him to call her back; the other from Squirrel.

D picked up car 10 days ago. drove 2 Waldara. No damage.

Natalie's car was stolen on the evening of the last day she'd been seen on toll cameras. This was huge. Mark ignored the note about the damage. He texted back his original query:

What time and where'd they pick it up from?

The answer came back within a minute. Mark pictured Squirrel's small fingers darting out the message:

Around 11 pm. Past the old school, Yielder's Track, Stone Town.

CHAPTER 18

Heart pounding, Mark brought up a map of Stone Town and the surrounding area on his phone. Yielder's Track wasn't listed, but Deference Road was. It ran to the back of Stone Town – parallel to the Stone Town Road he'd been driving on these last few days, but at the bottom of the properties of Jacqueline Matteson, Evan Williams, Pat Delaney, Sleeth and the co-op. Google Maps didn't always get country roads right. The technology couldn't match old colloquialisms and knowledge born from family history and gossip. All across the country in small towns there existed secret lanes, tracks, byways, side streets and closes, unknown to official sources. There was a Pudding Alley in Booralama. No official street name, no map would point to it – but everyone in town knew it ran from behind the old post office to the back of the butcher's on Ovens Street.

Yielder's Track. Mark took his information to Clare, who

immediately punched the details into her phone and sent them off.

'Great work,' she said, a growing excitement in her features as she stood up and paced around the room. 'Interesting.'

It *was* interesting. Whitsed's car had been found in the very same area a week before a local man's body was found shot in the bush. There was the phone ping. But still, Mark reminded himself, it could be nothing.

'It could be nothing.' *It's huge.*

'This Squirrel – can he be trusted? He looked pretty . . . Would he tell you the truth?'

The truth. On that note, Mark was not sure. Squirrel could be evasive, mysterious about the ways he earned money and with whom he kept company. Truthful was not a word Mark would use to describe Squirrel, no. But there were plenty of other words. Clever, yes. And loyal, now there was a word he'd use.

The only time anyone had ever called Mark a wog was at the Booralama swimming pool when he was in Year 6. The older kid who'd said it had made sure the word was directed loudly at him. He'd spat it out as they trod water, made Mark feel small for the first time in his life. *Wog.* Something shameful that put a name to sly glances, reactions to certain pronunciations, the way teachers sometimes called him Markos when he'd made a mistake. *Wog.* The whole pool, everyone in it, went quiet. And then out of nowhere, in a running leap, came Squirrel from the sides and, ignoring all safety rules, the small redhead was leaping high in the air, arms and legs open like a starfish before crashing into the water, bombing the offending kid. Squirrel smashed into him and then, as the dazed kid surfaced, pushed him underwater with his barrel body, dunking the bigger boy's head until a pool guard intervened.

'I think I can count on Squirrel,' Mark said, firm. 'And we've got to consider that Natalie's car could have been driven to Yielder's Track by someone else and *then* stolen by Dontay from there.'

Clare nodded. 'That's true, but still, the timing suggests that he stole it around the same time Nat went missing.'

But still.

'This could be the work of locals – someone shoots Nat by accident, covers up the body – maybe something to do with the car.' Clare's eyes were half closed as she ran through scenarios. 'A robbery gone wrong, maybe. This may have nothing whatsoever to do with Nat keeping an eye on the Scopellitis.' Clare stood up, began walking around. The new idea appealed to her.

'And Sleeth's death?' Mark asked. 'What about him, is it connected?'

'Someone had to shoot the both of them . . . Nat saw something . . . a hunter accidently kills Sleeth, sees Nat, turns the gun on her.' Clare trailed off, deep in thought. 'But what was she doing in Stone Town for a week, if she was there at all? Was she hiding? Injured or dead somewhere?'

The two officers sat deep in thought till the front doorbell sounded. A lady wanting to know if any keys were handed in, she'd lost them at the park.

No, they didn't have the keys. Mark wrote up a report for lost property.

It was nearing lunchtime. Mark let Clare know he was going down the street to get a sandwich. 'You want a coffee?' He asked it begrudgingly, the Jane Southern comment still fresh in his mind. His colleague shook her head, intent on her thoughts.

Outside, the world was fresh and bright, sunlight beaming through grey clouds, leaves on the old elms lush and green. Mark walked in a steady pace to the main street of Booralama and into the Fat Bean. Dennis the owner was there this time, his silver hair luxurious, his craggy features that of a fading rock star. Dennis had once hosted Stevie Nicks in his whiskey bar on Hamilton Island. Now, financially ruined and second divorce pending, he served up arancini balls with the air of a man who'd once had it all.

'What can I get you, Reets?' Dennis leaned on his counter and ran a hand through his mane. 'Mojito? Negroni?'

'Sorry, Dennis, just a sandwich please.'

Dennis rolled his eyes, then got to work on the multigrain and marge.

The Fat Bean was all heavy wood, glass and light bulbs hanging artistically from beams, a large oval mirror on the wall. The seating was a choice of stools by a high bench facing the street or cosy tables lining the sides. He chose the street view, added a coffee to his order and sat down. Fleetwood Mac's 'Tusk' played in the background, its heavy percussion and eerie vocals making him, as always, vaguely anxious. 'You mind turning it down, Den?' he called. The owner shook his head in disgust. The policeman, in his eyes, was not a connoisseur of all things fine and cool.

The song was abruptly turned off and a new track began. Acoustic, a clear voice strong and real, the lyrics speaking of regret and nostalgia. Mark listened to it as he watched the main street of his hometown, and was brought back to days when he was wild and reckless and did things he wasn't proud of but wouldn't take back. 'Jesus, Dennis,' he said when the song was finished, 'who's that singing?'

Dennis carried over his sandwich and coffee. 'Sam Fender,' he said. 'Geordie.'

'Got any more of his?'

'Got everything of his. Kids who work here, they bring it in. Get to like it after a while.'

Mark was brought back to the case. 'Isabelle Matteson work here?'

'Yeah – not much. Only as a fill-in. Her older sister did too. Forget her name.'

'Georgia.'

'That's it. You met the mother?' Dennis gave a low wolf whistle. 'Class.' He looked at his reflection in the mirror then back at Mark. 'Has this got something to do with Aidan Sleeth?'

Mark was momentarily taken aback. 'Yeah – how'd you know?'

'I see no other reason for you to be asking about young girls and their work habits. You're not the type. Plus, I know that Isabelle worked for Sleeth too. I asked her when she was in on Saturday. She was pretty shook up, I said she shouldn't have come in.'

'Shook up in what way?' Mark remembered her distraught face in his headlights, tears streaming down her face.

'I dunno. Sad? Anxious? Nervous? Who can tell with teenagers.'

Neither man had teenagers, or not any more. Dennis had a twenty-year-old son, rarely seen and now living in Brisbane; Mark had his boys in Adelaide. Each man yearned for lost moments. Ached. Mark thought of the two sisters and Evan, sitting at the Mattesons' kitchen table – their glances at each other, signals he knew nothing about.

'You know Aidan Sleeth at all, Dennis?'

'Not really. Never one for a chat. I think he was mostly in the city. Bit younger than us.'

Sam Fender kept playing. He had a touch of the Jeff Buckley.

'Bryan Ferry was one too.'

'What's that?' Mark said. 'Did I miss something here?'

'A Geordie, like Sam Fender.'

'Oh.'

'Went out with Jerry Hall, you know that? Now she's married to Rupert Murdoch, what a waste.'

'Isn't she, like, seventy?'

Dennis was lost in a dreamworld. 'Now there's a woman.'

Mark and Dennis reflected for a moment on women. Ex-wives, ex-girlfriends, old lovers, girls who they'd lusted after in Year 10, and women who they wished had stuck around. It wasn't great for the ego, but it helped to pass the time.

'You're a good-looking bloke,' Dennis mused. 'Why aren't you out and about yet?'

Mark took a big bite of his sandwich. 'It's a mystery.'

A man in acid-wash jeans rode past on a bike. It was too low for his tall frame, his back hunched over, knees almost reaching his chin with every turn of the wheel.

'Bet you wouldn't see that on Hamilton Island,' Mark said.

'No.' Dennis was distracted. 'They have golf carts there. And everyone wears white.'

A reflective pause and Dennis continued, 'Remember when we came runners-up in the semi-finals against Waldara? We must have been only thirteen, playing for the Under 16s. The coach bought us a slab and we drank it with the team out in the Stone Town bush. You and I rode our bikes to get to the assistant coach's house so he could drive us there.'

Dennis's voice had a sing-song rhythm to it, enhanced by the Geordie's lyrics. 'It was fun out there till someone brought in a stripper. Remember that?'

Mark was transported back almost forty years to a moment of unadulterated joy – men treating him and his mate like equals. The drinking, the drinking. And then, then something else, a craving unrecognised, frightening, and the feeling turning to shame when the older stripper came out to hoots and shouts of derision. 'Give us a break,' she said to someone. 'Just doing me job.' Wanting to watch, but also not wanting to. He and Dennis vomited. The shame, it was the same when he used to go spotlighting, holding the roo in the headlights, shotgun at the ready.

We few, we happy few, we band of brothers. Mark finished up, paid and said goodbye to Dennis.

As he closed the door behind him, 'Tusk' was back on the playlist.

CHAPTER 19

'Want to play a game?'

A game? She wants to cry, with fear and hunger and pain.
'What game?'

The last time he'd been here, when he brought her the teddy
bear, he took a photo. The horror when he'd made her hold it
up, when he said, 'Smile!' and the searing shock of the ensuing
flash – she's in agony thinking about what it was for. And now,
a game?

'Paper, scissors, rock.'

She doesn't know what to say.

The headtorch spins down, casts a beam on his hand, impossibly pale in the light.

'Come on,' he says.

They hold their fists aloft: paper, scissors, rock – she chooses
rock, he chooses scissors.

'You win,' the figure says, a small smile and white teeth
showing. 'Once again.'

Paper, scissors, rock: she chooses paper, he chooses rock. He breathes out heavily through his nose. Makes a tut-tut sound.

A pause. Heavy.

'One more?' she asks, querulous.

'Yes.'

Paper, scissors, rock: she watches him form the shape of scissors before she chooses paper. 'You win.'

'Yes,' he says, then coughs. 'I win.'

He coughs again. Runs a hand across his mouth.

'One thing . . . can I . . .'

He puts his headtorch on again, picks up the shiny blade thing. 'I have to go now.'

'Can I, can I come with you? Just for a little bit?' Small, needy.

He pats her on her cheek, runs his fingers down the back of her hair. The hand is soft and damp; the breath, like last time, is foul. 'Soon, soon.'

And then he backs out through the little hatch, again on his hands and knees, all the while watching.

She's watching him too.

And she listens as he leaves, closing the grille, and a whoomph sound as the air shuts in again. There must be a panel or something on the other side. A clinking sound, she is sure he is snapping a lock shut – and then he's gone.

Now, Natalie Whitsed, daughter of a woman who once took to her abuser with a cricket bat, rips out the plastic heart from the teddy bear, presses it to the wall of the cave and bends down hard on it with her foot till it snaps in two.

She picks the pieces up, feels the sharp edges with satisfaction. 'Come back again soon, fuckwit,' she says, 'I'll be waiting.'

CHAPTER 20

Back at the station, there was an air of busyness. Sergeant Finn Turner had returned from his search of Aidan Sleeth's office and was eager to talk. They'd waited for Mark's return to discuss what it was he'd found. Mark found himself begrudging his city counterparts less.

In his former office, he sat down on a chair against the window. Clare sat on the other, behind her desk. Finn stood, jittery, by the whiteboard that was filled with details of the case: Sleeth's picture, alive not dead (those ones were on file in case non-police walked in), photos of the crime scene sans body, a list of main contacts for Sleeth – his Adelaide lawyer, Lola Sleeth nee Hetherington, and Luke Howsley, his employee at the local real estate office. Other names too: locals from Stone Town who'd been spoken to, officially or not, and financial details of banking, loans, profits and recent sales. Forensics was a blank for now, but there was a note with 'five metres range/shotgun likely' at the bottom of the board.

Finn rubbed his hands together and began telling them about Sleeth's office. Nothing out of the ordinary at first – neat, usual stuff in the desks, no hidden panels or safes or tunnels behind the paintings leading to the sewers.

'Get on with it,' Clare said.

'I found two things,' Finn said. 'Firstly, I checked his computer. Easy enough to access. Found one folder I couldn't get into – blocked by encryption software. I've copied it and sent it to IT to pull apart. Rang Luke Howsley about it, and he said it's probably client details – sometimes they ask that their finances are hidden with extra encryption details. Everyone's that paranoid about cyber hacking and the richer you are, the bigger your target.'

Money, Mark thought, *it's what most crime boils down to.* He'd learned that in his five years working in Fraud. The rich were paranoid about people stealing from them. It made them suspicious of relatives, close friends and workers. Christmas break-ups were knife fights in party hats, funerals a total shitshow.

'Funny thing, in offices you usually see photos of people's family, right? Their dog on a blanket or whatever. Sleeth only had one photo, of himself standing in front of the Sydney Opera House. What a tosser.'

Mark didn't have any photos on his desk. When he worked in the city, in Fraud, he'd had one of Kelly and one of the boys. Now, nothing. There were photos of them in his Booralama house, ones his mother had taken and framed. Loads of family photos too: him in his school years, at his Deb, him and Prue as young kids beside a dam, each wearing a live yabby as a brooch, grandchildren, Kelly and him on their wedding day – the sodden hair and Kelly's running mascara making them both sad clowns. He should sort out the photos. Get one of the boys for his desk. There were so many albums his mother had collated over the years, images falling out of them, random memories shoved into plastic sleeves. What did you do with them all? The job was immense.

'And the second thing I found was this.' Finn held up a piece of paper. 'In an envelope on the bookcase just inside the door.'

'You're not meant to open mail, Finn.' Clare's voice had an edge to it. 'You know that.'

'It wasn't addressed – just an envelope sitting there, under some folders.'

'And?' Clare and Mark leaned forward. 'What's on it?'

Finn opened the plain A4 piece of paper and turned it to face them. On it a message was crudely written:

We are watching
We see you
GDWFB

They read it over a number of times, puzzling at the acronym.

'What's it mean, you reckon?' Mark asked.

'Not sure.' Finn turned the words to himself. 'But it's weird. *We are watching.* Looks like he was up to no good, maybe he owed money.'

'*We see you*, it's like whoever wrote this knows something about his conduct.'

'It's a warning,' Clare added. 'But that acronym. Something about Booralama and Waldara, places?'

'Or names,' Finn said.

'Maybe.' To Mark the message looked childish. Something from a *Hardy Boys* novel where the brothers received a note pinned to their clubhouse door and then set about searching for the author.

Finn and Clare began adding suggestions:

'WindFury, it's a gaming thing.'

'Wing Forward – basketball.'

'General Duty.'

'Facebook.'

'Follow Back.'

'Fuck buddy.'

'White female.'

For the first time since they'd arrived, Mark felt the beginnings of collegiality with Finn and Clare. The excitement of a new lead, the possibilities. Their station was a clubhouse; surely, in just a moment a mysterious stranger would appear telling them about an ancient legend of the town.

They looked at the sign again.

'"We" indicates a group, so the GDWFB sounds like the name of that group, not separate words,' Mark said.

'Good White Female Facebook.' Clare shrugged.

'General District Waldara Facebook,' Finn mouthed.

'Not everything's about Facebook,' Mark said, feeling his age.

'It's probably nothing.' Clare closed her notebook. 'Sleeth didn't exactly hide it. But even so, find out from Luke what he knows about this letter.'

'Well, he'd be the one to ask.'

'Why?'

'Because' – Finn's voice held an air of triumph – 'it wasn't in Sleeth's office. It was in Luke's.'

What? Mark was momentarily speechless.

'We didn't have a warrant for Luke's office,' Clare said.

'No, we had a warrant to search *Sleeth's offices* – you don't think he owns Luke's room too?'

They each considered the law they were bound by. The law which teetered, teetered and tipped depending on where you sat. They felt the waver.

Mark shrugged; Finn was technically right.

Clare coughed. 'The note is probably nothing. We're not looking into Luke.' She sounded deflated. 'Leave it for now.'

The clubhouse feeling was gone. The Hardy Boys grew up, got married and divorced.

'Anyway, we've had a development on the Whitsed case,' Mark said, and Finn brightened. As he told Finn about Squirrel and the news that Whitsed's car had been stolen from Yielder's Track, Stone Town, Clare was head down, taking notes. She was diligent, listening in, taking care that all dates and times were correct.

'Let's head out there,' Finn said, enthusiastic, when they'd finished. 'Go check out the spot.'

Clare and Mark agreed that, while it was unlikely they'd find anything after more than ten days, it was vital they check out the place where the missing policewoman's car was stolen on the day she was last seen.

Mark picked up his keys. 'You coming?' he asked Clare. Again, the careworn look took over her features and she shook her head.

'No. You two go. I'll call Homicide in Adelaide and let them know about the car being stolen from Yielder's Track. Got loads to do yet with Forensics and following up with Pathology. And I need to check out who Sleeth's cleaners were.'

'One of them was Isabelle Matteson,' Mark said.

'Right.' Clare wrote the name down. 'I'll find the others.'

Outside, the wind had whipped up. The two men sniffed at the air. 'Rain coming,' Mark said. 'Got a jacket?'

Finn hurried back into the station and came out again, half an arm already inside his coat. 'Tell you what, good time to get out. Clare's on the phone to her son again, and I swear one of these days I'll take the phone from her and give the little shit an earful.'

'She just got the one?' Mark unclicked the HiLux and they climbed in, put their seatbelts on.

'Daughter too, but you don't hear about her. It's all *Jackson, Jackson, Jackson.*'

Mark pulled out onto the road as the raindrops started, fine at the start and then a force. It reminded him of the time he was backpacking in Greece and he met an Irishman in some bar on Ios. After the talk of Australia and beaches and girls, Mark asked him what a typical day in Ireland looked like. 'Driving rain,' the man said, straight-faced. 'Three hundred and sixty-four days of the year, and the rest a fine mist.'

'What's up with Jackson then?' Mark enjoyed seeing this new side of Finn, conversational.

'Drugs. Into it big time. Stealing off the family, living rough, can't hold down a steady job. Bloke I know, and this is unconfirmed, says he's done casual work for Shane Spike. Clare wouldn't know that – don't let on I told you, her precious boy and all.' Finn shook his head. 'What a turd.'

Mark looked sideways at his passenger. The younger policeman was strangely judgemental for a man who, from what he'd heard, knew the hard side of life.

'Maybe it's a mental illness or something. You don't know what Jackson's gone through.'

Finn snorted and looked out the window. They were already out of Booralama, the long stretch to Stone Town, wizened trees and unruly scrub lining the side of the road. Big skies, heavy with cloud. The rain pelting, wind low.

'Plenty of people go through shit. It's not an excuse to act like one.'

Mark remembered what Angelo had told him about Finn's father – assault, theft, attempted murder – now housed in Morburn Prison with Tony Scopelliti. What did it do to a son, and a cop no less, to have his father in such a place?

'Take Nat.' Finn didn't turn to him. 'Her childhood was completely fucked up. In and out of foster homes, living on the streets and in shitty drug dens, one hundred different schools and no teacher that knows your name.' Unconsciously or not, Finn had shifted to the second person perspective. 'Yet, she got herself out of it, became a cop. A really, really great cop. So, poor old Jackson with his loving parents and his private school experience can get fucked.' Finn banged on the dashboard with the palm of his hand. 'He's twenty-three!'

The rain was easing and again a ray of sunshine speared the road, rendering it impossible to see. Mark slowed right down and waited till the clouds passed over before speeding up again. Paddocks were now giving way to the beginning of the Stone Town bush and already he could see thin tracks leading from the road into the thick of it.

'Were you and Natalie mates?'

'Yeah. We were, *are*. Good mates. I got her, you know? Even though she's older than me by like ten years. We've both had parents in jail – her mum got beaten up by an ex and when Nat told her he'd also felt her up, Nat's mother took to the bloke with a bat. Got eleven months for grievous bodily assault.'

Roz Whitsed. The wizened face from the television took on an extra dimension.

Finn continued, 'There's a heap of slimy bastards in the police force, not many that don't come from homes with Foxtel and four bedrooms plus two bathrooms and a butler's pantry. Whatever that shit is.'

'Don't ask me.'

'Nat's a good cop, a great one.' A hint of desperation had entered Finn's voice. 'She'd do anything for a case. Helped me when I started out, she's sort of like a sister to me. She worked all kinds of hours in surveillance, got right into everything she did. She's *resourceful*.'

'She sounds—'

Finn cut him off, his voice rose a level and he looked out the window. 'Not that it did her any favours. All the older ones, they treated her like shit. It's only now she's missing that they care. Didn't have her back when she was working; now, she's all they care about.'

'That might be true of your station, but seriously, Finn,' Mark said, 'we want to find her. When it all boils down to it, she's a cop. She's one of us,' he added, lamely.

We few, we merry few, we band of brothers.

'Ahh, that old bullshit.' Finn ran a hand across his eyes and sniffed.

'Yeah, that,' Mark said, sheepish.

They were passing the Mattesons' house. A ute and a small red car were out the front.

'We'd better find her, we . . .' Finn's voice cracked. 'She could be in some . . . with some . . .' He choked on his words, sniffed, and then, to Mark's dismay, the young man began weeping, big gulps of air, a mess of tears and snot.

'We'll find her,' Mark repeated, not knowing whether to pat his passenger's arm.

Again, he thought: *She's dead.*

'Yeah.' Finn's hands were fists, pressing into his eyes. He tried to stifle a sob. Failed. 'That's – what – Clare – says.'

'Clare knows her too, doesn't she?'

There was a pause while Finn sniffed and tried to slow his breathing. Mark stared studiously at the road. Finn's tears stopped and he wiped his nose on the back of his arm.

Mark leaned over to the dashboard and got out a pack of tissues, handing them over.

'Yeah, they used to work together.' Finn's voice was becoming gruff now. 'Nat liked her. And that was saying something.'

'Yeah?'

'Nat didn't get close to people easy. It's one of the effects.'

They drove past Pat Delaney's and the grand tree-lined driveway of the Sleeth house. The bush grew thicker on either side, the blackwood darkening things. Mark turned on his headlights and kept an eye out for roos.

'Effects?'

'Fozzies,' Finn said. 'We were both Fozzies, so we got each other from the start. Fozzies can spot another one from a mile away. We don't talk about the details, but we get it, you know? We get each other. Clare thought Nat called me Foz as a nickname, but really it was a code.' He wiped his face with a bunch of tissues in hard, uncaring strokes.

'What's a Fozzie?'

'Foster kids. Nat and me, we both grew up in and out of care. And' – there was pride in his voice – 'we both made it out.'

Mark was silent for a moment. He couldn't imagine being a foster child. Always he'd known that whatever he did, whatever trouble he found himself in, there would be someone to turn to. Family, close friends. His uncle once told him that when it came down to it, you can only truly count the people you can turn to on one hand. If you were left with nothing, if you were left destitute, each person had only five. Who were his five? His sister Prue, his ex-wife Kelly – did she still count? Did Jagdeep count? He'd only known her a relatively short time. Mark felt a vague anxiety. Who *were* his five? Angelo? Could he count on his slippery old friend? Dennis from the Fat Bean? Squirrel? Geez.

He needed to get out more. Make friends of his own. Real ones, not people he hung out with because Kelly knew their wives from uni.

He was thinking of himself again.

'You did well,' Mark said. 'Can't imagine what it would have been like.'

Finn didn't answer. He looked out the window as they passed the entrance to the co-op. Now the road turned to dirt, no signpost, and became Yielder's Track. It veered left in a wide turn and headed lower now, into a gully of rock and tough trees bent low. At the bottom, Stoney Creek flowed fast across the road, and Mark pulled up but kept the engine running.

'How deep do you reckon it is?' Finn said.

'Let's see.'

They got out and walked over rocks to where the water level began, high but not flood level. Mark bent down, picked up a rock and threw it in. A steady clunk indicated that the creek wasn't too deep – maybe just below the knee. No trees or big logs floating down; Stoney Creek was fairly clear. Mark walked back to the vehicle and heard another clunk. He turned to see Finn throwing a rock into the water. The simple pleasures, hearing that satisfying plunk. Finn threw another and Mark watched him, the former foster kid taking joy in the world. *Plunk.* Why not? When he turned the engine on, Finn returned, climbing into the passenger seat.

'Reckon we can cross it?' Finn's eyes were keen; the only sign of tears was his blotchy face.

'I do.' And not without a certain showmanship, Mark

revved the engine and drove expertly through the creek waters and up over the other side. Now the track continued, uphill and then back out of the bush onto flat country, paddocks. The track veered left again and here Yielder's Track widened, straightening along the backs of the properties owned by the families they'd just passed. Mark looked at his phone and the message Squirrel had later sent him when he asked for clarification. Past the old tennis courts and Stone Town school grounds – long since gone. Only two large pine trees remained, marking the entrance to what would have been an old school building – beside paddock gates, close to wild rose bushes, planted there, in all likelihood, by the last headmaster's wife.

They parked.

'This is where it was originally found. Natalie's car. Where it was stolen from.' Mark had seen the blurry photo of the car, taken from the toll cameras: a little grey Mazda. Natalie's blonde hair was just visible as she sped past, the last time anyone had seen her in ten days.

'Clare asked what your mate's nephew would be doing out here on a Friday night but . . .'

'Yeah.' Mark could see it. The appeal of the dirt track, long and straight, light dust at the edges and not in sight of any major roads or houses.

'It'd be perfect for motorbike riding, for coming here with mates and just hanging around, smoking dope, loud music, burn outs, drinking . . .' Finn mused.

'Drug deals.' Like every region in Australia, there was a drug problem in Booralama and its surrounding areas.

'Perfect for it. This track's not marked anywhere, it's only local knowledge—'

'And no prying eyes.'

They both looked around. Nothing to be seen, no sign of the missing cop. Bad weather had stripped the dirt area beside the track of any distinguishing marks.

'Where's that lead to, you reckon?'

There was a gate in the fence they had parked near, and beyond it a track, rougher than Yielder's, led straight up through the shorn fields to a couple of elms. Mark walked to the side, better to see into the distance beyond the branches of the trees. A red chimney came into view. He thought of where they'd driven and realised there was every chance they were at the back of Sleeth's property. It wasn't the co-op; they would have already passed that area once they'd gone over the creek. But this – this elm, the chimney and the strong fence line – was the property of someone with money. A spark of excitement lit in his stomach. Why would Natalie Whitsed's car be parked at the back of Sleeth's property? Dontay stole it from there on the evening she was last seen and drove it to Waldara. Why Yielder's Track?

As if he read Mark's mind, Finn spoke up, 'Nat's mother is from Broken Hill. She might have been going to visit her – this is kind of on the way.'

'Why stop here though?' Mark mused, 'What's wrong with a servo on the Barrier? She could have driven straight through Waldara on the highway, no need to go all the way out here.'

Finn shrugged.

Mark walked to the fence, pushed down the top wire and climbed over it.

'What you up to?' Finn asked, startled.

'I'm pretty sure this is where Sleeth's place is, we're at the back of it. Let's take a squiz.'

Finn followed and together they walked through the paddock to where the large elms began. A picket fence ran round the perimeter of a large old home, red brick with a wide veranda on all sides. Lavender, roses, hedges and a water fountain with statues of three Grecian women on it added to the air of gentility. Squattocracy, his mother used to call them, without spite. Families with gracious homes like this one, passed down through generations – whose children were shipped off to exclusive boarding schools, children who then invested in city apartments and first homes, who married others like them and, by the sheer fact of inheritance and current land prices, were destined to provide their children's children with funds that would keep them forever able to sail through life without any real care for what things really cost.

'I'll buy a raffle ticket for the struggling farmers,' his friend Stitcher used to say, 'but first let me know if they've got kids at Geelong Grammar.'

'Nice place,' Mark said by way of conversation.

'Yeah, this is the Sleeth house. We came here on Saturday and again on Sunday – took the front entrance. But this is it, yeah.' Finn's face was devoid of the earlier excitement. Natalie's car had been parked near this place ten days ago. *Where is she?* The younger man looked haunted as he darted around the yard, hunting for clues. The torment of those who love the vanished.

If one of his boys went missing, Mark would tear the world apart to find them. He'd never stop, he never would. The anguish, it ruined families and friends, left them wrecks of their former selves. Mark thought about Natalie's mother, teeth bared in rabid pain. Where was she? *Where was she?* The thought would destroy all who loved Natalie Whitsed, render sleep impossible, play havoc with their immune system. A doctor friend of Mark's once told him that intense grief alters the heart muscle and can cause 'broken heart syndrome', a serious form of heart disease.

Where is she, where is she? Mark continued to look around the empty property. There was a garage with a ute parked inside, but save for the gentle water lapping through the fountain, it was impossibly quiet. Sleeth was dead. This was all Lola's now.

Mark glanced back from where they'd come. He saw, perhaps five hundred metres away, their HiLux. It hadn't taken long to walk here. His watch told him it was almost 3 pm. There were things to do at the station, and he knew that Finn and Clare had already been through the Sleeth house after he'd gone home on Saturday. They'd found nothing of interest, save an empty plate and cutlery in the sink and a container of takeaway Thai food in the bin. Sleeth's last meal. But still. He walked up the steps to the back door and knocked. Waited. No one home, and why would there be? 'Hello!' he called out. 'Police!'

'We locked it back up,' Finn shouted from across the yard. 'Keys at the station.'

Mark studied the front entrance. A sturdy door, painted a dark blue. A mat on the floor for muddy boots. A large metal urn with a grey succulent weeping out.

He bent down, tipped the urn up an inch and deftly slid the spare key out from under it. Homeowners, no imagination. It was always the urn, the mat or a rock, slightly out of place.

Mark turned back to Finn. 'I'm going inside,' he called. 'Want to come?'

'You a robber in a past life?' The young man spoke without humour.

'Want to take another look inside?'

Finn shook his head. 'I'll check out the grounds again.'

Mark stepped into a long hallway, dark floorboards and paintings on the wall of horses and romantic landscapes. The smell was medicinal rather than musty and as he walked, Mark was aware of each footstep, loud on the wooden floor.

'Hello?' He entered a room to the right, a 'sitting room' or what his grandmother would have termed *the good room*. The room where you took guests: lace doilies, an old clock ticking loudly, a polished round table with uncomfortable chairs in green velvet and a single, large window covered in a lace curtain. If an old lady wearing a white Victorian gown walked in and began ringing a bell for the servants, Mark would not have been surprised. And this, he reminded himself, was where Sleeth grew up and lived – his primary place of residence for all of his forty-plus years. The room made him feel uneasy. Did Sleeth ever sit in here? Who would he entertain in the good room?

A shadow crossed the window and Mark spun around. A trick of light perhaps, but he could have sworn there was someone in the hall. He stepped back out of the room and looked left to right. 'Finn?' Nothing. 'Finn?' Nothing. Telling himself to get a grip, Mark searched through the rest of the house. It was much the same. Three bedrooms, each with a fireplace and tiny hand basin, a bathroom with a green clawfoot bath and faded brown around the sink hole, bronzed taps with the H half broken from the hot tap and a fading C on the cold.

The kitchen was large, neat and bare. In the fridge, a litre of low-fat milk, some butter in a dish and a loaf of bread. He sniffed: the milk was not yet off. Aidan's bedroom, the largest in the house, sat incongruously in comparison to the rest of the house: a king-sized bed, leopard-print doona cover, a huge television screen mounted on the wall, a large walk-in robe, and the walls painted what Mark guessed was a fashionable dark grey. The room was messy, but not unclean. A towel hung on the back of the door, a copy of *Think and Grow Rich* lay on the bedside table.

Mark continued looking: a large mirror in the bedroom and a small ensuite, tiled floor to ceiling in gun metal grey. The room made him uneasy, and after looking under the bed, for no particular reason, he walked quickly out of the room, back down the hallway and onto the verandah where the sun was making an effort to break through heavy cloud.

Finn was waiting near the fountain, deep in thought. Mark caught up with him and together they began walking back to the HiLux.

'Look what I found,' Finn said, holding up a tiny piece of pink plastic. 'It was out the front of the house, lying on the lawn. Didn't see it on the weekend, too focused on the house.' He showed Mark the corner of a piece of packaging.

Mark bent his face towards it. 'What's those letters say?' he wondered aloud, straining his eyes at the thing.

'E.N.D.U.R . . .' Finn spelled out. 'I've taken a photo of it.'

'A condom?'

'Could be.'

'Interesting,' Mark said, 'maybe Sleeth was in a relationship.'

'Probably just Tinder,' Finn replied.

Mark nodded, tried to hide the vague disdain he felt for such sites. *Don't be too dismissive*, he told himself. *Can't be too many months before you're taking profile pics and trying to hold your gut in.*

The men kept walking, out of the yard and towards the paddock.

'Sort of strange when you think that the house wasn't locked on Saturday when we looked,' Finn said.

Mark didn't think an unlocked house in Stone Town was unusual. Most people rarely bothered with the lock and key. His mother never locked the door in Booralama, not once. One time, they'd returned from a family trip in Port Lincoln to find the door wide open and leaves scattered up and down the hall. 'Well, that's a bonus,' his mother had said. 'Won't need to air everything out now, will we? And smell that eucalyptus!'

But it did merit further thinking: if the house was un-locked on Saturday, that meant on the Friday, when Sleeth left it, he either never locked it, or he was in a real rush.

'Did you move anything in the house?'

'Of course not.' Finn was retreating into himself again, becoming surly.

'Check for prints?'

'Obviously. On Sunday arvo too. So far, only Sleeth's that we could find, but we'll know more when we get the results back from Adelaide.'

Only Sleeth's. A man, then, who didn't have many visitors; family or friends.

'What did you think of the house?' Mark made a mental note to ask Lola about it. Was the house always so chilly and formal?

'Creepy,' Finn said. 'Those old clocks ticking, I hate them.' A beat. 'Once, I was at this foster home and on the first night I slept in a room with a clock like that. Tick, tock, tick, tock. All the house quiet except for that. Didn't sleep a wink.'

'Were they good to you?' Mark imagined his own boys in an unknown house with such a clock. 'The foster parents?'

'Very good. New clothes, nice food, gave me a bike to ride around.'

'Yeah?'

'Yeah.' Finn sniffed and turned away. 'I lasted three days before I ran away.'

'Why?'

'*Why?*' Finn looked at him as if he were mad. 'Because I wanted to go home, of course. Hey.' Finn stopped in his tracks. 'I didn't notice this before.'

Mark followed his line of sight. A thin single track, barely worn, led from the paddock fence line where they were standing to the property adjacent to Sleeth's. Pat Delaney's. Mark couldn't imagine Pat walking this path, her big frame negotiating fence lines, the rough track and the distance.

Still, a path linking the Sleeth and Delaney properties. That was interesting.

On their way back to the station, following Yielder's Track and finding that it came out, as he'd guessed, on Stone Town Road in a loop beside the Mattesons', Mark thought about the house he'd just walked through. Aidan Sleeth had been a successful property investor, healthy and single. And yet, after being alone in the man's home, Mark's lasting impression was of a person who blurred at the edges, inchoate and not fully formed.

CHAPTER 21

The Sam Fender song came back to Mark as he made himself a black coffee in the police station kitchen, the words on the things that linger and stick around. They came to him now, those things, as he drank his coffee and looked out to a birdless sky.

In Cutters End, a mining town up north, he'd had to make a decision that slashed and scraped at his conscience. Did Aidan Sleeth have anything like that, the thing that lingers? Did Natalie Whitsed? Because surely, in everyone's life there is a decision that gives pause, something that makes you ask in the middle of the night – did I do the right thing?

His phone beeped: Jagdeep. A text message.

Spoke to friend in Adelaide station. Homicide up your way checking possible link to Whitsed's car. Also, one of them has a son doing comm'y service 4 drug offences in East Adelaide, Scop recruitment territory.

Mark felt smug: he knew the first point already. He read the second part of the text again and felt less superior. Finn's words about Jackson reverberated. Did Clare's son work for the Scops? He texted Jag back:

Thanks. Shouldn't you be reading up on baby names?

A beep came back:

PISS OFF

Coffee almost finished, Mark was strangely comforted to see a maggie land on the fence outside the kitchen window. That reminded him, and taking his coffee back to his office, he fired up his laptop and googled *International Birders Conference, Oxford.*

It popped up immediately: a picture of a bird in flight and a profile image of Professor Aberdeen, keynote speaker. Mark clicked on the recorded live-stream of Professor Aberdeen and, while listening to her introduce the conference and welcome them all to the exciting and thrilling and important program, Mark pressed the link of participants. ('Make sure you introduce yourselves and let us know where you're streaming from and from what country!' Professor Aberdeen was saying. Her pointed nose and attractive dark features were those of a raven.) Mark scanned down the list. There were hundreds of names. He looked for the ones who'd listed themselves under 'AUS BIRDERS'.

Birdolife, Traralgon

Wingman45, Patchewollock

Birdbliss, Hunter Valley

Birdbox44, Adelaide Hills

Mark rubbed his eyes. There were too many names. The words on the screen blurred and he blinked, hunched towards the screen. Did he need glasses?

Urbanbird40, Melbourne

It was 4.45 pm, nearly time to go home. Mark scanned quickly over the other names:

Birdingrocks!44, Randwick

Chillbird25, Brunswick

Chillbird25 was too cool for school, Mark thought. Chillbird25 wouldn't be his friend.

Bins53, Stone Town

Gerald44, Stone Town

There they were. The two twitchers who were staying at the co-op that weekend. He scrolled down the chatroom as Professor Aberdeen and the other speakers presented. A steady line of conversation from across the world, the times mentioned in Australian Eastern Standard Time in a faint font at the top of each comment:

@Henharrier, Scotland – Had my first major dip today, Prof A makes it all seem OK!

@TwitchTwickenham – @Henharrier :(

It was another universe. Mark's head hurt and maybe he did need glasses. He could get *Top Gun* ones, hang out with Wingman45, wear a black leather jacket, pick up older women. Fly jets. Jump up and down on couches.

Mark stood up and moved his laptop to the window ledge. Clare popped in just to say she was heading off. She'd spoken to Homicide in Adelaide. Not time yet to break out the drones and high vis, they said. Not quite. Keep searching for clues. 'Look, but don't look like you're looking' was the general gist. It was bang on 5 pm. He waved her goodbye.

At 8.10 pm Bins53 had posted a photo of two men, including Gerald, with the message: *@Bins53, Stone Town – Birders from Aus, loving the twitch talk!*

In the photo, Mark could see Gerald and the twitcher who had run into him in the bush. Bins53 looked ecstatic to be streaming into the Birders Conference. Gerald seemed less enthralled, his smile uncertain, gaze elsewhere.

Getting out his notebook, Mark began copying the times and comments the Stone Town men made:

9.20 pm *@Gerald44, Stone Town – Pelagic species, not on my twitch list*

9.32 pm *@Bins53, Stone Town – Ha, ha! Nice one*

10.28 pm *@Bins53, Stone Town – That Willow Tit. Seriously.*

11.15 pm *@Bins53, Stone Town – Bye fly!! Ha, ha!*

There were comments from the two twitchers all the way through till the end of the presentation, at 12 am AEST. Mostly of the admiring sort, the men were clearly in their element among like-minded people. Inconclusive, but the timeline did suggest that Gerald and Bins had travelled up to Stone Town from Adelaide after work and then were typing at the conference from their co-op room from around the time Aidan Sleeth was supposed to have been shot. It didn't discount the idea that one of them could have typed for the other while they walked out into the bush and killed a man, but Mark was doubtful. The way Gerald had looked startled when he'd asked about friends: there was no sugges-tion of closeness. Even the photo of them together seemed

forced. The men were avid bird lovers, and therefore considered strange by those like himself who valued society and
company more than the solitary. Mark had thought that
Gerald exuded otherness, but surely that reflected more
on him than the man who only wished to find the Elegant
Parrot.

Mark took his mug back to the kitchen and washed it.

'You going soon?' It was Finn, standing in the door of the
small room.

'Yeah, just checking up on a few things.'

'Sleeth or Whitsed?'

A pause. The men stared at each other.

'They're connected aren't they?' Finn's voice was urgent,
eager for progress, action.

'We can't be sure, but—'

'Nat's car, the phone ping, Sleeth's body – all in the same
area and all in the same week. Come on! We should have
drones up, people out searching.'

Mark nodded. He wanted to add the mysterious element
of the cruising Chrysler registered to the business owned
by Tony Scopelliti but stopped himself. Remembered Finn's
father was in jail with the man.

'Well,' Finn said, 'I'm going back to the hotel to read up
on Sleeth's finances. We might have missed something and
it always—'

'Comes back to the money,' Mark said slowly. 'Okay, see
you tomorrow.'

The young detective waved and headed out. Mark put
his cup away and walked back to his space, thinking about

finance and his time in Fraud and all the white-collar criminals who when caught said, 'Well, if you had the chance to get rich, wouldn't you?'

Wouldn't you? He thought of it in regards to his own circumstances. In the grand scheme, he was a wealthy man. A house in Booralama, a not too shabby superannuation account and a stable wage. He couldn't buy a helicopter – but who cared? He thought of a quote he'd heard somewhere attributed to a celebrity – David Lee Roth maybe? 'Money can't buy you happiness, but it can buy you a yacht big enough to pull up right alongside it.' There was truth in it: money made things easier, gave you options. Dontay's mother with her grey hair and Grand Canyon wrinkles wouldn't be living in a caravan if she had the security of a home. Natalie Whitsed's mother could have had counselling and support and psychiatrists if she'd had the cash.

He sat again at his laptop. *But it's not just money*, he reminded himself: Clare's son Jackson, with his private school and his loving family, had a drug addiction. Nature or nurture?

CHAPTER 22

She's remembering: long ago, being trapped like this in a dark place. Twice, not exactly as punishment, more like retribution. That's often what it was about. Being too smart, saying something clever, upstaging a boy.

One of those times, in the darkness, she was with someone. Bigger than her, but not frightening. He was scared too. Tubby – was that his name? It was a mean name, she didn't call him that – not after he said he didn't like it.

She knew about names and what they could do. Povo, derro, tip rat. Memories of childhood spin out before her, light and dark with glinting edges. She's not sure if she's awake or asleep . . . She's remembering things: how every word had to count in childhood because if it was wrong, it could land you in bad places. Who you called Dad, for instance, could either mean smacks or laughs. If you told people you were hungry, you could get taken away.

At the thought of food, her stomach groans. Her brain is

fuddled with exhaustion and she struggles to recall exact details, but she's sure now: she knows who he is.

She's positive. It's the game, the paper, scissors, rock, that makes her recall the day she saw it being played. The boy and the girls. Her watching on, separated from them all. She's remembering other things, things from her childhood; a boy, way older than her and strange. She racks her brain to remember. Afternoons as a kid at someone's house, cubbies with a big boy who was kind and then, this one – always there, always watching.

Or were there two older boys who played the game with her? There might have been. One of them would come for her soon.

In the dark of the hole, hand clenched around the plastic, Natalie waits.

CHAPTER 23

On evenings like this one, with the sky a deep velvet grey, Mark wished he was still married. A shared beer on the verandah, mundane conversation about kids and work. Now, he was going home to an empty house. The evening stretched out long before him – and unable to shake off the rattled feeling the birders' chat had given him, Mark decided to walk home rather than take the HiLux. Ten minutes in, the smell of jasmine vine and family barbecues teasing him, he turned into the main street and was surprised to see Luke Howsley bending down low and talking with the youngest Matteson girl, Sarah. He called out hello and saw Luke straighten up, taller and thinner than he seemed in the station interview.

Mark reached them and stopped to say hello. 'What's up?' he asked.

'Tutoring,' Sarah said. 'He's helping me with my maths. But we went for ice cream first.'

'Yeah? What flavour?'

'Bubblegum.'

'Yuck. Should have gone for blueberry.'

'Blueberry's gross!' Sarah was delighted with the chat. '*You're* gross if you like blueberry!'

'*You're* gross.'

'*You* are.'

'*You* are.' Honestly, he could go on all day.

Sarah reached into her pocket and pulled out a chocolate in the shape of a star. 'And Luke gave me this for doing all my sums correctly!'

'Better and better.' Mark flicked a thumb at Luke. 'He a good teacher then?'

'Great.' The girl was emphatic. 'We think he could even be principal.'

Mark looked at Luke. 'You tutor in your office?'

'Just for today. Usually we go to the library, but the office is free now and you lot have checked it all out, so I told Sarah to meet me here after netball at school. It's quieter.'

Mark wondered what the Education Department would have to say about prospective teachers meeting young students in private workspaces, but neither Luke nor Sarah seemed bothered by the fact.

'Anyway,' Luke continued, 'I've been so busy with finishing up the final lot of sales, I couldn't leave the office. One week to go and without Aidan it's crazy.'

At Sleeth's name, Luke shifted awkwardly and looked at Sarah. She'd seen his former boss with half his head blown off not three nights before.

'I only went into school for half the day today,' Sarah explained in a new, serious voice. 'Mum said I could have the whole day off, but Mrs Ryburn said it's best to get back to normal.'

'The school counsellor,' Luke added.

'She's got a nose like this.' Sarah lifted up the tip of her nose and gave a pig snort. 'But she's nice.' Sarah was fidgety, eager to talk. Mark wondered if she, like him, was having trouble sleeping. He'd seen the back of Sleeth's head too.

A car pulled up, a little red Hyundai, and a young woman wound down the window. 'C'mon, Sarah!' she said. 'Get in.'

It had to be Georgia, the eldest of the Matteson girls. With her dark curls and slim features she was the spit of her mother.

Luke leaned towards the passenger window after Sarah climbed in. 'Hi, George, you back for long?'

'Just a couple more days.'

'Might see you then. Coming around to your house Wednesday. Got another tutoring session.'

Sarah looked grumpy. 'I don't know why. I just had one!'

'You missed one that time, remember?' Luke was mumbling. 'This one's a catch-up.'

Mark looked at his boots, hid a smile.

'Oh well, see you then!' Georgia pulled out from the kerb and, with a wave and a brilliant smile, she was on the road again. She drove slowly for someone her age.

'She,' Luke said, shaking his head, 'must be the hottest girl this side of Mount Gambier.'

'Haven't you got a girlfriend? I saw you jogging with someone . . .'

Luke looked at him strangely. 'That would have been Brooke. Yeah, I've just started seeing her, but it's nothing really serious.'

The little red Hyundai grew smaller and smaller till it became a dot and merged into the rest of the world.

'You known the Matteson girl long?'

The young man scratched his head. 'A year or so, just through the other girls. I tutored Emma too. But seriously, that one . . .'

A horrible thought came to Mark. The strange note – *We are watching, We see you* – the tutoring in the quiet office, the ice cream: 'Which one are you talking about?'

Luke looked startled. 'What?'

'Which of the Matteson girls are you keen on?'

An uncomfortable beat followed.

'What do you mean? Georgia, of course. Why would you . . .?' A look of disgust came over Luke. 'You thought I was after *Sarah*? Geez, mate, she's twelve!'

'I had to ask,' Mark said, relieved.

'That's not on, mate, I tutor the kid. It's her older sister that I'm interested in and she's, like, nineteen or twenty or something.'

'Yeah, okay. It's my job, I ask this stuff.'

Luke gave a short nod. 'Yeah, I s'pose, but—'

'Get over it, mate. I'm a cop.' Mark felt a headache coming on. What was this constant self-posturing he saw in males? He was sick of it. *I know it's common, but how could you suspect it of me? How could you suspect me of being a rapist, a paedophile, a wife-basher, a gang member, a vandaliser, a thief?*

Because, he wanted to say, *you're a man, mate, and that makes you fit the fucking bill, no matter how gelled back your hair is, or what car you drive, or who you play footy with. Suck it up, buddy.*

'And while we're at it, what can you tell me about a letter that was delivered to your office – sent from a person or group called GDWFB?'

Behind Luke, two older women strode past, walking gear on, arms pumping. They were two pairs of scissors, cutting at furious speed.

'Know anything about it?' Mark repeated the question as the swish-swish of the women's lycra faded away.

Luke sucked in his bottom lip. 'That note, yeah, I saw that one. Should I have told you about it?'

Mark didn't bother with a response.

'I don't even know when it arrived, it was just there, and on Friday I opened it – just a plain envelope, no stamp or anything.'

The policeman looked at his watch.

'I have no clue what it means.' Luke spoke in a rush. 'I thought maybe it could be some girls playing a trick? Some of the younger girls from the netball club?'

'What sort of trick?'

'I don't know.' The young man flushed. 'Flirting or something.'

Flirting? Mark could just about cast his mind back to the delicate dance of coy glances and charged repartee. Maybe. Mark considered: Luke was a good-looking man, a tutor, trainee teacher. Was this note a *Crucible* thing? A young girl, obsessed and furious with a man who dismisses her feelings?

'Look, I've got to go,' Luke said. 'I'll see you at footy training, yeah? Thursday night – we've asked all the old blokes to rock up.'

'Okay.' Mark thought that he and Luke regarded each other from opposite ends of a telescope, their generations hundreds of years apart rather than almost thirty.

Luke gave a half-wave and walked off in the opposite direction.

Mark's whole body ached with tiredness. The sky darkened further and became rich with fine insects and pollen. Where was Natalie Whitsed? Who killed Aidan Sleeth? A ute drove by, sagging mattress in the tray, not tied down properly. Mark walked on. Streetlights flickered to life and the main street of his hometown grew still. He could lie down in the middle of the road now and no one would know. He could throw a brick through the window of the bakery and be confident he wouldn't be caught. The quietness of small towns.

Mark turned down a side street and ended up by the river. The water was dark now, emitting a low rushing sound. Limbs of river red gums skimmed across the water and in the faint moonlight he could make out the ripples they made, circles that grew in silver lines before fading into the current.

Mark walked along the dirt path, the footbridge in the distance and the curling riverbank, thick with grasses and shrubs and empty bottles of beer. Once, he'd found a baby's hat on the muddy shore, small pink flowers on it still visible under the brown tannin dye. It made him think of that six-word short story that Hemingway allegedly wrote in a contest: 'For Sale, Baby Shoes, Never Worn.'

The sadness, the loss of young things dying.

Mark felt a deep sense of dread for the coming days.

He turned into his Booralama house, trees thick on either side of the path. He should cut them back. His mother would've liked that. His sister Prue called; again he ignored her. He ate some sausages and thought about the man who'd looked at him through binoculars in the Stone Town bush. He lay on his bed without getting beneath the covers. Sleep came like a slide down a steep embankment, swift into darkness, primed for anxious dreams.

CHAPTER 24

The beauty of the trees, the sky, the reflections meant nothing to Mark on his run the next morning. He ran in a haze of pain, sweat pouring, muscles searing and a drumming in his ears. Not time yet for drones and searchers in high vis, Adelaide Homicide had told Clare. Look, but don't look like you're looking. Cops were twitchers of humans. What Homicide meant was the same thing Gerald had told him in the Stone Town bush: Go quietly.

Natalie's car near Sleeth's house, her phone pinging, strange cars in town and men speaking Italian. Fragile information, but connections nonetheless. The drones and hi-vis would come.

There were no men in black suits today. The night before, Mark had slept poorly. He'd dreamed of Cutters End, girls tied to trees, lost girls, girls who wouldn't see their homes again. Now, on the run, he tried to shake it off. Over the footbridge on the return leg, Mark stumbled on a twig. It was a sickening feeling, like missing a step in the dark. He slowed down to a jog, a walk. *Look, but don't look like you're looking.* It's what cops did before the media hounds closed in. *Go quietly.* Find the evidence before it becomes tainted with innuendo, before potential jurors have their minds swayed when they watch *A Current Affair*. They'd say they knew nothing about a case, but it was never true. Bits and pieces filtered through.

In the distance Mark could see Lee approaching, green bag held aloft, Roxie straining at the leash. At his usual swimming spot, Mark gazed into the water. The sunlight sparkled on the surface, inviting him in. He wouldn't accept. When he'd run over the footbridge just before he'd seen a huge log float past, a *Titanic* iceberg, death for anyone in its path. He wouldn't swim today.

Avoiding Lee by taking a side street, Mark walked home, sweaty and in some pain. He should stretch, he really should.

Back home, Mark listened to the news on the radio. Nothing about Whitsed now. Only a body or a miraculous survival story could reignite the media's interest.

Kelly called. Was he definitely right to have the boys on Friday? Because she needed to get organising things . . . Mark faded out, listening to her mention again *Steven's thing in Perth* and, the main reason for this call, Sam's egg allergy. As always, when he spoke to Kelly these days, it was difficult to get past her new life: the boyfriend, the house, the holidays, the friends. He didn't love her the way he once had – that had been apparent for a few years – but the manner in which she'd moved on . . . It hurt a little, to hear of dinner parties with mutual friends where Steven replaced him beside her. But *were* those people mutual friends? He had to grudgingly accept that most of their social circle had been cultivated by Kelly, not him.

He fiddled with an old biscuit tin, an Anzac one his mother must have picked up in some op-shop. *This is the way the cookie crumbles,* he thought, and he couldn't deny that the probable loss of former mutual friends was grim justice for a lifetime of laziness in making new ones. Even the men he played squash with were the husbands of Kelly's university friends . . .

'Mark – are you listening?' Kelly's voice cut through his thoughts. 'You're always tuning out.'

'Yes, yes – Sam's EpiPen, I get it.'

He heard a groan, exasperation. 'I'll put it in his bag,' Kelly continued. 'He knows to take it with him if you go out.'

'Yeah, yeah. We'll have a great time. Looking forward to it.'

He'd forgotten about having his sons over the weekend, for three nights. It wasn't the best time for them to come. But, his boys! He'd already agreed to it. 'Might take them yabbying. It'll be fun.'

A pause. 'Hey, Mark?'

'Yeah?'

'You know those ads on TV where the wife is serious and practical and the husband does something stupid, acts like a kid and the wife smiles, all rueful as if she's thinking, "That's my hubby!"'

'Yeah.' There were at least five ads on TV like that at the moment. In the new Jeep one, the husband kept hiding the fact that he liked playing with toy cars till the wife held a keyring aloft and let him drive the family Jeep up a steep hill.

'Let's not be like those ads.'

He didn't know whether to be cross. 'Is this about the EpiPen?'

'I don't want to be the responsible, boring one and you be the fun one. Let's both be a bit of each.'

Mark reflected briefly on the mundane aspects of parenting, the parent–teacher interviews, pie drives, school camp notices, medical forms, dress-up days.

'Okay.' It was true. He never took charge of any of those things.

'And, Mark?'

He waited.

'Thank you. I mean it. I know this is hard for you, with Steven and being away from the boys. I appreciate it.'

He shrugged. It didn't mean her earlier words stung any less.

After they said their goodbyes and hung up, Mark felt a sharp gladness that he and Kelly were separated. She was too virtuous, too exacting. Her perfect husband would be Jesus. Mark pictured Steven wearing the Shroud of Turin and looking good in it; just standing there, eating activated almonds and signalling virtue.

Go quietly, that's what he needed to focus on today.

Dressed and ready for the day, Mark walked outside his front door and locked it. Then remembered his lunch of

STONE TOWN

ham sandwiches inside on the kitchen bench. He unlocked the door, collected the sandwiches and walked back outside, locking the door again, remembering why it was easier not to. A horn beeped loudly. It was Squirrel driving his tan Commodore, red head poking out the window like the end of a hotdog in a roll. 'Reets, you in the bouncer business now?'

'No, why's that?' It was hot. Mark regretted the coat he was wearing over the blue jumper. He might have to go back inside the house again and put it back.

'Dontay and his mates went back out to Yielder's Track yesterday – all kosher, just a place to meet . . .'

Right.

'This black car drives by and a bloke gets out, asks them what they're doing there, who they've seen, et cetera et cetera.'

Mark's skin prickled. 'Yeah? What make was it, this car?'

'Chrysler 300c SRT-8.'

'What time they out there?'

'Around lunchtime.'

'Dontay and his mates take a picnic out there, did they?' Mark thought back to Monday, his conversation with Clare, her tapping details into a phone.

'Yeah, fucken cheese sandwiches and lemonade.'

'Dontay talk to this bloke?'

'Not really. Gave him nothing. But, Reets, the man called him Dontay. I wouldn't be happy if you'd handed my nephew's name, or mine, to cops or otherwise.' He said it lightly, but there was an edge to Squirrel's voice.

'You know I wouldn't do that. Not on purpose, Squirrel.' Mark's brain raced. He *had* mentioned Dontay's name after the text from Squirrel about the car. But only to one person.

The small man considered him for a long moment. Nodded. 'Reets,' he said before driving off, 'Dontay said this bloke didn't look like a copper. Be careful, mate. All sorts out there.'

All sorts. Mark began walking. All sorts out there and in there and everywhere. The walk to the police station took ten minutes max. The sky was blue. Exhalation from the eucalyptus and mint bushes along the footpath gave him new energy as he strode towards his work. Things to do. Angelo had told him, and Clare intimated, that Finn Turner was a snitch, telling tales of the Whitsed files to his father inside Morburn Prison, who'd then pass them on to Tony Scopelliti. Images of the drug kingpin came to mind: thick-set and sturdy, face broad, with black eyes and a smashed and broken nose. Tony Scopelliti, at five foot ten inches, was, for five weeks, the heavyweight champion of Australia. Called the 'wrecking machine' for his punching power, he'd destroy bigger opponents with his agile moves, hand speed and devastating right hook. It was only when he was expelled from the sport for repeatedly punching an opponent after knockout that he retired for good. The guy he hit was left with permanent brain damage. Rumour had it, Scopelliti bought the man's family a house on the Gold Coast in compensation. One newspaper called it 'a generous act of contrition'.

Now, Tony Scopelliti's wife Charlene lived in their family apartment in the city, but his property portfolio reached from Port Douglas to Sardinia. Strip clubs, casinos, grey-hounds. Scopelliti was known to attend football games with political leaders and judges. His reach, it seemed, extended even as far as Booralama and Stone Town.

Mark arrived at the station to find the neighbourhood dog pissing in the westringias. The dog looked up at him with soulmate eyes. Dogs do that. He walked past it. Clare was already in the office, typing up something on her laptop, the phone on her shoulder. She gave him a wave and kept talking. Mark stood there, taking out his notebook and checking what he had there for today:

Evie Renner – check whereabouts for Fri night
Evan and Sue – Fri night
Forensics?
Lola – alibi for the pub – check
IGA graffiti, call back
Take mince out of freezer

Clare was still talking; blood splatter and formations. He started at the top of the list and rang the number that Evie Renner had given him. No answer. He left a message asking her to call him and hung up.

Clare was finished with her call too. 'Forensics,' she said.

Mark kept his face still.

After a beat, Clare continued. 'You were right: shotgun. Jane says twelve-gauge.'

The 12-gauge. Favoured by farmers and duck shooters all over the country. His father had a 12-gauge, though he'd no real need for it. Kept it in the boot when they travelled around Australia on their family holiday. It wasn't unusual. Now that Mark thought about it, that trip in the Holden, with the tents and the flat Lilos, wasn't all that fancy. A weapon in the boot, a father who smoked while driving, and *Pirates of Penzance* on the radio. It's a wonder they made it to Pinnaroo.

'Have to check gun licences around here, see who owns one,' Clare said.

'Every farmer will own one.'

'Yeah well, I'll get onto it.'

They would need to check the licences, but that didn't mean they'd find every gun. Not everyone handed in their weapons on the date of the amnesty in 1996 when the new rules were adopted. Guns were everywhere, hidden away in sheds, under beds, on top of the wardrobe, behind the TV. Prue had a friend whose brother handed in five guns, solemn-faced, on the day of the amnesty. Prue's friend was proud of him, thought that as a keen pig shooter, he'd never give them up. Later, back at the brother's house, he'd shown his sister the fake fridge in the garage. Behind the stacked warm beers was a crossbow, a handgun and a sawn-off pump action shotgun.

'Clare,' Mark said. 'Did your son ever do any work for the Crazy Cactus?'

Clare blanched. She opened her mouth to speak, closed it, looked like a rabbit caught in the spotlight.

'The Chrysler with the rego linking it to the strip club was seen at Yielder's Track. There was a guy from the city asking the kids who were there questions. Called one of them by name, Dontay.' Mark continued, 'How did the man know that was where Natalie's car was stolen from, let alone the kid's name who took it? It was too quick for the cops to get up here.'

'The leak . . .' Clare stammered. 'Someone must have . . .'

'I think that someone is you, not Finn,' Mark said. 'Jackson's in trouble with Scopelliti's men, isn't he? Did he do something to upset Shane Spike at the Crazy Cactus?'

'How . . . how would . . . why would you think that?'

'His drug addiction, his community service for drug offences in East Adelaide – right near the Crazy Cactus – Shane Spike a suspected dealer.' No need to mention Finn's earlier comments.

Clare crumpled. Her face turned a blotchy red and she reached for a tissue at the same time as a sob escaped her. For the second time in two days, Mark looked elsewhere while a colleague cried. *These Homicide cops, not as tough as they like to think they are.*

When she settled, Mark brought her a glass of water and sat down on the chair in front of her desk. 'I don't blame you for wanting to help out your son, but you must know that Scopelliti's men are hindering the investigation into finding Natalie. If they know what we're doing every time we find something they'll contaminate evidence, get to suspects before us – you know that.'

Clare nodded. She looked at him with a blank face. 'You've got kids, haven't you?'

'Two boys.'

'How old?'

'Six and eight.'

Clare sniffed and blew her nose. 'I remember that stage. It's cute. They still love you, want to hang around with you. It's middle childhood – experts call it the Golden Age, you know . . .'

Mark gestured towards her with both hands. 'Yes?'

'You wait. Your boys will grow up and they'll meet new friends, and not all of them will be good influences.'

A breeze blew in the open window and the images of Natalie and Charlene on the whiteboard lifted for a second before settling slightly askew.

'Jackson was a great kid. Loved hanging out with the family: Monopoly, charades, thumb wars, you name it. He played basketball, did swimming, Scouts – all of it. He was a real outdoors kid – we used to live in Bendigo, that old gold-mining town in Victoria – he'd spend hours exploring all the old places. And then we moved, and he met these older kids at his school – a good school, mind you, cost us a fortune. We started getting phone calls; he was wagging, he wasn't doing the work, he was disrupting others, had no organisational skills, lost his books, dropped his calculator, refused to wear a tie.'

It was a common enough story. In his line of work, Mark had heard it many times. Clare knew this too and her tone as she spoke was one of dry predictability.

'There was the vaping, the dope smoking, the drinking in the park. There was the stealing, the dropping out of school and having the police call around. Can you imagine how embarrassing that was?'

He couldn't. He really couldn't.

'Jackson started working for Shane Spiko – most know him as Shane Spike. Running drugs, errands I didn't want to know about. He got bashed up a few times. I sent him to live with my brother, but Jackson sold their new stereo system and bought ice with it. My brother kicked him out and we didn't know where he was for a month.'

Through the open window, Mark heard a car pull up.

'Jackson stole tips from one of the girls at the Crazy Cactus and Shane went mad. Got him to pick up a package of cocaine, sell it to a contact in Melbourne and bring home the takings. Jackson did all that, but stuffed up big time.'

Outside, Mark could hear Finn talking to someone. 'What happened?'

'He lost the money.'

'Lost it?'

'Yeah.' Clare gave a harsh laugh. 'Jackson's *always* losing things. He took a detour to Mount Gambier to look at the Blue Lake. Reckons he went for a walk, had a smoke, took some photos and went back to the car. That's the sort of person he is, a real nature lover. Doesn't seem to fit, does it, but it's true. Well anyway, in between his tourist activities, he lost Shane Spike's package of $20,000. Reckons he dropped it somewhere.'

'Jesus.' Mark whistled through his teeth. 'You believe him?'

'I do.' Clare was firm. 'Jackson wouldn't lie to me on something like that.'

Mothers and sons. Did his own mother really believe him at eighteen, when he told her that the dent in the new Holden was caused by someone backing into him at Kmart?

'So, that was around two weeks ago. Spike's mates roughed him up, sent a note to me saying they'd kill him if I didn't fill them in on police activities regarding the Scopellitis. Dates and times of raids, informants, gossip – all that. I had no choice but to snitch. Then when Natalie went missing and it was in the media that she'd been watching Charlene Scopelliti – they asked me to keep an eye on that too. It's one of the reasons I put my hand up for the case up here – that phone ping after she'd been reported missing . . . Really, I had no choice . . .'

Everyone has a choice. That's what parents and teachers used to say when you were kids. But was it true? In the Booralama police station, listening to Clare talk about her son, Mark wasn't sure. He had little doubt Scopelliti's men would kill Jackson if she didn't comply. The year before, a body was found in the Torrens river, almost camouflaged by the blue-green algae, which made it appear alien-like to the children who found it. But the method of death was all too human: hands and feet bound tight, mouth gagged, body thrown into the dirty water. The victim: Scott True, employee of the Scopellitis – petty drug thief, dealer and recently uncovered police informant.

'Are you going to let head office know?' Clare's voice was dull. 'I would if I were you.'

Mark didn't answer. The front door of the station slammed and Finn walked in, looking pleased with himself. 'Just met your friend Lee O'Brien and his dog.'

'Yeah?'

'He says to check out what he calls the Stone Town Crew. A bunch of scheming old women, he says.'

Clare was typing again, her blotchy face set hard.

'Lee has mentioned that.'

'Also, a woman in a car out there gave me this.' He held up a coat, folded and clean. 'Said she wouldn't bother you by coming in.'

Jacqueline Matteson. Mark walked out of the room, skipped perhaps, and made his way to the front porch of the station. He saw Lee O'Brien leaning into a parked red Hyundai. The older man straightened when he saw Mark. 'You know Jac and her daughter, don't you, Mark? They're right in the thick of things, Stone Town people, you know.'

Mark agreed aloud that they were Stone Town people. He looked into the driver's window, gave a wave. A stupid kind of wave, more like a salute. 'Hello!' he said. 'Been meaning to come around and get the coat, thanks for dropping it in. And I've still got yours,' he added.

Georgia, in the driver's seat, looked amused as her mother leaned over her to talk to Mark. 'We thought you might come around and collect it – we've seen your vehicle drive past often enough.'

'Didn't cross my mind, I'm afraid. But we will need to talk to you and the kids at some stage soon.'

'That would be fine. Anytime. And this is my eldest, Georgia.'

'We've met before, after Sarah's tutoring with Luke.' Mark and Georgia smiled at each other, nodding.

'Ah yes, that's right.'

'How're your two youngest? They coping okay?'

'Emma and Sarah, yes – remarkably well.'

'That's good.' Mark remembered Sarah making binocular shapes with her hands and then, yesterday, arguing the merits of ice cream flavours.

'We are worried about Evan, though.'

A pause. 'He's not coping?'

'It's more than that.' Jacqueline seemed hesitant. 'He's become very—'

'Anxious.' Georgia finished her mother's sentence. 'Always at our place. We have to chase him to go home.'

'Anxious.' Jacqueline repeated the word slowly. 'Yes, that's probably what it is.'

Mark thought about the day in front of him. The paperwork, alibi checks, local IGA manager to placate, videos to peruse, site searches to organise, forensics to consider, meetings, additional interviews, mince to defrost – now add the visit to Evan he'd taken note of earlier and forgotten until now.

'I'll see him as soon as I can. Hopefully he's getting some support?'

'The school offers counselling, but I'm not sure if he's taken up the offer. The girls did.'

Georgia turned the key in the ignition and started up the Hyundai. 'We have to get going, Mum. I've got a Zoom class.'

Mark thought about asking Jacqueline out, but he was so out of practice. He recalled his determination to make an effort to meet new people, hesitated for a moment, then dived in. 'Want to come yabbying this Friday night?' he blurted. 'You and the girls? My boys will be up for a few days and . . .' His voice trailed away and he felt a vague amazement that he'd even suggested the idea.

'I haven't been yabbying for years.' Jacqueline was smiling. 'It sounds fun, but I'll have to see what the girls are up to.'

Mark felt a swell of joy and relief. 'Well, come along if you can. No pressure.' He told her about Stitcher's farm. Stitcher wasn't home, he was on a trip around Australia with his family, but Mark knew his old friend wouldn't mind them having a night by the dam.

After they slowly drove off, Mark shook his head, surprised at himself.

'Seriously, a Stone Town woman?' It was Lee, disdain in his voice.

'What do you mean?'

'I've been trying to tell you – they're trouble! All of them. Always with the gossip and the planning and the scheming.'

Lee's eyes, Mark noted, were spaced far apart on his wizened face. With his skinny legs and green tracksuit, the man appeared reptilian. 'In what way? How do the "Stone Town women" scheme and gossip and lie?'

'The Booralama Show. Every year!'

'I'm busy, Lee.'

'And other things.' Lee pulled Roxie's leash close to him, so that the little dog was almost sitting on his shoe.

'Like what?'

'Like Jacqueline Matteson in a wheelchair after that car accident with her husband? He crashed them straight into a tree. Died at the scene. Jacqueline and the daughter in the car had blood all over them when the ambos finally turned up.'

Mark couldn't see why that was anything other than a tragic story. He began to walk into the station front yard once again.

'Rod Matteson was a drunk. No one ever says a bad word about him, certainly none of those Stone Town women, but those of us who've lived around here for a long time remember.'

The door to the station open, Mark turned to say a firm goodbye to Lee and Roxie.

'And there was that girl, you know, the one that died.'

Mark stopped, felt a drumming in his chest, waited.

'No one mentions her when they talk about Rodney Matteson, do they? All his fault, and yet he got off scot-free.' Lee walked off, satisfaction on his lizard face.

Mark stepped into the station, then waited a moment in the cool hallway. The building was quiet, save for the insistent tapping of a keyboard in his old office. *Everyone has a past*, he thought. *I do. But it's harder to hide one in the country.* A girl killed? He couldn't recall the story.

The door to Finn and Clare's room was shut so Mark walked to his office, closed the door and fired up his laptop.

It didn't take him long to find the information. Front page of the *Booralama Chronicle*, April 2001:

Stone Town man Rodney Matteson has been dismissed from Port Adelaide College after the court found the

*school guilty of negligence for the death of a 10-year-old
girl. The victim, Bella Lukic, died after anaphylactic shock
as a result of eating a peanut snack Matteson had given
her. Matteson expressed remorse for his failure to provide
proper attention to the victim's known medical needs and
wept as the judge found that Bella's death was directly
related to his failure to take reasonable steps to ensure
the health and safety of the children attending the camp.*

Two photos accompanied the article: Rod Matteson being
led into court, stricken; Jacqueline equally grim by his side.
The other, a young girl holding a puppy and sitting on the
knee of Santa Claus: the victim, Bella Lukic.

There were other articles which referred to the incident
and Matteson in particular: the South Australian Education
Department's policy change on anaphylaxis guidelines in
school camps, another on a drink-driving charge involving
Matteson, and one more on his work with the SES. A photo
of him in firefighting gear, weary after the bushfires that
almost claimed the locality twenty years prior.

A final article, dated four years previous:

*Local tragedy on Stone Town Road: Father of four Rodney
Matteson was killed in a tragic road accident at around
6 pm Saturday evening. His wife, Jacqueline Matteson,
was airlifted to Adelaide in a serious condition, and their
young daughter Georgia, 15, was left unharmed.*

Mark found and carefully read the initial accident report, filed
by the old Booralama copper. In the margins, a handwritten

note: *Good people.* Mark photocopied the report, underlined the key findings. He stood up and stretched, looked out the window to stony clouds and a brittle sky. *Good people*: the words wouldn't have been included in the official report, but they said much about how the investigation would have been handled. The old copper probably played footy with Rod; it shouldn't matter in policework, but it did. He read the newspaper reports again, closed the laptop and sat back in his chair. Country towns! Each tragedy magnified by the web of human connection. There was more space in rural communities, room for a veggie garden, a pool, a horse: but what the tree-changers didn't account for was the closeness of the links, the ties that bind and constrict and hold tight. Lee was wrong; Rod Matteson hadn't got off scot-free for the tragic death of Bella Lukic. Hindsight, remorse, regret – a cell doesn't need bars.

A tap at his door: Finn Turner. 'Got some more people coming up here today, Senior Sergeant Barrie and an Inspector Bithick.' He smiled. 'B1 and B2. They're from Investigations – doing a full search of Yielder's Track and the surrounding area. Official story is, they're checking out Sleeth's place; unofficial, searching for signs of Nat too.'

'That's good.' In his mind, Mark added another job to his list: have a story ready for the press. The editor of the *Booralama Chronicle*, not to mention larger papers, would perk up at the injection of new police in the town. He knew, too, that locals would begin to question the identity of the man in the black car cruising around, asking questions. Dontay, that unfortunate kid with the big mouth, might let it slip that he'd found a car in Yielder's Track. Yes. It was only a matter of time before people began to make tentative links between the two cases: Whitsed and Sleeth. Tenuous perhaps, but enough for a full spread in the local rag.

'I'm heading off down south today. I'll take the police vehicle – Clare's got her own car here so she doesn't need it,' Finn said. 'Going to be attending the autopsy and interviewing people connected to Sleeth in the city; neighbours in the house he had there, cleaners, people he drank with. I'll have a look at the finances of the business again. Not hopeful of finding anything in that regard. Besides that $1000 a month to his ex-wife, Sleeth looks to be in the clear.'

Mark nodded, taking it all in.

'We're still in the process of eliminating people as suspects, all those in the area on Friday night. Hunters, deer and whatnot look like they're not in the picture.'

The pelting rain, the isolated region, the lack of accommodation – it wasn't a surprise.

'There were four people who owned keys to Sleeth's offices: Sleeth, Luke Howsley, Lola and the main cleaner, Isabelle Matteson.'

The Mattesons again.

'You coming back up here?' Mark asked the young detective.

'Hope so. See what head office says. I can get this work done down there too. Anyway, B1 and B2 should be in this arvo to give you a run-down.'

Mark stood and shook Finn's hand. Despite the inauspicious start, he liked him. 'Good luck with it.'

'Yep, you too.'

'Hey,' Finn said, turning at the door, 'thanks for . . . well, thanks.'

Thanks for not laughing when I cried, thanks for listening to me go on about Nat, thanks for giving me time to come back down from the city-cop-arsehole act. Thanks for all of that.

'No worries.' Mark knew what he meant.

CHAPTER 25

*Natalie is remembering: her childhood, scattered and disjointed –
people coming and going – a tumble dryer of places and things.*

*Later, a short stint on the streets, a rehab place with too many
indoor plants, studying again, going to TAFE and joining the
police force. The thrill of working in surveillance, watching and
waiting.*

*Being placed on Charlene Scopelliti was a coup, her chance
to show the seniors what she was capable of. When she attended
the first briefing on the operation, older men around the table
relaxed their shoulders. She knew what they were thinking: cute
and young, which in their minds was the same as bubbly and
naive. But perhaps she was being unfair. Not every male she met
was like that. Finn wasn't like that – he was her friend. Where
was he now? Where was she?*

*In any case, after a few weeks she'd shattered her colleagues'
illusions. The cuteness appeal wore off and she wasn't that
young. Plus, she was assertive, determined and abrupt. It didn't*

make her popular, but it got results. She volunteered to watch Charlene full-time and a life spent being on guard meant that she was hyper-aware of the other woman's body language. In a way, she was actually looking out for Charlene, and there were times she felt the other woman knew it. Women were good at that.

Now, Natalie is waiting. She worries that her determination to fight is waning. She rarely sleeps. She hasn't eaten properly, and it scares her that her left arm doesn't hurt any more. She's conscious to move her fingers on that hand, but it's becoming harder. What does that mean?

Her mind is blurry and she hears herself whimper. The plastic shard in her hand is ready and she grips it so tight that the skin of her palm rips and tears. She doesn't care. Time is slipping away.

She strains her eyes in the dark. The inky surrounds feel closer, restrictive. A thought unbidden: I will die here, soon.

Natalie clenches the shard and welcomes the splintered bits that dig hard into her palm. Not today, she thinks, not today.

Hours later: a sodden thump. A scuffling at the wood. Rattling of the grate.

He has arrived.

CHAPTER 26

Ian Beard, the manager of the Booralama IGA, wasn't happy. Mark's insistence that the kid responsible for the graffiti wasn't going to be charged left the big man with a sour look on his face.

'Too easy on these kids, Mark,' he said. 'Now they'll be back with more spray paint and more balls. Probably paint the side of the cop station next.'

'No, they won't.'

'It costs me every time to remove this crap, and it's not cheap.'

'I've got some people who can help you with it.'

'Those dickheads on community service? Please, I'd rather not.'

It depressed Mark how few people in the town were willing to give the program a go. They didn't like the promising young kids moving away to the city, but they didn't support the programs designed to help the disadvantaged ones stay.

To appease him, Mark bought a Mars bar and a Coke. The man didn't look grateful as he scanned the items and handed them to the policeman.

'Never used to happen like this,' Beard said, jerking his head to the outside of the station in the direction of the graffitied wall. 'I blame drugs.'

Just after Finn left, and prior to his walk up the street to the IGA, Mark had told Clare he would not inform head office that she was the snitch, not yet anyway. He'd advised her to let them know and gave her a deadline of Friday. They both knew that after that, failing a miracle, her days in the force would be numbered. *Four days*, Mark said, and no communication with Scopelliti's man in that time.

Clare was subdued but grateful. It wasn't, however, compassion for her particular situation that stopped him from calling Angelo. Not entirely. Mark *was* sympathetic. If one of his boys was being threatened, he'd do anything, *anything* to keep them from harm.

No, the thing that stopped him from letting Angelo know that the leak in the force was Clare, not Finn, stemmed from his own history. Who was he to play judge on a fellow cop who was bending the rules to protect someone? Personal convictions mean less when family are involved. Look at the biggest advocates of state schools and how their values often wavered when their own children reached high school . . . *but, the opportunities!* In Cutters End, he'd kept important information from his boss and from his colleagues, Jagdeep and Darryl, in order to protect people who were not his family. Who knew how far he would go for a blood relation?

Mark ate his Mars bar and drank his Coke as he walked back to the station. Fairy wrens jostled along the picket fences and squabbled in the trees, little blue tails flicking as they went about their busy ways. He thought about his boys, and yabbying with Jacqueline and her girls. Felt a twist of anticipation. He checked the weather update on his phone – fine for Friday evening. They could have a little fire by the dam, cook up some sausages. His phone rang, and for a second Mark looked at it stupidly, half expecting or hoping it to be Jacqueline. It was an unknown number. He answered: Evie Renner.

'Hello. Mark?' she asked, voice warm. 'You called me earlier.'

'I did, I wanted to confirm something you told me when I saw you on Sunday.'

'Oh yes? What's that?'

'Can you tell me again where you were on Friday night.' Mark held the phone in between his shoulder and ear while he wrestled his notebook out of his back pocket.

There was a pause on the other end of the line.

'Evie?' Mark asked. 'You there?'

'Yes.'

'If you could just tell me where you were on Friday night.'

Evie cleared her throat. 'I was at Sue Williams's house. We had a meeting about the show.'

'Right.' Mark let the silence that followed thicken and grow. 'Because on Sunday you told me you were at home that night, in bed early.'

'It was a mistake. I was tired and, well – it had been a big weekend.'

'So, who else was at Sue's?'

'Jacqueline Matteson and her mother-in-law Beth, Pat Delaney and me.'

Mark jotted down the names in his pad. 'So, what's your specialty going to be for the show?'

'Specialty?'

'As in, what are you making? My mother always made jam. It was awful apparently.'

'Oh.' Evie gave a little laugh. 'Oh, I'll make a vegetarian slice. We've got plenty of veggies to choose from in the garden.'

'Vegan?'

'What?' Evie sounded startled. 'Yes, why not? Although it's difficult without the eggs.'

In the background, Mark could hear a car starting. 'Are you off somewhere?'

'Just to Adelaide Hills for the night, back to our unit there. John's thinking of ways we can raise money to buy the land back from Sleeth's business. Rattle the can under the noses of our richer friends. Failing that, we want Birds for Bush to buy it. Their CFO knows an old uni friend too – so we'll give everything a shot.'

'Sleeth's ex-wife will own the place now.'

'Well, whoever owns it, we'll try to come up with an offer.'

'Can you let me know if anything eventuates in that regard?'

'Of course.'

'Good luck.'

'You too,' she said – he wasn't sure why – before hanging up.

Did Evie forget the vegan slice Pat Delaney said she was planning to make for the show? It was a small thing, but Mark wrote it down in his notebook.

The sugary effects of the Mars bar and Coke made him jumpy. He knew it would wear off soon, but for now his brain raced with unpleasant possibilities. John Renner could have shot Sleeth in the bush on Friday night, in a rage at the other man's determination to develop Stone Town into a series of suburban blocks. Renner had no alibi now that Evie admitted to being at Pat's. The man was obviously a dedicated environmentalist. Mark considered eco-terrorism for a brief moment – in Australia there had been cases of tree-spiking causing injury, threats made to loggers, serious damage to infrastructure – but none of that seemed to apply to John Renner and the Stone Town bush, far away from any such activity. In truth, the man seemed to be mainly upset that a good chunk of his co-op, precious for its natural habitat and fond memories, had been sold to developers. Was that enough reason to shoot a man in the back of the head? Unfortunately, it was. Mark had heard tales in the police lunchroom of people shooting their spouses over a burnt roast, shooting their neighbours over a recycling bin dispute, shooting a passer-by out of boredom. Humans didn't always need a reason to kill. Sleeth could have been target practice.

CHAPTER 27

*She waits till his foul breath is upon her, and then she strikes —
hard with her good arm — stabbing him with the plastic piece of
heart. She aims for his chest but lands below his shoulder, and
while he cries out in shock and pain, she stabs again, this time
in his upper arm.*

*Already she's scrambling for the entrance, on her hands and
knees, head bent down.*

*She senses him rise, make an effort to grab her by the calf,
but she turns, kicking out at him, furious, harder this time. He
falls back in rage, wailing, and she's passed the iron grate and
wooden panel — not bothering to slam them shut but instead
standing up, feeling air.*

*She's in a hole — perhaps six metres below ground. Above her,
through the debris of leaves and branches, she can make out sky. Sky!
There's a tree root poking out above her, a handhold, a foothold,
but even though she can reach it, she'd never be able to pull herself
up with it — not with her bad arm, not in such a weakened state.*

Nevertheless, she jumps, grabs at it, hauls herself up for a second, only to fall back down again. She's too short! She's too short for this!

A moan from the den and movement, she's got to get out. But how?

She looks around wildly, sees a dark tunnel low and to her left. It scares her, terrifies her that it could be another cave, and she stares up at the sky once more.

The wood panel is moving, she sees the top of his head and, without thinking, she's bending down low, on hands and knees again, and is into the dark space. It's a tunnel, a crawl space, and when she hesitates for one moment about moving further into it, a hand grabs at her foot.

She kicks herself free and she's crawling, crawling and not thinking, and she's in another space – larger, she can stand up now, bent over – and she's running along the tunnel, touching the dank sides, and she can feel it's an incline, it's moving upward. There's light in front of her and she speeds forward. It's a space above her, a grate, and she can see blue sky and she's calling out, calling out – Help! Help! Help! But no one comes.

A sound – scrambling – and she knows he's following. It'll be hard for him with the low spaces and he's injured – but he's stronger than she is and she's so tired, so weak.

'Help!' she calls.

The sound of heavy breathing. Footsteps.

'Help!'

He's gaining.

CHAPTER 28

It was muggy in the office; Mark's shirt clung to him like a leech as he tried to focus on the Sleeth case. He needed to contact Birds for Bush and the local council to confirm Sleeth's dealings, in addition to managing the public leads. These were invariably the most tedious aspects of the investigation. Hundreds of people with suggestions, anecdotes, feelings and sightings to confirm. The Adelaide stations helped in this area, with Mark taking on the local calls. Jonno Cornell suspected hoons from Waldara, and although he could not name said hoons, felt free to give up his sister's children, who were going down the feral path. A truck driver in Sydney saw a group of bikies parked near a road stop south of Mildura and thought they could have something to do with it. *Just the way they looked,* the truck driver said, *there was something funny about it.* Edna Veery from South Booralama said the Stone Town bush was haunted with dead children, lost in the bush. When pressed if she thought one of the ghost children may have shot Aidan Sleeth, Edna clammed up, saying that anything was possible in purgatory. *I'm in purgatory now*, Mark thought, before thanking her and hanging up.

Clare's earlier gun licence search showed that twenty people owned a 12-gauge in Booralama and three in Stone Town; Jacqueline Matteson, Aidan Sleeth and John Renner. Inspector Bithick and Senior Sergeant Barrie were checking those guns that afternoon for signs of recent discharge. As expected, the editor of the *Booralama Chronicle* called for a statement. Mark gave excuses, held her at bay. Things were beginning to heat up, he could feel it.

Mark rang Sue Williams to ask if she could pop into the station after school with Evan, just for a chat. Sue was downcast. Just as Mark was remembering when he'd first met her that early Saturday morning, she said she didn't have her driving licence and could he come to her instead. He said he could, hung up and wondered at all the kilometres he'd driven since he first saw Aidan's body in the bush. Hundreds. Hundreds and hundreds of kilometres of driving on the Booralama–Stone Town road, watching the paddocks give way to bush and the houses melt into the trees. The country life. Another thing the tree-changers didn't consider: the road miles for work, for socialising, for catching up with family.

Mark picked up his keys, popped his head into Clare's office to let her know where he was going. He couldn't see her and felt glad he didn't have to talk. Once more, Mark climbed into the HiLux and headed south-west, along the now familiar road. He rolled through outer Booralama and passed the house where his school friend Joanne used to live. Two cypress trees stood sentinel on either side of the front path up to her door. Joanne's family had been religious. Were her parents alive? Mark couldn't remember. Dennis from the Fat Bean grew up in a little weatherboard around here somewhere too. Mark remembered trying to make smokes out of banana skin, choking on them while they sat on his garage roof. The houses gave way to paddocks and dams and low hills. Crops, flat now, and old Blakely's gums spread wide apart, remnants of an earlier place.

Natalie Whitsed was dead, Mark was sure of it. A week ago colleagues reported her missing when she didn't turn up for work on the Tuesday morning. She hadn't been seen since the week before. Scopelliti's men were scouring the countryside, police across the nation deep in search mode. There may be no connection to Sleeth. There could be many explanations: a snake bite, lost in the bush, fallen down a mine shaft, a gum collapsed on top of her. Mark thought of the missing children, years ago. Australians were obsessed with the idea – landscape swallowing the young. National poets, artists, journalists and film makers were dedicated to the trope – *Picnic at Hanging Rock* made it almost glamorous. *Miranda!* Azaria Chamberlain lent it truth. Was there ever a settled people so afraid of the land they lived in? 'White belonging', an old girlfriend used to call it. The unease that sits alongside.

The beginnings of bushland edging the wheat: Mark drove through Stone Town and the dark trees he knew to be acacias bent low. There was Jacqueline Matteson's house to the left, the red Hyundai nowhere to be seen. A dirt driveway further along, with a gate, a number and a name, 'Williams'. He stopped to open the gate and took care, once he passed through, to chain it back up again.

There were two cars out the front of Sue Williams's house. An old Holden and the red Hyundai. Why the crowd?

The house was a weatherboard in need of painting. A gravel path was skewed with mud and the steps to the porch bowed heavily to the right. A grey curtain flickered aside and a pale face looked out. Evan.

The door opened and his mother appeared, long hair limp and thin, face like porridge, attitude of weary resignation. She stood aside to let him in and he walked into what felt like a courtroom. A semi-circle of Stone Town women greeted him. Jacqueline Matteson, her mother-in-law Beth and daughter Georgia. Sue Williams and Pat Delaney gazed upon him: he was ten years old again, in trouble for something big.

'Interrupting you, am I?' He thrust his hands into his pockets and shuffled about. 'Sorry 'bout that.'

'Just a cuppa and a catch-up.' Pat Delaney spoke first, centre stage. 'Would you like one?'

'Be great,' he said, and Sue limped off to another room.

'Get him one of your fig bickies!' Pat called after the retreating woman before returning her gaze to Mark. 'Sue's fig bickies are second to none.'

What could Mark say to that? He gave what he hoped was a look of anticipation. 'All set for the show?' he asked.

'All set.' Jacqueline looked up at him, smiling, and he felt grateful for her presence. 'Will you be coming?'

'That's the plan.'

'The show!' Georgia scoffed. 'Rednecks and rides, that's what we used to call it.' With her black jeans and T-shirt emblazoned with a small flame on the sleeve, Georgia looked the archetypal arts student. Young, dismissive, smart.

'Kiddies love the show,' Pat said, ignoring her. 'Take them to see the lambs, they'll like that.'

He nodded.

'They can feed them with a bottle.'

Mark let out a sound. Signalling what, he didn't know.

'I've always said,' Pat continued, 'that good country shows are a sign of a thriving community.'

Beth in the corner of the room nodded. 'You do say that, Pat.'

There was a moment's silence. 'Is Evan here?' Mark asked. 'I want to follow up on a few things.'

'He's in the kitchen,' Jacqueline said. 'You could go in there and talk. Have your tea with him.'

Again, he was appreciative of her kindness. 'And the fig bickie,' he said. 'I don't want to miss out on that.'

The women around him chuckled and he felt now their warmth. His initial thoughts of being on trial as he entered the room faded away; it was their intimidating semi-circle that did it, he told himself. Nothing else.

Inside the kitchen, a steady hum emanated from an old Kelvinator fridge and the room smelled vaguely of damp lino. Evan was glued to a phone, the blue of the screen giving off a ghostly vibe in the dark room.

Mark re-introduced himself, shaking the boy's clammy hand once more. 'Here to ask a few questions, is that okay?'

'Yeah.'

'You can have someone with you if you like – want your mother to stay?'

'Nah, it's okay.' Evan said, and Sue, after placing a cuppa and a bickie on a saucer in front of him, shuffled out of the room.

'You don't have to talk with me if you don't want to.'

'It's okay.'

The boy's face was one of misery so strong Mark could feel it. Evan slumped over, forehead inches from the table. With his grey T-shirt and pale skin, the boy reminded Mark of a fish hook.

'Evan, Friday night – what were you doing out in the bush with Sarah and Emma Matteson?'

'What I told you that other time. I took them out there, I thought they might like to hear the Barking Owl.'

'In the pouring rain?'

'It wasn't always pouring – there was patches of it. When we started out it wasn't raining, just really damp.'

'Why at midnight?'

'That's around the time when I'd heard it before. I'd been looking for the nest, near the creek – a birder out there told me it was there. Barking Owls are creatures of habit. Plus, at midnight, more fun than, you know . . .' The boy kept his voice down. He grimaced, nodding towards the lounge room where his mother and the other women were.

'Yeah, I get it.' He used to sneak out of the house as a teenager, but for very different reasons. 'Know who this birder was?' Mark took a sip of his tea.

'No, just one of them. Lots of different birders come up here at different times. The one I know the most is named Gerald, but it wasn't him who told me. Gerald just told me about other stuff, like how the Barking Owl nests near creeks and how it's endangered and stuff like that.'

'You see him much?'

'No. Just out in the bush sometimes, or around the co-op. He's nice. People think birders are weird, but they're not. They just like being out in nature, they like the quiet. Gerald has always been nice to me. I don't know why people always give them a hard time.'

The lounge room containing all the women was quiet and the low hum from the fridge sounded louder as a result. Evan slapped the table with his hand and it stopped for a second, before starting up.

The slap surprised Mark, giving him a jolt. 'Did you see anything strange that night? Or hear anything besides the owl?'

The boy sniffed. Sniffed again.

Ever thought of a hanky, mate?

'Any detail, however minor, might help us. We're going back, asking questions – I'll talk to the girls too.'

Evan didn't seem to hear. 'It was weird that night I took the girls out there, different to the other nights I'd heard the owl. Like, the sound was different.'

'How?' Mark picked up the bickie, went to take a bite.

226

'Like, it was higher or something. Like, it went *yowwwwl* . . .' Evan cupped his hands over his mouth and made the sound. A high, sobbing wail.

Mark felt the terror. Put the bickie back down. God, what would it do to someone to hear that late at night?

'You seriously heard that sound on the Friday night you saw the body?'

'Yeah. It was like . . . I dunno. Freaky or something.'

Freaky wasn't the right word. Freaky suggested half fun: *Freaky Friday* with Jodie Foster in her mum's body. That was fun. In the seventies, it was fun.

'You hadn't heard that sound before?'

'When I heard it previously, the sound was less regular. Went from up high to down low, like crying and – I know it sounds stupid – like words being yelled almost. On the Friday night though,' Evan shuddered, 'it was different.'

'Words being yelled?'

'It wouldn't have been words, just that animals and birds sometimes . . . they sound so human.'

'Right.'

Mark hated the sound of rabbits caught in traps. On a clear, still night, their high wailing, born of extreme stress, made him sick with worry. Fear was what kept rabbits alive, he knew, and they were feral pests. But their screams, which signalled 'I am going to die' or 'I am afraid', never lost their horror.

'There was one more thing.' Evan raised his head, looked at Mark. Puzzled.

'What's that?'

227

'It's probably nothing.'

'Go on.'

'I couldn't find my hat. I left it by accident on the council webbing – that orange fence thing they put up to keep us off the path – three or four days earlier. It wasn't there on the Friday night.'

'You didn't just lose it or something?'

'No, my mum gave it to me for my birthday. It was a Billabong one.'

Mark wrote it down. Hesitated, pen hovering above his notepad. 'Your family and friends are worried about you. I know you've been offered counselling at school, but sometimes in my line of work I see it . . .' Mark paused.

'What?'

'A look. Like you're not telling me everything, but you want to. Innocent people tend to have that look.' He wasn't making it up. In his experience, Mark found that innocent people often appeared the most guilty. A friend in Customs called it the 'drugs in the suitcase' expression: innocent people walking through the scanners at airports who have a panicked manner about them, even though they've never been near a drug in their life. It was anxiety apparently, which manifests in the same way as guilt.

Evan cracked his knuckles nervously. He glanced at the door, where on the other side a low rumble of chatter began again.

'A few days before he was killed, I saw Aidan near the powder magazine. He asked me what I was doing there and I told him, looking for the Barking Owl, cos I'd heard the cry. I told him all about it and he was interested, really interested. Asked me to let him know if I heard it again.'

'And did you?'

'Yes. I heard it again on the Thursday night, really brief, not as loud. When I was waiting for the bus on Friday morning, Aidan drove past, and I told him about it. He said he was going to take a look. I didn't tell him a particular time or anything, but I did say they were nocturnal and creatures of habit. I said he should definitely go, even if it was raining – cos the sound they make, it's amazing!' Evan's face crumpled. 'That was the night he was killed! So, maybe if I didn't tell him . . .'

'You weren't to know,' Mark said, soothing. 'You did something he asked you to, and it was not your fault. Whatever happened to him out there wasn't your fault.'

The boy nodded, took in gulps of air. Collected himself. 'I thought he was interested in birds – maybe something to do with the subdivision or whatever. I heard that he was planning on not building around the powder magazine because of it, so that's why I thought he wanted to know. I was happy he was interested in it; no one ever really is aside from the birders. When I took the girls out there later that Friday night, I had no idea that Aidan had already been out and was, well . . . you saw him.'

Head smashed. Body curled neat. Blood and bone.

'Evan, you said that Aidan seemed really interested in the bird, like *really interested*. What did you mean?' Mark took a sip of his tea. Nice and hot, the right amount of milk.

'He was like, kind of weird about it. I dunno, excited or nervous or something. Asked random questions too, like had I been down the mines much or whatever. I haven't,' he added. 'Not safe.'

Mark nodded. Evan's voice was rising, his shoulders moving up and down with his breath.

'But it was mainly the bird and the sound that Aidan asked about. I didn't think anything of his behaviour – everyone doesn't always have to act the same. People are always calling others weird for no reason. Birders, old ladies, kids who don't have any money or kids who don't have too many friends . . .'

Like me. The words wavered in the air, unspoken and sad.

Mark felt a rush of sympathy for the awkward young man. 'You seem pretty all right to me, Evan,' he said. 'And you've got nothing to worry about, seriously.'

The boy's shoulders settled, moved back a little. He sniffed, looked about for a tissue and, finding one in his pocket, took a massive blow.

'There's one other thing I didn't tell you.'

'What?'

Evan hesitated. Mark waited, dread deep in his guts.

'I found this phone in the bush, near the powder magazine.' He showed Mark the phone he'd been fiddling with the whole time, an iPhone – a standard image of mountains in fog on the screen.

'Gerald told me about a nest near there and I wanted to check it out. It's an iPhone . . . a good one . . . it was just there, on the ground. I looked around for a bit, but no one was there. I took it.'

Was it Sleeth's? Aidan's phone hadn't been found yet. Let it be Sleeth's. Let it be Sleeth's.

'You should have told me about this, Evan, when I first spoke to you at the Mattesons' house.'

'I know, but – how could it be related? I found this phone like, five days before Aidan was shot.'

Shit. Not Sleeth's. Whose? Natalie's? The thought was almost too exciting. *Natalie's?*

'Someone's probably been looking for it, they cost a lot of money.' Kelly had a phone that cost her over a grand. 'It takes better photos,' she'd said in defense. 'And has a longer battery life.' *Well, sign me up,* he remembered thinking. *I'll take ten!*

'Has anyone called into the police station about it?' Evan asked.

'No,' Mark admitted. 'But you should hand it in to me now. It could prove important to the investigation. Once it's cleared, and if no one comes to claim it, I'll let you know.'

Reluctantly, the boy handed it over. A new version, shiny silver. Polished possibly, with love.

'Did you try to find out whose it was? Call the number or whatever?'

'I can't open it,' Evan flushed. 'I borrowed a charger from someone at school, so it opens to the home screen, but I don't know the passcode and, well . . . the phone torch works at least.'

Having a useless iPhone was probably better than having none in Evan's world. The ultimate status symbol. It said: I have money. I am cool. I am not some loser.

'You won't tell my mum about it, will you?' Evan glanced nervously at the door. 'She'd be so mad.'

'I won't.' At the moment, Mark had no need to.

He stood, pocketing the phone. 'One last question, Evan, were you here when your mother had all the ladies around for the CWA meeting?'

Evan said something unintelligible.

'What's that, mate?'

'I said, I was in my room, so I didn't see anybody.'

'No? But you must have heard them, right?'

'I heard them, I think.' Evan concentrated. 'Yeah, there were a few of them here. Mrs Delaney and Jacqueline and that.'

'Anyone else?'

'I dunno. Beth? She's usually here with them.'

'Evie from the co-op?'

'Not sure.'

The day was getting away, fast. Mark said his thanks, put his notepad and pencil in his pocket and held out his hand for the boy to shake.

Evan stood – almost the same height as him – and shook, his hand on the way to steady. There was promise in how firm it was. *Good.* He took a few more mouthfuls of tea and tipped the rest down the sink, washing the cup. Then, with Evan watching, he scoffed down the fig bickie. *Delicious!*

'Your mum can bake!' Mark said and the boy nodded, not cheered by the observation.

The chatter in the other room died down when he re-entered. 'Well,' he said, 'I'll be off. Thanks for the tea and the bickie, Sue, if I had a blue ribbon I'd give you one. It was top notch.'

Sue nodded. He turned to the rest of the women. 'Hope you ladies all win a prize for your jams or your scones or whatnot.'

Georgia made a scoffing sound, shaking her curls in derision. The rest of the women gazed at him. He smiled, uncertain. Once again, he was ten.

'It's not just about the prizes,' Beth said from her corner. 'The fundraising is the main thing.'

'Yes?' Mark looked at his watch. Too many things to do. Actual work!

'The new fire engine for the CFA, the renovations for the old folks' home, the playground at the school.' The old lady listed them off on her thin fingers.

'You want a job done,' he said, eyes on the door, 'ask a busy per—'

'And that woman who lives in a caravan,' Jacqueline added. 'We're trying to find housing for her.'

'Your mother,' Beth said, 'was terrible at jam, but wonderful at organising rosters and prizes for the hospital stall.'

'Baking scones' – Pat looked at him squarely – 'is the least of what we do.'

There was a silence. Mark looked around and saw the women clearly. Felt their collective power. This lounge room, like lounge rooms across the country, was where stuff got done. The setting up of the tables, the chairs, the booking of the hall, the filling out of forms, the applying for grants, the flowers, the jugs of water, the glasses, the stalls, the baking, the invoices. All the unseen and undervalued work. If a government wanted something done, some message rolled out, some national program – don't call in the academics or the Instagrammers, don't call the CEOs of marketing companies with their private educations and unfair elevations. No. Call the CWA and put the kettle on.

Suitably chastened, Mark thanked the women and raised a hand in farewell. Beth and Georgia stood, murmuring goodbyes.

If he was wearing a hat, Mark would have tipped it.

CHAPTER 29

She runs, definitely on an incline, and the tunnel takes a sharp left, becomes smaller again. Behind her the man is panting; she can hear it, his laboured breathing. And she runs, head bent low. Forget about the pain, she thinks. Forget about the pain. Run.

An entrance ahead, sticks and branches in the way. She scrambles to it, flinging debris behind her, crying now, trying to squeeze past a stone block covering the exit.

'You bitch!'

Behind her, the man comes at speed, crawling, and she sees his face for the first time – feels a sharp sting of recognition.

'Bitch!'

She pushes the stone, straining her weight against it, and squeezes her way through.

The man reaches out, trying to grab her foot, and she kicks twice, hard. She's out and, on instinct, shoves the stone back down the tunnel with as much force as she can – feels resistance as it pushes up against the oncoming figure.

Out now. Out of the tunnel and Natalie is stumbling through the bush. Aimless. No sound behind her and she stops for a second, panting hard.

She's wet all over, sopping with damp earth and dank water. Trees graze at her, the undergrowth is thick with spiky grass and her head thumps, it really thumps.

Stumbling on, she comes across a familiar sight – an orange council barricade fence, and a trail. She knows where she is.

There's a black hat lying on top of the fence and she jams it on as she moves ahead.

She knows where she's going. She heads there now.

CHAPTER 30

Driving home, Mark was bothered by something he couldn't name. There, back at the house, it was not just the feeling of being on trial. It was not in any way a clue, but a word or a phrase or the room itself. It was there, in the corner of his mind, fuzzy and unsure. *Think.* Nothing jumped out.

A voice on the radio urged him to buy a fridge with ice-making capabilities. It was getting late; the days were always too short in this job. Did the fridge also conduct investigations?

Mark flicked on the headlights. It was only 4 pm, but the dark road and uncertain sunlight breaking through the trees meant visibility was low. Coming up to the Mattesons' farm, a lump of something dead appeared on the road. Possum maybe? He swerved neatly around it, glancing into the bush to see the crows already lining up. Wasn't the collective term for them a 'murder'?

A glint of light flickered in the trees. A reflection, unnatural. Once, twice. Mark, without thinking, stopped the car and got out, peering into the bush. 'Hello!' he called out, listening. 'Hello!'

There was a crash to the side and Mark looked left to see a figure crouched low in the scrub, not five metres away. A jolt of fear in his stomach. A blur of green and the figure was up, darting into the thick of the bush, deeper into the trees and out of sight. Tall.

Without thinking, Mark took chase.

With branches clawing at his face, he leaped over fallen logs. Mark caught the figure again, darting over a rock, agile. Too fast for him. Still he pursued, feeling his knee ache and the wild thumping of his heart. Impossible. Breath ragged, he slowed, realising the futility of his actions. 'Anyone out there?' he called, knowing there was. He reached Stoney Creek, flowing higher now – leaves and sticks in its wake, red silver from the tannin in the leaves. Mark stopped.

The person could be anywhere, near or far. The lost children came to him now and he felt the strangeness of the day. In a slow arc, Mark turned around, looking into the trees. Was that a face there among the bracken? No, no it was not. He heard a sound nearby and strained his eyes to see a young joey eyeing him from afar, its whole being cautious and ready to flee. Briefly, Mark wondered if he'd imagined the crouching figure, the person dashing through the trees – but just as quickly he dismissed the idea. Someone had been there, and the reflective light was the tell-tale sign of glass. Binoculars? He thought so. Mark bent down, splashed some water from the creek onto his face. The coolness was a relief.

In the corner of his eye, he caught a movement: a coil unwinding and lengthening. And before he could escape it, the snake darted at him, biting him in the hand. Mark felt the fangs like two needles and, as he stood in panic, the thing hung from him, heavy, latching on. With his free hand he grabbed it behind the muscular, writhing neck and flung it away. A tiger, orange-brown.

'Fuck!' he cried in shock. 'What the fuck?!' He looked down at his hand where two red marks punctured the skin, ugly, already beginning to swell. Mark began walking back to the HiLux, not running. Never run with a snake bite. The instruction was hardwired into every country person since they could walk. When bitten, don't run. He stumbled over a log, nearly fell, told himself to calm down. *Calm down.*

Forearm resting across his midriff, he continued slowly back to the car.

Once in it, Mark pulled the first aid kit out of the glovebox and found a bandage, ripping the plastic covering open with his teeth. Taking care not to move his hand, he wrapped the gauze tight around it and then right up to his elbow and back again in the pressure immobilisation technique. With his right hand, and resting his phone on his knee, he punched in the number of Booralama Hospital, where he told the responder his name, where he was calling from and that he'd been bitten by a tiger snake.

'How long ago?'

'Five minutes. I'm on my way to you now, be there in thirty.'

'How are you feeling?'

'Fine. I've bandaged the area.'

'You alone?'

'Yes.'

'What do you weigh?'

'Ninety, ninety-two kgs.'

A second pause, where Mark knew the responder would be calculating the time for an ambulance to respond versus the drive himself.

'Drive safely. We'll be waiting.'

Kidney failure, respiratory failure, muscle damage.

Mark started up the engine, thinking about the venom pumping through his bloodstream and knew that if it was a serious bite, he'd have several hours before paralysis took hold. *God*, he thought, looking at the petrol gauge, *better not run out now.* He pulled out onto the Booralama–Stone Town road. *Steady, steady*, he told himself. A car drove past; the driver lifted a forefinger from the wheel, the signal for hello. Mark returned the gesture. It would be rude not to.

In Australia one person died each year from a tiger snake bite. Would he be that person? He never won the weekly meat tray at the pub and that seemed for the first time to be a very good thing.

He was out of the Stone Town bush now. His phone rang. Jagdeep.

'Hi,' she said. 'What's up?'

'Just been bitten by a tiger snake.'

There was a pause. 'You on your way to hospital?'

'Driving there now.'

'On your own?'

'Yep.'

'Feel all right?'

'Yep.' *Did* he feel all right? Was that sweat breaking out on his forehead because of the heat in the vehicle or the beginnings of a fever?

'Never a dull moment.'

'Say that again.'

'I'll call you in an hour.'

'No, Jag.' Mark put his foot on the accelerator, wound up the window, and flicked the air con on. 'Stay on the line.'

'Okay.' Jagdeep sounded cautious, concerned.

'What's up?'

'Sure you're all right?'

'Sure.'

'Well, I've found out a few more things about your man, Aidan Sleeth.'

'Tell me.'

'Complaint against him when he was at uni. Upheld, but no charges laid.'

'What for?' He passed a tractor, two bike riders in full lycra, a woman in a ute.

'Invasion of privacy. Sleeth filmed the lead singer of a band while she was changing. Claimed it wasn't meant to be offensive in any way, just recording the student concert as he was told to. Only, this was backstage, not onstage.'

'What happened?'

'The woman made an official complaint, then dropped it when it was pointed out that she regularly took her top off onstage.'

'Tricky.' Mark was thirsty. Was that a symptom of something? He should drink. Using his knee to steer straight, he grabbed his drink bottle and took a slug.

'She claimed that onstage it was performance and managed, backstage was private.'

Private and public life. Where to draw the distinction? Nowadays, people were fired for their Twitter feeds, for their drunken photos of vomiting, for their indiscretions years before.

'What happened?'

'Nothing. Sleeth graduated from Marketing with less than stellar grades, like most of his cohort.'

'How'd you find this out, Jag?' He was in the town now, the main street. Relief. He turned left for the small hospital.

'Got a friend who works at the uni. She looked through his student history for me.'

'You're a champ.'

'How's the hand?'

'At the hospital now. Speak soon.'

Jagdeep hung up without saying goodbye.

The speed with which he was treated in Emergency was impressive. A quick check of his vitals, confirmation of the type of snake and the injection of anti-venom, particular for tiger snakes.

Then the wait, hours it seemed after the initial treatment, for a final doctor's check.

He rang Clare to let her know where he was. Her shocked voice on the end of the line pleased him. He downplayed the event and his own horror at the curling ribbon of venom, which struck at him, hung writhing from his hand. When queried, Clare said she was out walking. She had a lot on her mind. Jackson, her job.

Clare had also briefly met with Inspector Bithick and Senior Sergeant Barrie, who'd earlier that morning checked the site at Yielder's Track where Natalie's car was first found. They, too, reported nothing as yet. Drone action was to come in the next few days over the Stone Town bush and surrounds. A major search of the area was being considered. The first significant lead for Natalie and the force was excited.

Clare didn't sound excited though. It was difficult to hear her over the sound of nature. She said something and he had to ask her to speak up.

'On the Sleeth financial front, everything seems legit.'

'Yeah?'

'Finn just called me.'

Clare's phone cut out and Mark hung up. There was only so much shouting into a phone you could do. He called Finn, who answered on the second ring.

'Yeah, Sleeth did go through a spate of buying flowers and chocolate.' The young man was chewing something as he walked along an East Adelaide street. 'About three months ago, bought them every couple of days for two weeks. Romantic type. The note said the same thing every time: "You don't know how gorgeous you are." I mean, gross.'

'Got an address for where he sent these flowers?'

'Not yet, it's a centralised booking place. We've got in contact with them – should have answers soon. But they say it'll definitely be in Adelaide – they don't deliver more than twenty k's outside Rundle Mall.'

'Sleeth have a girlfriend?'

'No, none that we can see and none that anyone he knew can tell us about.'

The men were silent for a moment, thinking.

'Hey,' Mark remembered, 'what sort of phone did Nat have?'

'Crappy one, nothing flash. Used to give her shit for it but she said it did the job. Why?'

Mark told him about the phone Evan found. An iPhone, latest version.

'Pity. Can't get much out of the newer ones. As well as de-indexing data, they're also encrypted, almost impossible to bypass. Probably won't get much out of it.'

'Yeah.' Mark rubbed his eyes.

'Fingerprints?'

'Not likely. The kid looks as if he hasn't had it out of his sight since he picked it up.'

Mark said goodbye, hung up and pondered first the lost phone, and then Sleeth's romantic life. Who bought chocolates and flowers? It was like something from a movie. Schmaltzy. He'd bought flowers for Kelly only a handful of times. He never rocked up to her work singing a dedication to her, or cried outside her window in the rain, or wrote love letters, or took off his jacket so she could stand on it when she walked over puddles. Maybe he would still be married if he'd done all of those things. That, or been divorced earlier.

The doctor arrived, her dark blonde hair in a ponytail,

smiley and interested. 'You're my first ever snake bite! And apparently you picked it up and threw the thing away. Are you Bear Grylls?'

'Yes,' Mark answered. 'I am.' He thought about his chase before the bite, running through the bush after someone, jumping over shrubs. 'But most call me Jason Bourne.'

The doctor studied her files, scanning down them fast. She looked into his eyes with a torch. She smelled vaguely of pears, or jasmine; nice nature-y things. A small gold chain glittered on her neck. When she leaned over to check his hand it dangled forward and back. He tried to see what was on the end of it. A cross? The holy grail?

'How are you feeling?' she asked.

He felt good. Better, in fact, than he had in a long time.

'You should buy a raffle ticket,' the doctor said. 'Bloods indicate the envenoming wasn't significant. You may still feel unwell tonight. If I were you, I'd go home now, have some Panadol and get some rest.'

'Are you new in town?' Mark asked. 'Usually it's just Dr Fogarty here and whoever is on their residency, or whatever you call it.'

'I've been up here for over a year,' she said. 'Meant to be here for six months, but now I'm playing tennis and, well, what can you do? Our Ladies B division is second on the ladder.'

'You're stuck. You can never leave now.'

Was he flirting? It felt a little like it. His mouth was beginning to hurt from smiling and it took some effort to pull it back into a straight line.

'Mark Ariti,' she said slowly, looking at his file again. 'Was your mother Helen?'

'Yes.'

'I looked after her before she went into palliative care. She was a lovely, lovely lady.'

Mark concentrated on the white wall behind her, felt the beginnings of a lump in the back of his throat. 'She was.'

'I'm sorry for your loss.' The doctor did something complex with her ponytail. Made it go from a hanging thing to a bun in less than a second. Mark blinked. It was miraculous.

'Come and see us if you experience any pain or illness,' the doctor said. 'But a big, strapping man like you – I think you'll be right.'

He squared his shoulders and nodded. And in the next instance, she was gone, the white curtain billowing in her wake.

CHAPTER 31

It was a desire he hadn't had for a long time: the need for a drink. Tired and wired from the day's events, Mark thought a couple of beers would do the trick. Tuesday night and the bottle shop wasn't open. He parked his car outside the Royal and entered the pub. An old bloke with a raspberry nose turned from his barstool to look at him before returning his gaze to his beer. 'Ariti,' he said. 'You here for the big party?'

'What big party?'

'No big party, you nong. There's never any parties.'

People in town called the man Doris Day on account of his negative outlook on life. It was a joke; newcomers rarely got it.

'Howzit going, Donald?' Mark remembered his proper name.

'Could be worse.'

'Yeah?'

'Could be yesterday.'

Rummaging in his wallet for a $50 note, Mark wondered how the man would cope living in Afghanistan. Doris Day owned a 1200-hectare property of prime land and was married with three children, all at university in Adelaide. 'What happened yesterday?'

'Header broke down. Had to get a bloke from Waldara to come and look at it. New part could take two weeks.'

'That's horrific.'

'Yeah well.' Doris Day stared into his pot, his big nose almost touching the glass. 'That's life, isn't it?'

Kill me now.

The bar manager, Michelle, finally came out of the kitchen. Mark asked for a six-pack of pale ale and paid, studying his phone screen while Doris Day sighed and sighed.

'Here you go, love.' Michelle passed him his drinks. 'Had an accident, have you?' she asked, nodding at his bandaged hand.

'Tiger snake,' he said. 'Bit me this arvo.'

Doris Day's face registered something like mild surprise before settling back to his comfortable state of morose. 'That'd be right. This country's going to the dogs.'

Michelle looked as if she wanted to hear the story. If there was another crowd in the pub, it might be good to stand around, let them hear about the time he grabbed a tiger snake and flung it across the creek. But for now, Mark backed out towards the door, clenching his beers like a life vest.

'Detective Senior Sergeant Mark Ariti!' A burst of energy, and Lola Sleeth, ex-wife of Aidan, entered the bar from the ladies as if she was crossing centre stage in a play. 'Are you here to arrest us?!' Her voice was high-pitched, excited.

'Just buying some drinks,' Mark answered.

Lola must have been applying make-up in the bathroom. Red lipstick ran thick around her mouth, bleeding into small cracks and staining her front teeth. Her hair, still curled, was dishevelled, and eyeliner clung to the corners of her eyes in lumps.

'Why don't you,' she sang, leaning in close, 'buy one for me?'

Mark stepped back. Lola smelled of stale beer and cigarettes. 'Have to get going.'

'Places to be, people to meet, is that it?' Her face loomed close, drunk. 'Or are you like me?'

Mark considered Lola, formerly Lee-Anne. In spite of her ditzy air, she was more perceptive than she let on. He'd known girls at school like this, who wore lots of make-up, talked only of clothes and gossip – but who, as it turned out, were sharp as whips, smarter than them all. It was an act of defence, often a triumph.

'Goodbye, Lola.' He opened the front door of the pub and suddenly Lola was beside him, hissing in his ear.

'All you care about is Aidan, Aidan, Aidan, isn't it? Never of anyone else in his life. Typical.'

He waited. In the background, Doris was slumping over his beer, Michelle was wiping tables at the other end of the bar.

'We're interested in all aspects of the case.'

'When we got married, I couldn't believe my luck. He was from one of the good families, the rich ones, and I was from the opposite. "Pov Town", they used to call our part of Booralama.'

Mark remembered it, the casual way they'd talk about who lived in Pov Town and who didn't.

'Aidan was so handsome and successful,' Lola continued. 'He took me to Adelaide to see a play. He bought me things, jewellery, clothes – so romantic! Not like the other boys I grew up with.' Lola exaggerated her mouth into a shape that suggested derision. 'We got married after six months.'

She was leaning on the door frame, swaying, slurring.

'But you know what happened after we said "I do" at St Patrick's in front of *two hundred* people no less?'

Mark rested his beers on a side table. 'I'm listening.'

'He didn't talk to me! Aidan barely spoke with me at all. Can you believe it?' Lola laughed, put her hand up to her mouth and wiped it, blurring the lipstick further. 'When I told my mother she was like, "Well, does he hit you?" and when I said no, she asked what the problem was.'

Lola picked up a beer coaster and began shredding it. 'After a while, I asked him if there was someone else, but he said no. He always said no.'

The beer coaster was a goner. Tiny cardboard pieces littered Lola's hand and dotted her black top like chunks of dead skin.

'There always was though. Someone. Someone to obsess over, spoil – like he spoilt me. There's a name for it, you know.'

'Yeah? What's that?'

'Love-bombing. That's what Aidan does. It's not as nice as it sounds.'

Mark didn't know what to say. He'd never heard of such a thing.

'He was always keen on someone, that's for sure. Used to tell me about them!'

'That must have been hard.'

Lola shrugged. Her face close up was a red myriad of blackheads and pits. It was the surface of Mars. Elon Musk and anyone else was welcome to it. 'Just a month or so ago he was telling me about someone.'

A beat. 'A month ago?'

'He always liked to tell me things like that. After we got divorced, he actually felt as if he was free to speak. Plus, I'm like a vault.' She mimicked zipping her mouth shut. 'Men like vaults.'

'Did you say he was with someone a month or so ago?'

'Yeah, a blonde. I saw a photo.'

A quickening of the heart. 'When did he show you the photo?'

'I don't know, two weeks, two months ago? Who cares?'

Heart thumping, Mark took out his phone and brought up a photo. 'Is this her?'

Lola raised her eyebrows. 'Her? I recognise her, the missing policewoman! She's all over the news! Why are you showing me that?' She stumbled, leaned in closer to the phone's screen. 'No, I don't think so. No.'

Mark put his phone back, regretting showing her Natalie's police profile photo. If Lola remembered, she could raise some serious interest in the press with his action.

'Although' – Lola had an exaggerated thinking look on her face – 'put some make-up on her, let her hair out – you never know. It *could* be her. She's pretty. Yeah.' Lola was almost talking to herself. 'It could seriously be her . . . Toilet!' she announced, and stumbled back to the ladies.

Mark called over to where Michelle was sweeping now. 'Should you be serving Lola alcohol? Looks as if she's had enough.'

Michelle rested her hand on the end of the broom. 'I barely serve her anything. I think she drinks in the bathroom.'

'She here much?'

'Every night. From seven till closing. It's sad. Tell you what though, she's always got money. Shouts the bar when she feels like it.'

'Want me to call her a taxi?'

'Thanks, love, it's what we have to do most nights. Either that, or she goes home with someone. But she likes it here and it's only early. I'll get her a cuppa and she can sit on the couch for a bit, have a chat.' Michelle's voice, husky from a nocturnal life in smoky bars, was kind. He could see why types like Lola and Doris chose the Royal.

'Was Lola here on Friday night, Michelle?'

The bar manager looked at him knowingly. 'Yes, she was. Everyone here that night will attest to it. From seven till closing, like I said. Around eleven-thirty.'

'Thanks.' Mark waited till Lola came out. He picked up his beers from the side table. She arrived, newly energised and smelling of bourbon. 'You happy here, or want me to call you a taxi now, Lola?'

Lola looked at him, uneven. 'No, love.'

'Well, goodnight.'

Suddenly, Sleeth's ex-wife grabbed him by the arm and pulled him in close, her breath hot and sickly in his face. 'Don't you want to know why Aidan paid me each month?' Mark did want to know that, very much, but every policing protocol warned him not to make enquiries while she was in this state. Again, he waited.

'It was so I wouldn't let anyone know what a weirdo he was. No sex, super tidy, shaving his whole body. No real friends, not close with his mother. Aidan wanted the facade of a successful country man and I gave it to him. The perfect couple. He wore chinos and RMs, I pruned white roses and bought *Country Style*. His house, have you been there? I hated it! It was like some sort of shrine to his ancestors, all doilies and white – no personality. He wouldn't let me redecorate. Said he liked it like that – wanted to preserve the Sleeth name in all aspects. Only his bedroom was semi-normal – but what went on in there wasn't. The man was obsessive over women and yet he didn't want to touch them. It was creepy, everything about him was.'

The Sleeth house, how bare it was. How strange and sterile, like the man himself.

'After a while,' Lola continued, 'I didn't mind. I mean – who would?' She flung her arms around as if the pub were a floating bar on the Mediterranean. As if Doris was really Leonardo DiCaprio and she was going home with George Clooney. 'I've got everything I need!'

'That's great.' He said it again, anxious now to be free of her. 'But I've really got to get home.' Three men arrived, locals nodding at him as they made their way into the pub.

Lola's attention was briefly diverted and Mark walked quickly out into the dusk.

'Look at you!' Lola was at the door now. Her voice shouted at him across the road, loud in the country town. 'You're all proper and professional, but really, you're just like me, Detective.'

'How's that?' he called back, wanting and not wanting to know.

'Isn't it obvious? We're alone. *Alone!*'

Back at home, after two Panadols, Mark tore open the lid of one of his beers. He liked the taste but didn't feel good about drinking it. *Alone*, Lola had said, and it was true. Feeling despondent and exhausted, Mark thought about dinner and realised the final blow: in all the day's events, he'd forgotten the last thing on his list, to get the bloody mince out.

CHAPTER 32

By morning the swelling in his arm was gone and Mark was pleased to see two small red dots on the skin between his fore-finger and thumb. He looked at his hand as he lay in bed, alarm clock pushed to snooze, the room a warm fug of himself. No run today. The doctor with the ponytail had told him to take it easy; he wanted to do as she said. He sat up and noted the greying hairs on his chest, the gut receding but persistent.

He recalled the night before and Lola's shriek: 'We're alone!'

She was right, but the jibe struck deep coming from someone who spent their nights drinking in the toilets of the Royal. Lola hadn't worked out for Lee-Anne. Perhaps she'd have been better off if she'd stuck with her true moniker, lived an honest life, married some bloke from the Booralama Pov Town, bought a big house in the 'burbs. Sleeth had done no favours for Lola. David Lee Roth was wrong: even if you have the yacht, you can still be a sad case.

Mark walked to the bathroom, turned the shower on hot and stepped in. It was a small shower, tacked on in the corner of the big bathroom where the old clawfoot bath still reigned supreme. He never used it. The shower was small and built for an older person, but for now he was grateful for the handrails on the sliding door, which he held on to while water pummelled his back.

A picture of Sleeth was emerging: antisocial despite a confident front, successful in business, obsessive, then careless in relationships; someone who professed to love the bush but bought it to subdivide and develop. He was a real estate agent who lived in a strange old-fashioned house. He had few friends but was possibly in, or pursuing, a new relationship.

Sleeth *looked* like a candidate for Prime Minister, Mark mused. Tall and fit, a private school boy, easy charm on first meeting, savvy in financial dealings, family money to back him up. But like most, the boy from Booralama was not as wholesome as he appeared.

Mark turned off the water, got dressed and fixed himself a mug of tea. He looked at the calendar on his wall; Charlie and Sam were arriving in two days. Yabbying with the Mattesons.

He ate two pieces of toast, three pieces, thick with butter and jam. *Steady, son*, he told himself. *You're one Snickers away from a place you'll find hard to crawl out of.*

On his way to the station, he looked at his phone. Another missed call from Prue. He texted her: *Will call tonight. Promise.*

First to arrive at the station, he made himself another cup

of tea and, enjoying the peace, took it into his office, firing up the laptop and opening the blinds. A bright, blue day despite the early chill.

There was an email from Finn Turner, sent late the night before:

Autopsy completed: full report to follow but main details – last known meal of Sleeth's was Thai takeaway. No alcohol or drugs. Level of digestion indicates he was killed between 7 pm and 10 pm on Friday night. Cause of death, gunshot to the back of the head. Right fingernail missing – old injury. Small scar on right thigh, recent.

Mark leaned back. Interesting, but not anything to get excited about. Everyone he knew had scars from crossing fence lines, standing on old nails, getting scratched by tree branches, or grazes from motorbike accidents. He rolled up the arm of his shirt. There it was – the zig-zag scar left from a barbed-wire fence he'd been trying to scale when being attacked by nesting plovers at his friend Stitcher's farm. Missing fingernails were nothing either. A hard bang with a hammer, getting it jammed in the door. The injuries weren't exciting. The whole autopsy drew a blank.

There was a light tap on the door. Clare. Any former attitude of superiority was gone. He knew she was a snitch. She knew she was a snitch. No matter what the circumstances, no matter whether it was the classroom or the boardroom or the cops, snitching was a low act. Clare had two more days to tell her seniors that she was the leak, not Finn. Then, he'd do the job – reluctant as he would be, hypocritical as he'd feel, given his own record of hiding things from the force.

For now, she was marking time – aware she'd not be trusted to go over any more details related to the Whitsed/Sleeth files, Clare was instead tidying the front office, updating the medical cabinet and staring gloomily out the window. Irritated by her heavy sighs, Mark went into his own office and rang Finn for an update.

'Been checking out Sleeth's movements in Adelaide and Stone Town,' the young man said, full of purpose.

Sleeth had been back and forth from his East Adelaide office as usual, but was spending a greater amount of time in Stone Town as he negotiated the sale of the co-op and the agreement with Birds for Bush that he'd keep the area around the powder magazine free from development. All that was expected. *Nothing to see here.*

'Now that Sleeth's dead, John and Evie Renner want to buy back the land,' Mark said as Finn finished speaking.

'So do Birds for Bush,' Finn said. 'They can buy it and keep it solely as public and protected land, not have to share with the co-op.'

'I don't think Evie and John would mind that as a solution. That it's not developed seems to be their main concern.'

One obstacle for the Renners and the nature society was Lola Sleeth. Would she agree to sell it back to them? Prices were higher now, demand at fever pitch – land, land, land. Would Lola hold the course, develop and then sell? *Buy land, they're not making it any more* was the slogan of the country's largest real estate agent. Behind the drive, Mark guessed, was not only FOMO, but something deeper. If it all goes to shit, if there's another pandemic, if there's a world war, if we run out of food, if some country invades – life is better on the land; the veggie garden, the space for the kids, the fresh air.

'Where's Clare?' Finn asked, after telling Mark he'd be back in Booralama the following morning. 'She's not picking up her phone.'

'Clare's not well,' Mark said. 'She's taking it easy for a bit.'

'Clare not well!' Finn sounded surprised. 'Since she's given up smoking, she's become so fit. Does triathlons and stuff.'

'Yeah well, she's probably going to go back to the motel for a rest.'

Mark *wished* that Clare would go back to the motel. Her drooping presence and frowns made him anxious. The men said their farewells and hung up.

There was work to do: send in the phone for prints, an update from IT on Sleeth's encrypted file from his office, nothing firm as yet. It looked to be mainly images, but IT couldn't confirm.

'What sort of images?' Mark asked. 'Do you mean photos?'

'Yes.' The IT person on the end of the line wouldn't budge. 'We'll let you know what they are as soon as we have all the details.'

Mark hung up, annoyed. What sort of details needed to be confirmed? He rubbed at his knee, looked with interest at the fading bite marks on his hand. It was easy to recall the horror of the writhing reptile, fangs in deep, the dry, smooth scales as he flung it over the creek.

The phone buzzed in the hallway and Clare answered, glancing at him briefly through the open door. Mark turned to his notes. In the background, his colleague spoke in a terse tone. 'Stay!' she was saying, annoyed. 'Watch TV, read or something.'

Mark zoned out, wondered how Jacqueline could go yabbying in a wheelchair. What was the deal with that? A snag of worry lodged itself in his mind. His grandmother used to come out to the dam when they were kids. Mark's uncle would pick her up, light as a bird, and carry her to the bank where one of the kids would have placed a chair for her. She was a stately woman, he remembered. His mother was always a little nervous of her.

The day rolled on, warm and humid. Mark went to ask Clare if she'd like anything from down the street, but was dissuaded by her vacant stare. With the medical cabinet laid out before her in the cleaning and sorting process, she looked like a deranged nurse.

By knock-off time Mark was well and truly ready to head home and put the chops on, when a loud ringing interrupted his plans. The station phone. At the same time, his own mobile began buzzing. Startled, Mark took two quick steps across to the front counter and picked up the phone. Clare's mobile also started – the whole office was abuzz.

'Is this the police?' A woman's voice, frantic.

'Yes.'

'There's been an accident. It's bad.'

'Where are you?'

'Stone Town Road, I've called an ambulance.'

'Who?'

'Luke Howsley. Oh God, I don't know. It's bad. He might be *dead*.'

'Who is this?'

'Sue Williams.'

'Stay there, Sue. I'll be there in thirty minutes.'

The line cut off.

Half an hour later: a country road and a mangled pushbike. Locals had gathered, waiting to see how they could assist. Sue Williams, Jacqueline Matteson and Pat Delaney bunched close together, John and Evie Renner slightly to the side. They all watched as a chopper airlifted Luke to Adelaide.

It had been Sue who first saw the young man, lying spreadeagled across the road, his face down, head bleeding. She was out shutting her front gate after Evan had forgotten to do so – and had seen Luke's body way up the road. At first she thought it was a roo, but the orange hi-vis cycling top told another story. She called triple zero. They'd sent the chopper. His mother was on the way to Adelaide, a long drive from Victoria, a hell trip.

None of the women had seen or heard anything amiss. Luke had finished tutoring young Sarah and had taken off on his bike on the way back to Booralama. He told the Mattesons that he was in training for a triathlon on the Gold Coast and was aiming to ride more.

What is it with triathlons? Mark thought. *Whatever happened to a nice walk around the block?*

Mark took photos of the bike. There were no skid marks on the road. He rang the nearby police stations and asked them to keep a lookout for a car with damage to the front. Call for dashcam footage. Hit and run, it was serious.

Luke had been hit between 5.30 pm and 6 pm. A car coming up from behind him, judging by the damage to the back wheel. Mark knew from experience that in the fierce late afternoon sun – the shadows switching and changing, the glare of the road – it would be relatively easy to hit someone and not even know. You wouldn't hear anything if you had the radio on full bore. You might feel a thump and think it a wombat or a wallaby. It happened all the time.

Sue Williams and Pat Delaney headed home, Sue walking back up her driveway, Pat getting into her old vehicle and pulling out. John and Evie Renner stood a little way down the road, heads bent together in what looked like quiet argument.

'You two see anything?' Mark asked, drawing close. 'The car that did this'll have some damage.'

John's head whipped around, irritated. 'No, saw none of that. Hope the kid's okay.'

'Will he be all right?' Evie asked, voice wavering.

'I'm not sure.'

'We were just driving back from Adelaide and saw all the cars. How awful! And Sue found him. I wonder if I should go around there – offer to cook or something . . .'

'Stop it, Evie!' John was red-faced. 'Stop pandering to these women, it'll get you nowhere.'

'They're my friends,' Evie protested, turning away.

'Some friends!'

'Shut up, John.'

'You tell him, Evie, or I will!' John would not shut up. He shoved his hands in his pockets and waited.

'It's nothing,' Evie said.

'All right – I'll do it then. Pat Delaney and her posse told Evie to say that she was with them on the night Sleeth died, when she was nothing of the sort. She was at home with me!'

A mob of cockatoos swirled across the sky, swooping and screeching. Evening time and they were returning home.

'John . . .' Evie warned.

'Evie's wanted to be part of their group for years – a real Stone Town community member – but what she doesn't realise is that, unless you've got a great-great-grandparent buried in the bush somewhere, then you're an interloper!'

'Stop it, John, for God's sake.' Evie's voice cut across the chaos of the sky. 'We're all worried about that poor young man and here you are, spouting nonsense. I've had it!'

John raised his eyebrows at Mark and walked off towards his car.

'Do you want to tell me what's going on, Evie?' Mark asked.

The older woman gave a sarcastic *Huh*.

'I've got to get back to the station, check up on Luke. So, can you tell me definitively where you were on the Friday night Sleeth was shot?'

'John's right.' Evie's tone was flat. 'I was at home with him all night. I didn't go out.'

'Did Pat ask you to say you were at Sue Williams's?'

'No. Sue did.'

'Why would she do that?' The Stone Town women were a mystery. He could see now why Lee had given them a collective name. He looked at the evening sky for a moment and wished himself a bird, wheeling into the deep blue.

'Because Pat had already told you I was there. Sue didn't want to make a fuss for Pat – have you going around there questioning her again and again. Pat's old, it tires her out. And anyway, what's it matter?'

'Well, it's illegal to lie when providing evidence to an investigation, for a start.'

'So she got mixed up, who cares? None of those women are involved in anything bad. Pat doesn't need the hassle. You know, with the cancer and all.' Mark blinked. 'You didn't know? Sorry – it's melanoma. Not good. Look, Sue was just being kind to Pat. Didn't want her to worry about who was there Friday night and who wasn't.'

Kind? Mark wasn't sure.

'John's right about one thing,' Evie said. 'I'll never be a local here, no matter how hard I try, what I do for them.'

'Being a local is overrated.' All the times he'd been told about his mother's looks and good humour, the people who stopped him at the Fat Bean to ask about Prue, the five hundred chats in the supermarket, the clucks of concern about his separation from Kelly. To be a local was to live a goldfish-bowl existence.

'Everyone wants it though, don't they? To belong, I mean.'

He couldn't deny it. 'Yeah.'

'Don't go too hard on Sue, she was only trying to help.'

'It's you who lied to me, Evie. Anything else you should add?'

'Nothing.'

'Okay.' Mark was sapped. 'I'll be off.' He issued a general farewell and walked with heavy steps back to his vehicle, already dreading the unpleasant reception his next job was sure to receive.

CHAPTER 33

The Matteson house smelled of paint and as he stepped inside – the door opened by a subdued Isabelle – and he saw the beginnings of a light grey wall with a white ceiling. Painting. A job for the cursed. He remembered his own renovation with Kelly in their first home and shuddered. Cool whites or warm whites, both could go to hell.

'Your mum in, is she?' Mark didn't have time for niceties. It was getting on for 7 pm. Behind Isabelle he could see the younger girls, Sarah and Emma, watching from the lounge room.

Jacqueline wheeled out and on seeing his serious look shooed the girls away.

'This is terrible, isn't it!' she said. 'Luke's poor mother, I keep thinking about her. God, I hope he's all right.'

'He's in intensive care,' Mark said. 'We won't know anything for a few hours.'

'One minute he was here, tutoring Sarah, then the

266

next . . . Who would do such a thing? Drive away and leave?'
Her voice held real anguish.

Mark gave her a look.

'What?' She caught his eye, puzzled.

'It's a pretty bad road,' Mark said. 'The time he was hit,
that late afternoon sun can blind you. Accidents happen.'

Jacqueline sat still.

'Were any of your girls out on the road, Jacqueline?'

'What do you mean?' A marked shift in tone.

'Were any of your girls driving? I know you let them drive
underage, even if it's just up the road.'

Jacqueline's face set hard. '*None* of us were driving.
Georgia's not even here. She went back to Adelaide this
morning and the girls have been at school all day.'

'After school then? He was hit around five-thirty. Was
anyone in your house driving at that time?'

'What? No. What are you . . .? Why are you coming
around here accusing them and me of . . . of . . .?'

'Negligent driving?'

Jacqueline narrowed her eyes. 'What *are* you going on
about?'

'I think' – Mark didn't enjoy saying it – 'that you've been
involved in a car accident before and didn't disclose exactly
what happened.'

Jacqueline opened her mouth to respond, then shut it
again, clenching her jaw.

'It was Georgia who was driving the night of the accident
when your husband Rod died, wasn't it?'

Jacqueline looked at her hands in her lap. Didn't speak.

'I had a look at the accident report. I don't think it was a miracle that Georgia survived relatively unscathed. It was because she was sitting in the part of the car that was the least damaged. According to the report, that was the driver's seat. The injuries Rod sustained weren't consistent with the crash report. He was sitting in the middle seat of the ute, wasn't he? He was beside Georgia, you were on the passenger side.'

An extended beat followed. Outside, a dog began barking.

'She was barely fifteen years old,' Mark said. 'Too young for a licence. I notice now that when she drives, it's so slowly and deliberately. I can't blame her; it would be difficult to get behind the wheel after something like that.'

Someone called out to the dog to shut up and it stopped. A good farm dog, obedient.

Jacqueline spoke quietly at first and then with conviction. 'In the moments after the crash – when I'd come to – it wasn't the sight of Rod dead beside me that made me the most scared. It wasn't even Georgia's screaming or the pain or me not feeling my legs. It was the thought of what she'd go through, what all the girls would go through, when they found out she was driving. I know what press intrusion and the constant scrutiny of community can do to a person. That, and the guilt, is what turned Rod into an alcoholic.'

Mark remembered the articles on the accident years before, when Rod was found guilty of negligence for the death of a young student in his care. What did that do to a relationship, to a family?

The moment she decided, Mark could almost see it: the one crystal-clear thought in all the chaos and din of the crash: *Georgia cannot be blamed for this.* And although her daughter must remember it, the pushing and shoving of her dead father into the driver's seat and her swapping into his, she would never have to endure the relentless glare of the accusatory finger of the public. Her sisters would never blame her for their father's death; her mother, complicit, would always be a support. It must have seemed a vital thing at the time, to push her dead father into the guilty seat. How long afterward would the psychological effects of such an act manifest physically and mentally?

And what of the old Booralama cop who'd written the report about the accident? What suspicions did he harbour? Those handwritten words, *Good people.* Mark leaned back, thinking of all the old cops everywhere and the collective knowledge they held, the secrets buried deep. A turn of the head here, a word they pretended to mishear, a gaze they averted, a road accident report they slightly doctored for a good family, *good people*, who'd already suffered so much.

'Georgia moved him into the driver's seat, didn't she? It couldn't have been you.' Mark was despondent more than anything else.

'My legs were trapped, so yes – it was her that moved her own dead father at my urging. So, will you report that?' Jacqueline was all ice now. 'You'll pull my nineteen-year-old daughter into this too?'

What good would it do? He'd be like his predecessor and look away. 'No.'

Jacqueline's shoulders slumped.

'But,' Mark said, 'you need to tell me where all your girls were earlier.'

'Not driving. I've told you that. Not driving.'

'You still let Isabelle drive,' Mark said. His voice was a monotone. 'After all that and you let her, a fifteen-year-old—'

'I live on a farm,' Jacqueline cut him off. 'I can't drive. You should know what it's like on farms – drivers are necessary, even if they're underage. Everyone knows that.'

All the pretending we do, Mark thought. To maintain the peace. Sentences that begin with 'Everyone knows that . . .' mostly end in complicity. Everyone knows that. Plus it was true. Farms need drivers.

Another awkwardness he had to broach. 'About this Friday night . . .'

'I don't think there'll be any yabbying, Mark.' Jacqueline studied the door, her face hard. 'My girls have found a dead body in the bush and now this. They've been through so much. I need to be here for them, just us. I don't have time for anyone else.'

He nodded. It was a release.

'And' – now he was here, he may as well dive in – 'can you confirm with me who was at Sue Williams's house on the night Aidan was shot?'

Jacqueline gave a scornful laugh. She held up her hands, ticking off the names one by one. 'Sue Williams, my mother-in-law Beth, myself and Pat Delaney.'

'Anyone else?' Mark felt the weight of his job.

'I'm telling you the truth.'

The smell of paint was making him feel woozy and claustrophobic. 'Evie Renner, was she there?'

A moment's hesitation. 'No.'

He passed the photo on the wall, of the Matteson family in happier times. Then turned to farewell Jacqueline, only to see that she had already left the room.

On his way home, the paddocks now dark, the wheat moving slowly in waves, he rang the hospital. No change. Intensive care. *Plenty of people recover from comas*, he told himself, *and not all with severe brain damage.*

Later, at home, he called again: stable. He left his name and number with one of the nurses.

A message arrived for him as he lay, unable to sleep, at one the next morning. It was from Luke's mother: *Greatly improved.*

Mark slept.

CHAPTER 34

Mark yawned, leaning back in his chair, tipping it. He used to do it as a kid.

'I knew someone whose friend broke their back doing that,' Senior Sergeant Rachel Barrie, or B1, said, frowning.

Everyone says that.

The two detectives, Barrie and Bithick, had finally called in to the station, rather than driving straight back to Adelaide after their searches in the Stone Town area. Inspector Leon Bithick had earlier informed Mark that drone searches were beginning in the afternoon, scanning the topography in the hope of seeing a sign of Whitsed, or – less excitingly in the eyes of the force – a clue that would solve Sleeth's murder.

There was serious money now being injected into the wider search for Natalie Whitsed. It would only be days, hours, before the story broke about her car being found near where Sleeth's body was discovered in the early hours of a rainy Saturday. Hours before they arrived: the press with clicking cameras, the jostling crowds, the amateur sleuths and those slavish for crime. They would come, they would all come.

The buzzer for the front counter sounded. It was a young woman wanting a Stat Dec signed. On days like this, Mark liked Stat Decs. You didn't have to think too hard, there was no pressure.

'Nice day out there, is it?' he asked, checking her credentials, pen ready to sign.

'S'pose.'

Her dark hair, eyeliner and black clothing made him wonder if there were still Goths in Booralama. When he was at school, they used to be semi-cool, mysterious and detached. Dedicated Catholics among his friends suspected they were Satanists and, he couldn't deny, at fifteen years of age, the thought turned him on.

The girl nodded her thanks and carefully put her signed Stat Dec back in a plastic pocket and then a folder.

He waved at her and watched as she walked back out the door, her black outfit incongruous against the blue sky. Something about her reminded him of someone. He couldn't place it and, giving the counter a half-hearted wipe, he began walking back down the hall.

Then it came to him, and he was rushing out the door of the station and looking left to right.

The girl in black was there, about to cross the road, and he called out, 'Hey! I need to ask you one thing!'

She turned around startled and dropped her folder, papers flying everywhere. He rushed to help, picking up handouts and notes, relieved she'd used a plastic pocket for the Stat Dec.

'What does the acronym on the back of your T-shirt mean?'

It was there, GDWFB, alongside a small image of a witch's hat. He'd recognised the small fire image on the sleeve.

'What? Oh! It's a meme. Or, well, a movement really.'

There was a *toot-toot* and a car pulled up alongside; a mother driving, looking concerned that her daughter was being accosted by a man on the street.

'What's it stand for?'

Toot-toot.

The girl smiled knowingly. 'It means: *Granddaughters of the Witches they Forgot to Burn.*'

Toot-toot.

'Is it a band or something?'

A smug grin. 'Educate yourself,' she said, sliding into the car.

Mark and Rachel Barrie, trained detectives both, consulted Google. The term, first coined in a young adult book, had now come to symbolise the continued misogyny and poor treatment of women who fitted outside social norms. It was a sign at #MeToo protests, a refrain on social media, and fast becoming a symbol of unity for women across the world.

Mark and Barrie had never heard of it.

Kelly, Mark's ex-wife, would know the term, he was sure of it. She would tell him: so many witches were burned and still burn today. Women who lose jobs and opportunities over unpopular opinions, who are shelved for speaking out, and whose experiences with violent men are diminished and decried. And even more so, the less privileged, less educated women and girls who are cast into surrogacy, sex work, trafficking, child marriage. It never ends, Kelly would say; it never, ever does.

He rang her: no answer.

Granddaughters of the Witches they Forgot to Burn. There was a power to it; the words scorched.

'Wish that had been around when I was just starting out,' Barrie said, staring out the window. 'My daughter's training to be a cop. Plenty of witches burned in the police force.'

'Georgia Matteson was wearing a T-shirt with it on,' Mark remembered. 'At Evan's mother's house. I didn't look too closely, but it was black and had the fire sign. I'm sure it was the same.'

The acronym, now that Luke Howsley was in hospital, took on a sinister light. Why did someone sign with it on a note that read *We Are Watching, We See You*?

Mark had an idea now of who he could ask. He checked his watch – 10 am, not too early for a coffee at the Fat Bean.

Dennis greeted him there, his tight black jeans and open-necked shirt giving out strong Bee Gees vibes. 'Reets,' the ageing lothario said. 'Bit early for a ham and cheese. You here for a Negroni?'

'Just a coffee, Den. Isabelle Matteson working?'

'She is, just got here,' he said. 'Everything okay?'

'Yep. Need to ask her something.'

Dennis wandered out to the kitchen, a casual stick insect, forever cool.

The day was clear and bright. He should go shopping, get some stuff for his boys. Zooper Doopers, chips, fruit.

Isabelle appeared. 'What's up?' she asked. 'I've got a heap of dishes to wash.'

Mark felt a bristle of annoyance. He would never have greeted an older person in that way when he was a kid. 'Good morning, Isabelle.'

'Hi.'

Young folk of today. 'How are you?'

She shrugged. 'It's been a really shit week.'

You're not wrong. 'Can I ask you about a note we found in Luke Howsley's office?'

Another shrug.

What's with all the shrugging? 'It was signed with the acronym GDWFB. Do you know anything about it? I know your sister Georgia was wearing a top with it written on the other day.'

Isabelle rolled her eyes, a world-weary expression born of assumed superiority and perfected by youth. 'Seems like you know more about my sister's wardrobe than I do.'

Dennis brought out his coffee, not in a takeaway mug but a ceramic cup. Mark would take it out of there, back to the station; Dennis wouldn't mind.

'So, can I like, help you with anything?' Isabelle asked, looking closely at her nails.

'Yes, you can.' Mark's patience was wearing thin. 'What can you tell me about the note with the acronym we found in Luke Howsley's office?'

Isabelle's face flushed and she bent to pick something up

from a table. 'Is he going to be okay?' she asked, voice small. 'Luke?'

'I hope so.'

Suddenly, the girl collapsed and fell into a chair. 'Everything's so crap, it's all so shit!' She held her arms up in despair. 'Aidan's dead and now this. I don't know how to . . . I don't know . . .'

Mark gave her time.

'He was my boss!' She was referring to Aidan. 'I never expected that he would . . .' Isabelle took a long drink of water and looked, impossibly glum, out the big glass windows of the Fat Bean.

'Were you . . .?' Mark didn't know how to phrase it. 'Did you, like, have a sort of thing for Aidan Sleeth?'

Isabelle gave him an incredulous look.

'It's just that,' Mark stumbled, 'on that night his body was found, I saw you driving back to your house and you were crying, really crying, and I thought . . .'

'You thought I *liked* him?' Isabelle's voice was brittle. 'You thought I *liked* Aidan Sleeth – what was he, thirty or forty or something? Bloody hell. Give me some credit.'

Mark made a helpless gesture. A shrug.

'Okay, look, *I* wrote that note. *I* wanted Sarah to put it in Aidan's desk, but she must have got distracted and put it in Luke's office when she visited him to talk about tutoring. Idiot, should have done it myself.'

Aidan's behaviour at the concert many years before – taking photos backstage. Lola's assertion that he 'love-bombed' people, that he had a new girlfriend, that he was weird. Mark felt a slow twist of fear deep in his stomach.

'Why did you write that note, Isabelle?'

The Fat Bean was suddenly very quiet. They were the only two left.

'Because Aidan Sleeth was a Grade A arsehole.' A pause. 'Because he was always staring at women and girls, offering to buy things for us, standing too close . . .'

Mark waited.

'Watching. He liked to watch. One time' – Isabelle spoke with revulsion – 'one time I was working there, cleaning the front window, and I looked up to see that the reflection of Aidan's face was right beside mine, almost touching. He was standing behind me, but I got the feeling he'd planned it and that he'd been standing there for a while. It was really creepy. He was so still.'

'Did he ever hurt you, Isabelle?'

'No.' She smoothed down her hair.

'Anyone that you know of?'

'No. Not exactly.'

'What do you mean by that?' Mark asked, sharp.

'Ask any girl in town. Aidan Sleeth used to perv at us. What a creep! I even saw him taking photos of Georgia when she was last up, and that's when I wrote the note. I wanted him to know that we knew about him, that we were watching too.'

'Does anyone else know about this?'

'The note? No. But his behaviour – well, only any female that's ever been within twenty kilometres of him knows about it. Pretty hard not to. We all know it. Girls, women – we talk.

Sleazy Sleeth we call him – behind his back – but you know, we all want to keep our jobs and it's not good to get on the bad side of the richest bloke in town, blah blah blah.'

'He was married for a while there, you know.'

Isabelle snorted. 'What difference does that make? Anyway, Lola's so pissed all the time now, he probably paid her to keep quiet.'

Too right he did.

'Look,' Isabelle said, 'it's not like he ever *did* anything to anyone, okay? I was just wanting to give him a warning and then when he died – when Sarah and Emma came back from the bush that night and said he'd been shot – I thought . . . Well, I thought it might have been something about the note. Like, a suicide or something, and it was all my fault.'

She was so young. Fifteen. His eldest son was only seven years off this age. Perceptive and innocent, that's what Isabelle was, and the combination seemed to fit anyone he'd ever known in the age bracket of fifteen to twenty-three. Out of the two qualities, Isabelle would lose the innocence first and it would make her safer, but with that came the arrival of the cynic and that in turn would make her less free.

'I'd like you to make a statement about this down at the station, please, Isabelle. You could bring your mother with you.'

She narrowed her eyes.

'Or not,' he stumbled. 'Just if it makes you feel more comfortable.'

'Okay.' Isabelle peered at something on her hand, picked at it. 'We're thinking of selling up, did you know? The farm's not going too well and with Georgia at uni, well – Mum thought it might be good to move back near her parents in the Adelaide Hills.'

The painting work at Jacqueline's house: they were getting ready to sell. The idea to move had merit; the Mattesons would get good money for their land, no matter how badly the farm was going. A smaller house on a manageable block, closer to city life: he could see it, but even so it stung, more so after the decline of the yabby invitation.

'Come down to the station soon, Isabelle,' Mark said by way of goodbye. 'We'll need to get that statement.'

Back at the station, and to his relief, Barrie had left to join Bithick with the drones in Stone Town. Less welcome was the fact that Clare had arrived. From the front window, Mark saw her hunched over the screen, pale and haggard. Luke Howsley's accident had rattled her, big time. The young man was around the same age as her wayward son Jackson. That, and the deadline bearing down on her when she must tell her seniors that she, not Finn Turner, was the snitch – the stress manifested physically, made her older than she was.

He walked into the office, sitting down on a chair beside the wall. 'How are you?'

Clare turned to him and he almost recoiled. She'd been crying hard; her face was a broad salt-lake, eyelids red and worn. She grabbed a tissue and dabbed at her face. 'Finn rang, he'll be here soon.'

'Yeah?' He looked to her desk, clear of papers now, and

her laptop screen, which showed an image of a cat sitting in a cup.

'Do you think that kid'll be okay?'

'Luke? I hope so. He's improving.'

'God, I'd love a smoke right now.' In the streaky-window light, Clare's face was one of defeat. 'I mean, what harm would it really do?'

'Cancer?'

Clare toyed with a heavy bracelet on her wrist, then made a dismissive motion with her hands. 'I know you don't trust me with the investigation any more,' she said. 'But I wanted to tell you something I noticed when I first looked at Natalie's surveillance files.'

'I'm not sure—'

'This was back in Adelaide, when I went over the first couple of files – no more. After the announcement of the ping, I made sure I got sent up here because, well, you know – I'd made a deal with the dark side,' Clare said bitterly. 'We were hoping to look over the rest of the recordings this week, haven't had time before this.'

'Finn and I are planning to look over them today.' They'd talked about it on the phone.

'You should.'

'What did you notice in the ones you saw?'

'Charlene Scopelliti liked to go to the hairdresser, *a lot*.'

Mark hesitated, unsure of whether to encourage her further.

'She goes there to get it washed. Not cut, not styled – washed!' Clare tried to rally. 'Every second day, she's there.'

'What a life.' Mark wondered why Clare was bothering with this.

'Be thankful you didn't have to look through the early ones where Charlene was filming some advertisement for herbal medicine outside Chemist Warehouse.'

'Okay . . .'

'The thing is,' Clare said, 'when I looked over the recordings, the ones in particular when she's at the hairdresser's – I think that Natalie put a listening device there.'

'What? Was there a warrant for audio?' His mind raced.

'No.'

Mark made a whistling sound through his teeth. If what Clare suspected was true, then Natalie had taken a serious risk.

'No evidence, just my initial thoughts based on what I saw in that one file. I was going to check it out more closely when I was up here. And' – Clare held up her hand – 'I'm going to be honest with you here, I did tell the Scopellitis. I needed to give them something, and even though it wasn't confirmed, I told them. I know it was wrong. I wanted to tell you, I . . .'

A ripple of anxiety washed over Mark. What would the suggestion of an audio tap mean to the Scopellitis?

'I think you should go home, Clare.'

'Please, please give me something to do here. Something separate from the Scopellitis and Nat. Please, Mark.'

They were under the pump, Mark admitted to himself. Perhaps there was something Clare could do.

'The vehicle that hit Luke Howsley, maybe see if anyone in Stone Town or the farms along the road remembers a car driving past, damaged, yesterday afternoon. Put the word out again for dashcam footage.'

Clare turned away. Mark knew she felt sidelined, but what did she expect? One more day and he'd tell the seniors what he knew.

When she'd left the room, Mark set up the surveillance recordings, put Natalie's digital files in order, and made a mug of tea. Finn arrived as he was rifling through the biscuit tin in the kitchen. Only stale ones left. Who'd eaten all the Monte Carlos? Had he?

After a debrief on Sleeth, Barrie and Bithick, and a general chit-chat about the weather, the men settled down to watch the recordings.

'Not exactly Village Cinemas Gold Class, but here we are,' Mark said, shifting in his seat.

'I mainly stream movies,' Finn said flatly.

'You wouldn't stream this one.' Mark nodded at the screen where Charlene had popped up, walking down the street, stopping to pat a dog, peering in a shop window. 'Although it is a lot like *Pretty Woman*.'

'I have no idea what you're talking about,' Finn said.

The men watched the recordings. Hours of them. Charlene at the hairdresser, Charlene shopping, Charlene on her way to the gym, Charlene on the phone, Charlene having lunch with girlfriends.

'Ever think we're in the wrong job?' Mark asked as they stopped for lunch.

Charlene out for drinks, Charlene back at the hairdresser's — one day with blonde hair, two days later, dark again. Charlene popping into a white building with a gold plate indicating Cosmetic Surgery. Charlene coming out with a bandage on her nose.

An update from Luke Howsley's mother: *Stable. Responding to stimuli.*

From the angle of the camera shots, it was obvious that Natalie Whitsed had chosen a variety of ways to keep tabs on Mrs Scopelliti. A car window, from a street corner, a chair by a table near Charlene. She was thorough in her work. The camera rarely wavered; Natalie never took a break.

Charlene at the hairdresser's again. Charlene getting her hair washed, Charlene coming out with shiny, bouncy locks. It seemed excessive. Mark mostly washed his hair with soap.

In the salon, a rare break: the camera stopped for a second, then settled – it had been placed or was resting on something. They could see the back of Natalie Whitsed walk into the hairdresser's and ask something at the desk, lean on it, then come out again, giving a very small smile at her camera.

'Clare mentioned this,' Mark said with growing excitement. 'What does that look like to you?' He wanted a second opinion.

They replayed it again, watched Natalie at the counter, leaning over it, resting her hand under the front lid, roughing her blonde hair up, holding a strand of it out as if seeking consultation.

They watched again.

'She's put something there!' Finn exclaimed. 'A listening device, under the counter. Holy, holy shit.'

It was a good theory, it fitted with what they saw, but

why would Natalie Whitsed do that when she was only told to survey Charlene's actions? And where were the records of the audio?

Finn Turner said that Natalie was a great cop. Great cops, Mark knew, were different from good cops. Great cops took risks, backed themselves. It could go either way, but they trusted their instincts. On television, in shows like *CSI* and *Law and Order*, the cops often took matters into their own hands and it mostly paid off. In real life, that was rare. But sometimes it did. Pay off.

Newly energised, Finn and Mark moved on to the other files, ones not seen by Clare, or anyone else to their knowledge.

In one recording, less than a week after the suspected listening device plant, Charlene got in her red Porsche and drove out of town. Natalie followed in her own car, filming again when they reached an outer suburb in East Adelaide. Here, Charlene exited the car, folder in hand, and walked up a line of seedy shops to a building lit with gaudy green lights. Out the front, two bouncers stood, huge in black, barely nodding as she looked side to side before walking in. Natalie panned the camera up so the name of the place was visible.

The Crazy Cactus.

There was a line-up of men snaking the entrance. Some ashamed to be there, married probably, on their lunchbreak. Others looked bored or nervous. One, near the front of the line, was jabbing into his phone, and when he glanced up, Mark saw with a jolt that it was Aidan Sleeth.

'Hang on!' Finn had seen it at the same time.

Aidan Sleeth, lining up, looking into the doorway of the Crazy Cactus, getting his wallet out, walking in. Finn and Mark stared at each other.

'His offices are in East Adelaide,' Finn conceded. 'Probably only a block or two away.'

They confirmed it on Google Maps: it was a twenty-minute walk from Aidan Sleeth's East Adelaide office to the Crazy Cactus, owned by Tony Scopelliti.

Another link.

Mark stepped out of the main office and into his own space, taking out his phone. Angelo answered on the second dial and Mark told him the news: Aidan Sleeth frequented the Crazy Cactus. He'd been there at least once in the weeks before he was shot in the Stone Town bush. A car, registered to Shane Spike, had been seen cruising around town. Natalie's own car was found at Yielder's Track, right by Sleeth's house, the night she disappeared. That put a definite link between the two cases.

'We also think Natalie may have put a listening device in the hairdresser's that Charlene goes to.'

There was a groan born of weariness and frustration from the other end of the line. Mark heard someone open a door, ask Angelo something, him barking at them to get out.

'Heard there was a hit and run up your way, could the Scopellitis be involved in that too?'

'I thought it looked like an accident. But maybe.'

'Fuck that family!' Angelo exploded. 'We bring in Charlene or Shane or any of their stooges and they come up clean. They don't speak to us.'

'Ever tried the big man himself?'

'Tony? Only every other day. "The Hook" doesn't talk to cops. He's the master of "no comment" bullshit.'

No comment, the worst thing you could ever say to an investigating cop. *Fuck off, pig* was *bless you* in comparison.

The two men fell into silence. 'You reckon she's alive?' Mark asked eventually.

'Not a chance. She'll be in some hole somewhere, rag in her mouth, bullet to her brain. I'm even more sure of that now you've told me about the listening device. No doubt Whitsed knew some serious shit. What the hell was Charlene talking about to her hairdresser?'

Mark's hairdresser was the local barber, who, for $25, would not only cut Mark's hair but also give him a precise summation of Port's chances in the upcoming season. It was ten minutes of valid information complete with a short back and sides.

'Search me. Didn't look like there was much talking at all. Just her going in there, brief chit-chat and over to the basins, then the blow dry.'

'I could do with a blow dry.'

'Couldn't we all.'

A silence. Glum.

'Heard anything up there, in your offices?'

Mark knew what Angelo was implying. 'Finn's okay. I've heard nothing to make me think otherwise.'

Angelo grunted in response. The man never wrote anything down; it was all in his head. Filed away, case after case over the years. 'You need anything?'

'Some assistance would be good. Now that there's this new information, we'll need more help. Barrie and Bithick are on the search of Stone Town, Finn and I are up to our necks in the rest. Clare too.' Mark didn't add that she'd soon, in all likelihood, be retired in disgrace from the force. 'Point is, now with this hit and run, it would be good to have an extra hand.'

'See what I can do.'

'Someone good, Angelo, someone we can trust.'

'Leave it to me.'

'Press will be onto us soon, if not already,' Mark said.

'Hold them off, I'll do my best down here with them too.'

'Is there anything else I should know?' Mark asked.

'Not that I can think of. I'll check with Internal Investigations, maybe even the Feds – see if there's anything we're not being told about Charlene's activities.'

After brief goodbyes, the men hung up.

The afternoon passed. Statements to take on the hit and run, another break-in at the church, two more Stat Decs to sign. Just after 5 pm, Mark walked into his little office, sat down and rested his head on the table. Images of the drones now flying above Stone Town sprang to his mind: digital eyes of the sky, police drones used thermal imaging and could continue into the night. Their vision sensed body heat, people buried under rubble or hidden in dense canopy. Police drones, Mark knew, were capable of detecting the slightest of movements, a chest cavity rising, a weak gesture of the arm.

Drones had their limits, of course. If Natalie was dead in the bush she could register to the machine flying above in the night as a fallen log, nothing more than nature's detritus.

Mark heard footsteps in the hall, the door to the kitchen slam.

What he wouldn't give for ten minutes' sleep right now, a tiny nap just to . . .

A sharp knock at the door and he raised his head, bleary and disorientated. 'Did I fall asleep?' he asked.

Finn looked at him with amusement. 'Only for ten. You often take a nanna nap?'

Mark looked around for his drink bottle, took a slug. 'I was meditating,' he said. 'Levitating, actually.'

'Levitate home,' Finn replied. 'You look like shit.'

CHAPTER 35

Football training. Luke's words, *We've asked all the old blokes to rock up.*

Despite the initial reluctance, something called him: loneliness, loyalty or the need for connection? Years after he'd given up the game for good, Mark found himself pulling on the boots again. Cinderella and her slipper: he felt it, a small piece of the magic as he tied up the laces.

The old blokes *were* there, sitting on the benches: Dennis, Squirrel and a man named Frank. Mark joined them. Four men in their fifties, Gen-Xers, trying to recapture some of their glory days. The young players arrived in groups as they always did. Sorrowful and angry and loyal. Friends and team-mates of Luke Howsley, not sure yet how to manage their thoughts. The night could end in tears, Mark thought. Or violence.

We few, we merry few, we band of brothers.

The coach, Mack Allen, spoke, and the boys were all ears:

'What happened to Howza was a fucken disgrace. Anyone knows anything, straight to the cops.' Heads turned to Mark, turned back again to Allen, spitting fury and magnificence in his pre-training speech. 'I talked with his mum, she says he's on the mend, but still in the coma. We're thinking of you, Howza.' He turned his gaze up to the ceiling and all eyes followed, noting the cracks, the asbestos, the filth. Howza wasn't up there, not yet. The coach urged them to go hard, and Mark was pleased for the wisdom. Young men needed this. They needed the release of energy and burning emotion, and they welcomed it too. The older blokes were less circumspect. The coach left them to their own devices. Frank practised kicking; he couldn't run – 'the hammy'. The others understood. 'Hammy' meant all manner of injuries, including being unfit and unwilling. Everyone did a hammy at some stage. No judgement.

They jogged around the oval, Dennis in the lead, Squirrel and Mark behind and wide of him in a holy trinity of pain and show. It had always been thus: Dennis the best player by far, best in the league, while Squirrel and Mark did their utmost to accommodate and support him in play. Even now, running behind him, Mark could glimpse their old selves. Dennis handsome and restless – a natural talent; Squirrel the small explosion of energy; and Mark following along, doing his best, mostly succeeding. So it had been all his life.

As his legs pounded the green grass of the oval, in time *almost* with his friends, Mark thought about what was coming in the cases of Whitsed and Sleeth, and now Howsley. All were tied together somehow, the line between metro and rural growing closer. Like the subdivisions that edged their way along the highway, city crime was reaching here. The Scopellitis were in town.

But was rural life always so bucolic? Squirrel spat to the side of him and Mark dodged. No, it wasn't – and the thought came to him: the bush equals the past. *Romantic fancy.* Stone Town and Booralama were growing, changing. The co-op would sell or shrink, the acacias and gums would be chopped.

'Get a move on, you fat old buggers!' the coach shouted at them.

Mark's breath grew ragged. Dennis sailed ahead.

After training there were drinks at the clubrooms before the pub. Frank bailed after two stubbies; his wife had a roast on. Squirrel's partner Donna, a champion jockey, joined them. In Year 10, Donna had punched a girl in the face for calling Squirrel a Ranga. The two had been together ever since.

On to the pub, and there was an energy in the Royal, frantic and dangerous. Music was thumping, Dire Straits boomed. The crowd was big for a Thursday night. Mark bought more beers for Dennis, Squirrel, Donna and himself. The Royal became a squeezebox, heaving in and out, the smell of stale beer, soggy carpet and sweat. He was finding it difficult to carry on a conversation, but didn't say no when Squirrel asked him if he wanted another drink. This was them – Generation X. *Say what you will about us,* Mark thought, *our mute acceptance at being shoved between showy Boomer parents and the outspoken ones after, but the men and women of Gen X are experts in the liquid field.* More drinks. Beer, a bourbon. More beer.

In his foggy haze, Mark saw Dennis sitting on a couch, arms spread wide over the headrest, two young women and a recent divorcee staring up at him like a god. Squirrel was dancing with Donna, their hands in each other's back jeans pockets like some poorly cast teen movie, and the old coach was one shot away from punchy.

As for Mark, he was standing in the corner, holding his Coopers Pale Ale like a chalice, trying not to think about the time.

The door burst open, and there was a huge roar as nurses and doctors filled the room, bursting onto the dance floor and lighting up the bar. *Who doesn't love a nurse?* Mark thought fondly as he watched them dance to 'Walking on Sunshine'. A warm sensation rushed through him and he emptied his beer. Good times.

'Bear Grylls, it's really you!' A woman was dancing towards him, wine glass aloft, oblivious to anyone in her path. 'Actually,' she said with delight, 'you're more like Steve Irwin. A good ol' Aussie wildlife wrangler.'

It was the doctor who'd treated him. Better than those mousy-faced whingers from that show that Kelly used to like, *Grey's Anatomy*.

'Not Bear Grylls *or* Steve Irwin – I'm Jason Bourne,' he reminded her. 'Besides, Steve Irwin died.' It seemed important to tell her.

'Oh yes,' she said, stumbling the final steps towards him and spilling the rest of her wine. 'That was really sad.' She stood stock still, arms down by her side, forlorn.

'Did you know Steve Irwin?' he asked.

'No,' she said. 'But I used to like his show. I used to really, really, really like it. And now he's dead!' She took two, three steps sidewards and nearly fell into Donna and Squirrel, who were returning from the dance floor.

'Steady, love!' Squirrel said, catching her. 'You okay?'

'Yes.' She gave him a wide gummy smile and then turned to Donna, beaming. 'I'm okay.'

Donna smiled back at the doctor and, taking her elbow, led her gently to a seat by the window. The doctor let herself be managed, sat down promptly and then held her hand up to Mark.

'Sit with me, Steve!' she said. 'I'm so lonely down here.'

Mark sat down and the two of them watched the dance floor, where a group of people now formed a wide circle and clapped, while one person took turns to perform on the inside.

'You're very handsome,' the doctor whispered, hot in his ear.

Mark felt a surge of happiness break through his swirling synapses.

Squirrel brought them both a glass of water, and Donna discreetly took their drinks away.

The senior assistant coach shouted for Icehouse and a minute later the dancing circle was moving in uncertain rhythm to 'We Can Get Together'. At some urging, Dennis took centre stage, his lithe body elastic to the music, hips impressive in their snaking moves.

'Wow.' The doctor, like most women, stared open-mouthed.

Then Squirrel was in the circle doing a worm, next Donna did one too, someone else did the robot, and soon the circle collapsed and became a heaving mass.

Jimmy Barnes started up, his screeching voice a thousand cockies with strep throat, the coach got kicked out, and Mark was vaguely aware of Dennis leaving with the divorcee.

'Do you want a drink?' he asked The Doctor. If he had a moniker, so would she.

'Why don't we have it at your place?' she said, gazing up at him. 'I can't stand to see another worm.'

Mark blinked in surprise. The Royal was suddenly a miraculous place, full of majesty and promise. Someone waved to him wildly from the corner of the room, the editor of the local paper.

'Let's go,' he said, taking The Doctor's hand.

CHAPTER 36

When Mark woke in agony the next morning, the first thing he saw was a white arm lying prostrate across the sheet. His immediate thought was horror: an arm, chopped off and left by the Scopellitis. His second thought: relief that the arm was attached to a body, long and lean. And his third was: *I am never drinking again.*

Mark slid out of bed as carefully as he could and slunk into his bathroom. He turned the shower on, freezing, standing under it for a brief moment before stepping out. All the Brut in the world couldn't mask his unpleasant bodily smells, but he sprayed a good deal of it anyway. As he towelled himself, vague memories of the previous night began to surface: The Doctor back in his house, them dancing in the lounge room, smooching on the couch. Smooching was a better word than pashing for what they'd been doing. He was over fifty, after all, and what was she, forty? A wave of nausea hit him and he turned back into the bathroom. The Brut combined

with other, more unsavoury odours almost blew his head
off. If he lit a match in that room, it would be Chernobyl,
Mark 2. He opened every window he could.

The Doctor was not yet awake. Dressing as quietly as he
could, he looked at her pale face and yellow hair streaming over
the pillow. Had she arranged it so? It was a delicate fan. Her
mouth opened and shut like a little goldfish. He hadn't slept
with her the whole night. He'd only come into the bedroom
at four or five am when the couch became unbearable. Even
then he'd barely acknowledged her presence as he collapsed,
confused and already hungover, onto the mattress beside her.

He didn't know her name. All night, he'd been calling her
'The Doctor'. She'd been calling him Steve since the pub. An
unfair equivalence, but there you go.

If Steve Irwin was in his place, he'd probably leave right
now and catch a fish with his bare hands before cooking it
for her over hot coals. He'd say, 'Crikey, love, I got you a
trout and it's a bewdy.'

What were the protocols in such a situation? The last
time he'd been in one like this, it had been Kelly, a year
before they'd married.

Mark found a piece of paper and wrote a note on it for
The Doctor to find if she woke up before he returned.

*Gone for a run, be back soon. Hope you are feeling OK. I feel
like absolute crap.*

He read the note and tore it up. She might read it and
think he regretted the night. Tried again:

*Hope you are feeling OK. I've gone for a run but will be
back soon. Bye.*

It wasn't Tolstoy, but it would do.

Outside, a spiteful wind was blowing, unpleasantly warm. His stomach churned. He'd lied when he'd written that he was going for a run. It was always going to be a walk today. He needed to wake up, get some air into his foggy brain. A low skein of mist fell across the river. It was higher again today: the rains up north meant that now the current was flowing strong, rising by the hour. Small brown waves lapped at the edges of the footpath, dangerous and steely cold. Mark thought about kneeling down, sticking his head into it, giving some respite to his heated, groggy brain – but then he worried he might vomit with the effort. *That*, he thought again, *was the last drinking session I will ever have. I swear it. I'm taking the pledge.*

Taking the pledge, it was something his mother and her friends used to say following too many wines after tennis, or at barbecues at someone's farm. He didn't know what it meant exactly, but he was taking it. By God he was.

On the path in front of him, a little dog was barking at a duck swimming close to the bank. The duck was saying, *Ha ha, I'm a duck and you can't get me,* when the little dog jumped in after it.

Mark looked around; no owner in sight. The dog paddled furiously, ears drooping into the water. Its head bobbed under, then up again.

Then he saw, coming down from the bank, a man in black pants and jacket. Mark recognised him immediately: the man speaking Italian into the phone, the suspected Scopelliti stooge.

Although it killed him, setting off a jazz band in his brain, Mark began to run and, as he did, he saw the man take off his jacket, shoes and pants, and wade into the water.

'Don't!' he called out ineffectually. '*Stop!*'

But the man didn't hear and now he was waist-deep and had got hold of the struggling dog, which promptly bit him on the forearm. The man howled and threw the dog back into the shallows, where it slunk up the riverbank.

The man looked at his arm and then, startled, at Mark, who was by now almost at his level on the bank. An old fence post floated past, grazing the man on the side.

In an instant, the man was pulled under water and Mark thought, even as he was taking his own shoes off, of the submerged wires connected to the post, snarled fencing discarded by some farmer long ago. Mark didn't have his phone. He looked around again – no one to call for help. Where was the dog's owner? Where were Lee and Roxie when he needed them?

The man emerged, shocked and bleeding ten metres down the river, his face stricken with fear. His feeble attempts to swim to the edge were useless; he wasn't going to make it. Mark dived in, shallow – arms out straight, feeling for debris. In a moment, he was hurtled downstream, reaching out for the flailing man, kicking hard towards the bank.

The man grabbed him with two hands, put them hard on Mark's shoulders, and tried to haul himself up out of the water. He was a thrashing beast, wild with panic: 'Help! Help!'

Mark was pushed under, submerged in the brown, swirling water, unable to rise as the man dug in hard. Mark kicked at him, stabbed his arms out, reaching for the man's torso, punching him with little effect. His ears rang with pressure, his lungs screamed, screamed. Something swirled past him and hit him in the leg. It got the other man too and, in shock or a growing weakness, Mark was freed of his clutch.

He was up to the surface again, big gulping breaths. He saw a willow tree in front of them, bent low. With one hand Mark grabbed the man's underarm, and with the other he reached out for the willow that was now speeding towards them in the current. Missed it.

He and the man gave each other a brief look. Fear? Resignation? Mark saw a coffee cup race past and it made him unbearably sad. Wasn't your life supposed to flash by in instances such as this? Where were the images of his sons? His parents, his sister?

A coffee cup? *That's* what he got?

It was difficult to catch his breath. He couldn't tell where the sky, the bank and the river began and ended.

Another willow tree. 'Reach out!' he called with supreme effort to the man, and as the leafy rope approached they each held an arm up – grabbing it. Grabbing it and holding on and holding on, and Mark edging closer to where he could stand up and then pulling the man by his elbow closer.

In the shallows, they kneeled like worshippers, and then, crawling up to the bank, the two men lay panting, sodden and growing cold.

After some time, the big man turned on his side and held out a hand.

'Joe.'

His grip was firm, true.

'Mark.'

'Yes, I know. Mark Ariti.' Of course, Scopelliti's people would know everyone who was investigating. 'Thank you, Sergeant.'

Mark nodded, too exhausted to answer. Sun speared through the clouds, some warmth at last.

'You've been watching me,' Mark said, chest still heaving. 'Here, when I run, and in town.'

Joe didn't deny it.

'And in the bush, out at Stone Town, I saw you there, looking at me through binoculars.'

'That wasn't me,' Joe said. 'I've driven around there, but I never got out.' The man sounded offended at the thought that anyone would assume he'd set foot in such a place.

Mark frowned. His tired mind tried to reassemble thoughts and timelines. The grainy sand beneath him was wet and cold.

'You Greek?' Joe sat up and ran a hand through his thick black hair.

Mark didn't know what to say. 'Dad's side.'

'You're Greek. Same as us.'

Mark slowly stood up, his pants clinging to his thighs. 'You lot are Italian, aren't you?'

'Scopelliti,' Joe answered. 'It's Calabrian, but originally Greek. Way back. There's an island that we used to live on, all of us, hundreds of years ago – you too probably.'

The man spoke as if he and his ancestors were the same, as if they could shake hands right here, today, by this river.

'I could've died out there.' Joe pointed to the swirling brown water. 'You saved me and I won't forget it. Tony won't forget it, he's my cousin.'

Thoughts came to Mark of horses' heads in beds, of concrete overcoats, of offers he couldn't refuse. 'I don't need anything,' he said, fast.

'Everyone needs something.'

It was true. 'What are you doing in Booralama?'

Joe looked up the bank for his shoes and jacket. 'Same as you. Searching.'

'What work do you do for Tony Scopelliti?'

'I do every kind of work. Bouncing, driving, looking for people.'

'You think Natalie Whitsed's here?'

Joe's big head turned to face him. 'We saw her, watching Charlene at the Crazy Cactus. Your cop wasn't as discreet as she thought. She was good, but not that good. We'd see her huddled up in her car watching us, eating snacks, playing with the camera. A little thing. We called her "Birdy" as a code. "Birdy's back today, Birdy at ten o'clock." We didn't always have eyes on her, but at the club I saw her often enough.' Joe took off his shirt, wrung it out, twisting and twisting it for every last drop.

Someone was always watching. Even if you were the one with the camera, there were eyes all about. It was the sort of thing civil libertarians went on about. Especially the ones with something to hide.

'When we heard that her car was found here and that a man had been shot, we put two and two together – like you did.'

302

Bouncers stand for long times in the one spot, barely moving. They're trained to notice things like agitation and detect early signs of aggression. In the long hours of waiting, they'd notice a woman in a parked car, feigning sleep or attention to their phone.

'I think Natalie's dead.' Mark said it aloud for the first time. A pause. 'Why do you want to find her so badly?' he asked. 'What's she got on you?'

Joe gave a slow chuckle and raised his hand, moving his forefinger from side to side. 'You don't get to ask me that.'

'I can if it goes to court.'

'We'll wait till then, then.' The man was genial, too relieved to be alive to be angry.

They began walking slowly up the bank to where their remaining dry clothes were. A couple passed by whispering, startled at their drenched appearance, the offending small dog now on a leash.

'Morning,' Joe said, and they scurried away.

'Did you know Aidan Sleeth?' Mark asked.

'I knew *of* him mostly. He had a real estate office nearby. I saw him at the club sometimes. Never spoke to him.'

'Was he there much?'

'On and off. Never stayed long.'

The Crazy Cactus spread its spines to all corners of the state. It was owned by the Scopellitis, surveyed by Natalie Whitsed and regularly visited by Aidan Sleeth. A meeting with manager Shane Spike loomed.

'What about Jackson Rendell, young bloke – ever heard of him?'

Joe shook his head. 'There's a lot of young blokes working for us.'

The men reached the place where they'd flung off shoes, jackets and wallets. All remained untouched.

'Listen,' Joe said when they'd collected their things, 'it wasn't us who ran over that kid. It's just me up here and I wasn't out there that day. It's a bad business. I hope the kid survives.'

'Me too.'

'I'm this way.' Joe jerked his thumb over his head. 'You're that way, aren't you?'

Of course he knew.

'Thank you again, Mark.' Joe was solemn. 'I mean it, we won't forget this.'

The two men shook hands and walked in opposite directions; each feeling the brisk wind, the sharpness of mud and wattle, aware of their own blood pumping strong.

Alive, Mark thought, watching a flock of cockatoos screech across the sky. *Life.*

CHAPTER 37

A pillow, a bed, sheets. Natalie wakes and for a moment thinks she is dreaming. But no: the pillow is real, the bed is real, the sheets are real. Her broken forearm is cleanly bandaged and there's a plaster across her forehead. She's in different clothes, but her Chapstick is in one of the pockets. She feels it. Pity it's empty, her lips are cracked.

When she sits up, her head pounds violently and she's horrified to see the face of a wild thing staring at her, open-mouthed and impossibly pale. It's her, she realises, a reflection from the mirror on the wall at the end of the bed. She looks at her image. The squinting creature looks back, dark lines under her eyes, cheekbones like chicken wings poking out. She's aged ten years or more. I'm my mother, she thinks, and the thought does not provide comfort.

All that effort, those years of study and hard work and moving away, and she's come back to her roots; rough-faced, stringy-haired and wild. She lies back down and thinks that

305

despite the horror of her looks, there's a sort of comfort in it too.
Genetics is what helped get her out of the hole. Nature.
   Footsteps up the hall. She tenses.
   There's a greeting, a familiar voice. Nurture.

CHAPTER 38

Back at home, The Doctor was gone. But there was a note on his bed:

God, I feel like crap! See you soon.

No phone number. If he had time, he could analyse that note all day. Did it mean she regretted the night? But the 'soon' gave hope. 'See you soon' was not always said with any meaning. Was it just a way of signing off and out? It probably was. But then again, Mark considered, it could be worse. It could be 'Keep in touch'.

One good thing about almost drowning: his hangover was gone. Glass half full.

There was a shiny HiLux vehicle parked out the front of the station when Mark arrived. Had Finn cleaned his? It wasn't Clare's, she'd driven her own car up and walked most days to the station. A murmur of conversation filtered through the windows, steady and intense.

'Morning!' he called as he walked up the hall, opening the door to his old office.

'Where've you been?' Jagdeep said, looking at her watch. 'It's eight thirty-five and we've got a lot to do.'

Jagdeep's bright orange turban lifted the grey of the room. Buoyant, that's how Mark felt when he saw her leaning back in his old chair. Buoyant.

'Give me a break!' he said, grinning. 'I nearly drowned this morning.' The wonder of it, his life in grave danger twice in two days. The world seemed a brittle, beautiful place.

'Drowning, snake bites, hit and runs, murders in the bush – what is this town, Midsomer?' Jagdeep turned to Clare, who looked confused.

'More of a Summer Bay, without the beach and bikinis,' Mark said.

'Awwww, but there's Alf?'

'Don't come the raw prawn with me, you flamin' galah.' Mark set down his laptop and leaned against the wall, smiling.

'It's good to be back,' Jagdeep sighed. 'Professional colleagues and intelligent discourse. I've missed it.' She put her hands together in a gesture of prayer. 'Thank you, Angelo! Desk work in Adelaide was driving me crazy.'

The resistance Mark felt to the whole case and its growing complexities lessened as he listened to Jagdeep and Clare talk about the findings so far. Jagdeep was mostly up to speed on all things to do with Whitsed and Sleeth. What she didn't know already, Angelo would have told her. Jagdeep was the most capable person he knew. She would be, if the powers could see her potential, a top cop. The very best, alongside and above Angelo Conti.

He told them both about the morning's events.

'Did you believe him when he denied the hit and run?' Jagdeep asked.

'I did actually.'

'But it has to be them! It fits with everything,' Clare said. 'Did we check out his vehicle yet?'

'A friend of mine saw it late yesterday near Sleeth's offices. No damage to it.' The moment he'd heard, Mark put out the feelers. Squirrel was the first to get back to him.

'Doesn't mean anything. We don't know there's only that one car up here. Tony Scopelliti could have dozens of men sniffing around. We should go and question your man again, Joe. Bring him in.'

Jagdeep looked at Clare thoughtfully. There was an air of panic about the older woman.

'If it was an accident, then there's a chance the driver doesn't even *know* about the victim yet.'

'That's highly unlikely,' Clare said.

'But not impossible,' Mark countered.

The number of times he'd bumped into something on the road – a wombat, a rabbit, a hare – and not thought much of it till he saw a slightly bent fender. It could have been a child and he wouldn't have guessed.

'It's also possible,' Jag said, 'that the person who did it has already escaped across state lines knowing they caused a serious accident and not knowing a thing about Sleeth or Whitsed.'

The three police officers were silent, thinking.

'Now,' Jag said. 'To the recordings.'

Clare stood up, indicating her phone. 'I'll call traffic squad, see what they can tell me about the accident report.' She walked out of the room.

'Sounds good,' Mark said. 'Anyone for a cuppa?'

'No time for cuppas.' Jag fastened her turban, business-like. 'Now, let's open this thing up.'

It was pleasant to be sitting beside Jagdeep, conducting police work. Her clear head and intelligent observations provided new insight into material and her calm presence was welcome, especially after the previous twenty-four hours. If it wasn't for his hangover and lack of warm tea, he'd be almost happy.

Mark filled her in on what they'd seen in the videos so far, and they started them again on the point where Natalie entered the hairdresser's. Jagdeep watched a couple of times, taking notes on the layout of the salon, on Natalie's actions.

'I think Clare's first impression was right,' she said slowly. 'A listening device.'

They continued watching: Charlene at the gym, Charlene back at the cosmetic surgery, Charlene at a cafe, Charlene getting her hair done. Charlene at the Crazy Cactus again, once more looking sideways before she walked inside.

'What's she looking for?' Jagdeep said. 'It's not as if everyone doesn't know she owns the place.'

Mark shrugged, kept looking.

The day after Charlene's last visit to the Crazy Cactus, she visited the gym and then the hairdresser's again.

'Is her life Groundhog Day?' Mark asked. 'It's like a portal into rich woman hell.'

'Quiet.' Jagdeep held her hand up. 'Look. Look at her face.'

Mark couldn't see anything interesting about her face. It had been sculpted and shaved and filled and fitted so much he couldn't tell what she was like.

Jagdeep zoomed in. 'Charlene's afraid.'

The woman loomed large, taking up the whole screen. Both cops leaned in.

As she exited the hairdresser's, Charlene stood for a moment and looked each way. What Mark initially thought was Charlene flicking her new hairstyle in show-off style he now saw was a nervous action, smoothing down her locks, fidgety and ill at ease.

Jagdeep zoomed in closer. Now Charlene's face filled the frame. Pale, and breathing shallow through her barely open mouth – the signs were there that she was alert to her surroundings. Jagdeep zoomed out again as Charlene clenched her handbag tight and hurried to her car.

'I wonder . . .' Jagdeep murmured as she went back through the footage. 'Let's see . . .'

It was there, in all the videos from two weeks before Natalie had gone missing. The palpable fear in Charlene's expression, the slight trembling as she went about her daily routine.

'She knows she's being watched,' Mark said.

'Yeah – but that's not what's making her scared. Those mob wives are always being watched by cops. They expect it.'

It was true. During the Melbourne gangland war in the nineties, wives and girlfriends poked fun at the cops watching them. One woman ordered takeaway for the surveillance crew outside her house, delivering it to them herself. Another played loud rap music, asking into the supposed hidden camera, 'Do you prefer this or R'n'B, cos I can change it if you like?'

Mark stood up, stretched and went to get a cup of tea. Jagdeep declined. As he walked into the little kitchen, he realised Clare wasn't in the station. He looked at his phone; no message from her. Outside, the sky was a bleached blue, thin clouds hurrying, rain chasing. A magpie sat on the fence outside and looked at him. He looked back. In a staring contest, the bird won. He made a cup of tea, put two big teaspoons of sugar in it – it's what he did after a night out drinking. Normally, he would find a kebab somewhere, but Booralama wasn't known for its Turkish cuisine.

His thoughts turned to The Doctor, her wild dancing at the pub and then later, her falling asleep in his lounge room and him carrying her into his bed, her hair a waterfall, her limp body translucent and lovely in the night. He remembered looking at her there for a moment, before covering her up in his doona and stumbling back into the other room. There had been kissing in the lounge room, he knew that. There was some fumbling and drunken moves. Should he be embarrassed? Probably, but he didn't feel it today. A fringe benefit of growing old. Self-consciousness becomes a thing of the past.

His phone buzzed again. This time a message from Evie Renner:

Lola Sleeth has offered to sell land back for $300,000. Pre-sub-division cost, so good deal, but still too much. Birds for Bush trying to raise $$ to go halves. Fingers crossed!!!

He texted:

Keep us updated.

Finn arrived, and after introductions with Jagdeep told them his news.

'Word in Adelaide is, Shane Spike's not happy. Cops all over the club since Nat went missing. Spike says the girls are getting hassled for visas, Health and Safety all over the place, and one of his bouncers was picked up for speeding when he swears he was under the limit. Safe to say the cops won't receive a Christmas card from the Crazy Cactus staff this year. Spike's seriously dirty. My mate says he rang the Adelaide station in a rage.'

Because it's our way, Mark knew. Put pressure on a place, squeeze them till they have to talk.

'He mention Aidan Sleeth at all?'

'Cops down there asked him that. Spike said he saw Sleeth around as a punter and as someone who worked close by. Never caused any hassle that he knew of. CCTV footage puts him at the club on four separate occasions in the last three weeks.'

'Give me those dates, can you?'

Finn read them out and Mark wrote them down in his notebook.

'How's the hit and run investigation going?' Finn asked.

'Clare's on it.'

A pause.

Jagdeep was still watching the videos, rewinding, pausing, taking notes.

'Notice anything?' Mark asked.

'I think . . .' she said. 'I think there is something, or someone. But I need you both to check.'

'Go on.'

She rewound to outside Charlene's apartment, a swanky joint by the sea complete with security gates and a camera. Mark pushed his chair closer to the screen; Finn leaned over his shoulder.

'Watch,' Jagdeep said.

Charlene's car approached the gates. She slowed, the gates activated, and she drove in. The gates shut.

'What?' Mark said. 'I don't see anything.'

'Look again.'

Mark remembered the birdwatcher Gerald's words – advice on how to spot the little and important details, *'Go quietly,'* he'd said. *'Remain still.'* Without fidgeting, Mark focused on the screen. The car, the gates. But this time, he noticed that there were other people in the frame. He was still, still, and he saw: a woman, waiting for Charlene's car to pass before continuing along the path, and a man, a tall man, on his phone for the thirty seconds it took for Charlene to enter through her gates.

'Is that Sleeth?' Jag asked.

With a deep unfurling in his chest, Mark recalled images of the man, both alive and dead; Sleeth's height, the build. 'It could be.'

Jagdeep fast-forwarded to the Crazy Cactus again, where

they'd already seen Sleeth. This time, they focused on his actions in regards to Charlene Scopelitti. She walked into the club, first looking side to side, then a minute later he walked in. She walked out, him close after her and out of frame.

'Is it definitely Sleeth?' Jagdeep asked.

'It is in this shot, but the other one outside her house, I can't be sure.'

'I think it's him,' Finn said.

Mark checked the dates of Sleeth's attendance at the club that Finn had provided, then cross-referenced them with Charlene's visits to the club in the video. Each time, Sleeth appeared at the same time she did – loitering in the background, hanging on the sidelines, watching.

They kept looking through the recordings, searching now for Sleeth's presence.

Another image: at the gym, and there was the man who could be Sleeth walking past the frame.

The hairdresser's again, and this time, as Charlene walked in, Natalie zeroed in on the front window. The focus was Charlene, talking to someone inside, but now Jag and Mark noticed a reflection in the salon's glass. A figure, tall and slim, the image woozy at the edges in the sunlight and refracted frame. Charlene appeared at the glass of the window for a second, looking out. Natalie zoomed in on her face as the figure walked quickly by. Charlene's face was pale, tired, and for the first time she appeared to stare directly into Natalie Whitsed's lens, tilting her head after the retreating figure in a gesture that looked less like the flick of a vain woman's hair and more like a naked appeal for help.

They sat in stunned silence.

'She's asking for help,' Finn said. 'Or pointing us to him.'

Jagdeep didn't answer; instead she was whizzing through the videos again, coming to a halt at the last few minutes of Natalie's surveillance. This time, Natalie must have been walking past with the camera – it was up close near the gates of Scopelliti's apartment.

Charlene drives up in her car, the gates open, she drives in, the gates close. Now, Natalie – from either across the road or on the same side but to the left – angles the powerful lens towards Charlene getting out of the car and walking away. It seems innocuous, the footage totally innocent, until the camera lingers. And lingers.

Charlene has left the driveway. There's a slight blurring to the left of screen. It's just the bins: two large bins and two smaller ones. Has Natalie forgotten to turn off the camera? And then – a movement behind one of the garbage bins and there it is: someone crouching there. Someone hiding behind the bins inside Charlene Scopelliti's apartment block. The camera zooms in fast, zig-zagging across the screen. The crouching figure emerges, slowly. Straightens and looks around, furtive.

Jagdeep, Mark and Finn look at each other for a long moment.

The figure is definitely Aidan Sleeth.

'Aidan was stalking Charlene,' Mark said, 'and Natalie knew it.'

'Maybe it's not stalking,' Jagdeep asked. 'Maybe he knew something about her, about the Scopellitis, and was looking for evidence or something.'

'Stalking fits in with the character profile we're building up.' Mark opened his notebook and read to Jagdeep the notes he'd made after talking to Lola and Isabelle. *Obsessive, buying gifts, watching, love-bombing.*

'Love-bombing sounds like stalking to me,' Finn said. 'Bastard.'

Mark had an idea, punched a number into his phone, rang it in front of the others while they waited, impatient.

'Lola,' Mark said. 'How are you?'

Lola was fine. She was having a few drinks at the Royal that evening and would Mark like to join her? Mark declined politely, asked if she wouldn't mind looking at a photo he was about to text through, and could she tell him if it was the woman who she said Sleeth had been obsessed with a while ago? Lola, with some disappointment at the nature of the call, agreed.

Mark took a photo of Charlene from the screen, the one where she had blonde hair for a brief time, and sent it to Lola.

A message came back: *Yes.*

Mark showed them the text. Put his phone away with a flourish.

Jagdeep was lost in her thoughts for a moment. 'Still,' she said. 'It doesn't seem enough. So, Aidan was stalking Charlene. He gets killed for it? Maybe Natalie too?'

'Or' – the detectives began throwing theories around – 'Nat shoots Aidan for stalking, then escapes somehow?'

'Or the Scopellitis take Natalie, keep her hostage, bring her up here to flush out Sleeth, then kill Aidan for stalking Charlene, and then lose her.'

317

'Could be . . .' That theory was probably the closest. But not definitive; something, something was always missing.

There were footsteps up to the front door – Clare had returned. 'What's up?' she asked, looking at their faces. 'What have you found?'

Mark shuffled through his papers. 'Not much,' he said.

An awkward beat followed.

Mark's phone rang: the editor of the *Booralama Chronicle*.

For a moment Mark stared stupidly at his phone. Did the press know about Sleeth's stalking already?

'They're onto the drones,' Clare said, looking at him. 'The search team called me. They said the press have been calling them too – a couple of journos starting to show up near the place Sleeth died.'

Mark let his phone ring out.

The drones had found nothing of interest, Sergeant Barrie had told Clare. What they were searching for was signs of soil disturbance, clothing, personal items. Cadaver dogs were being brought up, that would ring a few local alarm bells. But so far, the bush had not given up its secrets.

Mark's phone rang again; the editor of the local rag once more. He picked it up this time, looking at the other two.

'Got anything for me yet, Mark?' Janice said. 'Tell me you have, and I'll love you forever.'

'Police don't take bribes, Janice.'

'Come on, Mark, you're a local – be only fair to let me know what you've found.'

'Wheedling won't help.' Mark liked the word wheedling. He resolved to use it more.

'A statement then. In response to the growing task force of law enforcement and the use of drones in the Stone Town bush.'

'How's this for you? "*In response to a possible new line of inquiry, additional law enforcement personnel and equipment have been deployed to the Stone Town region in the hope of securing information about the death of local man Aidan Sleeth.*"'

There was a pause as Janice transcribed his words. 'Anything to say on the missing policewoman Natalie Whitsed?' The journo's voice was coy. She had been two years above him at school. Rumour had it that she'd blitzed the Year 12 English exam because she had wheedled – *yes, wheedled* – the main essay question out of the principal.

'No comment,' he said and hung up the phone.

They sat for a moment in silence, each preoccupied by different aspects of the case.

'Stone Town gun checks came back too,' Clare said, coughing. 'I forgot to tell you. All three clear in terms of licensing, two with signs of recent discharge: the co-op bloke, John Renner said he'd shot at a fox, Jacqueline Matteson fired twice into the air to scare cockatoos away from her berries. Sleeth's was obviously clean.'

'All valid reasons.' People shot guns all the time in the country: foxes, dying animals, rabbits, cockatoos, kangaroos, trespassers. It didn't mean they killed anyone.

'Yeah, it seems so.'

Clare's face was even more drawn than before. Her hair was pushed back from her face in a tight ponytail, flushed skin taut as if she'd been tortured on a rack. In a few hours she'd be either sacked or demoted.

'Why don't you head home, Clare?' Mark said. 'You look like you could use a break.' *Get on the phone to your superiors while you're at it*, he thought. *Fess up and spare us all.*

She smiled weakly, and he hoped she wouldn't begin crying again. She didn't. Instead, she began packing up her things.

'You'll be back later though, won't you?' Jagdeep, Mark knew, couldn't fathom an instance, save death or serious injury, where someone would choose to leave work in the middle of a serious case.

'Probably.' Clare's eyes were downcast and she muttered something about collecting her other things that afternoon or the next day.

When Clare left, when it was just the two of them, Jagdeep puzzled at Clare's behaviour. 'Is she stressed or something?'

'Personal stuff.'

'Why's she so fixated on the Scopellitis being the ones who ran over Luke Howsley?'

Mark shrugged. Clare had numerous reasons to be suspicious of the crime family, but he didn't voice them now. Instead, Mark suggested lunch at the Fat Bean.

At the cafe, Dennis greeted Jagdeep politely before turning to Mark with a knowing smile. 'Can I get you a Bloody Mary, Reets?'

'Just a coffee, Den.'

What Mark craved was a souva, lamb with garlic sauce and a Coke, or two Cokes. The night before and the morning's events were catching up with him and his heart raced. It was unpleasant. *I'm too old for this*, Mark thought, remembering the dancing and the drinks and the feverish kissing, and then the cold hardness of the river bearing him down.

Jagdeep, in contrast, had never looked better. Reading the menu with interest, she appeared pleased with everything she saw and gave a small jump from her seat when she read 'Paneer Tikka'.

'I'll have a serving of this, please,' she said to Dennis. 'It's one of my favourites.'

Dennis ran a hand through his mane. 'Mine too.'

Mark left the two of them talking cuisine while he checked his phone. Another text from Luke Howsley's mother: *Luke awake. V relieved and happy.*

Mark wanted to ask her whether the young man was up to talking to police. If Luke could identify the car that ran him over, they'd have an excellent chance of finding the driver.

Great news, he texted back. *Is he communicating with you?*

A little, came the response. *Doctors want him to rest.*

Soon, soon.

Dennis had wandered to the back with their orders and Jagdeep was looking out the window, her eyes closed against the warm sunlight.

In moving to Cutters End for six months, Jagdeep had taken a secondment from the city in the hope of bolstering her CV. Over a year later and she was still Senior Constable Jagdeep Kaur, working in the Adelaide station on small jobs, relegated to the desk. Her career, unlike others in her position, had stalled. She was newly married, pregnant, mortgaged to the hilt and frustrated by her job. This transfer to Booralama maybe felt like a break for her. It felt like one for him. *Thank you, Angelo.* His old colleague knew how much he respected and enjoyed working with her.

As if she could hear his thoughts, Jag opened her eyes and turned to him. 'It's so nice and quiet here; the river, the streets, the trees.'

Mark squared his shoulders and felt a sense of pride in his old hometown. 'It's not too shabby.'

'How are you going, Mark, living back here?'

It was the first time anyone had asked him outright. How he was: single, living in Booralama in his childhood home, his mother dead, his boys far away.

'Can't complain.' The old refrain, defensive and inadequate.

A beat followed. Jagdeep looked at him, frank. 'I was seventeen when my mother died. It was the most terrible thing that had ever happened to me. It was like a piece of me, a really significant chunk, was gone. And it is, forever. You don't get it back.'

Mark felt it, the void that appeared after his mother's death. It made him hollow, this chasm of grief. He could shout into it, rail at it – but his words would echo back. Helen was everywhere and nowhere. Everywhere and nowhere.

And still, he had not cried.

Dennis brought his coffee to him and patted him on the shoulder for no good reason. Had Dennis heard Jagdeep's words? Maybe. Either way, it was the sort of thing Dennis did. Mark took a sip of his drink, not trusting himself to speak.

'Anyway,' Jagdeep said, 'I'm glad to be here.'

He breathed out. 'It's good to see you, Jag.'

They smiled, two cops from different backgrounds who liked each other, a difficult case behind them, one more to follow up. Paneer Tikka to come, music at the Fat Bean. Steady work. The simple things.

Jagdeep's food came out, warm and colourful. She motioned for Mark to share it but he shook his head, instead enjoying watching his friend as she ate, praising Dennis in between mouthfuls, reminding the Fat Bean owner of other Punjabi dishes he could try.

Dennis leaned against the bar taking notes, an eager kid again, ready to learn.

'That,' Jagdeep said when she was finished, 'was very good. Even my aunts would approve.'

'They would?' Mark was doubtful. He imagined them as he always had, old ladies in grand saris, haughty and displeased.

'Maybe not the youngest one.'

Mark's phone buzzed: the officious bloke from IT.

'We've confirmed those images on the encrypted file from Aidan Sleeth's computer.'

'You said they were photos,' Mark said, impatient.

'Yes, we had to receive confirmation on sending them through to you – privacy issues. There are official channels to pass through before we can share.'

I'll pass through the gates of hell before long.

'Can you send them now, please?'

'Sending now.' The IT man was cool.

Mark held out his phone, showed it to Jagdeep.

'The photos on Sleeth's file,' he explained. 'They're finally sending them through.'

A series of beeps followed and over twenty images popped up.

Half were of Charlene Scopelliti: outside her house, walking in a park, sitting on a bench, talking with friends.

'Stalker,' Jagdeep said. 'Confirmed.'

The other photos were taken weeks earlier than the Charlene ones. A pretty girl outside the Booralama ice cream place, the same girl eating an apple, the girl talking on her phone, getting into her car, leaning against a tree, coming out of the IGA. More alarming, photos of the girl in Adelaide, standing out the front of what Mark recognised to be the university village apartments, another of her holding a bunch of flowers, her expression bemused.

The girl was Georgia Matteson. *Flowers, sent by Sleeth.*

Mark knew he should have been prepared for this after his conversation with Isabelle – but still, the images unnerved. The frankness in Georgia's expression showed absolutely no awareness that she was being followed.

Back at the station, Finn met them on the front porch. 'Shane Spike is going ballistic!' he said with real enthusiasm. 'Cops about to shut the Crazy Cactus, that other strip joint the Scopellitis own, plus that car-wash place, Soak City, that I didn't even know they had a stake in. Keeps saying he knows nothing.'

It wasn't Spike the cops were after though, they all knew that. Spike wasn't the keeper of secrets.

'And still,' Mark said, recalling Angelo's words, 'Tony Scopelliti won't talk.'

'Funny you say that,' Finn replied. 'Shane Spike says The Hook might finally be open to a chat.'

'Yeah?' This was good. If they could find out what information Natalie had on the crime family, even get a hint of it, it might assist in all sorts of cases; drugs, extortion, bikie gang info, the general shitty shit that goes alongside strip clubs. And closer to home, they could find out more about Sleeth and his dealings at the Cactus Club.

'Spike says the big man will talk, but only to you.'

A stunned pause. 'What?'

'He's asked for you,' Finn replied. 'Tony Scopelliti says he'll only talk to Sergeant Mark Ariti from Booralama.'

CHAPTER 39

Twenty minutes later Angelo confirmed it. In wonder, the Assistant Commissioner listened to how Mark had saved Tony's cousin Joe from drowning in the river that very morning.

'Well, you've got their trust now,' Angelo said. 'In saving his cousin, you've become someone Tony Scopelliti values.'

That gave Mark no special comfort. 'So, what, they're finally fed up with the cops swarming over their businesses?'

'It wasn't only that they wanted the heat taken off their everyday dealings. We think Natalie might have real evidence on them. Evidence that could bring them and significant others down in a big way.'

'Like what? Didn't you go over everything?'

'I spoke with Internal Investigations again, put the pressure on.'

Mark wondered briefly at the nature of the pressure. Angelo had sway; he knew people, *things about* people. In the man's head existed a catalogue of other people's secret shames and desires. Angelo Conti didn't need to bash anyone senseless in a ring to make his power known. There were other, more subtle and far more effective ways he did that.

'And?'

'The footage Natalie took inside the hairdresser's – when Charlene's under that blow dryer thing or getting her hair washed, there's usually a woman next to her getting the same thing done. Not always the *same* woman, but someone there nonetheless whose place of work has Internals just a bit excited.'

Mark waited.

'The state government's planning division. The two women getting their hair done next to Charlene Scopelliti at least three times a week all report to the Planning Minister. And there's some serious movement going on in that office, as you'd have seen in the press. All sorts of controversial deals underway, big money involved. Bet you thought they were just a bunch of rich women looking for idle ways to spend their time?'

He did. When he was watching, Mark had thought Charlene and the women who appeared alongside her led vacuous lives. It never occurred to him that under the hair dryers, land was being released, subdivisions approved, rezoning carried out and heritage overlays discarded. Again he was reminded, the new gold rush was a land rush.

'We want you to see him, Mark. Today.'

There was a sudden stab of fear deep in Mark's stomach. Morburn Prison, its reputation for menace and corruption.

People who lived nearby said it radiated a kind of sickness and now, in the Booralama station, Mark could imagine that was true. Serial killers, notorious rapists, paedophiles, armed robbers and terrorists called Morburn home. And what a home! Three acres of flat land with a twenty-metre wall and barbed wire in place of a picket fence. It had two hundred wardens equipped with tasers and batons and a deep hatred for the 1500 men whose crimes were the nightmares of everyday people across the world. Morburn.

'Get you to leave now, Mark, if that's okay.' Angelo's tone made it clear there was no other option.

'What do you want me to find out?'

'Just listen. Nothing else, make no promises. You're the first person he's spoken to outside the Scopelliti business. You don't know how important this could be.'

When the call ended, Mark rubbed his eyes, and wished for nothing more than to go home and fall asleep on his couch. While Jagdeep bustled about, downloading the official letter from Angelo to the Morburn Prison governor, arranging the visit and stipulating the terms (a non-contact visitor room, thirty minutes max, two guards in attendance, non-disclosure forms signed), Mark looked over the other police work he still had to do, unrelated to Sleeth (reschedule school visit, talk to a Mr Jakes about his stolen bike, connect an older homeless woman accused of stealing with care services), then made himself a strong coffee. No magpie arrived to join in a staring contest; the sky was a pale blue.

There was a sock lying on the concrete in the back yard though. A long, grey woollen sock with the heel bitten out.

Mark contemplated it. He imagined the foot that wore the sock as a pale and old thing, floppy with disuse, the toenails yellow and bent. He sculled half the coffee before pouring the rest down the drain. Usually, he washed and dried his mug. Today, he just didn't feel up to it.

CHAPTER 40

It was only thirty minutes into his drive, north and then east, along the Barrier Highway, that Mark remembered his boys were arriving that evening. Cursing the day he'd jumped in the river to rescue a Scopelliti, he called Jagdeep, who, in a calm and matter-of-fact tone, said that she'd meet Kelly at the halfway point and pick them up for him.

Mark tried calling Clare, to see if she'd contacted their seniors yet, but got no answer.

The Barrier stretched out in a long grey line to the horizon. That was the thing about South Australia: for hours there'd be ranges, or bushland or scrub, and then, before you'd even realise, a gradual stripping back to nothing but big sky and scrubby trees and a landscape that engulfed everything. If he continued on the Barrier, right to the end of it, he'd cross salt plains, dry creek beds and spinifex, and the state line into New South Wales, where the red dirt became low hills of sand. But for now, Mark was northbound, and the farmland gave way to small towns, then wheat country and, finally, the remnants of a massive plain, vast and still. Friday afternoon, no traffic on this road – and alongside him like a friend, the railroad called the Indian Pacific, its train travelling weekly from Sydney to Perth.

He passed Yarcowie, stopped for a cup of tea and a pie in Terowie. The pie was good, the tea was hot. Mark liked Terowie. At Oodla Wirra, Mark spoke to a truckie who told him about a recent land acquisition, further up the Barrier in New South Wales. Two stations bought by the government, almost 65,000 hectares for the purpose of creating a new outback reserve. The truckie was pleased with the buyback, said at least it didn't go to the foreigners and he hoped there'd be some shooting allowed. Mark pissed beside him at the urinal, drank some water and continued the drive.

After Yunta, and beyond the first sign for the new supermax prison, phone reception ceased. The remoteness of the area perhaps, but possibly telecommunication-jamming measures, taken by the prison to prevent coercion among the inmates. The desert lands rolled on and at the edge of the horizon Mark caught a first glance of Morburn. He wondered whether the incarcerated ever stopped to contemplate the vastness that awaited them outside the prison walls. It must be a kind of torture, he thought, knowing that just beyond the boundary of their confinement was a boundless land that cared for nothing of their heinous crimes and petty concerns.

The correctional centre was only three years old, given the supermax title for its world-class security and ability to house the most despised of criminals: terrorists, paedophiles and serial killers. Brick walls encircled the buildings, lookout towers on every corner. Any outside space was covered in metal mesh to deter drones and helicopters from flying above, and an inner steel wall went ten metres underground. Even if, on the rarest occasion, a prisoner might escape, where would they go? Without firm assistance, the land might offer freedom, but only for those who could endure it.

In the Morburn car park, rows of Toyota LandCruisers stood alongside each other like soldiers. Staff vehicles, Mark guessed. A dingy Holden, barely roadworthy and parked on the end, hinted at a visitor. Probably a mother, because who else would come to such a place?

Large steel doors stood at the entrance and, once opened, a security check took place. Physical body searches were no longer a requirement; at Morburn there was a hi-tech body-scanner, devised to identify any type of contraband a visitor, guard or new prisoner might bring in. Mark had heard the tales: guns, syringes, rings, mobile phones, razor blades, drugs, porn – it was incredible what could be shoved into small spaces. And not only orifices – a small nick in the lining of the mouth could provide a neat space for a SIM card; a caesarean scar – deftly reopened and sewn up again – could conceal a memory stick or a small pouch of cocaine.

Mark showed his police identification, gave up his keys, wallet, phone and watch, then entered the scanner. He came out the other side, innocent but not unsullied.

Two guards accompanied him to the agreed non-contact visitor room. A Perspex window encased in a steel door separated prisoner from guest. Two guards stood sentry behind him. A sign forbidding any language other than English was embedded into the Perspex; a smell of disinfectant and piss pervaded the air. *Anyone for tea?* Mark might have asked if he wasn't shaking like some poorly constructed shed in a storm.

Any earlier thoughts of Hollywood mob movies – black-and-white images of handsome men, Bond-like in suits and armed with short pistols – were dashed by Morburn and this room. An oppressive air made Mark weak with thirst and for a second he looked around wildly, as if it were he and not Scopelliti who was the prisoner. He used to snigger at the clichéd nickname 'The Hook'. He didn't snigger now.

'We'll be right here,' one of the guards said, not unkindly.

'Don't tell him anything about yourself,' the other said. 'Let him do the talking.'

The door clanged. Footsteps. A figure emerged.

Tony Scopelliti sat before him, and although a thick screen divided them, Mark felt his presence as closely as if they were touching. The Hook had grown fat in prison. Boxing fitness a thing of the past, Scopelliti was now an ill-formed pudding, doughy and bald. The eyes though, penetrating, still reflected the sharp intelligence that made him the current king of organised crime. A cold sore covered his lower lip, still in its early stage, pink and shiny. The sight of it made Mark relax just a little. His sister Prue got cold sores when she was anxious.

'You saved my cousin from drowning.' Tony's voice was thick, low.

Mark nodded.

'We appreciate this.' Tony spread his hands wide on the small bench in front of him. 'Joe is a cousin on my father's side.'

'He told me.'

'And you're Greek.' Tony nodded his big head.

'On my father's side.' Mark wondered briefly what his father, who had never set foot in Greece, would have thought of this.

'Markos Ariti.' Tony Scopelliti said his name slowly, drawing it out. 'Markos . . . it means "manly", did you know?'

This was not how Mark had thought the interview with Tony 'The Hook' would go.

'Not really.' Fact was, he *did* know. He'd looked it up one day as a kid, felt a sense of pride that 'Mark', derived from Mars, the god of war, was a manly name. Far better than 'Dennis', which meant 'The Dane'.

'Of course' – Tony spoke slowly – 'in Greek it might come from "malakoz", which means "soft and tender".'

Mark cleared his throat. 'You wanted to see me? What's this about?'

'I wanted to thank you. And to show you something.'

Behind him, Mark was aware that one of the guards shifted on his feet.

From his sleeve, Tony held up a small photo against the thick glass. It was of a young woman, hair in luxurious curls about her shoulders, pageant-queen beautiful in a strapless, gold top.

'My wife, Charlene.'

Mark nodded. He recognised her from the recordings and the photo on the station wall.

'Charlene is soft-hearted. She loves small animals, children, old people. She tells me, "Tony, look at that little boy playing on the swings, look at that fluffy bear there in the shop window."' Tony shook his head: his jowls moved from side to side. 'I want to keep Charlene happy. I look at the little boy on the swings, I buy her the fluffy bear, she keeps it on our bed.'

Mark felt his pulse thud in his neck.

'"Don't hurt people, anyone," Charlene says, and I say, "No, my love, I won't," because I can tell how much it means to her. Charlene wants no violence, no one harmed.' Tony moved in his seat, edging forward. 'Now, I give people chances. I watch them. I wait. But last week, my wife was sent this.'

Tony looked at each of the guards standing behind him and Mark felt, rather than saw, a subtle acknowledgement.

The prisoner, from his other chest pocket, took out a different photo and held it up to the glass. Mark looked at it, unsure of what it was. Tony's meaty hand pressed it against the glass and Mark shuffled forward in his seat, head bent towards the image.

He understood. Inhaled sharply and recoiled before looking once again.

There, in the small square, was a printed photo, taken in the dark, of a blonde woman, hunched in a dark space, staring at the lens. Her face, dirty and terrified, was without doubt Natalie Whitsed's. Clutched tight to her chest was a large fluffy teddy bear with a big love heart across the middle. On either side of the image were dark vertical lines.

'Who sent you this?'

'We don't know. It came to Charlene in an unmarked envelope.'

'Does she still have it? We'll need it for prints.'

Tony ignored the question. 'I bought Charlene that bear. It was in our house, in our bedroom.'

'We'll need—'

'We didn't take Natalie Whitsed. We knew she was watching us, but that's nothing new, we called her "Birdy" for how small and watchful she was. We want to talk to Birdy, that is true. We do. But on my word, we were never going to truly harm her. We don't hurt women.'

Mark looked into the other man's eyes. They didn't waver.

'But whoever took the policewoman has been in my house and this photo has greatly frightened my wife.'

A pause.

'Know this, Ariti: I will kill the person who took this photo and sent it to her.'

'You won't do that. We'll—'

'I'm showing you this photo because you saved my cousin, because you're Greek and because I want you to tell Angelo Conti: the policewoman was alive a week, a week and a half ago, being held somewhere dark. We would like to find the girl, it's true – but we did not take her. Tell Conti to call off the interest in my businesses. We have nothing to hide.'

Yeah right.

'A man was watching Charlene, stalking her,' Mark said. 'His name was Aidan Sleeth, he was shot dead a week ago.'

'We didn't kill him.'

'But you knew Sleeth was stalking Charlene?'

The man gave a low grunt. 'Only after he'd been killed. Charlene should have told me before. She didn't want to tell us in case we hurt him. And I would have . . .'

'Killed him yourself?'

'Yes.'

Tony Scopelliti was in a supermax prison, famed for its world-class security. Still, Mark didn't doubt that the man had the means to direct an execution on the outside.

'I think it was Aidan Sleeth who took the teddy bear from your house. Now he's dead.'

'I repeat. It wasn't us who did it. I'm glad he's dead if it was him in my bedroom and if he took the photo. Tell Angelo Conti – we didn't take the lady cop, tell him to stop his men swarming over my businesses.'

'But you're looking for Whitsed?'

'Of course.'

'What does she have on you?'

'That' – Tony smiled a little sadly – 'I cannot tell you.' The big man nodded at the guards and rose majestically from his seat.

'One more thing. That kid with the bike. Not us either.'

'You're telling me a lot of things you didn't do, Tony.'

The man's dark eyes turned to him, cold. They reminded him of the snake, clinging on, rage-filled and determined.

'I won't forget you saving my cousin, I'll repay you. But that doesn't mean you're part of us. You don't get to know everything, Sergeant Ariti.'

The guards beside Mark moved towards him; one touched his shoulder, indicating he should stand. Were they expected to bow? Mark didn't move.

Tony watched him for a second, weighing him up, before turning his bulk and walking out of the meeting room.

The tiny nod he'd given Mark felt like a benediction, and when one of the guards said, 'Let's go,' Mark had to stop himself from saying Amen.

Back in the Booralama station, Jagdeep was confused. Angelo had just called, asking for Mark. Mark was probably out of range, she told him. The outback, the prison phone-jamming mechanism. When pressed, Angelo admitted he was worried. Inspector Clare Rendell had just spoken with him, upset beyond all measure. She'd confessed to passing on information to the Scopellitis to protect her son, and to encouraging the suspicion that it was their colleague, Finn Turner, who was doing so. Deliberations were underway as to what to do with her – lengthy suspension or dismissal most likely – but Angelo was concerned at her emotional state. She'd had to have known that suspension was inevitable, but the way she'd sobbed over the phone, asking for privacy, pleading for a few days' rest . . . When did Jagdeep think that Mark would be contactable?

Jagdeep snorted. *Why ask for Mark? I'm here, I'm qualified, I'm keen: put me to work.*

Angelo told her to hold the fort. Not much to be done other than keep the press at bay and assist the Homicide team in the logistics of the drone and Forensics search. Finn Turner, along with other officers, was currently visiting the slowly recovering Luke Howsley in hospital. Information forthcoming.

Jagdeep hung up, deeply dissatisfied. What would it take, she thought, to be given some real responsibility? She was capable, highly so. What was all this 'hold the fort' crap?

It was growing hot inside the little station. Jagdeep opened a window, breathed in the fresh air of the country. Her husband, Adi, would probably be sleeping right now. Having one of his little afternoon naps on the couch. When he came home from his work in the mines, he liked to rest. She knew from an earlier text that one of her aunts was dropping him around dinner for tonight, *poor man with his wife up in the middle of nowhere, working when she should be at home looking after her husband*. Jagdeep snorted. Her aunts never brought around dinner for her, even though she was their sister's daughter, their only niece *and* pregnant. *Bloody Adi*, she thought. He knew perfectly well how to cook. The night before she'd left to join Mark in Booralama at Angelo's request, the youngest aunt said that she was becoming more and more like her mother. It was said sweetly, but Jagdeep felt the sting. Now, she reflected that perhaps Adi was becoming more like his father – accepting food from adoring elderly aunts, sleeping in the afternoons, unhappy with his wife's line of work.

Their arguments about her commitment to policework didn't seem like the sort you should have in your first year of marriage but perhaps that's just how it went.

Jagdeep looked up at the corkboard. Natalie Whitsed and Charlene Scopelliti smiled at her, encouraging.

She looked at her watch. There was time to pick up Mark's boys from Kelly at the designated halfway spot on the highway. Clare Rendell had made a grave error in providing police information to the Scopellitis. Jagdeep held no sympathy for her in that regard – and yet. And yet. The woman was, like her, a dedicated policewoman, hardworking and talented. Being told she could no longer work in the job she loved – or being demoted to administration and shamed by her colleagues – this was, for those who saw the job as a vocation, a devastating nightmare. Angelo admitted to grave concerns about Clare's emotional state.

Jagdeep slammed the window down and fastened the hatch before moving around the station, locking the doors and hanging up the little sign: 'Police currently out. Please call 000 in an emergency.'

She knew that, unlike her, Rendell was staying at the Comfort Inn in Booralama. Her accommodation was the Easy Rest Motel in Waldara, where for $145 guests received a continental breakfast and a $5 voucher for Chicken Time.

Google Maps told her the Comfort Inn was a five-minute drive and, aware that she'd need to be leaving shortly to pick up the boys, she got in the police-issued vehicle and drove down quiet streets to the inn.

The Comfort Inn was a neat, red-bricked two-storey motel surrounded by rose bushes and a pool. A 'No Vacancy' sign flashed a bilious shade of green. The young man on reception told her this was because of the Booralama Show; people were coming in from everywhere to attend. At first, he rightly refused to let her know which room Clare was staying in. When she showed him her police ID he held his arms up, blurted out the room number and backed out of the small office slowly.

Jagdeep shook her head: *Another cop show fan.*

A car was parked out the front of Clare's room, a blue Honda. Dirty. The blinds to Clare's room, unlike most others, were closed. Jagdeep knocked at the door.

Inside, there was the sound of a door slamming and footsteps.

'Hello!' Jagdeep knocked again, glanced back at the Honda and felt a growing uneasiness. *Is that a broken headlight?*

'Clare!' she called. 'It's Jagdeep Kaur, just here to check up on you, see if you're okay.'

A moment of waiting before the blind flickered and Clare's face appeared, pale. 'I'm fine,' she said. 'You don't have to check up on me.'

'Can I come in?'

'No.'

Now Jagdeep, senses ringing, put a hand on her gun belt. 'Let me in, Clare, I'll only stay for a moment.' Suddenly her phone started ringing, loud, and Clare's face disappeared from the window. A moment later, she opened the door, just a crack.

'Who's calling you?' Clare asked, and Jagdeep looked at her phone.

'Finn Turner.'

'Don't answer.' Clare spoke fast. 'He's been ringing me constantly and I'm fine, I'm *fine*!'

341

Jagdeep let the phone ring out and put her foot in the doorway. 'Are you alone?'

'Yes.' Clare's face was awash with misery. Pale and haggard, she looked as if she hadn't slept in days. In the background, there was a shifting noise, a cough.

'Who is with you, Clare?' Jagdeep's heartbeat raced.

'No one.'

Now she heard it again, the unmistakable sound of a deep groan. Without thinking Jagdeep forced her way inside, bursting past the distraught Clare and into the room.

The dimly lit room smelled of disinfectant and something more visceral – rotting skin, or blood.

A tall figure lay on the couch.

Behind her now, Clare loomed. 'You shouldn't have come here,' she said.

Once past Yunta, phone reception resumed, and Mark's phone began pinging with messages.

It's Finn, call me back.

It's Angelo, call me.

It's Finn. Ring me. Urgent.

Truck tyre marks in the road had created small canyons of water and mud. Mark negotiated his way around them, wondering at Australian country roads that were so full of hazards – tree branches, disappearing surfaces, drunken drivers, animals dead or alive.

He pulled over, went to text Finn back when his phone rang.

'Mark, it's Finn. How was Morburn?'

'The Hook says hi.'

A pause.

'Listen, Luke Howsley's awake. He's identified the car that ran him over.'

'Yeah?' Mark straightened. A flock of cockatoos flew overhead, screeching, and he almost missed what Luke was saying.

'Blue Honda Civic. It belongs to Clare.'

A sick feeling came over Mark. 'You sure about that? Lot of Honda Civics on the road.'

'As well as the make, Luke described a sticker on the rear window, a retro AFL Crows one, from early days when we made it into the AFL. You know it – crow in flight, beak open.'

Clare's demeanour, her behaviour after the crash. Her determination to pin it on the Scopellitis. Mark wound down the window; a hot breeze blew dust in his face. He wound it back up again.

'You speak to her yet?'

'I'm trying. She's not answering. Also, I've heard about how she was feeding info to the Scops.'

'Yeah.'

'She's not a bad person.'

Mark was silent. Finn may not be so generous if he knew she was blaming the snitching on him.

'Where are you?' Finn asked.

'About an hour away. Less, maybe fifty minutes. You?'

'Was on my way to Adelaide, but I'm turning around. Be there in forty.'

Mark called Angelo. His friend answered on the second ring,

'How'd it go with Scopelliti?' Mark filled him in. 'You're sure it was Whitsed in the photo?'

'One hundred per cent.'

'Whoever's got her is taunting Tony and his men. Information, or whatever it is she has. This is big, Mark. *Big.*'

Both men knew what was next: rows and rows of police, volunteers handing out coffee and sandwiches, sleepless nights, the press eager, pressure intense.

Mark spoke to his boss about the hit and run, Clare's car.

'This will not go down well,' Angelo said, grim. 'She'll be charged. No way they'll consider mere demotion for passing on info now. When she called me earlier, she was upset – hysterical almost. I told Jagdeep about it.'

'Anyone else know about the car?'

'Luke, obviously. Finn, you and me. Soon, everyone.'

'Not Jagdeep?'

'No, I didn't know about it then. Why?'

Mark was silent for a moment. Jagdeep wasn't one to sit and wait. If she'd heard about an upset colleague she might go around there for a check-up. He pressed his foot on the accelerator, a vague anxiety growing.

'I'm on my way home now, I'll go straight around to Clare's motel. Finn's on his way too.'

They hung up and Mark tried calling Jagdeep: nothing. Tried again: nothing.

He pressed harder on the accelerator, pushed the HiLux up to 130 kilometres per hour.

CHAPTER 41

A young man lay on a couch, unkempt and sweating. 'Why'd you let her in, you stupid bitch?' His breath came at short intervals and he made an effort to sit up.

'Jackson.' Clare moved across to him and touched him on the head. 'We need help.'

It was her son. Jagdeep saw concern and love flash across the other woman's face.

'Do you need an ambulance?' Jagdeep took her phone out of her pocket and instantly Clare was beside her, grabbing her arm.

'Not now,' she said wildly. 'We need a doctor, but no ambulance just yet.'

'Clare,' Jagdeep said slowly. 'The broken headlight on your car. It was Jackson who ran over Luke Howsley, wasn't it?'

'Yes.' Clare's face was haunted. 'But—'

'Shut up, you bitch!' Jackson shouted from the couch. 'Shut your mouth!'

He let out a groan of pain and Jagdeep could see that under his t-shirt, his upper arm was poorly bandaged, lumpy and grey at the edges.

'I'm going to call an ambulance,' Jagdeep said slowly. 'You're badly hurt, Jackson.' She began dialling when a tell-tale click made her look up.

Clare was pointing her gun at Jagdeep. 'Give me the phone,' she said. 'Now.'

Past Oodla Wirra, land whizzing by, the sky a blur, Mark tried again and again to call Jagdeep. No luck. From Angelo, he got the number of one of the Homicide cops who said she'd leave Stone Town and head straight to the motel. Finn should be almost there. Mark needed petrol, but didn't stop. He knew he could just make it on less than a quarter-tank. Through a small town he put the siren on and didn't slow. An old bloke in stubbies leaning against a caravan gave him an open-mouthed stare. Sheep paused to look up. A kid on a bike waved. Mark drove on.

'What're you planning to do, Clare?' Jagdeep asked. 'You know someone will identify the vehicle sooner or later.'

'It's not that.' Clare's voice was shaky, but her hands on the gun remained still. 'It's bigger than that, much bigger.'

'Shoot her!' Jackson's voice, deranged with pain, rang out from the other side of the room. 'We'll take her vehicle and leave. Shoot her, Mum!'

'He needs help, Clare, was he injured in the crash?' *Keep them talking, that's what you learned in police college. Stall for time.*

'I know what you're doing.' Clare's lips curled. 'It won't work with me.'

Jagdeep felt a rise of panic in her chest and fought to keep it at bay.

'Jackson,' Clare said in a new, flat voice, 'go to her car, I'll bring out the bags.' She leaned over and felt in Jagdeep's pocket for the HiLux keys. Her gun, close now, in Jag's face.

'You'll get caught, Clare,' Jagdeep said. 'The cops will find you.'

'It's not the cops I'm worried about.' Keys retrieved, she threw them to Jackson and pointed with the gun to the bathroom. 'In there,' she said to Jagdeep.

'Is it the Scopellitis?' Jagdeep asked. 'Are you in trouble with them?'

'Move!'

Don't let them take you to a second place, and that means a room. Fight. Run. Move. 'I'm pregnant,' Jagdeep said. 'You won't hurt me, Clare.'

Clare gave a short laugh. 'Give me a break. It doesn't work like that. We're all out for our own.'

There was sense to what she said. And Jagdeep, feeling acutely aware of the baby growing inside her, struck out hard with her right arm.

Clare gave a yelp of pain, and the gun flew into the air and across the room. Jagdeep took flight towards the front door but Clare launched herself at her, shoving her into the window and grabbing at her arm.

Jagdeep kicked back, repeatedly, trying to keep Clare at bay while the other woman, grunting with exertion, tried to gain some purchase.

Sirens? Yes – that was sirens in the distance.

Clare landed a wild punch into her back, the pain an almighty shock. For a second Jagdeep stood, bent over and stunned. Clare aimed again, but Jagdeep swerved out of the way and managed a flat-footed kick which landed hard in Clare's stomach.

The woman clenched at her middle, turned a deep shade of red.

As a police car pulled up, Jackson roared but his injuries kept him pinned to the couch. He made no attempt to leave, or help his mother.

Jagdeep took advantage of Clare turning to him to spin around, grab her by the back of one arm and push hard into her knees, forcing the woman to lie down. Kneeling on top of her, Jagdeep caught her swinging arms and handcuffed the enraged woman before sliding the fallen gun towards her with her foot.

The door opened and in rushed a policewoman, Senior Sergeant Rachel Barrie, who took in the scene and with a startled look on her face called for back-up. It wasn't needed: a moment later Finn arrived, and then, a few minutes later, Inspector Leon Bithick. Finally, Mark appeared, dishevelled, relief and worry etched across his face.

*

The small living space of room eleven of the Comfort Inn was crowded with bodies and all eyes turned to mother and son.

Bithick checked Jackson's injury. 'Is that a stab wound? It's badly infected, you need a hospital.'

'Ambulance is on its way,' Barrie said.

'You'll be charged for hit and run and for leaving the scene of an accident. That's the minimum,' Mark said to the young man.

'Fuck off.'

'And you, Clare.' Jagdeep sounded weary. 'You'll be charged with accessory after the fact, for false imprisonment and for assaulting a police officer.'

There was silence in the room, save for Jackson's increasingly laboured breathing.

Bithick, his face pale and freckled, looked from mother to son. 'Prison time for you, mate, and you too.'

'No,' Clare muttered from the floor. 'No.'

'Is it the Scopellitis you're afraid of?' Jagdeep asked. 'Why were you so keen to get away?'

Jackson began laughing, high-pitched, exaggerated and painful to hear. 'The Scopellitis will kill us both,' he said. 'You can't stop them.'

'What did you do to them?'

'I made them an offer they couldn't refuse.'

An awful coldness spread through Mark at Jackson's words. 'Was that offer Natalie Whitsed?'

Instantly, the atmosphere in the room changed, from slow simmer to boiling. All the officers waited on his reply.

We few, we merry few.

'It was.'

'Be quiet, Jackson!' Clare wailed from her place on the ground. 'Shut your mouth for once!'

'That's how you got your stab wound, isn't it? In a tussle with Natalie? She'd fight.' Finn's voice was low.

'Stupid bitch,' Jackson said. 'Stupid bitch stabbed me. I wasn't going to kill her – she was my ticket out.'

'You were going to hand her over to the Scopellitis.' Bithick mouthed the words slowly, menace in them.

Mark took a step closer to Jackson, protective or aggressive, he wasn't sure.

'You kept a cop locked up and you—' Barrie spoke in disgust.

'We don't know the whole story,' Mark interjected.

'We know *enough*.'

'We should fuck them up,' Bithick muttered, and no one reprimanded him.

'You killed Sleeth too, didn't you?' Mark asked.

'No! He didn't! He hasn't *killed* anyone!' Clare was struggling to sit up.

Where is the ambulance? Mark wondered. Jackson looked seriously ill. How long had he been like this?

'I didn't kill that guy,' he said breathlessly.

'That's hard to believe.'

'I didn't! Fuck it, I didn't!' He took a deep breath. 'But I saw him push the girl down the hole.'

There was a stunned silence broken only by Clare's low pleas of 'No, no, no'.

'You saw him what?' Mark asked. 'Tell us.'

'Wait for a lawyer!' Clare said, her old smoker's voice harsh. 'Don't say a thing.'

Jackson's breathing was erratic now and his face, slick with sweat, was turning an awful shade of grey.

'Lawyer's not going to do a fucking thing,' he said. 'I'm dead the moment I step out of here.'

In the distance, a siren.

'Tell us,' Finn said. 'What happened?'

Jackson looked at him, a strange smile on his face.

'He's going into shock,' Clare said. 'He doesn't know what he's saying.'

'*What happened?*' Finn repeated. 'Speak, for Christ's sake!'

'I was watching Natalie, like Charlene asked me to. Charlene knew she was being watched by a female cop, we called her the "Little Bird", or "Birdy". Chaz asked me to follow the Bird, see what she was up to. She didn't want me to let anyone else know – especially Shane or Tony. If they found out, Birdy'd be a goner. Chaz just wanted me to keep an eye on her.' Jackson felt underneath his bandage, grimaced. 'I followed her up here when she left in such a hurry that Friday. All the way up the highway to the middle of nowhere.'

Stone Town.

'I waited until she turned into some road and then followed. She'd parked out the back of a paddock – I could just make her out walking up to a big house. After a while, I followed. She thought she was so good at watching people, but she didn't know when I was watching *her*.' He took another long breath. 'I'm good at watching. It's all those fucking *opportunities* we had at that school you sent me to.' Jackson was looking at Clare, half laughing, maybe crying. 'Orienteering, outdoor ed – I mean, *Latin* for fuck's sake . . .'

The ambulance was pulling into the motel car park, its siren urgent.

'What happened, Jackson?' Mark asked quickly.

'Shut up, Jackson.' Clare's voice was flat.

'In the bush, she walked up a track and met that Sleeth guy near a stone building. I was watching from the trees. There was an argument. I couldn't hear . . .'

Paramedics entered the room and rushed straight to the injured man. Above the din, the growing anger, everyone moved in closer to hear Jackson more clearly.

'He pushed her and she fell down a hole, it was insane. Then he climbed in afterward and not long after came back out. Started throwing branches and sticks down there. Covered her up and walked away. But I saw! I saw it all.'

He was on a stretcher now, being carried out of the room. Jagdeep and Mark followed the ambos outside.

'What did you do, Jackson? What did you *do*?' Jagdeep was insistent, no anger in it.

He stared at her. 'I went down there afterward, thought at first she was dead. She looked it. But she wasn't! Her eyes moved when I opened them. She wasn't dead – unconscious but not dead. I rang Mum, who said to get her out of there. Couldn't lift her up, so shoved her to another tunnel right at the back, one with a door and grille at the entrance, they lock from the outside. There's loads of them down there. All tunnels, miles and miles of them. Remember in Bendigo, Mum? I used to love the mines. All those empty spaces so far underground. I was like a little rat when we lived there.' Jackson laughed loudly, joylessly. 'I kept Whitsed alive, you should be thanking me. Fucking *thanking* me! Sleeth left her for dead, but I wanted her alive.'

'Where was the mine shaft?' Finn said, pressing. 'Where exactly.'

'West from the front of the building, ten metres or so.' Jackson's voice was becoming slurry. 'Big tree just there.'

'Who shot Aidan Sleeth, Jackson?' Jagdeep's voice rose in urgency.

The man had either slipped into unconsciousness or was about to. The paramedics hooked him up to a drip and injected something near his wound.

'Got that teddy from the guy who pushed her, a big house – weird. Was going to take photo . . . but camera broken, typical! Got new one, from good old Mum. Took the photo with it.' Jackson gave a sickly grin. 'Bitch stabbed me . . . not bad at first . . . I couldn't find her . . . looked around . . .'

The man watching him in the bush – tall and thin – Jackson?

'Wound got bad, real bad, pus and fever, all kinds of fucked-up dreams. Ran over that kid . . . didn't mean it.'

'You're a dead man,' Bithick called to him from the motel doorway as the paramedics prepared to shut the ambulance doors. 'Kept a cop in a hole, went against the mob.

You're dead!'

Jackson mumbled something, sick and half grinning in a ghastly expression.

'What's that?' Mark leaned in.

'*Ego mortus.*'

Doors slammed. The ambulance drove off at speed.

Jagdeep repeated Jackson's words.

'What's he mean?' Mark asked. 'It was Latin, wasn't it?'

'I'm dead,' Jagdeep said. '*Ego mortus* – I'm dead.'

CHAPTER 42

It was quiet in the motel room, save for a low wheezing coming from Clare, who had now managed to stand and was leaning against the wall.

All eyes turned to her.

'Fucking snitch,' Bithick sneered. 'You're going *down*.'

'Please.' Clare was crying. 'He's only a boy.'

'He's a year younger than me!' Finn Turner said. 'He's no boy.'

'He was scared, the Scopellitis were onto him after he lost that money. Jackson wanted to pay me back for everything – he wasn't thinking . . . He thought if he handed her over . . . or bribed them or . . .'

It was the wrong thing to say.

'Your son will go to Morburn,' Barrie said with satisfaction.

If Jackson wasn't sent there, someone from up high would make sure a transfer took place soon enough.

Clare shook her head. 'We didn't kill anybody. No one

died because of us – I don't know who shot Sleeth, really I don't.'

Bithick clenched and unclenched his fist.

'The Scopellitis will kill him in Morburn, you know they will,' Clare continued. 'Tony will bribe someone to knife him in the yard.'

No one denied it. Prison guards would turn a blind eye for the second it took to stick a blade into his back. He'd kept a cop in a hole.

Fellow prisoners would offer no help. He'd stolen from and then tried to bribe the Scopellitis, power-mongers of the prison world.

The public wouldn't care. He'd run over a nice young man and left him to die.

Clare coughed, slow at first and then drawn out and hacking. Her long, lean body bent over, she rested her hands on her thighs like an athlete after a run. Mark remembered Finn telling him that Clare was the fittest person he knew.

'Clare,' he said slowly. 'How come you're coughing so badly?'

She said nothing, wiped her mouth and stood up to her full height. He'd never realised how tall she was.

'Is it because you've been spending time in the bush around Stone Town? All that blackwood wattle, it causes skin irritation and breathing difficulties.'

A tense pause filled the air.

'Jackson was wounded after Natalie stabbed him.' Mark chose his words carefully. 'But someone was watching me in the bush on the Sunday after Sleeth was killed, and then again on Tuesday when I got bitten by the snake. Someone who could run.' Mark looked at his hand where the fangs had dug in. 'Was it you, Clare?'

A slow smile came over the policewoman. Deeply unpleasant. 'Do you think,' she said, low and bitter, 'that my messed-up son is capable of looking for evidence, of where Natalie might be, of what traces he left of himself in the bush?' She gave a harsh laugh. 'He left a sleeping bag there, for Chrissake, he lost a phone! Of course it was me out there. Mothers do everything, we're always cleaning up our kids' shit.'

Everyone in the room held their breath.

'My stupid, stupid son,' Clare wheezed. 'When he told me he'd seen a man push Nat down a mine shaft, my first thought was to go straight to the Scopellitis. Feed them the information like they'd told me to.' She gave a mirthless laugh. 'But this was big. And I wanted it to stop. Once you're in debt to the Scopellitis they'll never let you go, ever. I thought – *we could use this*. Leverage some time and funds to move elsewhere, make a fresh start.'

Barrie's phone rang and she silenced it, put it back in her pocket.

'I drove Jackson back up to Stone Town with his swag, an old lock for the grate and essentials, the day after he'd seen the girl be pushed and moved her to the enclosed space. Told him to stay there, feed her, keep her alive. He's always been the outdoorsy type and it was only for a few days.'

There was an ugly hardness in the ease with which Clare had switched from 'Nat' to 'the girl'.

357

'You knew where she was the whole time, right from the day she went missing,' Barrie said, half in wonder.

Clare smirked, then gave a cough. 'Yeah, I knew. Watched you all scramble about for days trying to work out what happened.'

'You told Jackson to take the photo with the teddy, didn't you, Clare?' Mark asked.

Clare nodded, licking her dry lips. 'I know I told you I hadn't seen the files, but I had. Of course I had! Nat wasn't reported missing till the Tuesday, so I had from Saturday till then to make plans. I watched them all, I knew about Sleeth stalking Charlene. The photo with the teddy was meant to show Tony Scopelliti that we had the means to get close to him, that we had what he was looking for and we meant business. It was easy for Jackson to go and get it from Sleeth's house.'

Clare's face turned sour. 'But Jackson's phone had a cracked lens and he couldn't take a photo! I had to drive up with a replacement, a brand new one. He got the photo of her and sent it to me, but then lost the bloody phone!'

And Evan found it, Mark thought.

'He's hopeless,' Clare was coughing in between the wild laughing. 'His teachers were right – no organisational skills.' She wiped her mouth, took a ragged breath. 'The whole thing was already taking too long – then Jackson was stabbed when the girl escaped.'

'And then Sleeth was shot,' Jagdeep said.

But only Clare and Jackson knew that Natalie had somehow fled from her underground prison, Mark thought.

Clare must have hoped that the Scopellitis, on seeing the photo and thinking she was still captured somewhere, would put the feelers out and make an offer.

'But why'd you tell the Scops about the phone ping, the listening device and the place where Natalie's car got stolen from?'

'At first, I wanted to let them know I was still on their side – didn't want them to start looking at Jackson. But then, when Sleeth was shot, I thought what the hell? It was the perfect opportunity to be sent here. The Scopellitis didn't know that Nat had escaped from us. I could up the stakes, put the spotlight on them – make the cops think they were in the thick of it, make them sweat over the listening device. It all made Natalie worth more.'

Clare turned to Mark, her face blotchy. 'Then Jackson ran over Luke – thought he was going to find Nat. He drove out in a frenzy, half crazed in pain, and hit him on his bike. Then you save the cousin from drowning and get invited to Morburn. I bet Tony told you about the photo, yeah?'

'Yeah.'

'And now my stupid son has admitted to you that he let Natalie go. So, we have nothing. Nothing at all to bargain with. It was all meant to take just a few days: Tony gets the photo, puts out word he's willing to make a deal, we let Nat go and we get out of here.'

'You weren't going to let her go.' Bithick spat out. 'You would have given her up to the Scops.'

Clare shrugged. 'I did what I had to.'

'You took a big gamble,' Jagdeep said. 'Was it worth it?'

'You would all do the same.' Clare's voice was flat. 'You'd hide your kids, cover up for them. You would, and you know it.'

A long pause.

Only when it stopped was Mark aware of the rain that had been pounding on the tin roof for the last ten minutes. The change in atmosphere roused the officers into practicality.

At a nod from Barrie, Bithick began escorting Clare out of the room.

'Please!' she begged in a final appeal. 'Don't let him be sent to Morburn! He's made mistakes, but I love him, he's my boy.'

Finn – her colleague and the one she'd led others to believe was the informer – stepped forward and touched her arm. 'I'll ask Dad to watch out for him.' He said it low, determined. 'He'll do it for me.'

Blood ties, deep and visceral, Mark thought. *They make us and undo us and make us again. Oikogeni*, he remembered the Greek word for family. *Pateras*, father.

Rain pounded down the gutters in steady rhythm. Mark pictured the ones at his mother's house, clogged with leaves and nests. Another job he'd been late for.

Barrie left with a fired-up Bithick. The questioning of Clare would continue into the night, relentless.

Finn, Jagdeep and Mark remained in the dark room.

'I'm going out there,' Finn said. 'Jackson told us where she was.'

'Natalie escaped,' Jagdeep said. 'She's not there anymore.'

'She could be hurt somewhere down there. Dying, or lost or . . .'

Mark was already out the door, missing women from a past investigation on his mind. 'Let's go,' he said. Some of them were never found, some dead, two escaped.

Jagdeep sighed, rubbed her side. 'I'll drive.'

All was quiet in the Stone Town bush when the three police made their way to the powder factory. Most birds were settled into branches, sleeping. Time now for the nocturnal hunters to emerge. Bats, owls, snakes, feral foxes and cats. Dying rays of sunlight cast orange beams through the blackwood. Finn flicked his torch on and the others did the same.

'West of the front of the stone building,' he said. 'Ten metres . . .'

A thin path led that way. Jagdeep and Mark followed Finn, all three darting their torches around, looking for the mine shaft. Ten metres in, below a large tree, and Mark couldn't see a thing. He backtracked. Thick undergrowth covered the path, blackberry bushes ran wild up a small rise, strangling everything in their path.

'Is this it?' Jagdeep asked, leaning over the side of the trail further up. 'It's deep.'

Mark moved to where she was – focused his torch to where she was looking. A dark hole, one metre in diameter, ran deep into the ground. Grasses lined the sides, a tree root protruded from the sides. It would be so easy to miss it, or fall down by accident.

'I'm going in,' Finn said. 'You two coming?'

'Not me,' Jagdeep said, holding her stomach. 'This baby's had enough action for one day. I'll wait here.'

Mark felt heavy with trepidation. They had no ropes, no safety equipment. It was dangerous. *But Natalie could be down there*, a voice in his head said. *Or we could discover something to help us in the search.* He threw a stick down the hole. Heard a dull thud as it landed.

'Don't jump,' he said. 'Lower yourself down. I'll follow.'

It was easier than expected to climb down the length of the shaft. Tree roots provided hand holds and it was only the last part that he had to make a short leap, his knee straining at the effort. The bottom was thick with mud and a dank, cloying smell filled the space. Above, Jagdeep's head was visible as a dark blob straining over the hole.

'Take a look!' There was a touch of boyish wonder about Finn's voice and Mark followed his gaze to the left of the shaft, where a smaller tunnel led off the main one. He, too, felt a flicker of excitement.

'It's lengthy,' Mark said – his beam of light reaching into it. 'I can't see it turning anywhere.'

'That's where Nat escaped into!' Finn nodded. 'That's where we should go, it'll lead us to where she went.'

'We don't know that,' Mark said. There was another tunnel to the right, lower that the other one, less visible. He had to bend down to peer into it. The torch beam high-lighted the damp walls and muddy floor. It was a small space, a dead end, something ghastly about it. Mark blinked. A flat, curved object on the ground caught the light and he

362

bore the torch onto it. On hands and knees, he reached into the tunnel and grabbed it. Plastic. Sharp. Was that blood?

He backed out of the hole and stood up, showing it to Finn.

'The love heart she stabbed Jackson with,' the younger man breathed. 'This was where he kept her.' Already he was bent low, scrambling into the section where Mark pulled the jagged heart from. 'There's a door thing!' Finn exclaimed back from a short distance. 'And the grate he was talking about, shine your torch here. God, I can barely see a thing.'

Mark got on his hands and knees, focused his light onto the grate, wide open, a lock dangling from the very top of it. 'What's in there?' he shouted.

'A backpack, the teddy bear – I won't touch any of it don't worry – rubbish – it stinks. She was here!' Finn yelled back, loud with excitement. 'She was alive here!'

Finn's words reverberated through the tunnel, echoing. Mark backed out, into the main shaft. Above, he could barely make out Jagdeep, still looking over the top.

'We found where Natalie was kept!' he shouted back at her. 'We're coming up now!'

Jagdeep said something back, but he couldn't hear.

'We should go through the other tunnel while we're here.' Finn was filthy, making his way back into the main shaft. 'Let's do it now.'

'We will not,' Mark was firm. 'It's late. That can be done in the morning and when we've got the right equipment. These tunnels are like rabbit warrens, we could get lost.'

Again, Jagdeep shouted something down before backing away from the hole.

'What'd she say?' Mark asked.

Finn was grumpy. 'I dunno.'

A murmur of voices above ground startled them. The men eyed each other. Finn reached for the tree root lowest down, hauled himself up on it, Mark following at speed.

On the surface, any shred of daylight was gone. Mark spun his torch around, saw Jagdeep talking with a stooping figure. In the torchlight, his face appeared deathly pale.

'What are you doing here Gerald?' Mark asked.

'What do you think?' Gerald answered, mild.

'He's birdwatching,' Jagdeep said.

'Last week, a young man around here named Evan heard a bird call, I think it was the Barking Owl. I missed it on Friday night because of the conference – but I'm hoping tonight's the night.'

'That was Evan Matteson,' Mark said to the others.

'A fine young man,' Gerald said. 'Polite, intelligent.'

'This area is now part of a crime investigation,' Finn was jumpy, excited. 'You'll have to leave.'

Gerald nodded before cocking his ear, straightening, eyes wide. 'Listen!' he said quietly. 'Did you hear that?'

The three police stood still, mimicking Gerald's stance, hands by their side, head tilted.

'No,' Finn was impatient.

'Listen!' Gerald repeated. 'Be still.'

'I can't hear anything.' Jagdeep looked around.

'It's coming,' Gerald said, and in the few seconds that followed, Mark felt every hair on his body stand on end.

And then it started: a high-pitched, gurgling scream, intense and terrifying.

'What is it?' Finn looked around wildly. 'Where is she?'

'It's a bird.' Jagdeep's voice shook.

'God, it's horrible.' Mark wanted to run blindly through the bush to his car. The screams rang on.

Gerald's eyes were closed, a faint smile on his face. '*Ninox connivens*,' he murmured. 'The first time I've ever heard it.'

The bird cry stopped abruptly.

Mark breathed out. Jagdeep's hand had been clenched tight the whole time on his arm. She let it go, embarrassed.

'Is that what it always sounds like?' he asked Gerald.

'Sometimes it's more of a dog sound – like a "Woof, woof". Always regular.' Gerald did an impression. Finn raised his eyebrows. The man was good.

Evan had told Mark that during the days before Aidan Sleeth was shot, the bird sounded different, *like words being yelled almost . . . not regular.*

'Does the Barking Owl ever sound irregular, or like words being yelled?'

Gerald gave a brief laugh. 'Words being yelled? I don't think so. Birds aren't people, no matter what attributes we try to impose on them. Thank goodness for that. If you heard words being yelled out here, then I'd say it was human.'

*

Hours later, after he'd collected his boys from an irate Kelly; after they'd eaten takeaway pizza with Jagdeep; and minutes after she'd agreed to sleep in his mother's room rather than drive back to her Waldara motel, Mark brushed his teeth and lay on top of his bed. On the curtain, a moth was fighting for life, caught in a web. Mark watched it, saw the spider descend on the panicked wings, slow, slow. He closed his eyes.

Sleep came in a dark fluttering, strange noises outside, the hiss of things unseen.

CHAPTER 43

Despite the events of the previous day, despite high humidity, wind and rain, Booralama presented a stoic face for the annual show. Mindful of the rows of SES volunteers and police with rakes about to comb the Stone Town bush and its mines, and acutely aware he was not assisting, Mark paid and entered the racecourse grounds where the event was held.

It was an assault on the senses: fairy floss and Chiko Rolls, showbags and tight jeans, bad hairdos and the Ferris wheel and the Cha Cha and the Zipper – they were all there and they would be there at every show in every country till the end of time. Mark had a bad relationship with shows. When he was fourteen he'd taken Bernadette Grealy to this same one. He'd bought her a dagwood dog, which fell on the ground after she'd had one bite. He'd suggested the five-second rule, but her look of horror was such that he'd died of shame. On the dodgem cars they'd crashed into each other's shoulders so hard she started crying, and after he bought a showbag for $15, which contained only one chocolate bar and a plastic whistle, he said he couldn't afford the show any more and they agreed to call it quits.

His boys started wailing for a showbag. He lined up with them at the caravan to see that things had not improved. Now, the bags were edging up to the $50 mark and he knew, *he just knew*, there would be only one fun-sized chocolate bar or some shit Wizz Fizz and a plastic whistle in each one. He hurried them along to the Laughing Clowns, where a man with leering eyes said they were fine-looking boys. They attempted the Ferris wheel, but his youngest, Charlie, wasn't tall enough so they couldn't get on. People shouted in his ear. Someone spilled a milkshake on his shoe. He took his boys to the shooting range, where they each tried and failed to shoot a single rusted duck. Mark bought them a dagwood dog, which they hated. A scratchy voice on the PA system urging people to have fun and the jangling sound of arcade games combined to create the perfect storm of hell.

Perhaps this is it, Mark thought, woozy with the heat and smell of oil. *For my sins, I've ended up at the show. All is as it should be.*

He was ready to leave when he saw a shed with the sign 'Farm Produce and Animals'. A sanctuary. Steering his boys into it, Mark felt an immediate release when the smell of old straw and manure hit him. An exhibition of past show winners, a prize bull. Relative quietness, save for the soft bleating of lambs. *Jesus could be born in such a place,* Mark thought. *Pregnant women could give birth here and be presented with perfumed gifts.* Charlie asked if they could go back to the showbag van and he hurried them towards the pigs.

'Hello there, Mark!' It was spindly Beth Matteson, standing alongside big Pat Delaney. 'Who do we have here?'

Mark introduced his boys and the old women plied them with attention and lollies.

While Pat took the chattering boys to the lambs, Mark stood looking at the jams, thinking of his own mother and how she would have been the same with all children. It made him nostalgic to see jars with red ribbons around the lids and handwritten labels: 'Orange Marmalade', 'Quince Jelly' and 'Rhubarb'.

There was a list of the entrants, some familiar, on an A4 piece of paper: Pat Delaney, Sue Williams, Julie Mathers – his old girlfriend's aunt – and Lee O'Brien.

'Lee O'Brien!' Mark said. 'Good to see a man entering.'

'Ah yes, Lee,' Beth said, smiling. 'He enters every year. Very competitive.'

Remembering Lee's animosity towards the women of Stone Town, Mark nodded.

'One year, when Mr Sleeth – Aidan's father – entered with his fig jam, Lee accused us of robbing the man of first place!' Beth chuckled as she skilfully balanced three jars and moved them to a side table.

'Gosh.' Mark looked around for his sons. 'That's no good.'

'However, it *is* very easy to swap a name on the list of winners . . .'

With a start, Mark looked more closely at the old lady. She was fussing over the labels, but when she glanced up, he saw a sharpness in her eyes born of quick intelligence.

'*Did* you swap the names, Beth?'

Pat Delaney was returning with his sons, each holding one of the large woman's hands, their faces bright with excitement, mouths full of sugar.

'Mr Sleeth was up against Raelene from the caravan park. He had a new kitchen, a live-in cook and a Thermomix. Raelene had a four-burner stove. What do you think we did?' Her blue eyes were laughing at him and, as Pat joined them, Mark felt once again their strength. He cleared his throat. 'Did Evie end up making her vegan slice?'

Pat smiled, generous. 'She didn't get around to it in the end.'

'Come on, boys, let's get going.' Mark, although technically off for the day, itched to get out to Stone Town and the search for any signs of Natalie Whitsed. He was farming his sons off to Dennis for a few hours.

'Did you know, boys,' Pat addressed them seriously, 'that your dad once saved a young man?'

His sons perked up. 'No,' said Sam. 'Was he a superhero?'

'Pretty much.'

Mark had no idea what Pat was talking about.

'Tell us!' Charlie stood on one leg and wrapped his arm around Pat Delaney's waist to steady himself.

'About twenty years ago there were fires all through this area. Really bad bushfires.'

The boys nodded. All Australian kids knew about bushfires.

'Your dad was playing tennis at the Stone Town courts, near the old school.'

It came back; Mark remembered the day. A dry northerly, shrivelling heat and the smell of melting tar. He'd arrived early to set up, and only after he got there had the radio announcers begun declaring the extent of the situation: fast-moving bushfire approaching the Stone Town area, residents advised to leave or activate their bushfire plan.

'There was a photo of him in the paper!' Pat exclaimed.

That photo. It made him cringe to think of it. Janice Smith, annoying as ever, had arrived at the tennis courts in a hurry. 'Give me a shot, Mark!' she said. 'The paper will like a good-looking bloke like you on the front page.' Mark was busy packing his car with the racquets and tennis club ledgers. He couldn't think what else to do, but the old president would want them.

Suddenly an orange glow appeared above the hills to the west. 'Let's get out of here, Janice!' he cried above the din.

'One shot!' she called. 'Stand there with the hose, no need to turn it on – try to look as if you're about to fight the flames.'

'We've got to go!' Mark was winding up the hose but when he saw she wouldn't budge, he posed for her, trying, at her instruction, to look heroic and humble at the same time.

Janice took the shot then hurried to her car. 'See you in town. I'm sticking to Yielder's Track to get back on the highway. Stay safe!'

Pat continued her story: 'Your dad packed up the tennis gear as the fire was approaching, and drove through the smoke past the Stone Town houses.'

Janice had chosen the shorter route back to Booralama; Mark went the longer way, over the creek and along the Stone Town Road. There were people who lived along that way, people with kids and older women.

As he moved into a lower gear, Mark was surprised to see a silver Mercedes barrel down a grand drive at the same time as a branch from a gum tree smashed into his windscreen. The silver car sped to the end of the drive, turned a sharp right onto the Booralama road and accelerated away, spraying red dust all over Mark's window. He cursed, got out, cleared the branch, and used his arm to wipe off the dirt so he could see. Driving again, more cautious, and with the road in front alive with leaves and sparks, Mark saw in the distance a large man walking slowly by the side of the road.

'Your dad picked up my boy and drove him to safety,' Pat declared.

His sons were deeply unimpressed.

'There was nothing heroic about that,' Mark said. 'Anyone would have done the same.'

'But they didn't. Aidan Sleeth drove past Bob and didn't pick him up – even though Bob was madly waving at him to stop.'

Mark remembered picking up a young man who introduced himself as Robert. He recalled a deliberate slowness in Robert's voice and gesture, the bulk of him in the hot car.

'Some people stop to pick up the needy and others don't,' Pat said. 'You did.' The older woman gazed upon him like a gift. 'You were kind to him, and he didn't always have that.'

She picked up a jam, stared at its label. 'Bob died when he was twenty-two years old. Heart problems.'

'I'm sorry, Pat.' She had mentioned Bob at their first meeting; Mark was brought back to the informal interview on the porch, the axe, the creeping acacia.

'He came to me when he was three and I adopted him as soon as I could. Other children came and went, but Bob stayed.'

On top of all the other community work, she was a foster carer too then. Mark looked at her anew. He was guilty of clumping older women into the category of doddery and dull, but really – and it was true – they were the glue that held society together. Free childminders, foster carers, committee members, volunteers, theatregoers, workers, cleaners, gardeners, carers of those older than themselves, housekeepers, keepers of family stories and more. His mother was one of them. Now, without her sticking power, he was finding it more difficult to stay in contact with his sister Prue.

Mark's sons were by the pigs, watching the old sow lie exhausted while her piglets rambled all about her.

'Come on, boys,' he called to them. 'Time to go.'

They asked for a showbag. He said no.

They asked for a showbag. He said no.

They asked for a showbag. He said, a small one.

As they left, Pat clapped her hands together in a back-to-work gesture and the two women bent low over the jams.

CHAPTER 44

Back at the house, the boys coming down from a sugar rush, Mark made a cup of tea and checked his phone. Jagdeep had texted: *Search continuing, nothing as yet. Mine shafts all through the bush. Waiting for land survey to begin searching them.*

This length of time after her disappearance, Mark knew, it was a body they'd be looking for.

The night before, in the Stone Town bush, Jadgeep had commented on the way sound travelled up the mine shaft to above ground. When Finn was yelling below, the sound echoed through tunnels and came up via the different shafts. Unless she knew better, Jagdeep said, she could have sworn Finn was twenty metres underground to the right of her, not just below where she stood. Mark was brought back to the screams of the owl. He shuddered.

Dennis left a message: *Running late. Be home in an hour.*

Charlie and Sam were searching for something to do. He

gave them a pile of photo albums, ready for sorting, a job he'd been meaning to do for months.

'Find some nice pictures of Nanna,' he suggested. 'We'll put them in a frame.'

'Will there be photos of us in here?' His eldest son, Sam, liked to look at photos of himself as a baby.

'Heaps and heaps.' *I don't know.*

The boys weren't as sad about his mother's death as Mark thought they'd be. He'd felt conflicted when they ran around with water pistols after her funeral, and in the last year, he'd wondered at times if they'd forgotten her. But then, occasionally one would say something to stump him: 'Nanna said shit a lot of times but I didn't mind,' or 'In heaven, Nanna must be so sad without us.'

He stacked the boys up with albums, photos pouring out; life through Helen's eyes.

Another text, this one from the wheedling editor of the local rag, Janice:

Is it Natalie Whitsed they're looking for in Stone Town? Can you provide a statement? What is her connection to the area?

Mark sighed, slumping into the couch beside his boys.

'There's the lady with the jams! Nanna's there too.' Charlie was pointing to an old photo. Mark took a look. There she was, Beth Matteson, tall with strong arms, holding up a crate of vegetables. His own mother stood in the background grinning, her hand on a little girl's head.

'And there's the other lady!' Charlie held up another photo.

Mark sat down beside his boys on the couch. Photos of the show, of community events, of tennis, of fundraisers, of cake stalls. All the old faces. He recognised every one.

Mark drove out to Stone Town. The old settlement once teeming with gold-rush fever was again on the map. The news reports were full of it: the young policewoman's car, the Scopellitis, a man shot in the bush. It rained with intensity, the wind low. Strange to think that ten years ago, the country was in the grip of the worst drought on record. Now, everything was green and drooping, the land a giant soak.

Things floated to the surface, became visible.

Mark thought of his mother. If she were alive now, she'd be making sandwiches for the searchers and handing out plastic mugs of tea. In his own grief, he'd underestimated her importance to the community. She'd be thinking: *Who most needs my help here?*

Mark didn't know what his father would be thinking, although the man's edges were becoming more defined.

He pulled into the driveway, parked and made his way across the muddy path. There were no signs of a car. Up the creaking steps and onto the porch. Old boots rested against the wall, huge. An axe lay rusting on the wooden boards.

Mark knocked. No response. Knocked again. Nothing.

He moved to the window, cupped his hands and looked inside. A dark living room provided no answers.

He looked behind him. The Stone Town Road was as busy as it had ever been, police vehicles, volunteers all joining the search. Door knocking would commence soon.

There was a change in the light from the side of the closed door. Dark and then light. And now, two distinct shadows emanating underneath the door. Someone was standing behind it.

'I know you're in there.' Mark stood, face close to the door. 'It's me, Mark Ariti. I've been here before. I can help you.' A beat. 'I knew Bob.'

He took out a photo and slid it underneath the door; the shadows of the feet shifted again.

There was a pause and then the door opened a crack. 'Is it just you?' the voice said.

'It is.'

The door opened and Mark stepped inside.

'Natalie,' Mark said. 'I thought you might be here.'

CHAPTER 45

The woman looked different in the flesh: pale, thinner. Her blonde hair was tied back in a loose ponytail and her black jumper was too long. Her smile was not pleasant.

'Sergeant Ariti,' she said. 'I've heard of you.'

Her arm was wrapped in a sling, bandaged. 'You're hurt,' he said.

'Yes.'

'Did Sleeth do that to you?'

'Indirectly, yes.'

'There's so many people looking for you. Your mother, the whole force, the country.'

Natalie gave a snort. 'And that's just for a start.'

'The Scopellitis . . .'

'Them too.'

'I can help you.' Mark held his hands out in a gesture of peace. '*Let* me help you.'

'Cut the crap,' Natalie said, turning away. 'I only answered the door because of what Pat told me about you picking up Bob that time.'

'I think I remember you,' Mark said. 'Just. My boys found a photo with you in it. You were at the show one time, years ago, with a heap of kids and all the Stone Town women. My mother was there. You were a little blonde scarecrow.' Natalie's features loosened a little. 'I took you to see the lambs and you fed them with a bottle.' It was one of the times he had to help out his mother with the show.

A nod. 'Bob was there too,' she said, 'Robbie.' Natalie gave a faint smile.

Outside, the rain was starting again. Wind raced up the paddocks and into the trees. Gums swayed and bent north, like a thousand fingers pointing *this way, this way*.

'The police'll be door knocking soon. There'll be property searches – it's only a matter of time before they find you here.'

'I know.' Natalie looked at him, weighed him up. Unsure.

'My mother, Helen, had a bit to do with Pat.' Mark took a few steps up the hall. Natalie walked in front of him into an adjacent room and, after a brief moment, he followed. 'They were on all sorts of committees together. That photo I showed you, that's my mother and Pat and the other Stone Town women at the show. There's a bunch of kids in that photo, including Bob and you.'

'Pat told me about your mum. I think I remember her.'

The room was filled with a collection of memories: photos, a hundred of them, stood in frames about the room. Paintings of horses and trees and landscapes. Copies of Frederick McCubbin's *The Pioneer* and books piled up in the corner. A mirror. Trophies. Pot plants. A record player and a side table stacked with old cups and saucers. A sofa, blankets thrown over it and a small TV on a stand. Another side table held a wine bottle and three glasses. It was messy, but not dirty.

'This house' – Natalie threw her good arm wide – 'was the first one I ever stayed at for longer than five days.'

'How'd that come about?'

'Mum lived in Adelaide for a while, had a boyfriend in Elizabeth.'

Lizbef, snobs called it.

'Got removed from her after a few months. Sent to a family who already had a foster kid and didn't want another. There were always mix-ups like that. The system's completely overwhelmed.'

'How'd you end up here?'

'Pat was in Adelaide taking Robbie to see his biological mum. Somehow, I came back up with her to Stone Town. I'm not sure it was even official. Never any paperwork or social workers when I was with Pat.'

'And over the years, you kept coming back.'

'Yeah – every time Mum was losing her shit, she'd send me up here or Pat would come and get me. It was mad up here, up to five different kids at times. Always Robbie though.'

'You liked it here, in Stone Town with Pat?'

'Like it? I loved it. We all did. Everyone who stayed here did. We called her Nanna.'

Outside, an SES vehicle drove past, orange lights flashing. Natalie stepped away from the window.

'What happened, Natalie? Tell me.'

'I'll tell you, but I want something in return.'

'What?'

'Something big.' Natalie touched her bandaged arm. 'I want you to record what I'm going to say on your phone. Make it official.'

The rain was drumming now, a constant beat.

'Okay.' Mark made sure the recorder on his phone was working, confirmed there was enough charge. He nodded.

Natalie began to talk.

'Charlene was smarter than she let on. On her trips to the gym, the club, the plastic surgeon and the hairdresser's – she was always *on*. Tony Scopelliti's wife was polite and friendly to a fault – everyone from the bouncers to the doctors to the florists loved her. She listened, I could see that – she leaned in when people were talking. It showed a kindness, but it was calculated too. All the while, Charlene was filing information away. I could tell – in the moments when Charlene thought no one was watching, when she waited at the traffic lights, the moment before she threw her coffee cup in the bin, a second before she entered a shop: Charlene was planning every move. Some cops hate surveillance jobs, think of them as tedious and a waste of time. But me, I like to think of it as an honour. Where else do you get to see life through another person's lens? Go where they go, catch their hidden moments? And sometimes, *sometimes* on surveillance, you hit the jackpot.'

Mark checked his phone; all was in order. He held it out closer to where Natalie stood.

'In this case, it was the hairdresser's: the regularity of Charlene's visits, the other customers, the privacy afforded them when she entered the rooms. Watching the footage at night, over and over, recording dates and times and places and people, I began to recognise the same women getting their hair done at the same time as Charlene. Nothing overly surprising there – people often have regular appointments. But these women, I checked it out, were advisers to the Planning Minister, and the Scopellitis were long suspected to be laundering dirty money through construction and subdivisions. I didn't tell anyone about the listening device I then planted – I know that the seniors would have said no to it – not enough compelling evidence for it and so forth. So over time, I compiled my own evidence, proof of coercion between the Scopellitis and the government. Call it career building. I didn't go to uni with anyone in the senior ranks, I don't play golf, I don't have a father who writes news columns. I do my own networking, in my head.'

Another car sped past. Mark looked at his watch.

'But then,' Natalie continued, 'there was another break-through, and this time it was personal. It was a shock to see Aidan Sleeth at the Crazy Cactus the first time. Just standing there, in line, collar up like some dickhead. Why do they all wear their collars up? It's like a fucking vampire convention when private school boys get together. And there he was in my lens, Aidan: the blood-sucking arsehole from my youth. The one who bullied me, who locked me in a dark vault, who called me names like *pov* and *bogan*, *foz* and *feral*, and said my new shoes were street-kid specials. The one who told everyone I had AIDS and said that I stank.'

Faz has AIDS. The graffiti on the powder magazine wall. It was Foz has AIDS.

'The one who, when I was returned again and again to Pat Delaney, said, "Mother being a slut, is she? Off her face again?" If Aidan Sleeth turned up in the bush when we were playing, or when he came to one of the Stone Town events, I'd go all tense, like a fence wire pulled tight. It was the only bad thing about coming to stay here.'

Natalie spread the hand of her damaged arm out wide and flexed her wrist.

'But Aidan was worse to Robbie, the one who'd been with Nanna the longest. He made poor Robbie *do* things – wear jocks on his head and dance, showed him *Playboy* magazines and asked him which girl he liked best, called him a retard and a spaz and a mong.

'It wasn't just because Aidan was a rich kid that he was an arsehole. I'd come across nice rich kids, good families with lots of cash – it was something *in him*. Aidan was an only child with distant parents, shipped off to a boys' boarding school early on. He didn't know how to interact with people, with girls, with people different from him. Plus, he was cruel from the get-go. Whatever the case, Aidan Sleeth was a cock-head and here he was on tape, at the Crazy Cactus, looking at Charlene Scopelliti like she was a goddess. When I saw that, I remembered how much Aidan liked to watch. Girls, women. Sometimes in Stone Town I'd feel it, a shift in the weight of the air, a shadow passing. Aidan's face at the window, looking in as we ate our tea. He was mean, but it was the creepiness I remember most. And now, *I* was the one watching *him*.'

Natalie smiled in contempt. 'And it wasn't just at the Crazy Cactus I saw him. It was other places too – a peripheral figure, in places Charlene liked to go. Charlene was aware of it. The way she rubbed her palms down her sides before stepping outside, the glancing backwards as she walked home from a cafe. Just like how I could sense that Sleeth was nearby when I was younger, I'm sure that Charlene could feel his lurking presence. Once, she looked at me directly and nodded towards him. I knew exactly what she was doing. Women, we look out for each other with shit like this.'

Jagdeep had picked it up on the video, Mark thought. And who else had said something like that? Isabelle, when she wrote the warning note to Sleeth. Women talk.

Granddaughters of the Witches they Forgot to Burn.

'On the last day of surveillance, I sat in my car, eating takeaway and watching Charlene's house. Charlene pulled up into her gated driveway and parked and walked inside. And then, just as I was about to leave, I saw this movement behind the bins. Just slight, but I felt it – waited. And what do you know, Aidan Sleeth emerged, holding something, a teddy bear for God's sake. He looked left to right before slinking to the gate, pushing the open button and walking quickly up the footpath.'

He was in Charlene's apartment. Natalie had it on camera.

'So then,' Mark said, 'you made a decision.'

'I did. First, I checked that Charlene was okay – waited till I saw her moving about the house. Then, I thought about my mother, sick and living in a piece-of-shit housing commission unit, and I remembered all of Aidan's wealth and the property his family owned and I thought – I could make Mum's troubles all go away *and* I could warn him off Charlene for good.'

'You were going to blackmail him.'

'Call it what you will.' Natalie sniffed, dismissive. 'He had enough to share around, and I knew he'd hate the Sleeth name to be dragged through the mud. Are you still recording me?'

'Yes.'

'Good.' Natalie continued: 'I did some research, got his number from the Sleeth real estate site and sent Aidan a text on the Thursday afternoon asking him to meet me the following evening at his house in Stone Town. I wrote, "It's Foz. I know what you've been up to." That'd get his attention. It was perfect, I was planning on going up to see my mum in Broken Hill anyway. As a bonus, I could drop in on Nanna – I hadn't seen her for years. It would be a surprise for both of them.'

'You didn't tell anyone.'

'No, who would I tell? When I got close to Stone Town, I got another text from Aidan, asking to meet me near the powder magazine. That bloody arsehole, I bet he had it all planned.' Natalie grimaced and looked about. Finding a cup of water balanced on the windowsill, she leaned over, picked it up and took a few large mouthfuls.

'So, I parked behind Sleeth's house on Yielder's Track, near the old school – I didn't need anyone to see me going in there – and I walked up the paddock, through the house yards and into the Stone Town bush. There're loads of little trails there. I walked along, fairly sure of where I was going. But it was then that I started to feel something. That old sensation came back, that someone was watching me. Do you know what I mean? It's like a tingling feeling. I looked around me, thinking maybe Aidan was up to his old tricks, but no – he was there in front of the powder magazine, waiting. Now I know the person watching me was—'

'Jackson Rendell,' Mark said. 'A worker at the Crazy Cactus. He was following you.'

'Right, so that's his name. Bastard. His breath stank.'

'Addict.'

'That fits. The sweet energy sachets too – druggies love them.'

That piece of plastic Finn found on the lawn. He thought it was a condom wrapper – ENDUR. It could have been energy sachets, the type runners filled up on. ENDUR-ANCE. Jackson had been in there on Clare's orders: get the teddy – take the photo.

'Charlene asked him to follow you. She didn't want Tony to be the one keeping tabs,' Mark said.

In a way, Charlene was protecting Natalie from Tony, as Natalie was protecting her from Sleeth.

For a moment, Natalie was lost in thought. 'Anyway, I saw Aidan. Told him I knew everything, that he was stalking Charlene Scopelliti, that I had it on record and I'd show it to the cops and the media if he didn't give me $100,000. I knew that was nothing to him – and besides the fact that he'd be financially ruined if it all came out, the Scopellitis would hunt him down for preying on Charlene. I mean it. That's what they're like. Aidan would be in deep shit.'

Mark didn't doubt it.

'Aidan, surprisingly, agreed right away. He was still the smarmy shit I remembered as a kid, but he said he saw no other option. He was already paying off his ex-wife to be quiet. "What's another woman to be in debt to?" he said.' Natalie curled her lips in distaste.

The loud ring of a landline. Two rings then it stopped. Then three rings and it stopped again.

'That's Nanna,' Natalie said. 'Her signal that she'll be home soon.'

Mark looked at his watch. The farm produce part of the show would be closing up now. Time for the teenage boys in their tight jeans clutching Bundy cans to emerge from darkened rooms, ride the Zipper, slink around the dirty stalls, half crazed with lust unresolved.

'Aidan said he'd walk me back to the house. That he'd sign something – make it official. We started walking a few steps through the bush in the undergrowth, not a path. When I turned around, he said to keep going, that the trail was ahead. I had this feeling though, that something was up. I asked him where he was taking me and when he didn't answer, I started running – really running – but he chased me, just for a few metres more and then, he pushed me. At first, I stood my ground, kept one foot behind the other and bent low – but he pushed me again, hard with both hands, and I fell down into a mine shaft.'

Mark's phone buzzed. He didn't stop to read the message, kept his eyes on Natalie. 'Keep going.'

'Next thing I remember, I'm waking up in some hole underground. It's enclosed and covered with a grate – you know, you see them at the entrances of some old mine shafts. They were there to separate mines for those who owned the rights.'

Mark nodded.

'I'm guessing Jackson moved me there from the open mine shaft Sleeth pushed me into,' Natalie reflected. 'I was badly injured. Arm broken, maybe a rib or two. My head had a large bump on it – I think Sleeth hit me – and my phone was gone.'

Plenty of places to get rid of a phone in the bush. Rabbit holes, tunnels, tree hollows. Easy.

'I panicked when I came to, screamed – a lot.'

And Evan heard it and thought it was the Barking Owl.

'Then, some time later, someone came to check on me. Gave me food, energy sachets, water. Drugs. I know now it was Jackson Rendell.'

Yes, Jackson. Equipped by his mother for a few days to keep guard on her, take photos, bribe the Scops.

'I recognised him from the Crazy Cactus. He used to do the whole paper, scissors, rock thing with the strippers, like it was a joke. He took a photo of me with some stupid teddy bear . . .' Natalie paused. 'Was it the same one Sleeth took from Charlene?'

Mark nodded.

'He must have got it from Sleeth's at some stage . . .' Natalie paused again, thinking. 'Anyway, I pretended to be all weak and scared and helpless. In fact, I *was* most of those things – but not helpless, never that. I tore that plastic love heart thing out of the fluffy toy and stabbed him with it when he next came in. Not badly, but enough to slow him. Then, I ran. When I heard him coming for me, I climbed through another tunnel. I just ran through it, keeping low. He tried to follow me, but for once my height was an advantage. I got out and went straight to Pat's. Turned out I'd been underground for seven nights.'

And been hiding out, recovering at Pat's for another week.

Mark pointed at the hat on the side table, next to the empty bottle of whiskey. 'Where'd you get that hat, Natalie?'

Natalie gave a grin. 'Found it when I made my way out of the tunnels. Had a few stains on it – Nanna got them out. White wine vinegar, that's her answer to everything.'

Mark's phone buzzed. He ignored it again.

'Why didn't you let anyone know where you were?'

With disdain, Natalie shook her head. 'You *know* why. Once they knew where I was, the Scopellitis would come for me, wanting to know what I had on the files. Who knows what they'd do to get it? I realised when I was at Pat's that the media coverage on my disappearance was massive. I wanted to wait for a bit till things quietened down. Now, I want to make a deal: I'm not going down for Sleeth's death.'

So that's what she's after.

'What happened to Sleeth?'

389

'He must have panicked when he couldn't find me, especially when he heard people talking about screaming in the bush. The part of the mine where Jackson moved me was locked with a grate from the outside and covered with a wooden panel. If Sleeth jumped down to look in the spot he'd pushed me, if he even happened to find the space where I was trapped – which would have been difficult enough – there was no way he'd think I'd be in there. How could I lock myself in a closed den? Even if he saw it and tried to investigate, he wouldn't have been able to get in. He clearly thought I was in one of the tunnels, injured, or that I'd escaped. Sleeth came around here asking Pat if she'd seen me. Got a local kid to tell him if he heard the screams again, and the kid did. He went out the Friday night to find me. Safe to say, the man was in a bit of a panic.'

That was the Friday night he'd gone out into the bush with the Matteson girls. 'The sound was different,' Evan had said. That was because it was actually an owl calling that time, and not a woman crying for help.

'I saw Aidan go into the bush, there's a good view from here. I'd been watching most of the day. I took Pat's old gun and I went in there after him. He was peering down the grates of the mine shafts and calling out like a madman, saying he knew I was down there somewhere. We used to do that when we were kids, shout into the shafts so it would echo all around the tunnels. Beth says no one does it anymore, too unsafe.

Mark recalled Jagdeep's words on the sound of voices from the shafts.

Natalie continued, 'I thought of him stalking Charlene, then pushing me down the mine shaft and leaving me to die. I just said, "Look up, Sleeth," and he did. I said I'd be prepared to let it all go if he gave me $200,000 and left us all alone, Charlene included. I said if he told anyone, I'd release the files of him stalking her. There was a tussle, he grabbed the gun, it went off, I shot him. It was self-defence, he'd have killed me if he could.'

'He was shot in the back of the head, Natalie. From a distance of around five metres.'

'He was trying to grab the gun and I fell down. He twisted away with it, but I held tight, wrenched it away and shot him.' Natalie added, 'It wasn't five metres, more like two. Splatter formation estimates aren't absolute, you know that. You can turn off the recording now. That's it, the whole story.'

Mark did as she asked and saw that the text message on his phone was from Jagdeep:

Where are you?

His police vehicle was out the front of Pat's house. Jagdeep would work out his location. They would all be here soon, sirens on, copper adrenaline high. Boiling point.

An old Holden pulled up. Heavy footsteps on the porch. The sound of someone taking off their shoes and then the clap-clap as they were banged together.

'I'm not sure I believe you, Natalie,' Mark said.

Pat Delaney entered the room, regal in her purple kaftan. Suddenly, he knew who she reminded him of: Tony Scopelliti. Mark set his stance wide, kept a close eye on both women.

'What's going on?' Pat asked. Firm.

'I'm telling Natalie I don't believe her story.'

Natalie gave a bitter laugh. 'What about it don't you believe, Sergeant?'

'Unless you're Sarah Connor from *The Terminator*, it's highly unlikely you could, in a tussle, somehow move more than two metres away and fire a shotgun with a broken left arm – particularly as I know from the tapes you're left-handed – and shoot a man directly in the back of the head. So, *what happened to Sleeth*, Natalie?'

A pause.

'You've probably had a pretty nice life, haven't you, Mark?' Natalie studied him thoughtfully and Mark shifted on his feet, aware of his navy-blue chinos, RM boots and neat shirt bought by Kelly from some upmarket store in the city.

'You've had a stable upbringing and good schooling and you're not going to go hungry anytime soon, are you, Mark?'

He couldn't deny it.

'I don't resent you for that – I really don't. But there's something you don't get.' Her voice dropped; Mark had to lean in to listen.

'Foster kids are *always* on the lookout for danger. It's fight mode almost all the time, caused by early trauma. Any sense of trouble and your heart rate gets faster, which means more oxygen to your muscles, pain perception drops and hearing sharpens.' Natalie used her right arm to mimic firing a shotgun, balancing it straight on her bandaged arm. 'In foster care, you've got to be nimble, learn to use every part of your body – to run, to hit, to hide. I can't write with my right hand, but I can shoot with it.'

The silence in the room lengthened. Mark cleared his throat, went to say something, and stalled.

'Don't dismiss what foster kids are capable of. We're smarter, wilier and tougher than you'd think.'

It was difficult to argue with that.

'I've told you everything, that's it.' Natalie's chin was up, her small face set in defiance. 'It was self-defence, and I won't be doing any time for it. I won't be sanctioned, I won't be dismissed, I won't face charges for attempting blackmail. I love my job and I'm good at it.'

Mark nodded, slowly. 'You must have something to be that sure. What is it?'

'This.' Natalie held up a flash drive. 'Recordings of dozens of conversations between the Planning Minister's team and the Scopellitis in regards to rezoning of green lands beyond the city boundary. Charlene was knee-deep in the business. Everyone thought she was some bimbo, but she was the brains of the family. It's all here: buybacks of Crown land, land for dollars, schemes to undermine the Greens. It's big-time. All sorts of names implicated, right up high. If it gets out, I'm not safe from the Scopellitis *or* the government.'

'You sound very confident.'

'The material on this drive will blow up state politics for a long time. Yeah, you could say I'm confident.'

An SES vehicle drove past at speed. Window panes rattled. The room felt unreasonably hot.

A knock at the door. Police HiLux vehicles in the drive.

'Put the kettle on, Natty,' Pat said, 'looks like we've got company.'

CHAPTER 46

The Booralama Chronicle

WHITSED FOUND IN STONE TOWN
Janice Smith

*Detective Sergeant Natalie Whitsed was found safe and
well yesterday, in the house of her former carer, Stone Town
resident Ms Patricia Delaney. Whitsed, first reported missing
twelve days ago, has admitted to the shooting death of
Mr Aidan Sleeth, local real estate personality. In a statement
for the media, Assistant Commissioner Conti said the
shooting was found to be in self-defence. Investigations
are continuing.*

*In other developments, Mr Jackson Rendell of Adelaide,
former employee of the Scopelliti family, has been charged
with the offence of dangerous driving causing grievous*

*bodily harm, a crime which usually attracts a sentence
of seven to fourteen years. His mother, former Inspector
Clare Rendell, has been charged with aiding and abetting
after providing shelter to her son following the incident.*

*Rendell's victim, Luke Howsley, is expected to fully recover.
A GoFundMe page has been set up by the Booralama
Football Club to assist in his ongoing physical therapy.*

*In other news: Booralama-based Sergeant Ariti is calling
for patience on the roads as the Stone Town region attracts
visitors curious about the area. Young local Evan Williams
claims he has never seen so many people and is considering
opening a guide business to take people through the
historical surroundings.*

*Part-time resident John Renner has other views on the
recent boom: 'We sold our place in Adelaide for $400,000
to move up here, and now it's becoming busier and busier.
Might have to move back to the city for some peace
and quiet.'*

What Natalie Whitsed had captured on the listening device
was explosive. People at the highest paygrades agreed to her
condition of handing over the materials: no murder charges
laid, nothing on the blackmail. Pat Delaney was part of the
deal too – despite sheltering Whitsed after Sleeth's murder,
she was free to continue to live and work in the Stone Town

community. Mark wondered if, after all the years of service, Stone Town would look after Pat in return, as her cancer-riddled body gave way. Australia didn't have a good track record in caring for old people, particularly women.

And Pat Delaney *had* been a nanna – not biologically, but a nanna nonetheless. Mark, lying on the couch under the sunlit window, wondered about mothers and fathers and biology and love.

Clare Rendell, Jacqueline Matteson and Pat Delaney. When it came to it, all were acting out of love. He got up from his resting place and wandered to the pantry. He felt above to the highest shelves, ran his hands along the peeling surfaces till he came to a jar half full of mint-leaf lollies. He shook the jar; the lollies bumped about as one. He shook it again; one came loose and, popping it into his mouth, he tasted sticky sugar and the jelly candy, hardened with time. He looked out the window to where a little fairy wren hopped along the lawn. He watched its progress, *hop hop hop*, tail waggling, looking this way and that. *Hop hop.*

Mark and Jagdeep were unsure as to how much the other Stone Town women knew about Aidan Sleeth's shooting. Pat Delaney had gone to Sue Williams's house after Natalie blew the back of his head off. There was a whiskey bottle with three glasses on Pat's table. Who was joining Pat and Natalie for a drink? It could be any of them – it could be all. The way they stood around, shoulder to shoulder. *We few, we merry few.*

He'd passed it all on to his seniors – what he knew, any suspicions he harboured as to who had helped shelter Natalie. This time around, his conscience was clear.

The mint-leaf lolly stuck to the roof of his mouth and he had to gouge at it with his tongue to get it off. If his mother was here, she'd use the lollies on a cake, or chop them up into small pieces for the bees. The phone rang: it was Prue.

'I've got you!' she said. 'Finally. You are so crap at returning calls.'

'I did try.'

'Only once. I've called you thirty thousand times.'

The little wren was joined by others, five more.

'How are you, Prue?'

He could hear down the line a door slamming. 'I'm just hiding from the kids,' his sister said.

'Where are you?'

'Pantry.'

'I just found one of Mum's mint lollies in the pantry here, I'm eating it right now. Can't decide if it's disgusting or delicious.'

Prue laughed. It was good to hear his sister laugh. As kids, they'd be in hysterics over things they heard down the street, or *The Goodies*, or how they caught their mother's friend picking her nose.

'What have you been up to?' Prue asked.

Mark paused. 'Nothing much. You?'

A slight hesitation. 'Same.'

'Why'd you keep calling?' Parts of mint leaf stuck in his back tooth, and he eyed a stray knitting needle, wondering whether to use it to prise it out.

'I just . . . I've been thinking . . .'

'About what?'

'I miss Mum. And Dad. I just want to have a chat about them.'

It was interesting, Mark thought. When an elderly parent dies, people ask, 'How old were they?' and then when you tell them – seventy-five or eighty or ninety – they relax: they're thinking, 'It's not that bad.' And it's not, not in the scheme of things. But a sibling knows. Only the sibling knows the true grief of the death of a parent. In most instances, they're the only ones who've been as close and have known them for as long as you. Prue knew.

'We can talk about the mint lollies, how she never, ever threw them out,' Mark said.

'She really didn't. God, how unhygienic. You should chuck out all those old jars full of crap – it'll make you feel, I don't know, unburdened or something.'

'You really have lived too long with a Californian, Prue.' Mark liked Prue's husband, but the New Age stuff really wasn't his thing.

'Hashtag blessed,' Prue said, and they laughed.

It was a relief to talk with his sister, the sibling tie too deep to worry about entertaining or offending or impressing. Charlie and Lola, Hansel and Gretel, Jack and Jill: literature recognised it for years and was it Tolstoy who, in his old age, came to the conclusion that the simplest relationship was the one between brother and sister?

Their chat meandered pleasantly; fond recollections of their parents, people in the town. An old boyfriend had sent a drunk email to Prue, Mark was back training at football, the Royal still had spew-coloured carpet. Eventually they agreed without any awkwardness that they'd run out of things to say and hung up.

Mark sat for a while longer in the pantry, looking at all the old jars containing strange and rotting things. Then, in one motion, he swept up an armful of them and carried them outside to be emptied, cleaned and sent to recycling. It was funny, he thought after the job was done. He *did* feel lighter.

CHAPTER 47

On Sunday night, Mark took Jagdeep and the boys to Stitcher's farm. The yabbying was supposed to be good in the dam, but besides two small creatures, they hardly caught a thing. Both boys had a rod, small bits of chicken on the end, and they chattered on the edge of the water waiting for bites. Mark watched them in relief: their stay with him had not been a failure. Kelly wouldn't approve of all the baby-sitting they'd had over the weekend, but she'd approve of this.

As a boy, Mark had used an old stocking with a skinned fox leg as bait to catch yabbies. The stocking would be tied to a fishing line and cast out under a tree, but his boys liked the rods. And as his sons toppled semi-deliberately into the water, as they wore the captured yabbies on their T-shirts like brooches, as they ate sausages in bread and fought over lollies, Jagdeep and Mark quietly talked about the money.

The day after police had spirited Natalie away, an envelope appeared on the front of Mark's doorstep. No name, no distinguishing features. Inside: $290,000 in $100 bills. It was a clever amount. If he handed it in to the police, they'd forever suspect him of pocketing the additional ten grand. No matter if he was cleared, the underhand comments would remain. Tony Scopelliti was a smart man, Charlene probably smarter. Was $290,000 the price for saving a blood relative?

Jagdeep was worried, but Mark had already made up his mind: two anonymous donations. One to Birds for Bush, to help the fight to keep Stone Town free from rezoning. He imagined the fat envelope in Evie Renner's small hands, the weight of it, the promise. The other to the local CWA, to help that mother and kid in the caravan find housing – the capable women of the organisation would not let it go to waste.

That was one job for tomorrow – and another, to ring The Doctor, whose name, according to Dennis, was Rose.

Light shifted, and evening began to drift onto the saplings behind the dam. A faint orange, pink. They began to collect their things, ready for the trip home.

Fire had been through here, Mark remembered as he pulled the lines in; a small grassfire that threatened to grow huge with westerly winds. Houses north of Booralama were evacuated, a few sheds burned. Volunteers put it out. They came, the locals – armed with buckets and hoses and blankets. By the time the CFA turned up, they'd quashed the last of the embers and mopped up.

The dam took on a shimmery glow and the land was quiet. Mark waited a moment, felt the light shift, saw the outline of old gums on the hill. A dip in the water, a flutter on the surface. Was that a duck down there, a nest in the reeds? Mark took up his binoculars, raised them to his eye, focused.

'Gosh!' he whispered. 'It's a little wood duck.' And then he thought, *I'm sounding like my mother.* The lenses clouded, vision blurred. Mark blinked, blinked again, but still his eyes filled and the duck was a fleeting thing in his wavering, watery sight.

Mark put the bins down, patted them, felt their reassuring weight about his neck.

Jagdeep and his boys were packed and waiting in the car. Mark tucked the rods under his arm, picked up the esky and walked in the fading light towards them.

EPILOGUE

'Something needs to be done.' Beth downs the rest of her whiskey and sets her glasses straight. 'I've got three more granddaughters to think of.'

Pat nods, deep in reflection, and Natalie thinks that the two of them look like wise old owls. She's sitting up now, in the lounge room with Pat and Beth. The events of that morning – being chased, escaping through the tunnel and making her way back to Pat's house – feel like years ago. Her arm still hurts like crazy.

'These photos, did Isabelle say what they were of?' Pat asks.

'Georgia, all of Georgia. Her walking down the street, getting into her car, picking up Sarah from school. She saw them on his computer. There were dozens.'

'He stalks women,' Natalie says. 'We all know that. He won't stop.'

'And then there's the rest . . .' Pat adds, and the two owls give Natalie a long look. 'Pushing you into that mine, it's attempted murder.'

'The Charlene woman, Georgia and what he did to Natalie, Lola too – he was so cruel to her,' Beth lists. 'Something needs to be done.'

'And Bob. Don't forget him.'

The three women turn to the photo of Bob on the wall. Big and hulking, a gentle soul. Dead from a heart condition, twenty-two years old.

'We'll never forget your Robbie,' Beth says, and Natalie reaches over to stroke Pat's hand.

Pat clears her throat. 'How?'

'I'll go,' Natalie says. 'Let me get him, that prick tried to kill me.'

'Language,' Pat tuts, and Beth shakes her head.

'You're not well enough, love. Leave it to us.'

'Besides, someone might see you.'

A silence.

'Nat has rung Aidan, said she's prepared to meet him tonight at 7 pm near the powder magazine with a final deal that's more favourable to her. He'll think she's desperate for money.' Beth says quietly. 'She said she'll have someone with her so there'll be no repeat of last time.'

'You've already planned this,' Pat says, with no animosity.

'I have. When I came over here after you told me Nat had arrived, I thought of it immediately. We talked about it when I bandaged her arm . . .'

'Aidan might not go out at all, it's terrible weather,' Pat says. 'He might wait.'

'He'll go. He's desperate. All that walking in the bush, shouting down the mines, pretending to others he cares about the place. He wants to find her so badly, or make sure others don't.'

404

6.40 pm and the two women set out. Beth has her daughter-in-law's 12-gauge, Pat the .22 from behind the fridge. Natalie watches from the living room window. Later, she creeps outside to where a wattle, half alive, drapes over the side gate. There's a wooden rail there, perfect for leaning on. In the trees on the other side of the road, she sees the figure of Aidan Sleeth walk past, head darting this way and that like a snake. It starts raining again, hard. A car drives past, two men inside, and she steps back, into the leaves.

Beth and Pat don't take long.

They come back, guns hidden under dresses and raincoats.

'Is that you, Natty?' Pat asks as they pass through her front gate.

'Yep,' she says, lowering her own gun, the one kept under the porch. 'I had you covered in case something went wrong.'

It's only been twenty minutes at most, but her right arm is sore from balancing the gun on her damaged left one.

'Nothing was going to go wrong,' Beth says.

Natalie nods.

Pat smashes the man's phone with the axe, scoops up the pieces into her big hands and puts them into her apron pocket. She'll deposit them in one of the rabbit holes, she says.

Later, they'll decide that the best diversion is the co-op. Convoluted ownership and ongoing spats with developers mean that the police will waste time on John and Evie Renner. No harm done, they're good people. Stall for time, get Natalie well. Plan.

Natalie feels the Chapstick in her pocket – the flash drive concealed in it is her trump card.

That's all for later, but for now, Pat and Beth have a meeting to attend. There's the CFA and safe housing to raise money for, there's letters to be written, homeless people to cook for, blankets to knit and jams to make.

The women are tired; they need a cup of tea and then bed. It's been a big day.

'You want a job done' – Pat takes off her big boots and rests them by the door – 'you ask a nanna.'

ACKNOWLEDGEMENTS

It has been a joy to write a second Mark Ariti novel, and I owe this experience once more to the brilliant Bev Cousins at Penguin Random House Australia. A big thank you, too, to Kalhari Jayaweera, who again has elevated my writing through her kind insight and sage advice, and to Claire Gatzen for her eagle eye. I am grateful to senior publicist Hannah Ludbrook and to the proofreaders, designers, marketing, rights and sales teams. I am fortunate to be supported by Penguin Random House Australia.

I'd like to thank my colleagues at the regional school where I teach English. From the librarians who organise launches and allow me to write in the quiet space after school, to my friends in the office who offer advice on titles, and to the students who tell me they saw my book in a shop and might even read it one day – thank you. I'm glad I'm a teacher.

I've written this book with rural women in mind, and to those women – thank you for all the work you do, whether it be on the farm, in the community or in the home.

Lastly, thank you to Bernie and to my three sons.

AUTHOR'S NOTE

This book was written on the lands of the Waywurru and Dhudhuroa peoples, whom I would like to acknowledge as the Traditional Custodians and Storytellers of their country. I pay my respects to their Elders past and present, and celebrate all the histories, traditions and living cultures of Aboriginal and Torres Strait Islander people.

Margaret Hickey is an award-winning author and playwright from North East Victoria. She has a PhD in Creative Writing and is deeply interested in rural lives and communities. She is the author of *Cutters End* and *Stone Town*.